"There's the thrill that comes in discovering a terrific new mystery writer, and then there's the thrill that comes in discovering a terrific new—and different—mystery novel written by an already acknowledged master. . . . Superb . . . Another standout series . . . In Coleman's hands, all the standard elements seem as radiant and new as a freshly peroxided blonde. . . . *Where It Hurts* is one of those evocative mysteries that readers will remember as much for its charged sense of place as for any of its other considerable virtues."

—*The Washington Post*

"Coleman writes with . . . a rough beauty. . . . Coleman is a genius. . . . Fascinating reading and will richly entertain you."

—*The Huffington Post*

"Coleman's busy book—set far from the Hamptons in 'those ugly patches we Long Islanders like to pretend don't exist'—has plenty of robust regional flavor."

—*The New York Times Book Review*

"Coleman's poetic pulp fiction in *Where It Hurts* translates seamlessly to the here and now. . . . It's proof that the hard-boiled detective genre is timeless. His version of Sam Spade merely carries a cellphone and has a therapist."

—*The Dallas Morning News*

"A superb new series . . . The spare, hardboiled rhythms of its language, as well as its moody low rent Long Island setting have kept me thinking about *Where It Hurts* ever since its late winter debut."

—NPR's *Fresh Air*

"Sharp, clever dialogue, a dynamic cast of characters that represents a cross-section of Long Island cultures and an engaging plot keep *Where It Hurts* gripping and entertaining. Murphy's authenticity, his flaws and his complexity make him a character readers will eagerly anticipate in future books. An excellent beginning to a series with great potential."

—*Shelf Awareness*

TITLES BY REED FARREL COLEMAN

GUS MURPHY SERIES

Where It Hurts
What You Break

DYLAN KLEIN SERIES

Life Goes Sleeping
Little Easter
They Don't Play Stickball in Milwaukee

MOE PRAGER SERIES

Walking the Perfect Square
Redemption Street
The James Deans
Soul Patch
Empty Ever After
Innocent Monster
Hurt Machine
Onion Street
The Hollow Girl

JOE SERPE SERIES

Hose Monkey
The Fourth Victim

GULLIVER DOWD SERIES

Dirty Work
Valentino Pier
The Boardwalk
Love and Fear

ROBERT B. PARKER'S JESSE STONE

Blind Spot
The Devil Wins
Debt to Pay
The Hangman's Sonnet

STAND-ALONE NOVELS

Tower (with Ken Bruen)
Bronx Requiem (with John Roe)
Gun Church

WHAT YOU BREAK

REED FARREL COLEMAN

G. P. PUTNAM'S SONS / NEW YORK

PUTNAM

G. P. PUTNAM'S SONS
Publishers Since 1838
An imprint of Penguin Random House LLC
375 Hudson Street
New York, New York 10014

The Library of Congress has catalogued the G. P. Putnam's Sons hardcover edition as follows:

Names: Coleman, Reed Farrel, author.
Title: What you break / Reed Farrel Coleman.
Description: New York : G. P. Putnam's Sons, 2017. | Series: A Gus Murphy novel ; 2
Identifiers: LCCN 2016029299 | ISBN 9780399173042 (hardcover)
Subjects: LCSH: Ex-police officers—Fiction. |
Murder—Investigation—Fiction. | BISAC: FICTION / Mystery & Detective /
Hard-Boiled. | GSAFD: Suspense fiction. | Mystery fiction.
Classification: LCC PS3553.O47445 W47 2017 | DDC 813/.54—dc23
LC record available at https://lccn.loc.gov/2016029299
p.   cm.

First G. P. Putnam's Sons hardcover edition / February 2017
First G. P. Putam's Sons trade paperback edition / January 2018
G. P. Putnam's Sons trade paperback ISBN: 9780425283226

Printed in the United States of America
1   3   5   7   9   10   8   6   4   2

BOOK DESIGN BY MEIGHAN CAVANAUGH

FOR GARY SHULZE, MY FRIEND

What you break, you own . . . forever.

1

He was one of the chatty passengers, the type who wanted to be my pal, my best pal ever. Just my luck. I usually worked security at the club on Saturday nights, but with Fredo at his sister's wedding and our substitute driver out sick, I had to drive. For my first year on the job as the nightshift courtesy van driver for the Paragon Hotel, I hated guys like this. The compulsive talkers who dealt with their anxieties about flying or being near New York City or being away from the wife and kids by making nice with the poor schmuck who drove the three-stop route between Long Island MacArthur Airport, the hotel, and the Long Island Rail Road's Ronkonkoma station. And this guy had it bad. He was a determined sort.

"So—hey, what's your name, anyway?"

"Gus."

"So, Gus . . . Gus, huh? What's that short for? August? Gustave? Unusual names, either one, huh?"

I nodded, not bothering to tell him that Gus was an abbreviated version of my middle name, Augustus. What for? This wasn't an actual conversation. It was verbal smoke that would waft away and disperse into nothingness the moment I unloaded his bags and turned him over to the new night clerk for registration. It was a trick of time, a way to waste the empty minutes, to fill them up with something, anything other than reflection or thought. But I was onto the trick of time and I knew all there was to know about emptiness.

On and on it went. *Where did I come from? What did I do before this? Was I married? Did I have kids?*

That first year, either I wouldn't answer or I'd grunt or I'd make stuff up. Anything to deflect or to quiet the chatter, anything not to tell the truth. That I was from Smithtown. That I was three-plus years retired from the Suffolk County Police Department. That I was divorced. That I once had two kids, but now only had one. The last part, the part about losing a kid, that was really the answer to all of his questions, to any questions about me, because it defined me. Who I was, where I came from, all the answers, none of it mattered. I was once somebody, then my son John died, then I was somebody else. Before John Jr. During John Jr. After John Jr. It was like that. I was still becoming that somebody else. I supposed I would be becoming him until the moment I stopped drawing breath.

Thankfully, it was the short run I was driving, the one from the terminal at MacArthur back to the hotel, and I wouldn't have to deal with Mr. Curious for too much longer. Actually, I'd moved my focus away from Chatty before we'd made it out the airport exit and turned onto Vets Highway. No, my attention was fixed on my other passenger, the one half bathed in shadow in the last row of the van.

He hadn't said anything to me when I hoisted his beat-up blue duffel bag into the back of the van and had only nodded when I asked if he was going to the Paragon Hotel. He'd headed straight for the last row of seats, though the van had capacity for twelve people and there was only him and the talker along for the ride. I don't know why, exactly, but I got the sense he was a foreigner. I laughed at myself for thinking that word. "Foreigner," such an outdated term, like something my belligerent drunk of a father might've used or a word out of a '50s movie about marauding Commie spies in our midst.

Both my passengers had gotten off a Southwest flight from Fort Lauderdale. Not much intrigue in flights from Fort Lauderdale, just a lot of old snowbirds who split their time between New York and Florida. No intrigue on any flights into MacArthur because there were no international flights. There were barely any flights to anywhere anymore, and the place was down to two airlines. Word was that Islip Township, the authority that ran the airport, was trying like mad to lure an Icelandic airline to fly into MacArthur. If that failed, I guess they could always try for Burkina Faso Airlines with daily nonstop flights to Ouagadougou and Bobo-Dioulasso. Either way, it might add a little character to Suffolk County, certainly to the parts of Suffolk County that weren't the Hamptons. Which is to say, most of the county. For the vast majority of Suffolk residents, the Hamptons might as well have been as far away as Ouagadougou or Reykjavík.

I also got the sense that the foreigner was running. From what or from whom or to where, I couldn't say. But that he was a runner, I knew. A street cop, even one who worked the less-than-mean streets of East Northport and Commack, knows a runner when he sees one. Although his vacant blue eyes were hidden in the shadows, I felt them on me as I glanced back at him in my rearview mirror. I felt them darting from side to side, alert, on the lookout, assessing. *Where was the threat coming from? Who was a threat? Where could I run? Who could I trust?* And then there was his frayed blue duffel bag: faded, stitched—ragged, ugly unskilled stiches like drunken railroad tracks—taped and taped again. It hadn't been neatly packed, but was lumpy and unevenly weighted. It was the kind of bag a man who has to move on the spur of the moment might pack. He might just shove all of his things, his dirty laundry, his books, his family photos, his secrets into it, and go.

The chatter stopped, as it always did, when I pulled the van into the driveway of the Paragon and parked beneath its weirdly '80s-style portico that had somehow escaped remodeling. I flung the column-mounted gearshift into park, the van lurching forward. I used my left foot to kick the door open, hopped out of the driver's seat, ran around to the side of the van closest to the hotel entrance, and swung open both side doors to let my passengers out. I went to the rear of the van and unloaded the chatty guy's two roller bags and the runner's duffel. Chatty gave me two dollars and strolled toward the hotel without a word. I guess we weren't best pals anymore.

The runner didn't tip me. Didn't speak. He just picked up the duffel, his head on a swivel, and moved to the hotel entrance. I didn't care much about him beyond the potential for trouble that might surround any runner. I had to care about that much because I doubled as the hotel detective. That was part of my deal with the Bonacker family, the folks who currently owned the Paragon. I drove the van four nights a week, bounced at the Full Flaps Lounge on weekends, provided my police expertise and, when called for, my muscle. In return, I got paid a modest salary and a free room for as long as I was employed at the hotel. So far it had worked out well for us all, which was why I made sure to keep an eye on the runner as he made his way through the sliding doors.

It was when he got inside that I noticed something that piqued my interest in him even more than his duffel bag or his suspicious eyes. Slava, the night bellman and my friend, a man who worked nights because the dark helped hide his past, blanched at the sight of the runner. I didn't know much about where Slava had come from or why he'd come to the States. He refused to share those things with me because he was so ashamed by them that he didn't want to think about them himself. That much he'd shared. But one thing I knew about Slava, a big, ugly man with a jolly demeanor, was that there wasn't much in the world that scared him. So why, I wondered, was he scared now? What about the runner, a thin, weak-jawed man with high flat cheekbones, scared Slava?

Then I saw it, the subtle exchange between them. The runner smiled at Slava. It was a slight, sad smile of recognition, which Slava greeted with a frown and a quick shake of his large, nearly bald head. And that was it. *Snap!* Done. Over, just like that. If I had blinked or turned away for the briefest second, I would have missed it completely. The runner moved to the registration desk and Slava headed out of the hotel toward me, fishing a cigarette out of his jacket, fumbling for his lighter.

"Gus," Slava said, his still unlit cigarette dangling from the yellowed corner of his lips. "How is doing your night?"

I shrugged, not sure I wanted to give myself away or to put him on the spot. One of the deals Slava and I had made was that we would not pry into each other's lives, especially our past lives. We could share a meal together, drink together, even help each other out when it was called for, but it was strictly verboten to dig in yesterday's direction. Our lives, as far as our friendship was concerned, began the day we started working together at the Paragon. And until the runner did something that put the hotel, its guests, or its staff in danger, I wasn't going to ask Slava about him, though I'd be lying if I said I wasn't curious. Really curious.

"Same as always," I lied. "Same as always."

2

The next morning I woke up thinking about the runner and Slava. There was a time not too long ago when my first thought every morning was the same thought: John Jr. Well, that's not accurate, not completely. John would be at the center of my first thought, but the focus would shift. Sometimes the focus would be on remembering his death, all the horrible episodes surrounding it coming at me like the distinct flashes of a strobe light: the call from Annie, telling Krissy about her brother, the hospital, the wake, the burial. The cruelest thing in life, a parent putting a kid in the ground. Sometimes it was the emotions: the hurt, the rage, the sorrow, the grief. The grief . . . that was still present, like the background traffic noise when you lived close to the expressway. It had once been a blaring train horn blasting in my ears all day long until I'd wanted to surrender to it. But the warning horns were moot. The train had already run me down. There was no getting out of the way.

Sometimes they were good memories, though. I can't pretend there weren't good memories, too. Memories of John Jr. playing basketball—he was always at peace playing b-ball—John at the kitchen table checking his sister's homework, John as a little boy falling asleep in my lap at

Yankee Stadium. Annie reading with John before bedtime. Good or bad, they were relentless, giving me no rest, no escape, no peace. It was only when I'd begun to resent my dead son, to hate him for dying and haunting my every waking moment, that I turned to someone for help.

Doc Rosen had saved me from myself. He would deny it, had denied it when we'd spoken about it. But just because he refused to take credit didn't make it any less true. It was Dr. Rosen who'd gotten me out into the world again, who had basically drawn footstep patterns on the floor of his office and shown me how to put one foot before the other. *Right foot, then left foot. One step, then two steps, then, before you know it, you're walking. And only the living walk, John. Only the living.* And it was my appointment with Doc Rosen that I was headed to when I stopped down at the front desk to talk with Felix.

Felix, who ran the front desk during the day shift, was my friend, too, much in the same vein as Slava. Felix had come from the Philippines and had shared some of his story with me, but he also had his secrets, though seemingly less sinister ones than Slava. Felix was the kind of guy who would beat himself up with guilt over having once thought about stealing a piece of gum. He would never have taken the gum, not Felix, and there was something really cool about people like him. Honesty that wasn't self-serving or reflexive was in very short supply these days. Perhaps it always had been.

"Gus, good morning to you." Felix extended his short arm to me. We always shook hands. I liked that about him. "What is going on today?"

"Heading out for a little while. Hey, listen, a guy checked in last night around the same time as Mr. Logan. Both got off a Lauderdale flight."

Felix's smile vanished as he tapped the keyboard on the desk in front of him.

"Why, is there trouble with him? I mean, will there be trouble?" His Filipino inflection got intense when he became agitated.

Felix was a worrier, always looking for trouble, and finding it even when it wasn't there. This time, maybe it was there.

"Mr. Michael Smith," he said. "Room one eleven. Checked in right after Mr. Logan."

"Smith?" Unoriginal. I laughed a little laugh. "I doubt there'll be any problems, but I want to make sure. Can you print out all his particulars for me?"

"Certainly, Gus. Just give me a minute."

As Felix worked the keyboard I asked, "How long a stay is he down for?"

"Let me . . . Okay, no, wait . . ." He was talking more to himself. "Seems like it is an indefinite stay. At least that is what it says here."

I heard the high-pitched whine as his printer came to life, the soft chatter of its machinery, and then it went quiet.

"Here you go, Gus."

I took the sheet from Felix but didn't bother looking at it just yet. Instead, I folded the page once and then once again, sliding it into my back pocket.

"Something from the coffee shop?" I asked.

"No, thank you. I am fine."

"Later, Felix."

I walked into the hotel coffee shop, shaking my head at the wall mural by the entrance. I did that each time I walked by. The mural, like the front portico, was a vestige from the original hotel design. It marked great moments in Long Island's history in the field of aviation. It might as well have marked great moments in Long Island's whaling or bootleg-ging history, for they were all now in the past and equally irrelevant. Like a lot of the country, Long Island had turned rapidly from a place where things were produced into a place where they were consumed. Long Islanders had a particularly rabid appetite for consumption. If you lis-tened closely enough, you could almost hear the official island mantra beneath the crashing of the waves along the South Shore beaches: I want, I want, I want.

I thought I might get lucky and happen into Mr. Smith in the coffee shop, that I might engage him in conversation, to see if he was going to present an issue. No such luck. The place was already empty at a quarter past nine. It smelled of frying eggs, burnt toast, grilling onions from the home fries, and fresh roasted coffee. I had to hand it to the Bonackers. The Paragon wasn't the Waldorf, not by a long shot, but they didn't cheap out on the coffee. There were only small take-out cups, so I filled two of them up, added my Sweet'N Lows and half-and-half, and slurped a little off the top of each before lidding them. As I turned to leave, my cell buzzed in my pocket. I put the coffees down on the counter.

It was Bill Kilkenny.

"If it isn't my favorite ex-priest," I said. "What's up?"

"Good day to you, Gus Murphy."

Bill was Bronx born and to the bone, but affected a kind of B-movie Irish lilt. It was, as he told me, a thing he had started doing when he was an army chaplain in Vietnam. "It made me seem older and wiser than I was, and the guys seemed to want and need that from me." He had never gotten out of the habit, not even after taking off the collar.

"Back at you, Bill. Listen, I'm headed over to see Doc Rosen now, so—"

"I need to see you, to talk. Do you think you might be convinced to come my way after your appointment with the good doctor?"

I checked my watch. "Sure. Wanna meet for lunch over at All-American Burger on Merrick Road? Say around noon? My treat."

"A lovely offer, for sure, Gus, but I think I'd prefer us discussing the matter to be spoken of in a more private setting."

"Like your apartment?"

"Just so. Just so. Noon then."

"Noon it is."

I hung up, picked up my coffees, and went back into the lobby. Mr. Smith wasn't there, either.

"Felix, can you check the schedule? Is Slava on tonight?" I asked, passing by the registration desk on my way out.

He shook his head, his mop of black hair dancing. "Off."

"Okay, thanks."

I sat in the front seat of my new-used Mustang, sipping coffee against the morning chill. It had been that kind of April from the day it arrived, the weather only ever threatening warmth without delivering. Today there was no ambiguity, no promises or threats of warmth. It was turn-your-collar-up raw, a nasty gray mist enveloping the pudgy middle of Suffolk County. Even the cars along Vets Highway seemed to want to get in out of the weather. Jet engines droned and whined a mournful tune as the nose of a Southwest 737 emerged from the overcast above me. Another flight from Florida full of returning snowbirds. But the trick would be on them when they stepped out of the terminal into the current lies of springtime.

3

Bill Kilkenny, a lanky stick of a man, lived in a spare basement apartment in North Massapequa. It was as inglorious as it sounded, but Father Bill —I didn't call him that any longer, though I would always think of him that way—was used to having very little and didn't want for much. As he'd told me once, he was a prisoner of his past. *Who wasn't?* He said that a priest, unless he rises up through the ranks, learns possessions are cumbersome things that blind you to your calling. And it was the whole moving-up-the-ranks thing that had helped drive him out of the priesthood.

"When I rediscovered my faith, I found I had very little use for the mechanics and hierarchy of the church itself."

I supposed I owed as much to Bill as I did to Doc Rosen, for they were the two men who helped keep my head above water for the two years following John's death. It was almost as if Bill had handed me off to Doc after he'd done all he could do in that first year. Bill had the harder job, of course. Bill, he was still Father Bill then, walked into the raging shit storm in the immediate aftermath of John's death. He bore witness to Annie, Krissy, and me tearing ourselves apart because it was all we could do with our grief. I owed Bill Kilkenny for that. For other things, too, like literally saving my life. But the debt I owed for John Jr. was so great I could never fully repay it.

And there was Bill as I always found him, smoking a cigarette by the side of the beige, vinyl-sided ranch. He was a hopeless casualty of priestly fashion. He wore a ratty cable-knit sweater that had once been white but now matched the dirty beige siding. His pilled black slacks, worn shiny at the knees, hung off him like a scarecrow's, but worse were those ugly black priest shoes I could never get him to abandon. I'd even bought him a pair of running shoes at Costco, to no avail. When Bill saw me coming, he lifted his left foot and snuffed out his cigarette on the sole of his ugly shoe.

"Gus Murphy, prompt as always," he said, tossing the butt on the ground and wiping his palms together.

I took his right hand in mine. "Bill. Good to see you. What's this about?"

"I've got the wine opened and the glasses cleaned. We'll discuss it inside." He nodded toward the rear of the ranch.

"Sure, Bill."

Walking ahead, I turned back to see him bend over and scoop up the dead cigarette, cupping it in his hand like a fallen nestling.

"Go on." He shooed me away with his other hand. "The door's open."

I walked down the concrete steps and pulled back the door to his basement apartment. The place was much as it always was: neat, bare, musty. Beyond the dampness, there was an acrid petroleum tang of home heating oil from the boiler room. The boiler hummed on just the other side of the living room wall. The odor smacked me in the nose every time I walked in, but after a few minutes I got used to it and the stink seemed to vanish. The same could not be said of the scent of cigarette smoke. Although Bill never smoked in the house, he carried the smell with him on his clothes, his hair, his breath, and his skin. Of late, Bill's habit was worse. I suppose killing a man will do that to you, even if the man deserved killing.

When Bill came in a few seconds behind me, he headed straight to the kitchen. I heard the lid of the garbage can open and close. Heard him wash his hands in the sink. Heard the tinkling of glasses and the *glug glug glug* of wine being poured.

"Here we are, lad," he said, handing me a glass of red wine so dark it was nearly purple.

One glass of wine before we spoke. It was a ritual of ours established during my rage and grief. It was a way to step back from it, to put a fence around it for a few brief moments. The ritual became my sanctuary. The rage was gone, but the ritual remained.

"*Sláinte*, Gus."

"*Sláinte.*"

We clinked glasses and sipped.

"Christ, Bill, this stuff must've cost you a fortune."

"Amazing stuff, is it not? But I must confess to you that it was a gift from an old acquaintance."

"You must be keeping better company these days."

He shrugged. And we finished our glasses of wine slowly, savoring the wine's complexity, each sip revealing a different aspect of the wine from the one preceding it. It was rich with notes of berries and black pepper, and it tasted differently on the tip of your tongue from how it did at the back of your throat.

"Okay, Bill, we've had our wine. So, what's the deal?"

Just as I asked, there was the scratchy sound of grit caught between shoe soles and concrete on the stairs leading down to the apartment. A mischievous smile bent the corners of Bill's thin lips and there was a glint in his eyes. I got the sense that a spider might wear that same expression when it detected a stray termite stuck in its web.

"That'll be Micah now."

"Micah?"

"Micah Spears."

"Should I know that name?"

Before Bill could answer, the door opened. In stepped a man with a cruel mouth and cold green eyes, who looked like he was wearing sins in the pores of his skin, the deeply etched lines on his face, and in the pockets of his fancy green tweed and tan suede blazer. I didn't believe in God, but I believed in sin. Sin was real because there was wrong in the hearts of men and women, but it wasn't put there by a seductive serpent or because of apple eating out of turn. Sin was born the first time a human being wanted more than he had or deserved. And I didn't need to know anything about Spears to know he was nipple deep in hell. I knew because I had been there myself. Sometimes late at night, when I was alone in the van or half asleep, staring up at the ceiling of my room, I'd forget that I wasn't still there.

4

Spears was probably Bill's age, maybe a bit older, though he did not share Bill's priestly modesty or taste in clothing. His clothes were perfectly tailored to his still-athletic body. He was one of those guys who you just knew worked hard at cheating death. He ate right, spent hours on the treadmill, worked with a personal trainer. But all the fancy tailoring and gym time in the world could only hide so much and delay the inevitable just so long. It was my experience that these death-cheating types weren't so much in love with life as they were afraid of death. I laughed to myself, thinking that belief in God was a curse. To believe in him you had to believe in his judgment. Did people really imagine judgment awaited them? What judgment could be harsher than our own? And by the look of him, of his icy, distant green eyes, Micah Spears seemed impervious to judgment. God's or otherwise.

Bill pointed at me and then to Spears. "Gus Murphy, Micah Spears. Micah Spears, Gus Murphy."

Spears offered me his hand and I took it. He had a firm grip and he held on to my hand even as I tried to take it back. He was one of those guys, the type who thinks he can know you by your handshake. I didn't

possess that skill. It was like believing I could know a man by how he reacted to having me cuff his hands behind his back or how he blinked when
I recited the Miranda warning. *Do you understand these rights as I've read
them to you?* I had known cops who swore they knew someone was lying
by how the suspect's fingers twitched or whether the suspect looked up or
down when he answered their questions. It was all so much horseshit.

"Bill's told me a lot about you, Murphy," Spears said, turning his head
at an angle to take my measure.

More assessment. More horseshit.

"Then I'm at a disadvantage."

He nodded and clapped his hand on my right biceps. He smelled intensely of Old Spice aftershave, which, if it hadn't reminded me of my
drunk prick of a father, would have been a relief from the dank apartment's cigarette and home-heating-oil perfume.

"How'd you like the wine?" Spears asked, changing subjects.

Now I knew how Bill had come by it. A gift? An inducement? A
bribe? Sometimes three different words meant the same thing. But Bill
wasn't bribable. All a stranger had to do was look around his apartment
or at his clothes closet to know that. As a priest and confessor, Bill
Kilkenny knew things about important people that they would surely kill
for or, at a minimum, pay a lot to prevent from seeing the light of day, but
Bill had been the kind of priest to match his B-movie lilt. Even after
losing his faith, he was a diligent priest. I think he would sooner die than
break a trust. So if Bill had thought it important for me to meet Micah
Spears, I would listen.

Still, I took an immediate dislike to Spears. Was it his handshake test?
His belief that a fancy bottle of wine could buy Bill's favor? Or was it
something as petty as his aftershave reminding me of my father?

"Great wine," I said. "Must've cost you."

Bill answered for him. "Micah can afford it. He owns a . . . remind me
again, boyo, what it is that it's called?"

"An ESCO. An energy service company. I own three, actually. I buy and sell electricty and natural gas to commercial and residential consumers."

Bill shook his head at Spears. "And there's money in that, is there?"

"Horse-choking money, Bill."

"But I assume that's not why I'm here," I said, "to discuss your net worth or to watch you choke a horse with a stack of hundreds?"

"You were right about this guy, Bill." Spears pointed at me even as he looked at Kilkenny. "He's sharp and he already doesn't like me."

"You're a hard fella to like, Micah, if you don't mind me saying. You don't make it easy."

"Fuck easy, Bill. What's easy in this world?"

That much we agreed on.

"Okay, Bill asked me here. I'm here. I'm guessing it was to talk to you. So talk."

Micah Spears reached into his pants pocket and removed a sleek cell phone that looked more like a shrunken tablet. He tapped the screen a few times, then scrolled with his right index finger. He tapped again and handed me the phone.

"That's my granddaughter, Linh Trang," he said, as if that explained the universe. For him, maybe it did.

She was a pretty girl, slightly built, with a disarming smile. Her Asian eyes, overdone with blue eye shadow, black liner, and mascara, smiled to match her mouth. She had a button nose and black hair blown back by the wind. She wore a blue mortarboard atop her head, a gold tassel hanging off to one side.

"Pretty girl," I said, handing back his phone. "Graduation day?"

He nodded his gray head. "From Hofstra, last May. She was an accounting major. Top grades."

I asked, "Okay, so what about her?"

Spears stared down at Bill's threadbare carpeting. "She's dead."

That caught me by surprise. Bill crossed himself. That reflex had died in me long ago.

"I'm sorry, but how—"

Spears didn't seem to hear me.

"Murdered," Bill said. "She was murdered."

"Christ!" Spears said. "The fuckhead stabbed her twenty-three times. It was all over the news this last fall. I'm surprised you didn't read about it."

Bill spoke for me. "Gus isn't much for the news these days, Micah. And I was too long in the priesthood to venture too far beyond the needs of the people to whom I ministered."

I was a little curious. "And what is it you want from me?"

"I want you to look into it," Spears said, sneering at me as if I was a complete idiot. Maybe I was an idiot, because the longer I stood there, the less I liked the man and the less I cared what he wanted.

"That's what the Suffolk County Police Department is for. I would know. I worked for them for twenty years."

"I think you misunderstand me, Gus—may I call you Gus?"

"Sure. Gus works. So, what is it that I'm not getting?"

"I'm not asking you to find Linh's killer. The Suffolk cops caught him two days after she was murdered. His name's Rondo Salazar and he's in Riverhead, awaiting trial."

I looked to Bill, turning my palms up in confusion. "So what do you need me for? Do *you* understand, Bill? I'm missing something here, but maybe you get it."

Bill shook his head. "Micah, I know you told me before I arranged for you to meet Gus that it was to be about your granddaughter's murder, but I'm afraid I'm with Gus in that I'm not sure what you're asking of him. Is it that you don't think this Salazar fella was the man who murdered Linh Trang?"

"No, that motherfucker murdered her, all right. He's guilty and I'd kill him if I could."

"Is that what you're asking Gus to do, Micah? To gain access to this man so that he might kill him for you?" Bill was shouting, spit flying, his hollow cheeks fire red. "Have you dared use me as a conduit for such a deplorable thing?"

Spears waved his hands. "Relax, Bill. Relax. That's not what I'm asking, though I confess that if I thought Gus here could manage it and would consider it, I would ask. And not for nothing, but it's not like you don't have some blood on your hands there, Father Bill."

"Watch your mouth!" I shouted.

But Spears only laughed. "Temper, temper, Gus."

"Fuck you, asshole."

I lifted up my right hand to slap him across the face. Men detest being slapped. Punch them, they're okay with that. Slap them, and it somehow reflects on their manhood. But before I could slap him, Bill stepped between us, his back to me. Then he turned and pushed both of us apart. His anger, though, was directed at me.

"Stop it, the both of you. John Augustus Murphy, I fight my own battles. Always have and always will. I don't need defending by the likes of you. And to be truthful, I do have blood on my hands."

"On my account," I said. "It was my life you were saving when you shot that prick."

Bill wasn't having it. "And my life and the girl's as well. I did what needed doing."

"Besides, Gus," Spears said, reaching into his jacket pocket, pulling out two checks, "you wouldn't want to ruin this opportunity."

I shrugged. "I don't need your money and I don't want it. I've got half my pension, a steady job, and a pillow under my head."

"These checks aren't for you," he said. "Not directly, anyway."

"More nonsense."

He shook his head. "Not nonsense. One check is for fifty thousand dollars to start a youth sports foundation in your son's name and the other is for two hundred thousand to Stony Brook University Hospital to help fund research in . . . well, whatever you choose. I can rip them up and you can leave or I can hand them over to you right now."

"Okay," I said, "you've got my attention."

"Good."

"You've got my attention, but I don't see why you want it. And please don't give me that crap about looking into your granddaughter's murder. You said it yourself, the cops already have the guilty party."

He pursed the lips of his cruel mouth and tilted his head. "You're right. They have Salazar and he's guilty, but he won't talk. Hasn't said a word since he was arrested. The press and cops have theories about why he did it, but I'm not buying. I need to know why for Linh's sake, for her parents' sake. I need to know why."

The bastard had me and he knew it. Bill knew it, too. And I couldn't help but wonder how much of a part Bill had played in this beyond bringing the both of us together. Spears knew about John Jr. and the price I'd paid in the aftermath. It was clear Bill hadn't known the bloody details of Linh Trang's murder. I'd seen his shock at hearing them, but he understood what made me tick. That the magic word for me was "why." *Why? Why? Why?* I was haunted by it.

"You can give those checks to Bill for now," I said. "I believe in earning my keep. I'll ask around a little, and if I find anything, I'll be in touch."

He handed Bill the checks, handed me a business card. And for the first time since he came through the door, Micah Spears looked like a human being. All the sin, the cruelty, the snark and sneering seemed to have vanished.

"Thank you, Gus," he said, putting his hand out to me again.

This time he let it go without that extra beat of assessment. Apparently, I had passed the test.

5

Why?

The word went round and round in my head as I drove away from Bill's place. From the second I'd gotten the call from Annie about our son, "Why?" had been the central question in my life. The problem was there was no one available to answer the question. No one to see about it. No one to pay for it. No one to make it right. Doctors understand the mechanics of the why of death, but not the Zen of it. Why him? Why now? Why this? Why? And with all due respect to Bill, there was no God to ask. Even when I believed, God was mum. Paragon guests were always leaving books behind them in the van. I scavenged them to fill up the empty, lonely hours between runs. In one PI novel I read there was this character, a wise old man who claimed that God did answer prayers. He said God answered them all the time, but that his answer was mostly no. Sounded nice in a book, I guess. In real life it was just more crap. When it came to why, a cold, indifferent universe was more impenetrable than a mute God. It didn't explain itself. Not to me. Not to anyone.

After the initial tsunami of pain and grief there was rage. It fueled me, became the filter through which I experienced the world. Every feeling I had, especially love, became an iteration of rage. I wasn't alone in my rage. Annie and Krissy were just as furious in their way. It's what fueled us as we blew apart what was left of our family. Annie and Krissy had targets for their fury. Annie focused hers at me. Krissy's at herself. Me, I took on the universe. I wasn't usually an ambitious person, but I was ambitious in my rage.

We're complicated animals, us humans, but sometimes we're nothing more than little kids asking grown-ups why. All we want, all we need, is a reasonable explanation, even if it's wrong. Me, I needed something beyond "God has a plan for all of us." Something more than *When it's your time, it's your time.* Something more than a shrug. I'm more at peace now with the knowledge that I'm never going to get answers. That the question of why will hang in the air like a lazy fly ball that will never come down or a red balloon slipping out of a little girl's hand at the zoo.

It seemed to me that Micah Spears knew just what scab to pick at. Maybe Bill had coached him to go there or maybe Spears was genuinely interested in the true motive behind his granddaughter's murder. Now that I was committed, it didn't matter. I should have felt sympathy for the man and maybe I should have dug a little more deeply into his motives when I had the chance, but, Christ, I couldn't stand to be with Spears another minute. Were his checks an inducement? Of course they were. I'm not a fucking idiot. To have a foundation in John Jr.'s name meant he might live on beyond the memories of the people who loved him. We are all forgotten eventually, but I wanted John's memory to outlive me, Annie, and Krissy. And who wouldn't want to contribute to research that might prevent another family from going through what we went through?

For the moment, Micah Spears and his motives could wait. Sadly, his granddaughter wasn't going to be any more or less dead if I started looking into her death immediately or in the morning. Death was as much a constant as pi or the speed of light. The dead could afford to be patient and so could I. I pulled my car into a parking spot at the edge of the

Paragon's parking lot. Although I fished out the sheet with Michael Smith's particulars from my back pocket, I ignored it.

I took a minute to check out the cabin of the 2010 Mustang I'd owned for about a week. I was still getting used to it. Since last Christmas, when three bikers tried to kill me, destroying my car instead, I'd made do with insurance rentals, borrowed cars, lifts, and the spare Paragon courtesy van. I wasn't a procrastinator by nature, but I wasn't sure what my nature was anymore. For the last twenty plus years, I'd owned family cars. A minivan when the kids were young. An Accord. A Taurus. I was a man and I had the remnants of a family, but I wasn't a family man anymore. I guess it finally took a kick in my ass from Magdalena to get me to buy something.

"I'm not Cinderella and no one knows better than me that money isn't anything next to love, but it's a little weird when you leave the courtesy van in my guest parking spot overnight. I'm not a woman who needs a limo. Still, I prefer something a little sexier than an airport shuttle."

She was right. Maggie was right about a lot of things. So when Tino, the night-shift van driver at the Clarion Hotel down Vets Highway from the Paragon, told me he was selling his Mustang, I checked it out and bought it the next day. One of the things that was different about me now was that I thought about my impulses, about what I wanted and why. I had never been a man who wanted for much, because I didn't want much. Funny how that works. That much about me hadn't changed. I still didn't want much. But in the week since I'd gotten the car, I found myself wondering if I'd bought it because I'd never had a sporty car or because John Jr. never had one and never would.

Doc Rosen and I had talked about that earlier. He didn't have much to say on the subject. He doesn't usually have a lot to say except to ask how I feel about things, yet somehow he manages to get his point across. Today's point was that it didn't matter why I bought the Mustang. The car was mine, and like everything else in life that a person brings on himself or is thrown his way, it's how you move forward. The weird thing about Rosen was that he could make me feel better just by asking me a question.

"How do you think John Jr. would feel about you buying the car?"

When I smiled, he smiled. We both had our answers.

Before I got around to looking at the sheet of paper Felix had printed out, Magdalena called.

"Hey, babe."

"Hey, Gus."

"What's going on?"

"Can we switch plans to tomorrow night?"

"Why, what's up? You get a bartending gig?"

"Better than that. A callback audition in the morning."

When Maggie was in her twenties she had a recurring role on a popular soap opera, but her career stalled and she wound up marrying some asshole personal-injury lawyer. By the time their marriage ended, all Maggie had to show for it was a beat-up old Mercedes, an eighth of a bottle of custom-made perfume, and a condo. By then, as she told me, she'd lost her chops, her confidence, and her agent.

"I wasn't Meryl Streep to begin with," she said. "Playing the hot blond bad girl served me well when I was twenty-two. At thirty-two, not so much."

When we met, Magdalena was bartending in an after-hours club in an industrial park in Hauppauge, a place called Malo. I'd been brought there by Pete McCann, a Suffolk County detective who'd once been a close friend. We were close until he started fucking my now ex-wife a few months after John's death. Pete had slept with Maggie, too. That was the thing about Pete: Unlike me, he was a guy who wanted things, especially things that weren't his to have. Pete was dead now. It was Pete who Bill Kilkenny had been forced to kill in order to save me, a woman named Katie Smalls, and himself. There was a lot of blood spilled that night. Only some of it was Pete's.

In any case, Maggie and I had been seeing each other since we'd met. We were good for each other. She still tended bar. She also had started taking acting classes and auditioning. Me, I don't know. I felt almost human again when we were together. Almost. We came to each other as damaged goods, but we didn't dwell on the damage done to us and the dents we'd put into other people's lives. We didn't talk about the future, either. We just tried to be. Whatever that meant.

"What kind of part?" I asked.

"Let's not talk about it, okay? I don't want to jinx it."

"Sure. I can shift my schedule around."

When I hung up, I noticed a car zipping past me into the Paragon parking lot and pulling under the portico. It was Slava's old green Honda Civic with the mismatched fenders. I knew it because I'd borrowed it many times since Christmas. Normally, I wouldn't have paid it any mind, but Felix told me Slava had the night off. Even if he had been scheduled, his shift wouldn't've started for several more hours. But what really got my attention was the man quickly getting into the front seat beside Slava. It was the mysterious Michael Smith. Since Maggie had just canceled on me, I decided on my new plans for the evening. I waited for Slava to leave and to get about a quarter mile ahead of me on Vets Highway before I pulled out to follow him.

6

Slava must have been distracted, because he didn't seem to notice me behind him. If he had, he would have ditched my ass without much effort. Following a car is a lot more complicated than it's portrayed in the movies. To do it right, you usually need multiple cars. Since I'd spent most of my career in uniform, driving a white-and-blue cruiser with the words SUFFOLK COUNTY POLICE written in big bold letters on its flanks and a light bar on the roof, I wasn't exactly an expert at it. When I was chasing you, you knew it.

Slava wouldn't talk about his past, but there was some stuff I'd figured out about him. For one, he wasn't who or what he seemed. With his booming voice and broken English, cigarette and vodka breath, big belly, veined and bulbous nose, Warsaw Pact dental work, and thrift-store wardrobe, he looked the part of the buffoon. With a little greasepaint, maybe even the clown. He was no buffoon, no clown. Behind the back-slapping and favorite-uncle routine was a serious man with a dark past.

He carried a Russian-made Makarov pistol and an old-fashioned leather-and-lead sap on him. He was skilled with them both. I'd seen it for myself. He had known where to look to find a hidden tracking device in my car and, unlike me, knew how to trail a car without being spotted or lost. It was an unusual skill set for a Polish émigré bellman. Until last December, I had accepted his story that he was just a poor peasant from Warsaw. Now I was less sure about that.

As Slava's Civic approached Sunrise Highway, I'd foolishly let myself get within that quarter-mile window. I half expected him to speed up or hang a fast U-turn or do something to lose me. He did nothing evasive, instead making a lazy turn onto Sunrise and working his way to the Southern State Parkway heading west. Given that we were starting out almost as far east in the United States as it was possible to be, our direction didn't give me much insight into where Slava and his passenger might be going. For all I knew, it might as well be to Anaheim as Amityville.

For the first part of the trip along the Southern State, a twisty, old tree-lined highway with low stone overpasses, it was easy to keep my distance and still keep Slava in sight. But as the rush-hour traffic built up and the already gray skies deepened, both tasks became more difficult. There were whole stretches of stop-and-go, bumper-to-bumper traffic followed by moments of clear sailing and higher speeds. But I managed to stay with him through all of Nassau County, into Queens, and onto the Belt Parkway. The traffic on the Belt was a nightmare, though it eased when we passed Kennedy Airport. And after Slava zipped by the Cross Bay Boulevard exit, I figured we were headed at least as far as Brooklyn.

When Slava exited at Coney Island Avenue, it seemed that Brooklyn was indeed where we were going. Brighton Beach, to be exact. Brighton Beach was now almost completely a Ukrainian and Russian enclave. I'd heard stories from city cops about how the neighborhood was run by the Russian mob and how it was impossible to get them to roll over on one another. I knew Brooklyn a little bit because my parents and grandparents were from here, but not this side of the borough. They came from neighborhoods like Greenpoint, Flatbush, East New York, and Red Hook. I'd been around this side of Brooklyn maybe five times in my life, mostly as a teenager with my friends at Coney Island, and maybe once or twice when I went drinking with cop buddies in Bay Ridge.

The ride up Coney Island Avenue toward the beach was a brief one, and when Slava turned right under the elevated subway tracks along Brighton Beach Avenue, the sky blackened into permanent night. Above my head trains thundered, their wheels, their brakes screeching and squealing, random sparks raining down on the cars below. The air smelling like burnt metal sparklers on the Fourth of July. It smelled of the ocean, too. It was the same ocean smell we got in Suffolk County, same ocean, only somehow it smelled dirtier here, with sour, rotting notes beneath the brine. Slava was stopped at a light a block ahead of me, so I pulled over by a fire hydrant and waited.

With the El tracks, the little shops at street level, and two stories of rental apartments above them, the streets crowded with people, I felt like I was looking into the past at old New York. But in the past, the signs would have been in English or maybe Italian or Yiddish. Not the signs here. Not now. In Brighton Beach, the signs were written in Russian. Maybe it was Ukrainian. How the hell would I know the difference? I knew it wasn't English. Lucky for me that I looked away from the signage just in time to see a man come running out of one of the stores on the street, a produce market, I think, and get into the backseat of Slava's car. I couldn't make out much about him except that he wore a torn black leather jacket and seemed to be about Slava's age and size.

Emerging from the artificial night beneath the tracks and into real darkness, I followed the car down Brighton Beach Avenue until it turned left onto Surf Avenue. I stayed as close behind as I dared, worried that I might lose sight of the Civic along the swooping swan neck curve of Surf Avenue that was kind of the gateway to Coney Island. Suddenly, the boardwalk was visible to my left, the Atlantic maybe fifty or a hundred yards beyond it. I still couldn't hear the ocean for the rumble of subways at my back. I passed a park with a band shell, handball courts, and the New York Aquarium. The Cyclone roller coaster was lit up for business, but there was no business. The gray mist of the day had transformed itself into a steady, miserable rain.

I could hang back because Slava's taillights were easy to see with so little traffic. Then, just before he got to Nathan's Famous, he hung a quick right onto Stillwell Avenue, heading back beneath the elevated tracks. But when I turned onto Stillwell, his taillights were nowhere in sight. I kicked myself for having gotten this far without being spotted and for losing him because my success to that point had made me complacent. Isn't it always the way?

The thing was that I had pretty much already exhausted my local knowledge of the streets. Once I was off Surf Avenue, I was out of my depth, so I did the only thing I could do. I slowed down, looking left and right and ahead of me for the old Civic with the wrong-colored fenders. I turned left onto Mermaid Avenue and began a search pattern, driving along Mermaid, turning down the side streets—West 15th, West 16th, and so on—until I hit Neptune Avenue and back up the next street. Then, on West 21st Street between Mermaid and Neptune, I found Slava's car. It was empty, of course, because a good fifteen minutes had passed since I'd lost him. I backed down the street, pulled into an empty spot, and waited.

7

As I waited, I put my cell phone to work in a way I hardly ever used it, Googling Linh Trang Spears. Though I realized Spears might not be her last name, I thought I'd try it. I realized a lot of things as I sat there in my front seat, waiting, watching. For one, I realized I was a fucking idiot. That I had finally gotten a piece of my life back. That I'd found an incredible woman I could love and who could return love to the man I was becoming. I was on good terms with Annie. Krissy was back at Stony Brook. I had a steady job, such as it was, and new friends. Yet here I was at the ass end of Brooklyn on my night off, following around a friend who probably didn't want or need me following him around. But the worst of it was agreeing to help Micah Spears. I wanted to bang my forehead into the steering wheel for being a fool.

I realized that accepting his checks as a trade-off was a remnant of the magical thinking I had tried so hard to shed. Sure, the foundation and the research were worthy things, and of course I had jumped at them. Of course they were a means to keep John's memory alive, but I'd had time to think as I'd driven here. I'd fallen into my own old pattern, the belief that if I just wished hard enough and did all the right things, and if I clicked the ruby slippers together three times, that maybe Humpty

Dumpty could be put back together again. I was past hoping. I thought I had finally gotten past wishing. And each time I thought it, I would prove myself wrong. I would never get fully past it. I would always wish John Jr. back alive and wish all of it undone. Dead was dead and gone was gone and that was that. But I guess there was still a part of me that didn't want to accept it. Maybe a part of me that never would.

Just the same, I'd given my word. That meant something to me, even if handshakes and promises no longer seemed to matter much to the rest of the world. So I looked at the screen, waiting for the results to come up. Linh Trang's last name *had* been Spears and I got lots of hits. She was the adopted daughter of Kevin and Victoria Spears of Bellport, New York. There were plenty of photos of her. Some better than the one her grandfather had shown me. Some older ones, too, grainy black-and-white newspaper reprints of her as a teenager. Despite the relative quality of the photos, there was no spinning the brutality of her murder. Just as Micah Spears had said, Linh Trang had been stabbed twenty-three times. She'd been reported missing by her parents early on the Sunday before Thanksgiving, and her body had been discovered by a Great River couple out for an early-morning walk in Heckscher State Park later that day.

I got a sick feeling in my belly, remembering our first Thanksgiving and Christmas after John's death. Holidays were the worst. There wasn't a single thing in the house—the smell of roasting turkey, a dent in the hallway wall, the creaking of the basement stairs—that didn't evoke his memory. The air was so thick with him, we all choked on it. Those first holidays were the final straw. We knew there was no future for us together after that, and we knew we could never live in that house again. Remembering the horror of those first holidays, it took everything I had in me not to cry for her parents and for myself. They had the added horror of Linh Trang's death being so violent. I read on.

The unnamed police spokesman said the body had been moved to the park and that Linh Trang had been killed in a different location. I searched through all the stories but could find no mention of the actual murder scene having been located. I went back and read the stuff on the pursuit and capture of Rondo Salazar. Other than stating that he was a prime suspect in the unrelated homicide of a drug dealer, there was no specific mention of how the SCPD tracked him down. But I knew how to hear the words that weren't spoken, and how to read between the lines. Either they had surveillance footage, they got an anonymous tip, or an informant gave Salazar up. My bet was on a tip or an informant. A lot of brilliant detective work came down to good sources and good luck. I'd be able to find that out easily enough. I'd been off the job for three-plus years, but I still had sources inside the department.

Micah Spears might have been a bit of a belligerent asshole, but he hadn't lied to me. So far the little he had told me about his granddaughter's murder had been spot on. The test would come when I looked into Salazar's motives. I was just about to scan through the *Newsday* stories about Salazar when I noticed movement down the block. The front door to a crummy little row house opened only a few feet to the left from where Slava's car was parked. Most of the houses on the street fit that description. Their façades were mostly beige brick—many chipped and dirty—with little stoops three or four cracked steps up from the sidewalk. The majority had bars on their first-floor windows. Some of the weary houses had dirty aluminum siding covering their brick façades and unattached flanks. A few had narrow little driveways.

The rain had stopped by the time Slava and Michael Smith came out onto the stoop. They did not walk down the steps. Instead, they stood on the stoop, facing inside the house from which they had just come. I assumed they were speaking to the third man, the one with the torn leather jacket, though the open door blocked me from seeing who it was. They were too far away for me to make out much of their facial expressions, yet there was something about how they stood that told me this hadn't been a happy reunion of old friends. Their shoulders were slumped and, like the houses on the block, their bodies sagged. No, there wasn't anything cheery going on here. Then, quickly and unceremoniously, Slava and

WHAT YOU BREAK / 33

Smith turned, trundled down the steps, and got into the old Civic. Neither looked back at the still-open door. There were no fond farewell waves. Slava started the car, popped on his lights, and pulled away.

I stayed behind, watching. I was curious about the man blocked by the door. I figured that I'd give him a minute to close the door and go back inside. Then I would drive up closer to the house, see what I could see, jot down the address, maybe take a photo with my cell. The door didn't close. Instead, the third man, wearing that torn jacket, stepped out onto the stoop. He lit a cigarette, the flame of his lighter illuminating his face for a brief second. It was a cruel face, the cruelty enhanced by the red flame. He had a flattened nose, pitted skin, and a nasty-looking mouth. Standing there, he surveyed the street. His gaze wasn't casual. It was a wary stare, not dissimilar to the stare I'd seen in my rearview mirror when I'd looked back at Michael Smith as I drove him from MacArthur to the Paragon. He was looking for danger that might come at him out of the dark.

At one point, he turned in my direction and seemed to focus his full attention on me. It was only after I caught sight of headlights in my sideview mirror and heard the telltale splash of tires kicking up water behind me that I understood the man on the stoop was looking over the roof of my car at another vehicle coming up the street, a white Dodge van. I kept switching my gaze from the man on the stoop to the van and back again. There was something about the white van he didn't like. I could tell by how his body stiffened and how he tossed his cigarette. I didn't like it, either. This Dodge was driving slowly, too slowly. I thought of how a cat moved when it was hunting. I tried to get a look at the driver as it rolled past me, but the windows were tinted nearly black. I focused on the rear of the van, staring at the New York tag number ENK 4771. I repeated the tag number aloud to myself.

The world got very quiet, the way it does when your body is going into fight-or-flight mode. My throat was suddenly dry and my heart was pounding. But the van rolling down the street kept going right on by the man on the stoop. My eyes, his eyes, stayed locked on it as it moved to the end of the street and turned left onto Mermaid. Even at this distance I could see him relax and breathe out a huge sigh. There was even a smile on his cruel mouth as he lit up another cigarette. As he relaxed, I relaxed, too. Then things changed. Everything changed. Neither the smoker nor I had noticed the man walking down the street in the opposite direction as the van, and by the time we noticed him, it was already too late. He was dressed in matte black and wore a silky black balaclava that covered his face.

In one balletic act, he reached behind him, drew a pistol, dropped to one knee, and fired. I lost count of the shots at five, and the fire spewing from the tip of the sound suppressor seemed continuous. The man on the stoop didn't have a chance, his body tumbling awkwardly down the four front steps and onto the wet pavement. Calmly, coldly, the shooter let his empty clip slide out of his weapon and clink to the sidewalk. He quickly reloaded, racked the slide, walked over to the wrecked body of the smoker—the glowing red tip of the still-lit cigarette on the concrete beside the victim—and fired two shots into his head.

I was out of my car now, Glock drawn, moving toward him. As I moved, I used stoops for cover and tried to keep as quiet as possible. I didn't shout a warning. No "Police! Drop your weapon!" Nothing like that. This guy was a pro, and pros knew that once you got caught in the act, you might as well keep killing. Innocent passersby or cops or retired cops, it didn't matter. Amateurs didn't dress in matte black, didn't wear balaclavas or use sound suppressors. And they didn't usually have the presence of mind to tap their victims twice in the head just to make sure the job was done right. Pro or not, I counted on his being too concerned about the task at hand and making a clean exit to notice me. It worked three row houses' worth.

He looked up and must have seen my hair above the ledge of a stoop. He didn't hesitate, firing three shots—*Pop! Pop! Pop!*—splintering the bricks above my head. I kept my head down and didn't return fire. I was a good shot, but he was better and clearly more experienced. I didn't want to risk a ricochet and have one of my shots careening off a sidewalk or lamppost and crashing through some kid's bedroom window. He may not have cared about killing an innocent, but I did. And I didn't want to give him a reason to come at me. As it was, he knew I couldn't identify him, and my guess was he just wanted to get out of there. If I fired at him, he might feel compelled to finish me in order to cover his exit.

When I worked up the nerve to peek over the ledge again, I saw that he was running back in the direction he'd come, toward Mermaid Avenue. I stood and calculated that even at full stride it would be more than a block before I'd be able to get close to him. When he reached the corner of Mermaid and West 21st, he rendered my calculations moot. There was the white van waiting for him, its side door open. He dove through the open door. The door closed. The van was gone. Then, as distant sirens filled up the night, so was I.

8

'd zipped out of my spot, backed down the block, and onto Neptune Avenue. I didn't stick around to see if those sirens were headed in my direction. I knew they were. I found my way to a shopping center parking lot a few blocks away, dimmed my lights, and tried to orient myself. It wasn't like I'd never seen anyone killed before. I had, and I'd seen plenty of dead bodies, but I had never witnessed anything that calculated or cold-blooded.

I was torn between going back to the crime scene and getting completely out of there. The old cop in me wanted to go back, felt an obligation to, but what could I have told the cops? I couldn't identify the killer. I hadn't even been close enough to identify the weapon he'd used. I didn't know the victim. I had only the barest description of the van, though I did have its tag number. It was probably rented or stolen. I suppose I could have explained my leaving the scene by saying I'd tried to chase the van. The cops would have bought that. The problem would have been explaining what the hell I was doing there in the first place. *I always drive into Coney Island on rainy nights and park on a block where I don't know anyone.* And even if I could have explained my presence, I didn't want to risk bringing Slava into it, at least not yet. Not until I had some idea of what was going on. I owed him that because I owed him my life, literally. Slava had saved my life at least twice.

I called Slava's cell. He didn't pick up and it went to voice mail. I left a vague message, hinting at potential danger, but not coming out and saying it. I wanted to leave both of us wiggle room if the cops ever got hold of his phone. I texted him: Call my cell, now! He didn't call. He didn't text back. I figured to give him a few minutes before trying his number again. As I sat there I wondered if Slava and Michael Smith were in danger, too, or if the hit—and there was no doubt that's what it was—was specific to the cruel-faced man with the torn jacket. I wondered a lot of things. There was a lot to wonder about. I wondered if Smith's arrival at the Paragon, his driving into Brooklyn, and the meeting with the now dead man were related to the dark and shameful past life Slava had only ever alluded to.

I remembered his first mention of it. We were at breakfast on a Saturday morning at the Airport Diner near the Paragon. I thought about that breakfast sometimes when I saw hints of who Slava really was behind his ugly, gap-tooth smile and goofy broken English. It was at that breakfast when he'd shown me his Makarov and the leather sap. It was also the first time he'd warned me away from asking too many questions about him. That conversation now echoed in my head.

"It would not be good to be curious about Slava," he said.

"For you or for me?"

His face turned headstone cold. "For both, I am thinking."

I had let that go for a few minutes, but came back to it.

"But maybe someday you'll tell me your story."

His expression was as mournful and haunted as any I had ever seen. As mournful as my own face in the mirror. "No, Gus," he said. "I am never telling you this. I am shamed in my soul."

Shamed in my soul. That phrase has never left me. I don't think it ever will.

I looked at my cell phone for the time and saw that five painful minutes had crept past since I'd called his cell. I was about to dial him again when that sick feeling in my belly returned. What if Slava and Michael Smith weren't in any danger at all, but had been the ones to set up the hit? Shame came in many forms. You could earn it in any number of ways. As anyone who had experienced it knew, shame could hurt like a bastard, but that if there was incentive enough, you would risk the pain. Bee stings hurt, too, but they didn't stop people from collecting honey.

When the phone buzzed in my hand, I startled. It was Slava.

"Gus, why are making call to—"

I cut him off. "Don't go home. Don't go back to the Paragon. Find a landline and text me the number."

I hung up without explaining. Even if he didn't fully understand, I knew he would do as I said. I got out of my car and searched the stores in the shopping center for a pay phone. There was one in the pizzeria. The Mexican kid behind the counter tried to sell me a slice, but I waved him off. He shrugged and went back to watching a soccer match, the play-by-play announcer's voice rising and falling in rapid-fire Spanish. Pay phones weren't easy to find, and I figured Slava would have had to pull off the Belt Parkway to look for one, so I reconsidered and took the kid up on the slice. I had a Coke with it and was just polishing off the crust when Slava called.

"Hold on."

I asked the kid behind the counter for a pencil and a piece of paper. He flipped the takeout order pad to me, a stubby pencil wedged under a few sheets. He went back to his match.

"Give me the number," I said. "I'll call you right back."

He picked up on the first ring.

"What is happening, Gus?"

"I'll explain when I see you. Whatever you do, don't drop your passenger back at the hotel and don't go back to your apartment until I see you. Go to Eleven Pinetree Court in Commack," I said. "Do you think you'll be able to find it?"

"I am finding it, no problem. We talk then?"

"Yeah, I'll meet you there in about two hours or so. The keypad code for the garage door is one-seven-five-five-six. There's a mountain bike hung up on the garage wall. Taped under the seat is a key that will get you into the house through the garage. Sit tight."

"We are sitting tight," he said.

"And Slava . . ."

"Yes, Gus."

There's a closed bedroom door on the ground floor. Please don't go—"

"Slava and no one else is going in your boy's room. I am promising you that."

I hung up, threw ten dollars on the counter, and told the kid to keep the change. He was too busy with *fútbol* to thank me. I was too worried about murder to care.

9

Eleven Pinetree Court was the house Annie and I still owned in spite of ourselves. It was the house we had raised our kids in. The house we were planning to live out our lives in. Annie and me, we weren't the move-down-south-after-retirement types. We were Long Islanders and we didn't figure Florida or the Carolinas held any particular magic for us. I don't know, but lower taxes and insurance rates didn't sing to me. I was born here and always figured to be buried here, too. Like my son. After John Jr. died, I knew I would never leave, not while I was breathing. Anyway, the house became a nightmare for us. We couldn't live in it and we couldn't bear to sell it.

Funny thing is that there's a cemetery behind the house, a Polish cemetery owned by a parish in Greenpoint, Brooklyn. Since there's a thick patch of trees and shrubs between the graves and our back fence, it was easy enough for us to ignore it, to forget it was even there. If the parish in Brooklyn hadn't started to build a church on the property a few years back, one they haven't finished, you might not know there was a graveyard there at all. And hardly anyone got buried back there these days. My mom once told me that's what people from the Old Country—whichever Old Country that happened to be—did. They would band together and buy land for cemeteries on Long Island, so they could be buried with their own kind.

The island was once a place of "out there" with potato and sod farms and lots of empty land. Not anymore. The "out there-ness" of Long Island had been swallowed up by tracts of split ranches and strip malls. The irony was in the power of our own denial. That Annie and Krissy and me, we pretended that the cemetery's existence in our backyard had nothing to do with our inability to live here. *Yeah, right.* The crazy thing is that it took me years to recognize the role the cemetery played in our need to escape from 11 Pinetree Court.

For about a year, we were renting it to the Shermans. Nice people with two kids and two Siamese cats. But after the house got broken into last year, they turned and ran. I didn't blame them. People don't realize the sense of violation a crime victim feels. It didn't have to be rape or murder. Any crime reminds us of how fragile we are, how vulnerable. It reminds us of how much we really do depend on everyone around us to play by the rules. I knew. I understood. When you're in uniform like I had been for twenty years, you are the first person the victim deals with. It isn't easy. After the Shermans left, we had a month-to-month rental, but he'd left at the beginning of April. Now, at least for the next little while, we had some new tenants coming soon.

The house was dark, but they were there. Slava would know to keep the lights out as a precaution. See, it wasn't only that Slava carried a big Makarov and a sap that told me he was someone very different from the man he showed to the guests and the rest of the staff at the Paragon. Any thug can carry a gun and a sap. Any thug can use them. It was that he knew things that a laborer from the poorest part of Warsaw couldn't have known: how to follow cars and people without being seen, where to hide a tracking device, how to disarm and incapacitate men larger than himself. I didn't know what side of the law he had been on back home, wherever that really was, but he was more than a simple thug.

I found them sitting quietly in the kitchen with the lights off. They had unlatched and opened the French doors off the kitchen in the event they had to run for it. I turned on the kitchen lights. Both men held Makarovs in their right hands.

I made a gun of my index finger and thumb and said, "You can put those away now."

Slava holstered his and nodded at Smith to do the same. When Smith hesitated, Slava glared at him. Smith put his Russian-made semiautomatic away. That done, he was fidgeting with his fingers.

I tilted my head at Smith. "You want to smoke, do it in the backyard."

Slava said something in a language that might have been Polish. It might not have been. I knew it was Slavic, but that was about all I knew. It must have meant "Go outside and smoke. I have to talk with my friend." It must have meant that, because that's exactly what happened.

"You are following Slava tonight?" he asked, referring to himself in the third person, as he often did.

I nodded. "Coney Island is beautiful in the rain."

He grunted, shaking his head. "Why you are doing this, following us?"

I pointed out the door to where Smith was standing on the wooden steps leading to the backyard, smoking the hell out of a cigarette. "Him. I saw the look you two gave each other last night when he checked in. I have to protect the guests and he looked like trouble to me. Seems I was right."

"Or maybe you are only thinking you are right. Maybe this is not so."

"Well, after you two guys left the house on West Twenty-first Street, the guy with the torn jacket, he was shot."

"We are knowing this might happen. Goran, he is dead?"

"Yes, very," I said. "As dead as it gets."

Slava didn't quite smile, but he conveyed a sense of satisfaction.

"He was executed in cold blood, Slava. The killer put two in his head just to make sure."

"You have seen killer's face?"

"He was wearing a mask."

"Goran is a man who is deserving to die many deaths in ways much worse. This death was kind to him. He was not so kind."

I pointed back outside again. "Then what were you and him doing with Goran?"

"I cannot say. Gus, once I am asking you to make me a promise that you will never ask about Slava's past."

"I will keep my word. I won't ask about your past."

Slava smiled at me with his ugly mouth.

"But I can't have the hotel guests put at risk. Will there be more violence?"

Slava rubbed his thick, flat fingers against his stubbly cheeks. They made a rasping, sandpapery sound. The sound of Slava thinking.

"Can maybe Mikel—that is his name—stay here?"

"But his last name's not Smith?"

Slava laughed, shaking his head. "No, is not Smith."

"Not any more than yours is Slava Podalak?"

Slava wasn't laughing now.

"If you want him to stay here, it must mean there is going to be more violence."

"Some maybe, yes. Goran was a terrible man, but we are meeting so he can make warning to us."

"Will my neighbors be in danger?"

"Slava would not ask this if it would be making trouble for you or harm for your friends. I am swearing this on the souls of my ancestors."

"Okay, he can stay," I said, "but he has to be out by the end of the month. We have someone interested in renting the place from May to September. Remember, keep him out of—"

Slava raised his right hand. "No one will go in John Junior's room. We have respect."

"I don't suppose you want to tell me what this is all about?" I asked, not expecting an answer.

I was wrong.

"There is trouble from the past. What was being done to Goran, it is possible to be done to Slava and Mikel someday."

"There are people who would harm you?"

"Many, but only some are having the right to do so. Not Goran or his people. They are wearing our shame. They are stinking of it."

"Shame." There was that word again.

"Look, Slava, I owe you. We are friends and you've never lied to me that I know of. Promise me that what you're telling me tonight is the truth."

He put his huge right hand out to me. "My handshake is my word to you. No one of your neighbors is being hurt and the blood that has come to Brooklyn tonight. It is coming for many years."

I shook Slava's hand.

"I will collect Mikel's things and bring them here. Maybe you should stay here, too, and not come to work for a while."

"Slava is losing his job, then."

I shook my head. "You call Alton and see if he can fill in for you. If he can, I'll fix it with the boss."

"How you are doing this?"

"I'll tell him you had a death in the family and you had to go back to Poland. Even if he doesn't believe it, he'll accept it."

Slava shook my hand again and gripped my biceps with his other hand.

"I'll call my neighbors and I'll let Annie know, too."

"I am owing to you much, Gus Murphy. I will repay for this."

I shook my head at him. "Just keep your word about keeping the neighbors and the guests safe. Yourself, too. Now, go have that cigarette with your pal. I'll call you tomorrow."

"No." Slava looked around the kitchen. He found a pen on the counter, took a dollar bill out of his wallet, and wrote a number down on the dollar bill. "Don't call Slava's number. Call this one."

When I got back into the Mustang, I turned the rearview mirror to face me. I stared at my reflection for what felt like a long time. I still looked like me. My hair had gone grief gray—that's what my sister called it—but otherwise the same. *Who the fuck are you, Gus Murphy? Who are you?* I had asked myself this question many, many times in the last few years, but I don't think I had ever felt further away from who I once was than I did at that moment. I once defined myself by my uniform, blue even under my skin. Now here I was, a witness to an execution, but hiding two men who were possibly complicit in the murder. I turned the car on and the mirror away. I would not find my answers here or in the mirror.

10

S leep wouldn't come to me. It was like that sometimes on days off because of my night-bird schedule. Even when I worked the door and security on weekends, downstairs at the Full Flaps Lounge, I often didn't get to bed until five or six. Some nights, like tonight, it was about adrenaline and a busy head. I watched TV and saw all the reports on the execution-style murder in Coney Island. None mentioned a Kona blue Mustang backing down the block, nor did they mention anything about the victim beyond the fact that he was a man between fifty and sixty years of age.

It didn't sound as if anyone had witnessed the whole incident except the killer and me, though that might not mean anything. The cops might well have a witness, maybe several, but they weren't going to announce it to the world, certainly not to the media. There was always holdback to help sort out the crazies. And detectives were, by nature, withholders, very proprietary and territorial. Their cases became *their* cases because they were judged on their ability to close them and make for nice statistical reports. That's what law enforcement was all about these days: statistics. It was impossible for me to make firm judgments about what the cops actually knew and didn't know, but if a few days went by without me getting a visit from the NYPD, I'd be clear of it.

I got tired of listening to the reports for anything new and watching *SportsCenter*. I'd already squeezed all the available joy out of the Yankees' win and the Mets' loss. I got tired of the same four walls, the cheap art, and the popcorn finish of the ceiling above my bed. If there was a major downside to living in a hotel room, it was the claustrophobic nature of it. The walls close in on you. They just do. I couldn't imagine doing time; what a prolonged nightmare life in a cell must be. So I threw on my Kirkland jeans, slipped on my beat-up old Nikes, and went downstairs to the business center in the lobby.

The lobby was just how I liked it at this time of morning: empty, silent. It would be hours before jets could use the runways at MacArthur again and there were no restless guests roaming about. Martina, the new night desk clerk, was in the office to the side of the front desk. I didn't hear her stirring in there, so I figured she was napping. I didn't know much about her yet and she didn't seem anxious for me or anyone else to get to know her. She fit right in. Night work at the Paragon was for people with secrets and stories not to tell. The lobby itself was okay, if you didn't look too closely. Some places were frayed around the edges. Some were just frayed. The Paragon lobby was like that. Frayed. The sofa cushions were no longer cushiony. The chairs were unsteady. The decor, dark granite and terrazzo, mirrors, and big fake potted plants had grown chipped, dull, and dusty. I guess the Paragon was a pretty dumpy hotel, but the rooms were clean and cheap. And for me, there was comfort here.

At least Kurt, the boss, had gotten some updated computers and connected us to a speedy network. I put one terminal to good use, first reading whatever reports I could about the murder in Brooklyn and then going back to my reading on the murder of Linh Trang Spears. It was an early morning for murder. There was nothing new on Goran's execution. I didn't guess there would be.

I reread some of the stuff on Linh Trang I had gone over earlier and then moved on to what there was on the alleged murderer. There wasn't a whole lot. What there was wasn't pretty. Rondo Salazar was, to put it mildly, a real piece of shit. A soldier in the notorious Asesinos gang, he'd been in trouble with the cops since he was eight years old. But when I saw the photos of him doing the perp walk and then in his jail jumpsuit, I thought there had to be a mistake. I'd been expecting a big, broad-shouldered tough guy with a thick neck, arms like tree limbs, and dead eyes. Yet the man in the photos above his name was a little skinny guy who couldn't've been five-foot-six. He had the tats. You could see them everywhere his skin was exposed. His eyes were buggy, nervous eyes, crazy eyes.

I knew better than to judge a man's potential for violence by his size or the bug in his eyes. The toughest motherfuckers I'd ever come across were little men, but it wouldn't have taken a big man to subdue a slight girl like Linh Trang and stick her. A sharp knife and a violent heart were all that was required. Still, for all the details on Salazar's violent past and his trouble with the SCPD, there was little on his motive for killing Linh Trang. Only some speculation that he had admired her from afar and that when he approached her, she had rejected his advances. This seemed mostly the concoction of a *Newsday* reporter. When the investigating detectives were asked about it, they weren't exactly effusive.

"No comment."

Which didn't mean they thought the reporter was wrong. All it meant was there was no need to establish motive because they had him on blood and tissue evidence. His attack had been so brutal that he had cut himself in the process. His skin cells were found under Linh's fingernails. And when they arrested Salazar, he had scratches on his face and cuts on his hands. It was as neat and clear-cut a case as any detective could dream of. No need to establish motive if you had the embarrassment of evidence the SCPD had.

The media was different, though. For them to wring as much mileage out of it as they could, they needed a motive. The more salacious or squalid, the better. So they speculated, based on the scant fact that Linh Trang and Salazar were the same age and had attended the same elementary school for a few years. That was the thing about the media. They could throw questions out there and make them sound like answers. *Had poor little Rondo from the wrong side of the tracks had a crush on the cute Asian girl since they were kids? Had his crush turned into an obsession? Had the obsession turned finally to violence?* There was no evidence for any of it, but neither party was available to deny it. Linh Trang was dead and Salazar hadn't volunteered to comment. According to all reports, Salazar had not spoken a single word about the crime since his arrest. Not to the cops. Not to his court-appointed attorney. Not to his family. Not to anyone.

I understood Micah Spear's frustration. At least I thought I did. It was all very tidy in a clinical, statistical sense, but utterly messy and unsatisfying in a human sense. Oh, I understood that very well. And it all came back to that haunting question: Why? It was our curse and salvation as animals, the need to understand. Do birds need to understand? Do ants? Do they grieve? Some animals do. Elephants do, but do they haunt themselves with *Why?* And are they luckier for their big brains and what Bill Kilkenny would call their souls? I wasn't so sure.

When I stepped out of the business center, the first light of day was reflecting off the brown mirrored windows of the tech company building across Vets Highway from the Paragon. I finally felt drained and ready for a few hours of sleep. I had dinner with Maggie to look forward to, but some other less enjoyable things to do between now and then. I rode up to the second floor, and when I stepped back into my room, the claustrophobia was gone. The only thing closing in on me was sleep.

11

made some phone calls and left some messages before heading out. Downstairs, I stopped by Kurt Bonacker's office to square Slava's temporary absence with him. Like I thought he would, he accepted my explanation. He didn't believe it. Kurt was a smart guy. Some people think smart people are the ones who ask all the questions all the time. My experience was that the smartest people know when to shut up and shake their heads yes. Kurt was like that. He trusted me. The explanation about Slava's dead relative was just something he could hang his hat on if the need arose.

I waved at Felix on my way out to see Annie. She always got a bit crazed when we discussed 11 Pinetree Court. Less so now, but it was always better to discuss stuff about the house with her in person. Early on, after we'd split up, when I'd moved into the Paragon and she'd taken Krissy to live with her brother in East Setauket, our conversations about the house were fraught with all sorts of baggage not directly related to the house. There are smooth divorces, but no such things as easy ones. Ours was neither, but the one thing we had agreed on was our refusal to sell the house. Our attorneys were not pleased.

Although we both knew neither one of us could carry what was left of the mortgage and afford not to live there, Annie hated renting the place. I didn't much care for the idea myself, but since I was the one shelling out the monthly payments, the reality of the situation hit me the hardest. Her one condition for renting the house was that we padlock John Jr.'s old room, keeping it as it was on the day he died playing pickup basketball in East Northport. I thought it was kind of creepy, like something out of a gothic novel. Creepy or not, who was I to not indulge her grief? She had indulged mine. I had forced her to bury our son in a small graveyard in Smithtown so I could keep him close to me even though there would be no room for the rest of us to join him. I would not be budged on that. She would not give on the room as a kind of shrine and time capsule. It was a way for her to keep her son alive in her heart.

Then last year, when the house was broken into and ransacked, the shrine had been defiled. Annie and Krissy had worked hard to put the room back as it was, but just as there was no bringing John back, there was no recapturing the untouched nature of the room itself. After her initial anger had worn off, Annie had softened her stance about the possibility of selling the house. Until she came all the way around, I wouldn't press her on it. She wouldn't like the fact that I was renting the house on a weekly basis. Didn't think it attracted the right kind of people. *If she only knew!* I believed Slava when he told me there would be no trouble at the house. He was a man of his word. It was the rest of the world I was less certain about, so I didn't want Annie or Krissy anywhere near the place until Slava and Mikel were gone.

The radio went silent in the car, replaced by the ringing of a phone. I picked up.

"Gus Murphy here."

"I know who it is, you prick," said Al Roussis. "I'm the one who called *you*."

"Well, the one who returned my call, if you want to get technical about it."

Al Roussis was an old friend. Sometimes a reluctant one. We'd spent years together at the Second Precinct. More important, he was a Suffolk County Homicide detective.

He'd already run out of patience with me. "What? What is it now?"

"Linh Trang Spears."

There were a few seconds of dead air as Al searched his memory.

"Last November," he said, his voice softening. "Her body was a mess. Something like twenty stab wounds—"

"Twenty-three."

"If you know so much about the case, Gus, what the hell do you need me for?"

"We can talk about it over lunch if you'd like."

More dead air.

"The last time you bought me lunch, someone tried to shoot you in the head. You're a dangerous man to eat with."

"But an inexpensive one for you. We'll go somewhere else."

"Zin's Deli by the mall," he said.

"Kosher deli? Your Greek ancestors are spinning in their graves."

"Jews, Greeks, same thing. Our flags are white and blue. See you there at noon."

He was off the phone. I was glad for that. I had expected a lecture from him about keeping my nose out of other people's business. Maybe he was saving the lecture for lunch, or maybe he didn't think I could do much harm with such an open-and-shut case of murder.

As I pulled up to the Airport Diner, Annie was walking up the stairs. It was hard for me to see her and not wonder how we had gotten to where we were. To wonder if it was only John's death that had torn us apart or whether there were already cracks and fractures in our marriage. Even now, with all the grief and pain and hard feelings, my heart skipped a little at the sight of her lean, streamlined body and feline face with her perfect nose and lush, dark brown hair. The way she walked still knocked me out. I think I once described her as an arrow built to slice through the air. An arrow, the perfect way to describe my ex.

She smiled when she saw me. It wasn't the old, unfreighted smile, but there was love in it. There were other things in it, too, things that outweighed the love. Yet we had come to an understanding. We would always be connected through our kids and what we had shared. We wouldn't pretend that the pain and fury hadn't existed. We had kind of agreed to put it aside. That life was too short to hold on to the wrong things, the things that shortened it even more.

I leaned over and kissed her on the cheek. She smelled of citrus— fresh-cut oranges and limes—and mildly of cigarettes. She had gone back to smoking after John's death and had tried to stop, but as she once said, "Stopping would be like forgetting and I can't do that."

I didn't agree. That was another battle for someone else to have with her. Threads of gray appeared in her hair. I thought they suited her. She wouldn't have agreed with that, either. She was drumming her piano fingers on the tabletop, the surface of her black coffee vibrating in kind. She seemed anxious or poised for a fight.

"So what's this about, Gus?"

"Relax, Annie. I just haven't seen you in a while and I wanted to tell you that there'll be two guys in the old house for a few weeks. I know you don't like weekly rentals, but it's some cash."

I didn't get the reaction I thought I would.

"Fine" was all she said, distracted.

"Hey, what's up with you? Usually when I mention the house, you—"

She reached her left hand across the table and took my right. "Let's put it on the market."

I wanted to say something, but no words would come out of my mouth. Luckily, the waitress arrived with a cup of coffee and placed it in front of me. She dropped off some creamers as well. I fixed the coffee up the way I liked it, sipped some, sipped some more, but what I was really doing was stalling. I had always been the one to push putting the house on the market. Annie had been the one to move toward my way of thinking by the inch, and now here she was proposing we sell the house we thought we'd live in for the rest of our lives. My guts twisted up, and much worse than they had the night before in Coney Island.

"But what about John's room?"

Silent tears rolled down her cheeks and she squeezed my hand. "He's gone, Gus. And after what happened last year . . . I mean . . . he's just gone and he's never coming home. I don't want to hope anymore. It hurts too much."

"I know." My voice was brittle. "Have you talked to Krissy about this?"

Annie shook her head. "She'll be good with it. Don't worry."

"Okay, I'll talk to the real estate lady when I get a chance."

She squeezed my hand even more tightly. "Can we get out of here, Gus, please?"

"Sure." I pulled free of her grasp, stood up, and threw a ten-dollar bill on the table. "Where do you want to go?"

When she looked up at me the way she did, I knew the answer.

I'D MADE MY ROOM as dark as I could manage in midmorning, not because it would help me pretend I wasn't backsliding or risking everything I had with Magdalena, but because the artificial twilight blurred the lines between right and wrong just enough to let me do this. I knew what was on the line. I also knew that we each needed this to let go of the house and of each other, finally. The last time we'd slept together was December and it had been angry and spiteful and marvelous, too. Annie had shown up at my door naked beneath a long leather coat I had bought for her birthday years before. She said that day was about goodbye. What it really was about was punishment for us both. This, though, really did feel like goodbye.

Almost an hour had passed since we walked through the door and we hadn't uttered a single intelligible word since. We undressed each other in silence, though the sex had been noisy and urgent. We laid in bed next to each other, her shoulder in the nook under my left arm. Her hair against my chest and cheek. The room smelling so intensely of her that I felt myself getting hard again. She noticed and used her mouth to encourage me. Then a strange and intimate thing happened. As Annie went down on me, she cried, her tears raining down on me. I didn't try to stop her or comfort her and she seemed not to want to be stopped or comforted. I lifted her up at the hips, careful not to slam her legs against the headboard, and pressed my lips to her. We both came almost immediately.

After she collected herself, Annie got up and showered. I didn't join her. She didn't want me to and I knew better. I knew a real goodbye when I saw one. As the water ran, I called our real estate agent and left a message about putting the house on the market. There would be time to change our minds, but that wouldn't happen. Still, it would be good to do it as soon as possible. Magical thinking and hope are persistent powerful things. It was best to treat them both with strong doses of reality. In this case, reality would come in the form of a SOLD sign dangling from the FOR SALE sign astride the mailbox at 11 Pinetree Court.

Annie came out of the bathroom, a towel wrapped around her, an odd expression on her face. It was an appropriate day for an odd expression. I didn't need to look at a mirror to know I had the same expression on my face. I thought she might simply get dressed and leave without a word, but no, Annie had something to say. I wasn't sure I wanted to hear it, though I wasn't going to stop her. There was no stopping her. She sat down on the edge of the bed.

"Rob asked me to marry him."

I thought I heard someone ask, "What did you say?"

"I didn't answer him yet. I couldn't until . . . I just couldn't yet."

"I think I understand." There was that someone's voice again. "But you don't really love him, do you?"

"He makes me happy, Gus. I want to be happy."

"You don't need my approval." I recognized the voice as mine.

"I want it."

"Then you have it. He's a good guy."

I sat up, leaned over, and kissed her on the cheek. I hugged her hard, very hard.

"So you've talked about it with Krissy?" I asked.

"She was harder to convince than you."

I laughed. "Let's not go there, okay."

She laughed, too.

"I just have one question, Annie. Did the decision about the house have anything to do with Rob's proposing?"

She thought about it for a second and said, "No. Until you mentioned renting the house, I hadn't even thought about it. It just seemed right, you know? I have to let go."

"Okay."

Ten minutes later, Annie was gone. I almost hung the DO NOT DISTURB placard on the door handle outside my room because I didn't want the sheets cleaned or the room aired out. I didn't do it, though. Annie wasn't the only one who had to let go.

12

(MONDAY NOON)

had about an hour before I was to meet Al Roussis, and it would only take me about fifteen minutes to get to the Smith Haven Mall in Lake Grove, so I went down to Michael—Mikel—Smith's room to collect his things and pack them in his blue duffel bag. I figured I'd bring it over to the house after lunch with Al. One of the privileges afforded me as the house detective was a passkey card. I only used the thing once, and that was when I'd mislaid the keycard for my own room. The Paragon wasn't the kind of place that attracted trouble, not the kind that required me getting into people's rooms. We had some drunks on the weekends at the Full Flaps. That was about it.

The Paragon was a convenient way station, a hotel used by cheap businessmen or bargain-hunting travelers to spend the night before early-morning or late-night flights. Not the kind of clientele who attracted the assholes and dirt bags you'd find fifty miles west, lurking around Manhattan hotels. That said, someone did try to shotgun me in my sleep last year. The only casualties were the mattress and the bedding. But so many people had tried to kill me last December that I would have needed a scorecard to keep up.

As I left my room, I noticed the maid's cart two doors over to my right, heard her vacuuming. I thought about going back into my room and blasting the AC, but I didn't. Nor did I strip the bed and bundle up the sheets to obscure the stains. I guess I was beyond embarrassment if not beyond guilt. I wasn't feeling guilty, not exactly. It hit me in the shower that although I understood what had just happened between Annie and me, that there was an inevitability to it, there would be no way for Maggie to see it as anything but a betrayal. Maybe it was. Maybe it wasn't. Sometimes there are things between people that defy the usual moral judgments. I didn't try to fool myself or give myself an out because Maggie and I had never made declarations of eternal love or pledges of monogamy. We had only one spoken rule: no rantings about our exes. So it was easy to see how this situation would be particularly touchy.

I took the stairs down to the first floor, turned left out of the exit door, and headed for room 111. There wasn't much happening on this floor, or anywhere else in the hotel for that matter. We were about a third full. Business would pick up in May as we headed toward summer. The nature of the business changed in the summer because vacation travel would pick up and because we were a convenient stop for people on their way to or back from the Hamptons. A few hours stuck in traffic on the LIE on a ninety-degree day made the Paragon look like Eden. There were Thursday, Friday, Sunday, and Monday nights when we'd be almost full. But now it was the usual crowd of returning snowbirds and business travelers.

As I approached room 111, I got the sense that something wasn't right: a noise that seemed out of place coming from a row of empty rooms. Or maybe it was too quiet. It was hard to know, but I wasn't imagining it. Something was up. I reached down, pulled out the little Glock 26 that I carried on my ankle, and pressed my ear to the wall outside 111. Nothing. With the Glock in my right hand and the passkey in my left, I moved slowly toward the door, the carpeting swallowing up the sound of my footsteps. I moved past the door. Listened. Nothing. I gently slid the card into the lock and pulled it out. The green light popped with its accompanying electronic tune, the door unlatched, and I pushed the paddle.

Just as I stepped into the darkened room, a jet thundered over the roof of the Paragon. No matter how many times a day you experience it, that roar is distracting. I knew I should have waited or stepped back until the jet passed. Too late. My eyes were still adjusting to the change in light between the hallway and the dark room, my ears to the renewed quiet when a metal baton slammed down across my right wrist. Burning pain radiated both ways along my arm, the Glock tumbling out of my hand to the floor in spite of me trying to will my fingers to stay locked around its grip.

I dropped down to my knees and felt the breeze of the baton swishing over my head. I rocked back on my heels, coiled, and sprang at the shadowy figure to my left. My shoulder plowed into his midsection, some air going out of him. More air went out of me when he whacked me in the ribs with a jackhammer fist. We toppled backward, bouncing off the side of the bed, then crashing onto the floor. I landed on top of him. Between the pain in my wrist and ribs, I was unable to put my advantage to much use. I caught my breath and tried kneeing him in the balls. No good. He pushed me up off him as if I was a bag of leaves, and he slid out from under me.

He staggered some getting to his feet, and that gave me time to get myself upright, too. I threw a chopping left lead at where I thought his jaw would be and connected. That did two things: It hurt my knuckles and made him laugh. It wasn't like I was a small man or that I didn't know how to make an impression with my fists, but this guy had a jaw like a stone wall and a perverse sense of humor. When he stopped laughing I knew I was fucked. Before I could even try to get in a defensive stance, something like a baseball bat, his shin, thumped me across the liver. I went down again. He was behind me, on me. His arms locked around my neck and the already dark room went black.

I don't think I was out very long, but it was long enough for the guy with the sick sense of humor to have gone. I got up in stages and was still a little dizzy when I wobbled over to the wall switch. The room had been tossed, but neatly so. Neither the chair cushions nor the mattress had been slit. The drawers were open, but not pulled out and dumped. The closet door was ajar. The ratty blue duffel bag was gone, as were its contents. At least my gun was there on the floor where I'd dropped it. My attacker had also left his telescoping metal baton behind as a kind of parting gift. I collected my gun, put it back in my ankle holster, and reached for the baton, pressed the tip of it against the floor to fold it up, and placed it in my back pocket.

Before heading to the ice machine, I took one last look around the room. And there, peeking out from under a fallen pillow, was the corner of a newspaper article. I nudged the pillow aside with my foot and picked up the strip of print. It was yellowed with age, dry and brittle to the touch, and not many years away from disintegrating into dust. The fading print on the paper was like the signs on the stores in Brighton Beach, Cyrillic and totally incomprehensible to me. There was a black-and-white photograph of a man above the print. I didn't recognize his face, not that I expected I would. I carefully folded it and put it in my shirt pocket. At the moment my wrist and ribs were screaming at me. I also had to get to my meeting with Al Roussis.

13

I laid down for a few minutes to recover, an old T-shirt tied around the makeshift ice bag to hold it to my wrist. Gravity held the other ice bag to my ribs. I called Al Roussis and told him I'd be a half-hour late. He said he was willing to wait for a free meal. My next call was to Slava. I dialed the number one digit at a time as I read it off the dollar bill on which he'd written it. The phone rang four, five, six times but didn't go to voice mail. I hung up, figuring Slava's phone would capture the number, he would recognize it, and he would know to call me back. Five minutes later he did just that.

"Something is going wrong?" Slava said, dispensing with hellos.

"When I went to get Mikel's things from his room, there was already someone in there."

"He is hurting you, this man?"

"I didn't say it was a man."

"Gus, now is not time for playing the games, I think. Are you hurt?"

"My wrist and ribs a little bit, but mostly my pride. Nothing's broken. He hit me with an ASP. You know what an—"

"Is metal stick like police are using."

"He was a tough motherfucker, Slava. I hit him flush in the jaw with everything I had and all he did was laugh at me. Then he kicked me in the liver and choked me out the same way you choked out that Jamal guy last year."

That seemed to get Slava's attention, because he went quiet.

"Whatever Mikel had in that duffel bag of his is gone," I said, to break the silence. "He cleaned out the room."

"Is all gone?"

"All of it," I lied, remembering the folded newspaper clipping in my shirt pocket.

I owed Slava a lot, but not everything. I realized he was never going to tell me about his past. He wasn't ever going to volunteer information about why he and Mikel had been involved in last night's execution. Or even information on who the hell Mikel was. Slava and I had made promises to each other that we would keep, but I had never promised not to look into things on my own. And besides, this was now personal. Somebody fucks around in my hotel and attacks me, I'm not going to sit on my hands. I'm just not.

"This man who is attacking you, he is big man?"

"It was pretty dark. You know how rooms in that part of the hotel get no light. And it happened fast. Took maybe fifteen, twenty seconds before he choked me out. But I guess he was pretty big, yeah. He would have been about my height. Maybe an inch taller."

"You are seeing his face?"

"No. Do you know who it was?"

"I do not know, Gus. Maybe."

"Well, maybe you and Mikel need to keep an even lower profile than you planned."

He grunted, then said, "Slava is sorry to causing you trouble."

"I'll live."

"So will I. I must. Surviving is Slava's punishment."

The phone went dead. Slava had said all he was going to say.

14

The mall was located on the borders of the towns of Smithtown and Brookhaven, hence the name Smith Haven. And when I was growing up, the mall was where we hung out on most weekends. The place had a multiplex and some character back then. There were Calder mobiles hanging from the ceilings and the food court, Calder Court, had a big orange stabile right in the middle of all the tables. The birds that got trapped inside the mall used to perch on it and crap all over that thing. It was kind of neat how sparrows would come beg french fries and pizza crust from you. I liked that.

The Calder stuff had been auctioned off years ago. The movie theaters were gone, too. I'm not misty-eyed about any of that. Still, it is kind of sad that the Smith Haven Mall was now like any other mall in any other suburb anywhere. I'm not a fan of sameness. I mean, I like Cheesecake Factory and P.F. Chang's as much as the next guy, but who wants sameness to define a place that once meant so much to him?

But the mall had a new significance to me that had nothing to do with teenage Gus hooking up with girls from Sachem North or Ward Melville. Nothing to do with getting high outside Sears or setting off firecrackers in the theater. The mall was where I took my first footsteps away from the edge of John Jr.'s grave. Doc Rosen had pretty much told me to get out of my room on my days off, to get back into the world again. *Go to the mall. The mall,* I thought. *Why not?* It was a safe choice. For a Long Islander, going to the mall was like going to Mass. Turned out the mall was the least safe choice I could have made and Doc knew it. Because as I zombie-walked the mall I was confronted with the reality of men who would have been my son's age. Breathing, laughing, walking men with friends and girlfriends and lives ahead of them. At first, I hated them. I hated that they had something my son was robbed of: a future. Then came a period when I wanted to scream at them, to shout at them about how lucky they were. That they had a gift not to be thrown away or taken for granted. Eventually I stopped seeing them at all. That was when I knew I was living again.

Zin's was in a strip shopping center on the Route 347 side of the Smith Haven Mall. When I pulled up to the place, Al Roussis, a somewhat dour, athletic man about five-foot-nine, was pacing a rut in the concrete out front. Al was a good guy who was on the job because he believed in the job and in doing right. Homicide was the perfect place for him to be. He took his job speaking for the dead very seriously. If Al had a fault, it was that he took too much too seriously. One of the things he took too seriously was eating. Athletic and fit as he was, he ate like a moose. When I took Al out, it cost.

We hugged hello. Pushing back from the embrace, his moist brown eyes were full of suspicion. I must've winced a little.

"What happened to you?"

"If I told you, you wouldn't believe me."

He held his palms up to me like he was on traffic duty. "Forget it. I don't want to know. Just tell me it's got nothing to do with this Spears case."

I slashed my index finger over my chest. "Cross my heart."

"Should I believe you?"

"About this, yeah. Let's eat."

The inside of Zin's smelled like the Lower East Side of Manhattan. It was perfumed with the scents of sour pickles and steaming meats, of drying salamis hanging like red wind chimes over the counter. The walls were covered in badly painted murals of the home country—Brooklyn. Nearly all the folks on the island my parents' age came from the city. A lot of people my age were born in the city and had moved out here, most of them from one Brooklyn neighborhood or another. Some from Queens, too. Very few from the Bronx or Manhattan. Almost none from New York City's stepchild, Staten Island.

Neither Al nor I bothered with the menus. As usual, Al ordered enough food to feed a family of four. He had matzo ball soup, a pastrami sandwich, a potato knish, pickles, coleslaw, and a sour tomato. My last name *was* Murphy, so I had a corned beef sandwich. We didn't talk much during the meal, because when Al ate, he concentrated on chewing. But in between courses we managed to catch up a little. His family was fine. Work was good. Like that.

"So," he said when I ordered us coffee, "what do you want to know about the Spears murder?"

"Your case?"

He shook his head. "Not mine, no. Guys who caught it had a suspect in like fifteen minutes. Once there was a blood-type match, they arrested him. The DNA results confirmed it."

"Rondo Salazar?"

He nodded. "Real piece of shit."

"I know," I said. "The Asesinos, from the womb to the Tombs."

"If we were in the city, yeah. Now he's in Riverhead. Some bad motherfuckers, the Asesinos. Really prey on their own."

"What gang doesn't? For them their people are low-hanging fruit."

"Good point. So, is that it?"

"Almost."

Al rolled his eyes. "Uh-oh, here we go."

"What?" I made a face.

"Don't give me the innocent look, Gus. Last time you stuck your nose where it didn't belong a lot of people got dead."

"Some of them deserved it."

"But not all."

I couldn't argue with that.

"So who you working for? And don't give me any shit about privileged information. All you got a license to do is carry a gun and drive a van."

"The vic's grandfather."

The downturn at the corners of Al's lips was even more pronounced than usual. "Sad, really sad for the family when a kid dies."

"Tell me about it."

"Oh, shit! Gus, I wasn't thinking. I'm—"

"It's okay, Al. I know what you meant."

"So, what, he doesn't believe Salazar is guilty, because I gotta tell you, this guy's as guilty as sin."

"That's not it. He believes the guy's guilty. That's not why he asked me to help."

"Then what?"

"He wants to know why."

Al nodded, but without being aware of it. "Yeah, Salazar won't talk."

"There's all this speculation in the papers about unrequited love and stalking, but the grandfather thinks it's bullshit and the family needs some real answers. They want to know why. He's a real piece of work, the grandfather, a mercenary SOB. I don't blame him, though. Still haunts me."

"No need to tell me about it, Gus. I deal with victims' families all the time. They ask me why first a lot of the time, even before who."

"Then help me out here, Al."

"If I can I will. Ask your questions."

The waitress brought our coffees, but neither one of us drank. We just kind of played with them, stirring and stirring. I asked for the check.

I said, "How did the guys who caught the case get onto Salazar so fast?"

Al shrugged. "They were already looking at him for this drug thing, but my guess is either he was snitched out or they got an anonymous tip."

"That's what I was thinking, too. But you don't know for sure?"

"Nope."

"Can you get me a sit down with the detectives who caught it?"

Al suddenly looked as uncomfortable as if I'd asked him to give me head.

"I'm not sure, Gus. I know that you did the right thing last year by exposing Chief Regan and Pete McCann for the corrupt, murdering pricks they were, but they're dead. And it's easy to make heroes and martyrs out of the dead. There are still a lot of guys on the job who looked up to Pete as Mr. Cool Guy and others who owe a lot of loyalty to Regan."

"So that's a no?" I said, slipping my credit card into the black check folder.

"That's an 'I'll see what I can do.' May cost you another meal."

"Thanks, Al."

Outside, Al headed right for his car. I stood there on the sidewalk for a moment, letting the sun warm my face. It was one of the first days of spring that actually felt like spring. I didn't know whether April was the cruelest month, but it was a liar. That much I was sure of.

15

I f you look up the expression "wrong side of the tracks," you might find an accompanying photograph and map of North Bellport. North Bellport was largely poor, largely African-American and Hispanic, and basically shit out of luck. And the thing about the wrong side of the tracks was literal in North Bellport, because once you crossed south over the Long Island Rail Road tracks into Bellport proper, you were in a different world, a white one. One featuring a yacht club, the Gateway Playhouse, and a country club with a nineteenth-century golf course bordered by the Great South Bay. A cozy place that held free concerts on summer nights at a band shell down by the water. Across the Great South Bay was Fire Island and the Atlantic beyond.

Bellport was a picture postcard village of white picket fences and quaint houses sided in cedar shingles gone silver and black with age. There were great restaurants, art galleries, and little shops along Main Street. It was like a little slice of Sag Harbor had been carved out of the Hamptons and transported thirty-eight miles to the southwest. North Bellport . . . well, it had its unique charms, too: 7-Eleven and Spicy's Barbecue. Spicy's kind of looked like the devil's concept of a McDonald's. Its squat, freestanding building across from the railroad tracks was painted white and Hey-look-at-me-right-the-fuck-now red with like colored, cat ear–shaped arches on either side. Spicy's chicken, ribs, and collards were top shelf, according to the cops who worked the Fifth Precinct. And the place was probably the only spot where the citizens of North Bellport and Bellport crossed paths. Those railroad tracks might just as well have been a wall or a moat, but you didn't need physical barriers when economic ones were just as effective and far less conspicuous. That was how segregation worked on Long Island.

I drove with my windows down to take advantage of the rare warmth of the day. Only a few seconds after taking the right fork off Montauk onto South Country Road, I could smell the ocean almost as if I was standing on the beach. I didn't know whether it was because we were surrounded by Long Island Sound on the north and the Atlantic on the south that we were nose-blind to the smell of sea water or because most of us lived along the spine of the island, just one side or the other off the LIE, far away from any body of water larger than an in-ground pool. There were days you could smell it inland, but not many. I forgot all about the smell of the sea in the few minutes it took me to get into Bellport proper.

My attention had been drawn away by the sight of greening hedges, big old houses on fat pieces of property, and thoughts of the inevitably painful conversation I was going to have with Linh Trang Spears's family. I hadn't asked Micah Spears for his family's contact information because I wanted as little direct contact with him as possible. I wasn't a brown-noser by nature and didn't feel I had anything to prove, not to anyone, not anymore. When you've sat with the muzzle of a Glock nestled up under the fleshy part of your chin, your finger on the trigger, you get past giving a shit about what the world thinks of you. In that way, the last two years had been liberating. Liberation wasn't worth the cost of my son's life, but the nature of the universe isn't transactional. The universe isn't like some large-scale version of *Let's Make A Deal*. No one, not God, not Monty Hall, had offered me a choice. *You can have liberation, your son's life, or what's behind door number two.* No one had given John the choice. So I figured that word would get back to Micah Spears indirectly. And if he didn't like that, well, he could go fuck himself. I didn't know what it was exactly, but there was something about that man beyond his brusque manner and fine clothing that rubbed me wrong, very wrong.

I turned off South Country onto Browns Lane, a lovely straight street that ran downhill to the water's edge. But the house I was looking for was a few hundred yards north of the water, across the way from the Mary Immaculate Church complex. It was a lovely slate-blue-and-white Victorian with one turret, a side portico, and only a bit of whimsy. Lovely as the house was, it looked tired and lived in. Maybe I was projecting, but probably not. The painted rows of clapboards and shingles were chipped, flecked, and faded. I could see down the pebbled driveway into the backyard where the detached garage was sagging, seeming in the midst of a decision whether to collapse this way or that. There was a white Toyota RAV4, a girl's car, I thought, parked under the portico. Krissy had always wanted a RAV4. The lawn and garden, such as they were, were overgrown and weedy.

The porch boards creaked under my weight. I pressed the nib of the old-fashioned doorbell and heard it buzz inside the house. At first, there was nothing, but as I raised my finger to the bell again, I heard footsteps.

"Coming!" promised a muffled woman's voice on the other side of the door.

There was a click, another, and the door pulled back. Standing there in front of me was a heavyset girl with a pretty face and Micah Spears's green eyes. Only on her, they were warm and welcoming. She was twenty, maybe younger, and she smiled an uncertain smile at me with a mouth of perfectly straight white teeth and curvy lips. She was the type of girl my mom would shake her head at and whisper under her breath, *What a catch she'd be if she would only lose the baby fat.* My mom was born here but was old-school.

"Hi," she said, tucking some stray black hairs behind her right ear. "What can I do for you? Because if you're selling anything, I—"

I smiled back at her. "I've got nothing to sell."

The smile vanished from her face, but the uncertainty remained. "Then what?"

"My name is Gus Murphy and I used to be a Suffolk County police officer."

That didn't have the intended effect.

"Oh, Christ! Oh, no. Is it my mom? Is it—"

I reached out and placed my hand on her shoulder and smiled as reassuring a smile as I could manage these days. "No, no." I pulled my hand back when I felt her relax. "It's nothing like that. I'm a retired cop. I've been hired by your grandfather."

That also got an unexpected reaction.

"But Grandpa Frank is dead. How could he hire you?" She grabbed the door, ready to slam it shut.

I held my hands up. "Not that grandfather," I said. "Micah Spears."

She didn't slam the door, but she didn't let go of it, either. That was something, at least. She tilted her forehead toward me, challenging me. I could see she wanted to ask me a question. She just couldn't seem to decide which one.

"What did you say your name was again?" she asked. I supposed to give herself more time to sort through the others.

"Gus Murphy. What's yours?"

She wasn't expecting that and smiled in spite of herself. "Abigail. Everyone calls me Abby."

"You're Linh Trang's sister?"

Abby ignored the question, sort of. "Is that what this is about, LT?"

I nodded.

"But they have her killer."

"Rondo Salazar. I know."

"Then . . . I don't understand. My folks—we don't really have much to do with my grandfather, with the man who hired you."

"Why's that?"

"My dad doesn't talk about it much, but he says Micah isn't anyone we want to have anything to do with."

"And your mom, what does she say?"

Abby rolled her pretty eyes. "She likes him even less than my dad."

I thought back to my meeting with Micah Spears and remembered the photo he'd shown me from Linh Trang's graduation. If he wasn't at the graduation, and it didn't sound like he would have been welcomed there, someone must've forwarded him the photo. I tried something that I hoped would get me off the front porch and into the house, something that would help me get some answers instead of having to answer them myself.

"But you keep in touch with Micah, don't you? You sent him pictures from Linh Trang's graduation."

That did it. Abby swiveled her head, searching for anyone who might be within earshot. This was a secret, one nobody could know about. When she was satisfied it was safe, her face twisted up and turned red with anger.

"Micah swore to me he wouldn't tell anybody. I—"

"He didn't tell me, Abby. I figured it out. Like I said, I used to be a cop. Now, can I come inside so we can have a talk?"

She hesitated. She was smart to hesitate. Who was I, anyway? Some guy who showed up at her front door claiming to be an ex-cop hired by a man her family hated to look into what was probably the most traumatic and horrible event in her young life. I pushed her to decide.

"Call him," I said, taking the business card he'd given me out of my wallet. "Here." I offered her the card. "Call your grandfather. I'll wait."

"Come in, Mr. Murphy. Come in."

As she closed the door behind me I got the sense that the secret between Abby and her grandfather was just tip-of-the-iceberg stuff. Abby showed me into the parlor—her word, not mine—gesturing toward a leather wing chair. She asked me if I wanted anything to drink, listing beer, soda, and water among the choices.

"Coke," I said.

When she left, I looked around the room. Mostly it was dark. I got the sense that there were a lot of things in this house hiding in the darkness behind the drawn window shades. There was much to wonder about in the old blue house on Browns Lane. And when I asked Abby about some of those things I was wondering about, she didn't shed much light on them. Like when I asked her about Linh Trang's ethnicity.

Abby shrugged. "I don't know. They could've adopted from anywhere, I guess, but it wasn't something we ever talked about. She was my sister and that was that. It was weird sometimes, them trying to make her American and also make her Vietnamese. It was almost like they felt guilty and tried to do too much. You know what I mean?"

I didn't know, but I could guess. Leaving the house, I realized I had more questions on the way out than I did when Abby let me in.

16

(MONDAY, LATE AFTERNOON)

I didn't have to be at Maggie's until eight, so I picked up some Spicy's Barbecue and headed to Bill's apartment in North Massapequa. The contrast between Bellport and North Bellport was the most egregious example of the north and south haves and have-nots, but it certainly wasn't the only one. See, the north/south town contrast was a reoccurring phenomenon all along the South Shore of Long Island. Sometimes, like in Bellport, the dividing line was the railroad track. Most frequently, though, it was Montauk Highway. The towns and villages south of Montauk, the ones closer to the water, were the haves. The ones north of Montauk Highway were the have-nots or, in the case of places like North Massapequa, the have-lesses. And in Massapequa not only was the contrast less drastic, it was less to do with ethnicity and more to do with salary.

"This is unexpected," Bill said as I walked through the door of his basement apartment, his eyes locked on the bags in my hands. "Smells wonderful."

"We'll see soon enough."

We were well into the meal and our second glasses of red wine before

Bill asked the inevitable question: "To what do I owe the pleasure of your company, boyo?"

"Two things."

"The first?"

I wiped my fingers, reached into my shirt pocket, noted my wrist was still tender, and pulled out the yellowed newspaper clipping I'd found in Mikel's room at the Paragon. I handed it to Bill. He stared at it, one eyebrow raised.

"I understand Latin, speak some Spanish, some Vietnamese and Thai, but I haven't a clue at Russian."

"But you do know some people who would be able to read it?" I said. "I don't need a verbatim translation. Just who the guy in the photo is and what the piece is about."

"I suppose I do know someone who could help. Yes, I will have a chat with Brother Vassily. And what is second, may I ask?"

I didn't answer directly. "I was just over in Bellport."

"I can see that," he said pointing at the Spicy's bag. "The food is grand, by the way. Thank you."

"You're welcome. Late lunch was a by-product of my being in Bellport already."

"So you've said. I take it this is where I am to ask about your reasons for being in Bellport in the first place."

"I was as Kevin and Victoria Spears's house. They were Linh Trang's parents."

Bill frowned but didn't speak.

"I had a long talk with Spears's other granddaughter, Abby. Do you know Micah's family?"

"Not at all, I'm afraid. I know only Micah, and not intimately, at least not in the way you might expect. So what did the girl have to say?"

"Look, Bill, my list of debts to you is a long one. Don't bother denying or deflecting. I owe you, and that's that. So when you introduced me to this man who needed my help, in spite of his being a rude prick and try-ing to bribe and manipulate me by playing the dead-son card, I agreed. I figured it was part of the debt I owed you. And I guess I can't deny that at the moment he pulled those two checks out of his pocket, the thought of keeping John's name alive even for ten minutes longer got to me."

"But . . ."

"But after my talk with Abby, Micah Spears's grieving-grandpa rou-tine rings like a papier-mâché bell. According to Abby, Micah Spears is estranged from his family. His son won't talk to him and his daughter-in-law can barely stand sharing the same area code with the man. Abby's relationship with him is so limited and secretive that she couldn't bring herself to do more than whisper Micah's name to me, even though no one else was in the house. The photo he showed us on his cell phone, the one from Linh Trang's graduation, was sent to him by Abby.

"Now, here's the weird thing, Bill. Abby says her parents won't talk about why they're estranged from Spears. They just say stuff about Micah being a bad man or that he's a man who's done bad things. They warned Abby against having anything to do with him, but they absolutely for-bade Linh Trang to have any contact with him. In my family, believe me, there were long-standing feuds. There was a whole branch of his family my dad would have nothing to do with because of some petty bullshit over a forty-square-foot parcel of land back in Ireland. As stupid as it was, at least we knew what it was about. Do you know what the deal is?"

Bill looked as if the food he had just eaten had turned rotten in his belly.

"You said to me not two minutes ago that you took this on because in your eyes you owe me a debt. I might be inclined to argue the debt you say you owe to me you actually owe to Christ, that I was his instrument in saving your life and the girl's. And that I was only his messenger when I comforted your family after your lad's passing." Bill waved his bony hands at me. "I know you're not a believer, Gus, and this isn't me preach-ing. I'm beyond preaching to you and you're beyond hearing . . . for now, anyway. But if you feel you owe me that debt, then don't ask me about Micah and do as you promised. Do his bidding on my account, for I owe him an old debt, one that goes back to my days in Vietnam."

"Can you give me something, Bill? Anything more than that?"

He thought about it, tapping a single finger to the tip of his nose.

"I'll say this. Whatever godliness lives within me now had its roots in my meeting Micah Spears all those years ago. After I lost my faith, my dealings with Micah in those days sustained me for many years until God's love reawakened in me."

Of course there were a thousand more questions I had for Bill, and of course I wouldn't ask them. One of the first things Bill—he was Father Bill then—ever discussed with me was the loss of faith, his and mine. I had lost mine many years before losing John Jr. His death only cemented what I had long held as fact: We were alone and here but once. There was no Heavenly Father waiting in judgment, to guide us, to watch over us, to pull this lever or that. For me, it was the drip, drip, drip of being on the job that diminished my faith. The daily grind and the senselessness of crime and poverty. Police work has a polarizing effect on a person when it comes to God. It drives you to his bosom, to the bottle, or straight into disbelief.

It hadn't been that simple for Bill. As a chaplain in Vietnam, he'd been forced to pick up an M16 and kill a fifteen-year-old girl who was tossing grenades into the surgical tent at an Army field hospital. That was enough to shake anybody's faith. And as Bill had confessed to me, the incident had vanished his faith, which he claimed had always been powerful in him.

"Gus, I tell you, as the girl collapsed, the grenade in her hand blowing her body apart, so too was my faith in all things holy blown apart. So it is no wonder to me that you've no belief in a God who punishes the seemingly innocent and places unfair burdens on the likes of you, Annie, and Krissy."

Bill had never run away or tried to deny his loss of faith with me. It was what had bonded us together. The reason he had continued to act as a priest for a cause and a God he no longer had faith in, those he had always kept to himself. Now I knew it had something to do with Micah Spears, but what? That's what I was thinking about as I headed back to the Paragon.

17

Magdalena hadn't yet seen the Mustang, and since she was partially the motivation behind my purchasing it, I stopped at a car wash on the way back from Bill's and bought the platinum package. The car wasn't particularly dirty, but there was something about what had gone on over the last few days that made me feel like it needed a wash. Would getting the rugs vacuumed and a coat of wax over the paint get the image of Goran being executed out of my head? Was it going to take the ache out of my wrist? Was it going to answer any of my questions about Micah Spears or Rondo Salazar or Bill Kilkenny? No. But it still made me feel better when I slipped the detail guy two fives and drove away, the smell of artificial vanilla filling my head. That and the image of Maggie's exquisite body next to mine.

The mental reverie lasted until I walked through the Paragon's front entrance. I winked hello to Felix. He didn't wink back, but rather shook his head at me, then tilted his brow at the coffee shop.

"What is it, Felix?"

"In the coffee shop, two police detectives from New York City."

"When did they get here?"

"About an hour ago."

"Men?"

"A man about your age and a younger woman. They warned me not to call you or I would have. I am sorry, Gus, but—"

I reached across the front desk and patted his shoulder. "It's okay, Felix. I'll handle it."

"Is it trouble?"

"Your favorite question." I laughed. "When the cops are involved it's always trouble for somebody. Relax."

I was still laughing as I walked toward the coffee shop. But I think Felix knew my confidence and laugh were just me pumping myself up. In the end, there was nothing the cops could do to me, even if they had me on video at the crime scene in Coney Island. I hadn't killed Goran. I never discharged my weapon. The worst they could do was bust my balls for being a retired cop who didn't report what he had seen. I could live with that. I wasn't the first person, retired cop or ordinary schmo, who didn't want to get involved. What concerned me was the chance of anyone connecting me to Slava and Slava to the murder. Outside of the job, I had been a bad liar, but testifying in court teaches you how to deal with difficult questions. Stick as close to the truth as possible without telling too much of it. Don't answer questions that aren't asked. Don't expound and elaborate. "Yes," "No," "Maybe," and "I can't recall" are your best allies.

There was a fair amount of activity in the coffee shop at that hour, as all the Paragon offered in terms of dining choices was the coffee shop. But no one had to point out the NYPD detectives to me. They were seated at a booth facing the stupid Great Moments in Aviation mural, their expressions a mixture of wary curiosity and false weariness. The fact that they were the only man and woman seated together kind of helped me pick them out. *There was just no fooling Gus Murphy.* The man looked like a hard-ass. He was a squatty Hispanic dude in his mid-forties with salt-and-pepper hair and a crooked nose. The woman detective, thirty-five, maybe younger, had short, mousy brown hair and pale, freckled skin. She was cute in an Irish sort of way, but her face was more difficult to read than her partner's.

"Front desk says you're looking for me," I said, walking up to the edge of their wingtip-shaped table. "Should I sit, or you guys want to go talk somewhere else?"

"You John Murphy?" the guy asked.

I nodded. "Gus Murphy. Everybody calls me Gus."

The woman scooched over to make room for me. Her partner didn't like it.

I sat down.

They showed me their gold-and-blue-enamel NYPD detective shields.

"I'm Detective Narvaez. She's Detective Dwyer. We're from Brooklyn South Homicide."

I figured to play dumb for as long as I could. "Homicide, huh? What's this got to do with me?"

"Cut the shit, Murphy," Narvaez said. "We know you used to be on the job, even if it was just jerking off in Suffolk fucking County."

Suffolk cops are used to getting our horns busted about our salaries and benefits, which are better than in most departments. The disparity between NYPD and SCPD salaries used to be enormous. It was still pretty sizable, though less so than in the past. No matter. City cops resented the shit out of us.

I turned to Dwyer, who was fighting back a smile. "Your partner always this diplomatic?"

"Only when he's in a good mood," she said. "Usually, he just growls and foams at the mouth."

"So," I suggested, "should we start over, or is this just going to go downhill from here?"

Narvaez snorted, but Dwyer opened up her notepad.

"Do you own a blue 2010 Mustang coupe?"

"Yes." I almost asked why, but stopped myself. *Only answer what's asked.*

Dwyer nodded. "That's something. This past Sunday evening, April fifth, was your Mustang parked on West Twenty-first Street between Neptune Avenue and Mermaid Avenue in the Coney Island section of Brooklyn?"

"Maybe."

Narvaez really didn't like that answer. "What the fuck kind of answer is that, Murphy? Your car was either there or it wasn't. Where's there room for 'maybe' in that?"

I tried not to laugh or antagonize them, because in the end it wasn't in my self-interest, but Narvaez wasn't making it easy.

"There's plenty of room for maybe. How about if I loaned my car to a friend? Then I wouldn't know if the car was there or not, would I? So my only truthful answer would be maybe."

"Well, did you?" Narvaez asked.

"Did I what, Detective Narvaez?"

"Did you lend your car to a friend?"

"I don't recall."

Narvaez turned red and pounded his fist on the table.

"Relax, Detective, I was only giving you shit. Now let me ask you guys this again. Can we start over? And maybe a good place for you to start would be with telling me why you're here and why you're talking to me. 'Cause otherwise you're gonna hear a lot of 'maybes' and 'I can't recalls' and then I'll have you talk to me through my lawyer. And please don't give me any nonsense about how only guilty people lawyer up. Smart people lawyer up, guilty or not."

Dwyer smiled. "Fair enough." She looked back down at her notepad. "At eight thirty-seven p.m. on April fifth, nine-one-one received several calls from residents of West Twenty-first Street in the Coney Island section of Brooklyn. The responding units from the Sixtieth Precinct discovered the body of a fifty-five-year-old male Caucasian identified as Goran Ivanovich. Mr. Ivanovich had been shot multiple times, including twice in the head at very close range. It was an execution. Ballistics reports confirm eyewitness accounts that the weapon used was a forty-caliber semiautomatic handgun."

I sat there impassively, aware that Narvaez was eyeballing me to gauge my reactions.

"Eyewitnesses also agree on the shooter wearing a black fabric mask that covered his entire face and that he was dressed in what some described as dark military garb and one described as a ninja-like outfit. Now, here's the interesting part, Mr. Murphy," she said, looking up from her pad. "At least two of the witnesses describe a man fitting your physical description approaching the shooter. This man, the one who matches your description, was carrying a handgun as he approached. Several witnesses say that the shooter noticed the man fitting your description and fired two rounds at him. Ballistics and crime scene evidence bears this out. Not thirty seconds after those shots were fired, a blue Mustang was seen pulling out of a parking spot on West Twenty-first Street, backing down the block, and turning onto Neptune Avenue. One of the witnesses got a partial plate number, and that's why we're sitting here together today. Any comment?"

"No."

Narvaez laughed in frustration. It was a staccato, barking laugh. "Can you believe this fucking guy?" he said to Dwyer. He turned to me. "Listen, Murphy, what were you doing there? What's your connection to Goran Ivanovich? And why didn't you come forward?"

I sat back. "Let me answer that second question for you. I had no connection whatsoever to this Ivanovich guy. I've never heard his name before your partner just mentioned it." It was only half a lie. Slava had never mentioned Goran's last name.

Dwyer jumped at that. "But you're not denying that you were there and that our witness statements are inaccurate?"

"Let me answer you this way, Detective Dwyer. If I would have been inclined to be in Coney Island that night, it would have been because I just purchased my Mustang and hadn't really gotten a chance to drive it. Why Coney Island?" I shrugged. "I don't know. Maybe because I like how the neon lights look in the rain. And if I was on West Twenty-first Street, and I'm not saying I was, it might've been because I don't know the area that well once I get off Surf Avenue."

"And the rest of it, Murphy?" Narvaez said, his voice unexpectedly calm.

"Like your witnesses say, the shooter had on a dark balaclava and black clothing. So even if I had been there, I couldn't give you a better description than what you already have. And if I had been shot at, but wasn't hit, what could I add?"

Dwyer smiled a cool smile. "Maybe you caught a tag number or saw the shooter's escape route. Who knows what information you might have?"

I agreed. "Yes, who knows?"

"Why are you being such an asshole, Murphy?" Dwyer wanted to know. "We checked you out. You were a really good cop."

"You mean for a Suffolk PD jerk-off, right?"

Narvaez was barking his machine-gun laugh. Dwyer wasn't laughing.

"Look," I said, "if you checked me out, then you know I've gotten a lot of ink lately about some bad shit that went down out here. The guys who got killed . . . most people think they got what was coming to them, but there are some who still admire them. I didn't need that stuff in my life, but it landed on my doorstep. I've had enough turmoil in the last few years to last me a lifetime."

Dwyer stared at me. I could feel her eyes on the side of my face like the summer sun through a car window. "Yeah, we heard about your son. Tough."

"'Tough' doesn't begin to describe it. So do me a favor, read between the lines of what I said to you. If I had been there and there was something I thought I could give you that would help, I would."

"If you were there?" Narvaez repeated.

"Exactly."

Dwyer and Narvaez gave each other a little nod. They were done with me.

"Okay, Gus," Narvaez said, suddenly friendly, standing up. "That's all for now."

I slid out of the booth to let Dwyer out. She stood and was taller than I expected, but just as hard to read as she was when I first saw her. They handed me their textured white business cards, their shields embossed on the left side of the card. The address of their unit was printed beneath the shield, contact info on the opposite end of the card.

Dwyer said, "You think of anything else that might have happened if you had been there, please call."

Then I did a stupid thing. I extended the conversation.

"This Ivanovich guy, the vic . . ."

"Yeah," Dwyer said. "What about him?"

"Who was he, anyway?"

"A naturalized citizen originally from Chechnya," Narvaez said. "Wherever the fuck that is. Owned a produce mart on Brighton Beach Avenue and owned the row house on West Twenty-first. He has a jacket. Some minor Russian mob–related stuff. Anything else?"

I shook my head and they were gone, but I got a feeling their absence would be temporary.

18

Maggie's condo, I guess it was really a co-op—not that I understood or cared about the differences—was in a towering apartment complex in Nassau County near the Queens border. The buildings were about as appropriate to the context of their surroundings as the Chrysler Building in the middle of a Kansas cornfield. The buildings themselves were fairly ugly, but the units were expensive. And in New York, expensive counted. It counted for a lot. In New York, expense was a drug, an aphrodisiac. In some places the important questions were: How big? How are the schools? How close to the water? How close to shopping? Here the truly meaningful question was: How much?

The security guard at the gate perked up when he recognized me.

"Where's the courtesy van tonight?" he said, smirking. "The janitor lend you his car or something?"

You had to love this place. Even the asshole square badge making minimum wage had an attitude like he was somehow better than the peons beyond the gates. I wasn't in the mood, not tonight. Not after the day I'd had.

"Yeah, that's right." I gave him my best fish-eyed stare. "And by the way, go fuck yourself."

He wasn't smirking anymore as I drove past.

I could tell the second she let me into her apartment that there was something going on with Maggie. What, exactly, was hard to know. Naturally blond, full-breasted, and curvy, with a stunning face, she had a great mid-twentieth-century kind of look. She told me that was what had gotten her noticed during her early acting career.

"At auditions, the rest of the girls had figures like this," she said, holding up her index finger. "Many of them were prettier than me, but I didn't look like they did. I had curves and breasts and I could even act a little. I was Scarlett Johansson before Scarlett Johansson, only ten years too soon and three inches too tall."

I loved that she could laugh at herself and look at herself without false modesty, but she wasn't laughing tonight. I got the dumb idea in my head that she had somehow found out about what had gone on between Annie and me. That was just my own craziness, though. And it wasn't like I was feeling any intense guilt or regret over it. No matter who was in my life, there would always be Annie in it, too, in one form or another. Even if I was fooling myself and was feeling guilty below the surface, I hadn't been inside her door long enough to give myself away. No, this was not in my head.

Maggie was fully made up and dressed about as suggestively as she could be without being undressed. She was wearing a tight, sheer black top with no bra underneath. She had on a short black leather skirt, sheer black stockings with a thick seam running along the back of her legs, and shiny black stilettos. This was similar to how she was dressed the night we met, but she was working then, her outfit a means to tip money. There was a nude dancer at the club that night, a beautiful black woman covered in a light sheen of sweat, robotically going through her routine. I remembered thinking that Magdalena seemed so much more naked than the black chick, so much more exposed, because Maggie could not hide her heart behind a performance. Tonight was the first time since that night last December that she was emitting that vibe.

She kissed me hard on the mouth and I kissed her back harder, but she pulled out of my grasp.

"I'll be right back," she said, disappearing into the kitchen.

When she reappeared she did so with a bottle of Moët and two flutes. She handed me the bottle and leaned in close to me, her breath warm on my neck, her raw herbal perfume filling up the room, her breasts pressing against me.

"Make it pop, Gus," she whispered in my ear, then licked my neck. "I want to hear it. Make it pop."

I did as she asked, the cork bouncing off the ceiling and a wall. Some of the wine foamed out the top. But if Maggie was upset about it getting on the rug, she wasn't letting on. I filled our glasses. We clinked. We drank.

"You got the part! That's fantastic."

"I did, but I don't want to talk about that now," she said, taking my hand, pulling me toward the bedroom. "I don't want to talk at all."

Inside the bedroom, she poured us more champagne. We drank. She nudged me gently onto the edge of the bed. She placed the bottle between my feet, her empty glass on the dresser. She began to sway and dance to music that was in her head. As she danced, she slipped out of her skirt, revealing a silky black thong and lacy garter. The dance grew more fevered. Me, too, frankly. And bit by bit the clothing came off her body but for her sheer top.

Maggie leaned over and undressed me, kissing me, rubbing me as she went. When I was nude, she reached for the bottle, took a swallow, and knelt down in front of me. Before taking me in her mouth, she let the still-cool champagne leak out of her mouth and onto me. Her mouth was warm and cold at the same time and my entire body tensed. A minute later, satisfied that I was hard enough, she reached for the bottle again, took another mouthful, and straddled me. She sat still with me inside her, leaned her head forward, and placed her lips over mine, the champagne pouring into my mouth from hers. That was about the last fully conscious act between us for the next ninety minutes.

As we lay there in the now black room, the air smelling of slightly sour champagne, sweat, musk, and crushed green herbs, my head throbbed, but in a good way. My whole body pulsed with the slowing beat of my heart. The curves of Maggie's body found comfortable niches in mine.

"You're leaving," I said, breaking the quiet. "That's what this was all about."

"Not all of it." Maggie shimmied up my body, resting her head under my chin. "Most of it was about loving you."

"How long?"

"Three months, at least. It's a big part, Gus. The play's about Marilyn Monroe waiting to be judged before God. I play the older Marilyn, the one who would have moved forward had she not killed herself. Another actress plays younger Marilyn, Norma Jean. And another one plays Marilyn at the gates. That's what the play's called, *Marilyn at the Gates*."

"So," I said, "you're kinda like the ghost of Christmas that never was."

"I never thought of it like that." She kissed me hard again and squeezed me tight. "That's brilliant. I can use that."

"When do you leave?"

"Next week. Friday, I think."

"Where to?"

"The rehearsals will be in Detroit."

"Detroit?"

"The producers got all these concessions from the city. They're trying to revitalize theater there. We'll do a few weeks in Detroit after rehearsals, then we're doing a couple of weeks in smaller cities before opening in L.A."

I opened my mouth to say something, but nothing came out. What could I say? I had been Maggie's biggest backer, pushing her to go to classes and to auditions, but I naively assumed any part she would get would be in New York. I guess I'd never considered the possibility she would take a part that would take her away from me. The universe liked reminding me that all things were fleeting. I was sick inside.

"Say something," she said. "Anything."

"Break a leg."

She laughed too loudly. Then said, "With some feeling, Gus."

"You don't want to know what I'm feeling right now," I heard myself say, easing out from under her. I sat up on the side of the bed, my back to her. "You really don't."

She put her arms around me, resting her head on my shoulder, and whispered, "I won't take it, Gus. I'll stay here and we'll get married."

"Don't be stupid, Maggie. You'll be on that plane next Friday if I have to drive you to the airport myself. The ghost of Marilyn awaits."

The quiet in the room turned angry and cold. I stood up and went into the bathroom before I blurted something out that we'd both regret. It took everything I had in me not to scream at her that I'd just fucked my ex-wife. There would be no taking that back and no coming back from it. I stayed under the shower head for what seemed a very long time. Long enough that the urge to strike out at Maggie had passed.

When I finally came back into the bedroom, Maggie was gone. I found her in the living room, smoking, drinking a scotch, her cheeks streaked black with mascara tears. Her eyes got big when she turned to look at me.

"Those bruises, Christ! Where did you get those bruises?"

I looked at my wrist, looked down at my ribs and abdomen. We'd both been too caught up in things to notice them before.

"I had to get rough with a guy at the Paragon today," I said, leaving it at that.

She didn't pursue it. "What do you want from me, Gus? You've been the one supporting me, telling me to keep going when I got laughed out of auditions, and now . . . I don't know what I'm supposed to do."

"Yes, you do, Maggie. You know exactly what to do. You'll take the part and follow the dream. You won't be any good to me or to yourself if you are always looking back at what might've been."

"But you're so angry with me."

I said, "You'd think loss would prepare you for more loss, but it doesn't. I'm gonna go."

While I was in the bedroom getting dressed, Maggie came in.

"Don't go, Gus. Stay with me tonight."

I shook my head.

She said, "How about we do half of my plan?"

"How's that?" I tilted my head at her like a confused puppy.

"I'll go out with the show, but let's get married first."

"No. I don't want that. I don't need that from you, some gesture of your faithfulness. We're adults, Maggie. You'll be on the road. I don't want you to be lonely. I don't need you to prove anything to me. I'm just not ready to lose somebody else. It's my issue, not yours."

"But I've fallen in love with you, Gus Murphy."

I kissed her on the forehead. "That was your first mistake. I've gotta go."

"Will I see you before Friday?"

"Of course. Maybe I'll drive you to the airport. It's my chosen profession, you know. Besides, you haven't seen my new car."

"You know you can live here while I'm gone. I would like that. You've got the key. You could get out of the hotel and live a more normal life."

"You know, Maggie, just before we met, I was sort of seeing someone. At one point in my life, she would have been everything I would have ever wanted. She was very pretty, had a stable job helping special-needs kids. Owned a nice little house and she could really cook. We even slept together once and it was pretty good in an awkward sort of way. We could have had the kind of life I once had with Annie, but it was too late. I'd changed. If I wanted a normal life, I wouldn't date a beautiful actress.

I once had a normal life. That was taken from me. I won't let that happen again." I kissed her softly on the lips. "I'm very proud of you, Maggie. I gotta go."

When I left the parking lot, I made sure to use the side gate. I wasn't in the mood to see that same smug security guard on the way out. A snide remark or smirk and I might have shot him in the kneecap.

On the way back to the Paragon, I called Slava. He picked up this time. I let him know that the cops had tracked me down. That got his attention. I could tell by the fact that his usual cheery tone went straight out of his voice.

"Are you thinking they have Slava's plate number?"

"I don't think so. You and Mikel were just two guys talking to Goran on his stoop. Even if the neighbors had noticed you guys, they wouldn't have taken any particular interest. But once the bullets started flying, people paid attention. The cops told me this Goran guy was from Chechnya," I said, just to see how Slava would react or if he would react at all.

"From Grozny, is the capital, but he was—how you are saying this— ethnic Russian, not like the Chechens."

"You mean he wasn't a Muslim."

That surprised Slava, not a man easily surprised. "You are knowing about Chechnya?"

I didn't answer directly. "Can't a Muslim be Russian?"

"The Muslims, the Chechens, they hate Russia. They are not wanting to be Russians."

"You know a lot about Russia and Chechnya for a Pole."

He turned it around on me. "And you, Gus . . . I am thinking Americans are not knowing anything of these places."

"I used to read the papers and watch the news. I know about the terrorism, about the kids and teachers murdered at the school and the theater in Moscow."

That was met was a tense silence. Then, "Do police suspect you of anything?"

"Well, they know I'm full of shit, but I don't think they believe I was involved in Goran's killing. I think they believe I just didn't want to get involved because of all the stuff that happened last year. They believed that."

"Thank you, Gus. What is wrong with you? Slava is hearing something bad in your voice."

"Bad! You mean besides getting whacked with a metal baton, being choked briefly into unconsciousness, and getting questioned by the cops?" Only at the end did I realize I was screaming at him. "You think I have reason to feel bad?"

Slava didn't bother apologizing and just hung up. He was savvy that way. But of course, he was right. He *had* heard something in my voice that had very little to do with the things I listed and everything to do with Maggie leaving.

19

(TUESDAY MORNING)

I met Charlie Prince at Maureen's Kitchen on Terry Road in Smithtown. When I was younger, Maureen's was little more than a shack on the side of the road, serving the best breakfasts and lunch sandwiches in town. The restaurant had since moved across the street from its original locale into a converted house and it was no longer Smithtown's best-kept secret. Sometimes the wait for a table was so long you'd think the whole county got hungry for Oreo–peanut butter pancakes at the same time. You couldn't miss Maureen's. There was a full-size black-and-white cow sculpture out front and a giant cow head sticking out the side of its mansard roof.

Charlie Prince was taking a selfie with the cow sculpture when I walked up to him.

"My wife'll love this," he said.

I knew Charlie by name and rep, knew what he looked like from photos. Although our careers on the SCPD overlapped, we'd never crossed paths. He was about ten years my junior and was in the Third Precinct when I was in the Second. We had friends in common, friends like Al Roussis. Charlie Prince was a stout African-American man with close-cropped hair and a happy demeanor. And about that happy demeanor and broad white smile, I didn't let it fool me. Charlie's rep was that he was a tough bastard, stubborn, and shrewd. Even the most racist guys on the job admitted, without much prompting, that Charlie was a good cop. According to Al, he was a better detective.

"Charlie," I said, offering my right hand.

He took it. "Gus. Nice to meet you. I heard a lot about you from Al."

"Only the good parts are true."

"There were only good parts."

"Then either you or Al is full of shit."

We both laughed at that.

"C'mon, Gus, there's no wait. Let's get us a table."

I was happy to be meeting with Charlie. Less happy about it being for breakfast. I was scheduled to work my regular shift for the next two nights, from six p.m. to six a.m. And getting up before noon on days I drove the van made me cranky. Given the previous day's events, I suppose I would have been in a shitty mood no matter what.

When Al called at eight that morning to tell me he'd set up the meeting, I was already aching—inside and out. I was mourning Maggie, though there was more than a week before she was to leave. In a way, she was already gone. I wasn't at all sure I wouldn't have been better off if she had just taken off and left me a note. The goodbye sex was otherworldly, but it made the hurt that much worse. It wasn't her fault and there was no way she could have known that her leaving would bring the ugliness and pain back to me. When I got home to my room at the Paragon last night, I'd spent an hour staring at John Jr.'s photo and having intimate relations with the minibar. I didn't remember passing out.

I wasn't tiptop physically. My head was throbbing. My wrist was swollen and hurt like a son of a bitch. My gut and ribs were sore. After I got off the phone with Al, I swallowed a fistful of aspirins. My next thoughts were of the guy who'd attacked me in Mikel's room. At that moment, I would have given a lot to have had a chance to go another round with him. I wanted to make him pay. I wanted to make him pay for a lot of things, for the wounds he'd inflicted and the ones he had not. I wanted someone to pay other than me.

"Mmmm, smells great in here," Charlie said as we sat down at a two-top table with a cow-print tablecloth. "I'm hungry, man."

"The smell of frying bacon'll get you every time."

A cute redheaded waitress came by, poured coffees, gave us the specials, and left. I guzzled my coffee, flagged down a guy carrying coffeepots, and begged a refill. Guzzled that, too.

"You're lookin' a little green around the gills this morning. Rough night, Gus?"

"You got no idea, Charlie."

"A woman?"

I nodded, not wanting to go into the whole opera of Maggie, bad memories, and the minibar. "Did Al tell you why I asked to talk with you?"

"He did. You want to discuss the Spears homicide."

"Not so much the homicide itself," I said. "I'm more interested in Rondo Salazar."

"That piece of shit? Why you interested in him?"

The waitress came by before I could answer. Charlie went the whole nine yards: banana-walnut pancakes, scrambled eggs, bacon, and sausages. It was all I could do not to puke just listening to his order.

"Just some scrambled eggs and whole-wheat toast."

The waitress took a good look at me and smiled sympathetically. "You look like you could use more coffee," she said. "I'll make sure it keeps coming."

The guy with the coffeepots showed up ten seconds later.

"Well, not so much Salazar himself," I explained after Coffeepots left. "I'm more interested in why he did it."

"Million-dollar question, ain't it, though? Glad I don't have to answer it on this case. Why you interested, anyway?"

I had a decision to make. I was acting like a PI on Micah Spears's behalf, but I didn't have a license. I didn't necessarily have an obligation to protect my client's identity. Even if I had, I didn't have the right. I wasn't a doctor, a lawyer, or a priest. On the other hand, I didn't want to shout it to the world. So I played it halfway.

"I'm doing a favor for someone."

He made a face, thinking about my answer. "You getting paid for this favor?"

"Sort of. Does it matter?"

"What do you think?"

"Okay," I said. "If I do this favor, the person I'm doing it for is going to start a foundation in my son's name and donate money for medical research."

"Yeah, I heard about your kid. Sorry. That musta been hard on you."

"'Hard' doesn't begin to describe it. But you can see why I'm motivated to see what I can see, right?"

Charlie Prince leaned forward. "Gus, we don't know why he did it, and that's the God's-honest truth. All that stuff in the papers about his being rejected and the stalking . . . we think that's just some bullshit to sell papers."

"Any guesses?"

"They'd just be guesses and I really have no idea."

"Could it be gang-related?"

"Maybe, but I'm no expert on the Asesinos, MS-Thirteen, the Latin Kings, the Bloods, Crips, or any of those assholes."

"I have someone else to talk to about that," I said.

"Who, Alvaro Peña?"

I laughed. "He's the man. We go way back."

"I love that guy. Give that bastard a kick in the nuts from me."

Cops have a twisted sense of humor and ways of expressing affection.

"By all reports, Salazar hasn't said a word to you guys about the murder. Is that true or an exaggeration?"

Charlie held up his right hand. "No exaggeration. The prick wouldn't even talk to his lawyer about it in our presence. He hasn't said a word. My guess is he ain't even talking to his lawyer when no one's around."

"You think that's his choice, or that he's been ordered to keep quiet?"

Charlie shrugged. "Anything I say would be a guess, and I have nothing to base it on."

"Has the DA tried to get him to cop a plea to save the trouble of a trial? I mean, he sounds as guilty as guilty can be."

"They've tried, but any plea would have to come with an allocution and there's no way this motherfucka is gonna do that. Anyways, the DA wants to make an example of this guy, so the trial is a win-win for him. It won't last very long and it will get a lot of press."

Our food came and we ate without discussing the case. We talked some baseball, family stuff, told some stories about guys we knew whom we had both served with. The food did me some good, the pounding in my head retreating. The distraction did me good, too. It was a relief to go a half-hour without thinking about Maggie or John.

After the plates were cleared, I asked, "Have you made any progress in finding the actual murder scene?"

"None, Gus. Fact is, unless Salazar starts talking, we don't have a shot at finding it. Maybe if we knew where he killed her, we might begin to know why. I guess that's along the lines you were thinking."

"Exactly. At least it would be a start. If I knew where and when, I could trace it backward to how and why."

Charlie smiled a sad smile. "If only . . ."

"Now I'm going to ask you a tough question that you had to know I would ask. I know you won't want to answer it. I wouldn't want to if I was in your shoes, but I hope you will. It would really help."

Charlie Prince nodded at me. "You're gonna ask how me and my partner got onto Rondo Salazar in the first place, right? If we didn't know where the murder scene was and we didn't have a motive, how did we come up with a suspect so fast?"

"I sort of know the answer," I said. "I know you were looking at him already for another unrelated homicide, but to get to where he was, it had to be a tip or intel from a CI. Problem is, knowing only that doesn't do me any good. I need a name."

"Gus, Al said you were a good man and that I'd like you. He told me you woulda made a helluva detective. He was right all the way around. But even if I had a name for you, I wouldn't give it to you. However we found Salazar came via my partner, so that's all off-limits."

"Fair enough. I had to ask."

"I know you did."

"Who's your partner, anyway?"

Charlie Prince suddenly looked like I'd felt when I woke up that morning and said, "Tony Palumbo."

I understood the sick look on Prince's face. Tony Palumbo had been a protégé of the late chief of police, Jimmy Regan, and a close friend of the late Pete McCann. Both were late because of me. Regan indirectly—he'd shot himself because I'd discovered things about his past that would have ruined his career and family. Pete McCann directly—I shot him in the neck after Bill Kilkenny shot him in the legs.

"I take it you didn't mention our breakfast meeting to Tony," I said.

"You got that shit right. I did not."

"Yeah, he's got no love for me."

"That prick McCann had my partner snowed. Tony really loved the guy, thought he was so cool. Loved his stories about all the women he'd bedded. Even after all the rumors circulated about the bad shit he did, Tony defended him to anybody who would listen. Then everyone stopped listening."

"Pete McCann had everybody fooled. Me, too, at least until he started fucking my wife a few months after my kid died."

Charlie shook his head. "I don't even know what to say to that. What an asshole. And Chief Regan was grooming Tony for big things. Now he's got no rabbi to look out for him, nobody with any juice to pull him up. I love my partner. He's a good man, but now he's got this chip on his shoulder. Anything goes wrong for him or me, he blames it on the fact that the brass knows he was close to Regan. You should steer clear of him, Gus."

"So why'd you agree to meet me?"

"Because Al Roussis is a good guy and I owe him," Charlie said.

"And?"

"And because I wanted to know if all those rumors about Regan and Pete McCann are true."

"Pretty much, Charlie."

"They ran drugs?"

"Heroin, a lot of it."

"They really murdered people?"

I nodded. "I saw Pete gun down a dealer in Wyandanch and stood a few feet away from Regan as he shot a barely conscious man in cold blood. Pete also killed an ex-cop and Regan confessed to me that he beat his ex-mistress to death. The body count is probably higher, but I can't be sure. You know Father Bill Kilkenny?"

Charlie smiled at the mention of Bill's name. "Everybody knows Father Bill."

"You don't believe me, ask him."

"I believe you. I think I believed it before I even asked."

We stopped talking after that. I took care of the check. We walked out to the parking lot together in silence and shook hands. As I turned to head to my car, Charlie grabbed my forearm to stop me.

"A CI with Asesinos connections snitched Salazar out," he said, leaning in close to me so that only I could hear. "I don't have a name for you. And like I said, I wouldn't tell you if I did. You find out why that piece of shit murdered such a sweet girl, you let me know. The system may not demand a motive, but I sure would like one. No matter what people think, most of the time murder makes some kind of sense even if it's an all-twisted-up kind of sense. This one just doesn't. I mean, there was no sexual assault aspect to it, but it was vicious."

It was my turn to stop Prince from going to his car. "Fair is fair. My client, the guy I'm doing the favor for, is Micah Spears, the girl's paternal grandfather."

"Guy creeps me out."

I was confused. "You interviewed the grandfather? Why would you interview the grandfather?"

"Nah, it wasn't like that. He showed up one day wanting to speak to Tony and me about the case. At first we were polite about it. We understand that families sometimes need to know stuff, to try to understand what can't be understood. Comes with the territory. We explained that we were a hundred percent sure we had the killer, but that we weren't gonna discuss details of the case with him. You know, we told him that if there was anything to come out, it would come out at trial. But the fucker wouldn't take no for an answer, so we basically escorted him out of the building. When we called Linh Trang's father to ask him to keep the old man away from us, he told us they no longer had any contact with Micah Spears and that we shouldn't feel obliged to even talk to him. I'll tell you what, Gus, there's something not right with that guy. My gut tells me he's got a dark side bigger than the moon's."

"I agree with you, but I'm not doing this because I like the guy."

"I feel you, but you be careful."

"You do the same."

I watched Charlie Prince get in his car and drive out of the lot onto Terry Road south. I stood there for a few more minutes, frozen, thinking about everything and nothing. Then I knew exactly what I needed to do. There was someone I needed to see.

20

John was buried in a narrow corner of St. Pat's Cemetery on Mount Pleasant off the Smithtown Bypass. St. Pat's was a vaguely triangular patch of grass, dirt, and mostly tasteful headstones less than a mile west of Maureen's. He hadn't been meant to rest here, but rest here he did. That was my doing, mine and Father Bill's. The plan had been for us all to be buried together in the family plot in a big Catholic cemetery in Queens. But what the fuck did plans matter, anyhow? The world is cold and doesn't care about plans or what's supposed to be. *Supposed to be.* What does that even mean? It's easy to fool yourself that plans matter right up until the moment they don't. You tell yourself you're in control, that the things you think, things you believe count. They count, all right. They count for shit.

And when I realized that, when that lesson was dropped on my head like a grand piano from a hundred stories up, I took control of the one thing left to me: where my son was to be buried. I didn't want him far from me while I was still breathing. After I was dead, too, so what? Then I would be beyond caring. I didn't want him thirty miles away from me in a place where I'd need a map to find him among thousands of other dead. Where his headstone would be just another cornstalk in a field of corn. So with Bill's help, we wrangled a small plot in St. Pat's. Annie hated me for it because there would be no place for the rest of us when our turns came. I think sometimes that Annie's hate made it easier for her to spread her legs for Pete McCann. Or maybe I'm fooling myself about that. Wouldn't be the first time. Wouldn't be the last.

There was a burial going on at the opposite end of the cemetery, but what was that—fifty or sixty yards away? Less? So I parked on Mount Pleasant out of respect and walked through the far gate to John's grave. Yet as I walked I could not help but stare at the ceremony going on, at the priest, the coffin. I could not help staring at the mourners, at their tears. I stared at those with no tears, too. At the bored and busy men checking their watches and their phones, counting the seconds until they could go, until they could get away from the unpleasant reminder of what awaited them. I always thought it strange, checking the time at a funeral. Tick . . . tick . . . tick. Then I stopped staring.

Most of the time when I came to see John, the caretaker would come over and stand by me. Sometimes we talked. Not always. And when we talked, he would tell me who had been by to visit or who had left flowers. Not today. Today he was busy at the other end of the cemetery. One thing having this odd friendship with the caretaker ensured was that John's grave was always seen to. There were fresh flowers laid against the headstone. Flowers meant Annie had been here, probably to tell John she was getting married. Flowers were Annie's MO. She always brought flowers. Other things, toys, books, stuff like that, those were Krissy's doing. Me, I just tended to stand and remember. I was out of tears, out of anger at him for dying, out of words to say to him.

"What should I do, John?" said someone who sounded like me. "Maggie's leaving and I'm afraid she's not coming back."

I laughed at myself. Even if John was still alive, he wouldn't have known what to say. He was twenty when he died. What do twenty-year-olds know? Which is a different question from what they think they know. Why do we imbue the dead with wisdom? Why would they know anything the living don't? I think it's mostly that they can't answer. The wisdom is in their silence.

As I was leaving the cemetery, one of the mourners going to her car stopped me. She was a handsome woman, a little older than me, perfectly made up, and somberly dressed in a dark gray dress and black shawl. Her expression was neutral. She asked me if I had a spare cigarette.

"Sorry. I don't smoke," I said, pointing to where the burial had been. "Who was it?"

"A business associate's mother."

"Sad."

"Is it?" she said, seeming to talk more to herself than to me. "Is it always sad? For her family, it was sad, but it isn't always sad for the family. Sometimes it's a relief. I was obliged to be here, so was it sad for me?"

I interrupted her contemplation on sadness. "You didn't know her?"

"Not at all. Thanks."

She walked on, her car parked a few spaces ahead of mine.

As I sat in the front seat of my car, it occurred to me that I might be approaching my task for Micah Spears all wrong. If there was no obvious why in the killer's behavior, maybe I should start looking at the victim more closely. Maybe she was where the secret was hidden.

21

Before I dived headlong into the too-short life of Linh Trang Spears, I had one or two last cards to play in terms of Rondo Salazar. Although they were unlikely to get me any further than I'd already gotten, I thought it was probably a good idea to see what those last chances would net me. So when I got back to the Paragon, I called Alvaro Peña.

As witnessed by my conversation with Charlie Prince, if you wanted to know anything about gang-related activities in Suffolk County, you went to Alvaro Peña. For most of his career on the SCPD, Alvaro had worked on gang stuff in one capacity or other. He'd been on every local, state, and federal task force in the last fifteen years that dealt with gang activities in the New York metropolitan area. That meant he had sources not only on the streets of Central Islip and New York City, but on the streets of San Juan, Santo Domingo, and San Salvador as well. He also had powerful connections at the NYPD and in D.C.

"I figured you'd be calling," Alvaro said when he heard my voice.

"How'd you figure that?"

"C'mon, Gus. How long you think it would be before I heard you been sniffin' around about the Spears homicide?"

"There's no surprising you, huh, Alvaro?"

"Not with this shit."

"So . . ."

"So."

"You got anything for me at all that's not in the press?"

"You talk to Palumbo and Prince?"

"Charlie Prince, yeah. This morning."

"What'd he say?"

"To call you."

Alvaro laughed a squeaky laugh, the one he laughed when he wasn't really amused.

"So I'm calling," I said.

"Why didn't you talk to Palumbo? He caught the case."

"Palumbo was chummy with Pete and he was one of Regan's golden boys."

"Those are good reasons. He'd probably spit in your face."

"Anything about Rondo Salazar on the street that isn't public knowledge?"

"Nada."

"Isn't that a little unusual?"

"Very," he said. "There's usually a lot of bravado and dick waving connected to gang stuff, but not with this one. No one's talking."

"You think they're ashamed of Salazar because of the victim and the brutality?"

I swear I could almost hear him shrug. "Maybe. I mean, the girl had no gang affiliation or connections at all. Believe me, I checked. And the Asesinos don't usually have an issue with brutality or negative press, but could be there is so much bad press this time that they're clamming up."

"Could it have been an initiation ritual gone wrong? I know that some gangs require you to kill a random person to get in. You know, like what happened with those girls at that mall on the South Shore a few years ago."

He didn't like it. "Salazar is a lifer. No need to have him kill randomly. Besides, they were already looking at him for a drug dispute homicide with MS-Thirteen."

"Maybe they were questioning his loyalty and he had to do it. Was he a snitch?"

"You think I didn't check that shit out? Believe me, Gus. No one inside the gang, not here or in Latin America, is questioning his loyalty. I would hear about it. Salazar was no snitch."

"Let's go back to my initiation theory again, just for a second."

"Okay."

"You're right. Salazar is a lifer and didn't need to prove his loyalty, but maybe it wasn't his initiation. Maybe it was somebody else's, some kid or his brother or cousin he was sponsoring who fucked up and Rondo is taking the fall."

Alvaro was almost always quick to answer, especially to refute something he thought I got wrong. So when he was quiet, I knew that maybe, just maybe, I had hit on a possibility he hadn't given much thought to.

"But what about the DNA?" he asked, finally. "And the cuts and scratches?"

"I can't explain any of it away, but remember, they found the girl in Heckscher State Park. She wasn't killed there. You find where the killing actually happened, maybe you'll find out there was someone else involved. Think about this scenario, Alvaro. He sponsors this kid and the kid stabs the girl once, twice, but the kid can't go through with it. He freaks, but it's already too late. The girl's got to die. Rondo is furious, loses it, and takes it out on the girl which accounts for the vicious nature of the attack."

"That's a whole lot of what-ifs and maybes and could've-beens, Gus. A whole lot based on what? Your imagination? Evidence. Where's the evidence?"

"Good question. Where's the murder scene?"

"Gus, you're a fuckin' pain in my *cojones*, you know that? But you've given me something to check into. I wouldn't get my hopes up, though, amigo."

"Hoping's not something I do a lot of these days."

"Anything else, Gus?"

"You should've learned your lesson by now, bro. Never ask me that."

"What?" He packed a lot of exasperation into one syllable.

"If I need to, and I probably won't, can you get me in to see Salazar?"

"Are you fuckin' with me now, Gus?"

"No."

"If I had to, I guess I could, but it would cost me a lot of goodwill and capital. So make sure this is something you're desperate for, or don't ask."

"I probably won't ask."

"*Jefe*, you'll forgive me if I don't have much faith in that."

"You're forgiven, Alvaro. One other thing."

"How did I know you were going to say that? What else?"

"Anything going on with the Asesinos? Nothing related to this. I mean, generally," I asked, not expecting him to come back with any revelations. I was wrong.

"As a matter of fact, yes. They've had more money to put out on the street lately, like they've had a big infusion of cash."

"Drug money? They were looking at Salazar for a drug killing, right?"

"Doesn't seem that way," he said. "No big increase in drug activity from them, and if there was, I'd hear about it. No, Gus, this is something else. They've got some other business we're not onto yet."

"Money from back home? Are they laundering cash?"

"Maybe, but I doubt it. Money usually gets kicked upstairs, not down."

He knew better than to extend the conversation again, said goodbye, and hung up. As interesting as my theory was, I didn't believe that's how or why Linh Trang was murdered any more than Alvaro believed it. But like me, he was curious. His curiosity was different from mine. As Alvaro once told me, gang behavior, as irrational and violent as it seemed to outsiders, was governed by a twisted kind of logic and tradition. Gangs had all sorts of rituals, rites, and rules, a litany of dos and don'ts. What ate at him about the Spears homicide was his inability to make it align with his understanding of how gangs functioned. Me, I just wanted to know why.

22

No alarms. No phone calls. I got up all on my own at about one in the afternoon the next day. My shift had been unremarkable. Three trips to Ronkonkoma station and two to the airport. By midnight, there was nothing to do. So I used the computer in the business center to do a background check on Linh Trang. Not on her death, but on her life. Except for the autopsy photos and the ME's report—which I could get from Al Roussis or Charlie Prince for the asking—I knew what there was to know about her death. No, if there was something I was missing, it was in the folds and creases of her too-short life, not in the depth of the twenty-three puncture wounds.

It was odd how publicly people, especially kids, lived today. I had kids. I knew how it was, that the expectation of privacy was as much a thing of the past as covered wagons and rotary phones. I'd always been uncomfortable with how much of their lives John and Krissy shared, how much their friends shared, of things I would have never wanted anyone to know. The hardest thing for me to swallow was how much Krissy shared of her struggles after her brother's death. She posted stuff about her drinking, her drug use, her careless dating, and anonymous sex. There were times I wasn't sure which was worse, her posting about it or having to listen to people report the details of her activities to me. That was all over now, but remembering those days still made me wince.

Linh Trang Spears left a social-media footprint behind her. I guess everybody does. She had a personal website she must've created when she was barely a teenager. Maybe her parents couldn't bear to cancel the hosting fees or maybe they paid their credit card bills blind to those few dollars appearing as a charge month after month. Who knows? On the site there was some awful poetry about boys and unicorns, rainbows and clouds. There were drawings, too. Better than the poetry, much better, and a lot of old photos. The photos were mostly of her and her pals, some of her family. I thought it was kind of odd how few photos there were of her and her sister. When I spoke to Abby, I sensed that she and Linh weren't the closest sisters ever. But so what? I guess I kind of liked that Abby didn't act all guilty and regretful about it. Murder, at least in Abby's eyes, hadn't turned her sister into a saint. I saw there was a contact page, but didn't go there. It just felt creepy.

I had a Facebook account that went back as far as John's freshman year in college. His idea, not mine. These days I used it occasionally to check in with Krissy at school, even though her school was a fifteen-minute drive from the Paragon. I went to my page and typed Linh Trang's name into the Facebook search box. Her page was still there and, by my figuring, was current up to the day before she was murdered. Her last post was about her being bored at work and wanting to do real accounting after she got her CPA. Many of her posts were similar to Krissy's: photos with friends at the wineries with wiseass comments below, photos at ballgames, a shot of her cat sleeping in a weird position. There were links to videos, funny and political, and shares of friends' posts. There were some photos of her with men—"Jerry and me on midnight cruise around Manhattan." Like that. To judge by her Facebook page, she dated several men, but none seriously or for very long. Maybe there was something in that. Probably not. None of them had killed her.

What I was most interested in were her friends. I'd always believed that if you wanted to know someone, you talked to her friends. Friends knew a person in a way his or her family never would or could. I believed it, but I wasn't sure that it was true of me anymore. So many of my old friends, friends that were our friends, Annie's and mine, had disappeared. Even before the divorce, they seemed to have evaporated. It was John's death. Tragedy frightens people. It shakes the ground under their feet and they don't know what to do with it, so they run. Don't misunderstand, our friends didn't abandon us. They were there for us during the worst of it, but then . . . *pffft!* Gone.

I had some old cop friends like Al Roussis, though many of the people I had been so close to while I was on the job were out of my life. No one knows better than a cop the difference between work friends and friends. To my shame, my closest friend on the job had been Pete McCann. I didn't like to think about what that said for me. Bottom line was, what my old friends would say about me wouldn't be valid because I wasn't who I used to be. They didn't really know me, not really, not anymore. Now my friends were Slava, Felix, Bill, and this funny-looking ex-con named Smudge. They could tell you who I was.

Systematically, I clicked on her friends' photos, went to their pages, and sent them brief messages explaining who I was and what I wanted of them. That I'd been hired by Linh Trang's family to try to learn as much about her as I could so they could remember her and not just her death. Technically, I was telling a stretched version of the truth. I gave them my cell number, my e-mail address, and the option of just messaging me back on Facebook. I expected to simply leave messages and that I'd check back in the morning to see if I had any takers, but her Facebook friends began answering me nearly immediately. Message boxes appeared on my screen and my cell phone was buzzing madly in my pocket. I was sure that if I checked my e-mail, there would have been replies there, too. I forgot how people in their twenties could be night owls. I was one by default. Twenty years of rotating shifts and driving the night-shift shuttle will do that to you.

WHAT YOU BREAK / 113

I ignored the phone calls and answered the three people messaging me back on Facebook. They all seemed eager to talk about Linh Trang. I answered each one with a thank you and explained that messaging on Facebook was probably not the most efficient way to accomplish what I had in mind. That a phone call was better and that meeting in person was best. I suggested a place closest to them would be best, a public place where they felt comfortable, like a local Starbucks or bar. I said anyplace would work for me as long as it was in the New York metro area. I made sure not to sound too pushy. Sound pushy and you push people away. Two of the three agreed to meet, said they'd think about where to meet and when and then get back to me. I had similar results when I returned calls to the messages left on my phone. And like I thought, there were e-mails from a few of her friends in my inbox.

It was nearly three-thirty when I was done working through Linh Trang's Facebook friends and exchanging messages. I was about to click out of Facebook and go back out into the lobby. Then I recalled Linh Trang's old website and Facebook page, and I hesitated. I went back to the Facebook search box and typed in John Murphy Jr. When a hotel guest came into the business center, I looked at my watch. Five o'clock had already come and gone.

23

I met Jim Bogart at Grandpa Tino's in Nesconset. The place was a Long Island classic because below the green, white, and red lights that spelled out GRANDPA TINO'S PIZZA was a red neon sign that flashed FROM BROOKLYN. The essential message being the pizza didn't suck like the rest of the crap in Suffolk County because Grandpa Tino came from Bay Ridge. I wasn't sure I bought that. I had relatives from Bay Ridge, too, and none of them could make pizza worth a damn as far as I could tell. But I had to admit, the pizza was pretty good and they did keep it traditional. No garlic knots or Caesar-salad pizza with pretzel crust here. No Sicilian—square—pizza, either. Just old-fashioned flat, round Neapolitan pizza with lots of red sauce, shredded mozzarella, oregano, olive oil, and a dusting of Parmigiano cheese. I hadn't had a slice of Grandpa Tino's pizza for a while because I hadn't been in Nesconset since last December.

Bogart was a tall, slender young man with an earnest face, killer blue eyes, and the fading red traces of the acne wars. I recognized him from his Facebook photo. Even in the photo there was a sadness about him, which was more evident in person.

"Jim," I said, walking up to him and patting his shoulder. "I'm Gus Murphy."

He smiled an uneasy smile and offered me his hand. His handshake was like his smile, uneasy. But I wasn't Micah Spears and chose not to make any judgments based on the relative firmness of his handshake.

"C'mon, Jim, let's get a table."

Linh Trang didn't have a steady boyfriend, not that I could figure. Jim Bogart was as close as she got, although she had apparently broken up with him a month before she was murdered. Bogart was one of the first of Linh Trang's Facebook friends to respond to my request. He'd been one of the callers, and his voice mail message to me was full of eagerness and grief.

I ordered a pie and a bottle of Coke from the waitress.

"That okay with you, Jim?"

"Great. Perfect," he said, though his words belied his unease.

I wondered why'd he had picked Grandpa Tino's to meet.

"I work about a mile or two from here in the frozen-food department at the Stop and Shop in Ronkonkoma." He snorted and shook his head. "See what a three-six-five GPA and a BS from Hofstra gets you these days. I'll be done paying off my student loans about the time we establish a second Mars colony and unify quantum mechanics with Newtonian physics."

"You're too young to be so cynical. Leave that stuff to old people like me."

He relaxed a little, laughed. "You're not old. You're probably younger than my dad."

"I was twenty years on the job, Jim. That'll make you a cynic."

But I didn't believe it even as the words came out of my mouth. The job hadn't made me cynical. Other things had done that. I was always the cop knee-deep in shit who still believed in people. I was the good neighbor. The guy on the block who mowed other people's lawns when they were away or shoveled their driveways just because I was already out shoveling mine. Not because I thought it would buy me anything, but because it felt right to do. Nor did Jim have to remind me that I wasn't old. I knew that. And being with Maggie made me feel really young. Christ, I was young! Maybe that's why I worried about her. I didn't want to go backward, returning to the lonely days in my hotel room watching hours of *SportsCenter*. I went back to the conversation before my mind drifted off the subject at hand and into my own regrets.

"Don't let it get to you, kid," I said, as much for my own sake as for his. "Things'll work out."

"They didn't for LT."

"No, they didn't. They don't always, not for everyone. So, Jim, you're the second person who called Linh Trang LT. In fact, a lot of the people who responded to my message about her called her that. Why?"

"She hated her name."

"Did she? It means beautiful spring, right?" I said, proving only that I could Google Vietnamese names as well as the next guy.

"She felt like it marked her. Like, 'Hey, if you can't already tell I'm Vietnamese by birth by the way I look, just listen to my name.' It was like that. She said that if she didn't love her dad so much, she would have changed her name in a second. She said her mom didn't care, but that her dad got really pissed if she brought it up. So LT was kinda like a compromise."

"Was there any more to it than that?"

"Nah, I think she felt very American on the inside and that she was already saddled with having to explain her adoption to people all the time when they found out her parents were white. She felt like the name made it harder for her to just be who she was."

"How did you guys meet?"

His lips shaped themselves into a sad smile. "At a party off campus. We both were bored and standing around, and we just started talking. I asked her to dinner and she said yes. It was no great romance or anything. We didn't see each other from across the room or anything."

As we ate, Jim told me more about their relationship, trying the whole time to convince me and maybe himself that LT wasn't the great love of his life. Neither one of us was convinced.

"So," I said, "what happened between you guys?"

He looked as if the cheese had caught in his throat, but he could see I wasn't going to let him change the subject or move on to the next question.

"She could be very cruel sometimes."

"Cruel how?"

"After I told her that I loved her, she would never say she loved me back." He held up his hands to stop me from speaking. "I know that that happens, that there's no guarantee that just because you love somebody, they're gonna love you back. But the thing is, I think she did. I know she did. She just wouldn't say it. So this one time we were in bed and I said it to her again, I love you, and she got really mad. She like jumped out of bed and began shaking her ass at me and rubbing herself and screaming at me, 'Is this where I'm supposed to tell you I love you, too?'"

"That's rough, Jim."

"That's not the worst part. You ever see the movie *Full Metal Jacket*?"

I nodded.

"You know the first scene after they get out of boot camp and they're at an outdoor table in Saigon and this Vietnamese prostitute approaches them and—"

"I know the scene," I said.

"So after she asked me if she was supposed to tell me she loved me, I got really frustrated and told her yes, that it would be nice to hear once. I mean, I'm human. I just wanted to hear her say it, you know?"

"I know."

"She said, 'You want me to say it? Okay, I'll say it.' Then she started touching herself again and in a bad Vietnamese accent she said, 'Me love you long time.' And kept repeating it. After that, Gus . . . it was never the same. It wasn't right between us. She wasn't cruel to me, but to herself."

I didn't speak again for a few minutes. I let the kid finish his slices in peace. When he was done, I told him he could take the rest of the pie home with him. He seemed happy about that.

"One more thing, Jim. This is the tough question. Can you think of any reason Rondo Salazar would murder her? Did she ever mention his name or the Asesinos? Can you think of any connection between them?"

He thought about it, searching his memory. "Sorry, Gus. I can't think of her ever mentioning him or that gang or any connection between them. I just can't. You know what's fucked up?"

"A lot of things, but what are you talking about?"

"On the night she went missing, I went to her house."

"In Bellport?"

He nodded. "Yeah. I waited down the street for her to come home. I wanted to try and make things right between us. To tell her that I didn't care if she never told me she loved me and that I could deal with whatever she had to deal with."

"How long did you wait?"

"Most of the afternoon and until about one the next morning. Then I left. I never got to tell her, Gus. I never got to say the things I wanted to say."

Boy, did I understand the pain of that. There were things I'd wanted to say to John that I never got to say. The crazy thing is, there were things I wanted to say to him every day. These days I said them, even if he wasn't ever going to hear them.

24

Although I had another of Linh Trang's friend's to see, I found myself driving deeper into the heart of Nesconset. Nesconset was a quiet area of neat, small houses and big, old trees at the southeastern corner of Smithtown. It was a nice if unremarkable place. I wouldn't have even given the place a second thought but for the fact that TJ Delcamino's battered body had been discovered in a wooded lot there last August. I guess I could sugarcoat things or deny that Delcamino's murder hadn't played a major role in my return to the living, but where had denial ever gotten me?

I never knew TJ, not while he was still breathing, anyway. I'd known his dad, Tommy D, a petty thief, and not a very good one. I can't say I really knew the father either, not in any meaningful sense. Until a Tuesday morning late last year, my contact with Tommy D had been limited to cuffing his wrists behind his back and reciting his rights. That all changed when he showed up at the Paragon to beg for my help in finding the people who had murdered his boy. He said the SCPD was dragging its feet, that they didn't care because he was a fuckup and his kid was no better. I threw him the hell out. The way I figured it, he was playing the dead-kid card. *Your boy's dead. My boy, too. You'll help me because that's a tie that binds, ain't it?*

I was wrong on many counts, but that's not why I was parked on Browns Road, leaning against my car's fender, peering through the tangle of suffocating vines, leaf litter, and dwarf trees starved of light by the huge oaks and maples along the lot's borders. It was still early enough in spring so that I could see through the vegetation and the crap the neighbors too lazy or cheap to go to the town facility had dumped there late at night. I could see all the way to the left-hand corner of the lot where TJ Delcamino's body had been left.

I really wasn't sure why I was there after all these months. Not to pay homage, certainly. The kid hadn't been tortured to death so I could live again. That wasn't the way things worked. I was no longer a big fan of magical thinking, because whenever I looked for it, I could never find any magic in it. The only things I ever found when I looked for the magic were wishes, hopes, and prayers. All unanswered. TJ Delcamino had been murdered because he took something that didn't belong to him from the kind of people you didn't take things from without paying a price. Where was the magic in that?

I stopped staring, checked my watch, and realized I had to get a move on if I was going to make my appointment. As I walked back to the driver's side of the car, my cell buzzed in my pocket. It was a seven-one-eight number I didn't recognize, and I let it go to voice mail. I wasn't in the mood for a robocall about lowering my credit card interest rate or winning a free trip to the Caribbean. I wasn't in the mood for much of anything. But the only person interested in my mood seemed to be me, because the phone buzzed again even before I could start the car. It was the same seven-one-eight number. Robocalls, as annoying as they are, don't usually cycle through that quickly, so I picked up.

"Gus Murphy."

"Mr. Murphy, this is Detective Dwyer. You remember me?"

"How could I forget?"

She laughed at that, but like everything else about her, it was guarded.

"How is your charming partner, Detective Narvaez?" I asked.

"Funny you should mention him."

"Yeah, why's that?"

"Because he's standing right next to me and he's not in a very charming mood. Fact is, that's why I'm calling."

"That was my next question. Why are you calling?"

"We'd like you to come in to talk to us."

"What for? You're not lonely, are you?"

She ignored that. "To answer some questions," Dwyer said, her voice neutral.

"We've already done that, haven't we?"

"New day, new questions. Look, Murphy, we can go round and round on this and I'm asking nicely. Don't make me be a prick about it."

You could tell she had the capacity for extreme pricky-ness and no hesitation about displaying it. Still, I wasn't going to jump through her hoops just on her say so or because her partner was a nasty SOB.

"I don't want to get on your bad side, Dwyer, but you're gonna have to do better than a 'new day, new questions' before I come in."

"Hold on."

I could hear her putting her palm over the mouthpiece of the phone. No doubt she was consulting with Narvaez.

She tried, "We've got new information that we need to ask you about."

"C'mon, Dwyer, that wasn't even close. Try a little harder. Give me a reason."

There was a moment of hesitation, then she said, "Slava Podalak."

I couldn't afford to overreact and took a breath before responding.

"What about him?"

"You have any idea where he is?"

"Told me he was going back to Poland to a relative's funeral."

"Now it's you who isn't trying, Murphy. When can we expect you in here?"

"Tomorrow noon."

"How about now?"

"Sorry, tomorrow noon is the best I can do. I'm already late for an appointment and I work six to six."

"Brooklyn South Homicide on Mermaid Avenue at noon. We'll be waiting, and don't stall us, Murphy. Retired cop or not, we won't give you that much leeway on this. We got a case to close. Do we understand each other?"

"Tomorrow noon," I said and clicked off.

Now I had a call to make. I reached into my wallet and fished out that dollar bill with Slava's number on it.

25

The entrance to Hauser Hall was guarded by two pairs of chubby concrete pillars. The building itself was a funky brown brick that looked like it had been carelessly spray-painted in a shade of concrete gray to match the pillars. But I was there to speak to Kaitlin Fine, not to critique the architecture on the South Campus at Hofstra University. Hofstra was a private school in Nassau County about a forty-minute drive from Nesconset on a good traffic day. Of course the next good traffic day on Long Island would come only after the apocalypse. So it had taken me an hour to get there, and an aggravating one at that. The aggravation was only partially the result of the traffic. Some of it was thinking about Maggie, about how she hadn't called. Most of it was to do with Slava.

He hadn't sounded at all surprised when I told him that the detectives had his name. Nor did he seem caught off guard or annoyed when I suggested it might be a good idea for him and Mikel to clear out of my old house in Commack.

"This morning we are already going from there," he said.

"Where to?"

"It is better for all if you do not know, Slava is thinking."

I didn't argue the point.

"Gus . . ." he said, just before I was about to break the connection, "there is being more blood. You should not be surprised tomorrow when cops are telling this to you."

Whose blood? Why more? Where? He hung up before I could ask. It was just as well. I wouldn't have known what to say if he had answered me. I didn't like being in the middle of something I didn't understand. Who did? But sometimes it was better not to know. That's what I told myself. It would have been even better if I could've made myself believe it.

First I went up to the main office of the Psychology Department on the second floor, where we'd been scheduled to meet, but she wasn't there. I asked a woman working at a computer if she could tell me where Kaitlin Fine was. First she shrugged and then said I should try one of the labs in the basement.

"The grad students are always down there futzing around in the labs."

Labs. The word conjured up all sorts of images in my head. Images of flashing red lights and behemoth machines shooting white sparks through the air, of test tubes filled with rainbow-colored liquids and beakers bubbling over blue-flamed burners. Images straight out of old monster movies I used to watch when I was a little boy. But the lab in which I found Kaitlin Fine was empty of nearly anything but her. It was a drab little space with a few chairs and a single Photoshopped poster on the wall of Sigmund Freud dressed in a shocking pink suit.

"Pink Freud," I said, pointing at the poster. "Funny."

She closed her laptop and walked up to me. "Mr. Murphy?"

"Gus. Call me Gus. Sorry I'm late. Traffic."

On Long Island, that was the one excuse that carried more weight than any other, and it was accepted without question.

"That's okay," she said, gesturing at the chair across from her. "Please sit down."

I sat.

Kaitlin Fine had a serious but unthreatening demeanor and her looks were kind of nondescript. Dressed in faded jeans, running shoes, and a black-and-white T-shirt with a diagram of a dopamine molecule on it, she kept her brown hair short. It wasn't styled in any particular way, nor was it messy. She wore a light coating of makeup over the fair skin of her face. There wasn't anything beautiful or ugly about her, nothing that screamed "Look at me" or "Look away from me." There was nothing that would make you pick her face out of a crowd, yet I doubted she lacked for companionship. Some people just have a pull about them, and she had it. Dr. Rosen had it, too, a kind of welcoming magnetism.

"You wanted to talk about LT, Mr.—excuse me, Gus?"

"You were her roommate?"

"For four years," she said, the flicker of a smile crossing her serious lips. "First two years in the dorms and then with a bunch of other people off campus in a rental."

"You guys hit it off, then?"

She nodded. "Immediately. Look, Gus, I think we need to establish some ground rules before we start."

"You sound like my shrink."

She smiled in spite of herself.

"Ground rules like what?" I wanted to know.

"One ground rule, really: the truth. I may be young, Gus, but I'm not gullible. I agreed to meet with you because I was curious about what you were really after. I've known LT's family for a while now and I don't believe they would have hired you as you portrayed in your message. She's dead and they want to move on. So you can either tell me exactly why you're here or we can shake hands goodbye."

It didn't take me long to decide. I told her the truth, all of it. Right down to Micah Spears's offer of the checks.

"I'm sorry about your son," she said, not because it was the right thing to say.

"Thank you. So can we keep talking?"

"Sure, but first I want you to know LT didn't really have much of a relationship with her grandfather. In our junior year, there seemed to be a thawing. They even met a few times, secretly. LT's folks hated the old man. But they wouldn't have needed to worry because the détente didn't last. It fell apart before it really got started. She wouldn't talk about it, no matter how I tried to get it out of her. She just said he was a monster and that was all she ever said."

I thought about that for a second, about what her proclamation of Micah Spears as a monster could mean, but that was another issue for another time. I repeated to Kaitlin the same question I'd asked Jim Bogart. "LT, why not Linh Trang?"

Kaitlin's lips turned down at the corners. "She despised her name. She felt trapped by it. In fact, LT's struggle with her identity inspired a subject I am researching: the dynamics of self-image versus ethnic identity and public perception. That's why I was down here, trying to design a reliable and valid model for data collection."

"Sounds fascinating."

"Data collection, not so much." She laughed. "It's the stuff that comes of it that will be interesting."

"You said she struggled with her identity. How?"

Kaitlin was amazingly well versed in Linh Trang's struggles. She explained that college was weird for LT because it's a time when most people are looking for a way to be different and to be seen to be different, but that all LT wanted to do was fit in.

"Obviously, the name didn't help with that," Kaitlin said. "It got so that she simply started introducing herself as LT and wouldn't tell people her name. But there was no escaping her looks. She was pretty and she was Asian and there's a lot of guys, regardless of their own race, who have a thing for Asian girls. Bad combination—pretty, intelligent, friendly Asian girl on a campus of horny college boys."

"She dated, though."

Kaitlin was also well versed on that subject and needed little prompting from me to slide from LT's dating history into her sexual escapades.

"She was complicated. It was complicated. She liked all the attention. Who doesn't like attention? But she didn't trust it. Were they actually attracted to her, her sense of humor, and her wit, or were they attracted to their fetish about Asian girls? She would have sex with a lot of them on the first dates and then taunt them. She would play the subservient, submissive girl and do whatever the guys wanted and then she would abuse them. She used to describe stuff to me in detail. It was hard to listen to sometimes because she did it under the guise of punishing the boys she was with, but she was punishing herself."

I thought I had hit on something. As I sat there listening to Kaitlin Fine describe her old roommate's self-destructive behavior, I formulated possible scenarios in my head. I pictured LT in a particularly low mood, going to the wrong bar at the wrong time and hooking up with just the wrong guy. A guy like Rondo Salazar wouldn't take kindly to a woman taunting him, not about sex, not about anything. She hadn't had sex, hadn't been raped before her murder. But maybe it hadn't gotten that far. Of course, I had to guard against jumping to conclusions, guard against creating likelihoods out of possibilities. That's why it was so important to find out where Linh Trang had been before she was killed. I had to talk to Charlie Prince again.

"I spoke to Abby, LT's sister," I said after Kaitlin had stopped talking. "They didn't seem close. Why is that, do you think?"

"LT loved Abby and Abby loved her big sister."

"But."

"But it was the classic case of the miracle baby."

I screwed up my face. "Huh? The miracle baby."

"Well, I can only tell you what LT told me and stuff I heard from Abby, but it rings true to me. LT and Abby's mom had had several miscarriages. And that was when their parents decided to adopt LT. The year after they adopted LT, her mom got pregnant and for the first time successfully carried the baby to term."

"Abby?"

"Abby. But instead of seeing Abby as the miracle, they saw LT as the magical ingredient and she was clearly their favorite. Abby resented it, understandably. She was their biological child, after all. She was the miracle, but her parents really focused on LT."

"People are complicated."

"Incredibly so," Kaitlin said. "I don't think people realize how complicated we all are."

I told her about my earlier conversation with Jim Bogart and waited for her reaction.

"Really nice guy, but it ended ugly," she said.

"I heard. Did she love him?"

"If she ever loved any guy she dated, it was Jim, but I suppose in the end she didn't even trust his love for her."

"Sad."

Then I asked her the same closing questions I'd asked Jim. Kaitlin's answers were the same. She couldn't think of any reason that LT would have had contact with Rondo Salazar.

As I stood to go, she stopped me.

She asked, "Have you spoken to anyone at her work?"

"Not yet."

"You should. She was really unhappy there." Kaitlin shrugged. "Maybe someone there knew LT in a way her friends didn't. It's worth exploring."

"I'll do that," I said, and shook her hand. "It's been a pleasure."

"Good luck, Gus. I hope you find out why this happened. Why things happen is what I'm all about."

"If I find out, I'll definitely let you know."

It didn't escape her notice or mine that I'd said "if." Even with my newly conjured scenario, I wasn't at all sure I was any closer to an answer than I was the day I started.

26

There were some nights that driving the van was a chore, but on nights like tonight, it was a relief. When I'd first moved into the Paragon, my life was a simple one, my room a vampire's coffin. Locked away in it until dark, I emerged to perform very robotic tasks in a van that sometimes smelled like wet socks and a mildewed closet, the air outside the van stinking of hot metal and spent jet fuel. It was a safe world to operate in, one that kept the grief from completely choking the life out of me. But as I'd taken the small steps forward to gradually reclaim my place among the living, the simplicity of my monastic vampire existence faded away. It was gone now, completely. The last several days had stamped out any flicker of belief that I could uncomplicate things by taking two giant steps backward. There was nothing I wanted back there, not really.

It was a pretty busy night, too, one that had me doing several runs to the train station, the airport, and back to the Paragon. Still, even at its busiest, driving a courtesy van isn't all-consuming. It gave me time to think. Well, at least when there weren't any chatty passengers making small talk or asking nervous questions about the big, bad city forty miles to the west. And I had a lot to think about: Linh Trang Spears's self-torment, the new blood Slava had talked about, my pending interview with Detectives Narvaez and Dwyer, what Micah Spears had done to earn the label of monster, and what Maggie's departure would mean. But I kept thinking back to my trip to the wooded lot on Browns Road and wondering what had drawn me there after all these months.

Deep down I knew what it was. Why I hadn't gone back there and then why I had, finally. My reasons were selfish and ugly. One of the aspects I liked about who I used to be was that I wasn't jealous or resentful by nature. When you don't want for much and have what you want, there really isn't fuel to feed those toxic, gnawing feelings. That was me. Among my family, my friends, my house, my pension, and time to enjoy them all, I had everything I'd ever wanted. More. Then I didn't. I'd never understood people like Pete McCann, people with a hunger who filled in their own emptiness with other people's possessions. I understood them better now. I had gone to the lot on Browns Road because I resented Tommy D. Not the most rational feeling, resenting a murdered man whose only child had been murdered a few months before him. What was even more irrational was what I resented him for.

Since the day Tommy D had walked into the Paragon to ask for my help, I'd been discussing my resentment with Doc Rosen. The crux of my resentment was simple enough. There were answers to be had about his boy's death. There were people responsible for it. People to answer for it. Who could I see about my son's death? Where were my answers? Who was going to pay? Although therapy had helped heal me, the resentment persisted. Worse. It had only grown more intense. There was a brief period there after I'd found out why TJ Delcamino had been killed and by whom, when the men responsible for it had met their fates, that I thought I'd beaten it back. I'd been fooling myself, and now, with this search for the cause of Linh Trang's murder at the hands of Rondo Salazar, it was back with a vengeance.

I was hanging out between runs, resting my eyes, lying back on one of the defeated lobby sofas, when I heard the phone ring at the front desk.

The ringing stopped me from going any further down the resentment rabbit hole.

"Gus, you have a guest to pick up at the station," Martina called to me from behind the desk. "Name's Gordon. Says he'll be looking for the van."

"Thanks."

I went straight out to the van and started it up. It was only after I had turned right onto Ronkonkoma Avenue from Vets that I realized the timing was all wrong, that a train wasn't due in for another forty minutes. It happened. Sometimes people took the train out from the city without first booking a hotel for the night. For all I knew, Mr. Gordon had spent the last half-hour calling around to the area hotels looking for a vacant room or, more likely, looking for a room at a rate he was willing to pay. One thing about the Paragon, our rooms were cheap compared to some of the other places near the airport.

Pulling into the courtesy van spot, I saw the station was pretty deserted. The Dunkin' Donuts shop was closed, as were all the other businesses that, like brick-and-mortar mosquitoes, fed off the commuters. Even the cab stand was empty but for a single old Crown Vic with a duct-taped front fender. Its driver was probably trying to catch some zees in between calls. I'd been known to do the same thing on occasion.

Almost immediately after the van stopped, a big man stepped out of the shadows and waved to me. I hopped out of the driver's seat, ran around to the passenger side, and opened the double cabin doors.

"Mr. Gordon?"

He nodded. I expected him to step back into the shadows to retrieve his luggage, but he climbed directly into the van instead. This, too, was unusual, though not unique. Sometimes people made last-minute plans or got great travel deals and decided they would shop at the airport or at their destination. If he asked, I would have advised Mr. Gordon to wait until he got to where he was going or at least to shop at the next airport. MacArthur Airport's wardrobe choices ranged from Yankees hats and

Mets T-shirts to I heart Long Island sweatshirts. No Brooks Brothers or
Johnston & Murphy here. He didn't ask. Instead he settled into the first
row of seats, over my right shoulder.

Making the U-turn out of my spot and heading back toward Ronkonkoma Avenue, I checked him out in my rearview. His eyes were focused
on the mirror. Our eyes met. And though I'd never seen Mr. Gordon
before, there was something familiar about him, especially his gray eyes.
He turned his head and I turned mine. I was searching my memory for
where I might have met him or for the person he reminded me of. It was
no good, yet I couldn't shake the feeling. So I did something I rarely did.
I struck up a conversation.

"So how long will you be staying with us, Mr. Gordon?" I peeked back
at the mirror to see him smiling at me. It wasn't the kind of smile to give
you comfort. More like the feral smile of an imaginary cat. One sizing up
its prey.

"A single night, maybe. We shall see," he said, his thick Russian accent
making my guts seize up.

I tried not to react, but I wasn't completely successful. The Russian's
cat smile broadened.

"Maybe I don't stay at all. Maybe I just want to have talk, one old
friend to another."

"You wanna talk?" I said, my voice steadying. "Talk."

"Where is the man you know as Slava Podalak?"

"Not that it's any of your business, but I don't have time for this bullshit. He's in Poland, Warsaw, I think, at the funeral of a relative."

My passenger laughed, shaking his head.

"I have no time for bullshit, either, so now that you have fed me some,
we can be past it, yes?"

I shrugged. "It may be bullshit, but it's all I got."

When I looked back in the mirror, Mr. Gordon was holding a
Makarov in his hand for me to see. I hit the accelerator as hard as I could.

WHAT YOU BREAK / 133

"Go ahead and shoot me. At this speed, you're gonna die, too. Too bad you didn't put your seat belt on, huh?"

He raised the weapon and slid it back where it came from. "No one is shooting anybody," he said, laughing. "Besides, Mr. Murphy, if I had wanted to kill you, I wouldn't have missed you in Coney Island the other night. I don't miss unless I am trying. And how is your wrist feeling? That encounter in Mikel's room was unfortunate, but necessary."

So now I knew where I recognized him from.

"My ribs hurt worse than my wrist. You know my name, but—"

"I could give you another name, but it wouldn't be mine. Mr. Gordon will do as good as any other."

I backtracked. "Easy not to miss when your target is bleeding out on the sidewalk and you put two in his head."

He laughed again. "True, but don't feel sorrow for that man. Very few people deserved to die more than Goran. I was merciful to him, much more merciful than he was to the many people he killed."

He wasn't laughing by the time he finished talking. In fact, there was real anger and sorrow in the things he said. Things that matched what Slava had said previously. He was looking out the window now.

"Was Goran a policeman, too?"

"Yes, like the man you know as Slava also. I have worked with many such men, policemen in Grozny."

"Chechnya?"

"Very good. I didn't think Americans would know it." Mr. Gordon didn't wait for me to speak. "So, now you know something of the man calling himself Slava, but maybe already you knew this."

"We're not close," I lied, sort of.

Slava and I were close, but not in any conventional sense. I didn't know where he lived. We went out for meals every now and then besides our regular Saturday breakfast. When we talked, we talked about my past, never his. We discussed Maggie and how Krissy was doing at school.

Sometimes Bill came along and we would let him carry the conversation. Yet we had an unshakable bond that was only partially based on his saving my life. I couldn't have explained it to Mr. Gordon or anyone else. I wasn't sure I understood it myself.

My passenger didn't challenge me, but re-asked an earlier question.

"Where is Slava?"

"Same answer as before."

"Maybe you would not be so stubborn or so loyal if you knew the things your friend has done in his life."

"Maybe. Try me."

"I don't think so," he said as we pulled into the Paragon's lot. "Your friend Slava is not what he seems."

"Who is?"

"You make a good point, Gus Murphy. Be warned, he cannot hide forever. Do not risk your life and those closest to you to protect this man. He is not worth it, I can assure you."

I wasn't happy about that line involving "those closest to me." Not happy at all. So I slid my Glock out of my ankle holster and turned to show him the muzzle when we came to a stop in front of the hotel.

"Did you just threaten me? Because I can do some assuring myself. Let me assure you that I will eagerly empty my clip into you if you come near anyone close to me. Don't think because you choked me out so easily that you'll be able to do it again. Next time, I'll see you coming. You have an issue with Slava, deal with him. Leave me out of it."

"No, Gus Murphy, you won't," he said, opening the van door closest to him.

"No, I won't what?"

"See me coming. Good night. Thank you for the ride and the conversation, but I have decided not to stay here. I think maybe it would not be good for my long-term health or yours. What do you think?"

I didn't answer.

He climbed out of the van, and when he did, a familiar white van with darkly tinted windows, the same one he'd used to escape in at Coney Island, pulled up next to the courtesy van. He opened the passenger door to get in, but stopped and turned. He motioned for me to roll down my window.

I did, making sure to place the bottom of the Glock's barrel on the windowsill.

"What?"

"I am a big fan of Marilyn Monroe," he said, his voice cold as mid-winter. "Too bad she had to die the way she did, alone in bed. Such a tragedy." Then he smiled that smile at me. "Remember, don't risk what isn't yours for a man such as Slava."

Before I could get out of my van, his was gone. But his words rang loudly in my ears, louder than any jet that had ever passed over the Paragon.

27

I didn't sleep well. And there was no soul searching needed to hit on the reasons why. A man who I'd watched assassinate someone as if he was stepping on a cockroach had just made a not-so-veiled threat against Maggie. This was a dangerous man, a man who had overpowered me and could just as easily have choked me to death as into unconsciousness. It also gave me no comfort that when I called the number Slava had given me, there was no answer. It rang and rang and rang.

What I didn't do was make a panicked call to Maggie. I felt sure she was safe from Mr. Gordon for the moment. He was only letting me know that he knew where I was vulnerable and that if he came back to ask me more questions, I'd better answer truthfully. And what would my calling Maggie have accomplished other than frighten her? Frightened people do stupid things, so for the moment it was better for only me to worry.

All of a sudden, my pending interview with the NYPD didn't seem all that worrisome. It did present me with a dilemma, though. I was no longer just passively stalling the cops to keep them away from Slava until this thing he was involved in worked itself out. If it wasn't personal with me before, it sure as shit was now. Until I picked Mr. Gordon up at the station, I'd been perfectly willing to play dumb, to take all the crap from the cops I had to. Things had changed. I could still try to keep Slava out of it while throwing the cops a bone. It would be simple enough. When I was with Narvaez and Dwyer, I could pretend to have remembered something from the night Goran was killed. I practiced the exchange in my head.

After they busted my chops for being uncooperative, I'd say, "If you two would give me a break, I think I might have something for you."

"What?" they would ask.

"There was a white Dodge van that I remember driving slowly down the block before . . . well, before whatever happened happened."

"Not much of a help, Murphy," they would say. "There's probably a thousand of those in Brooklyn alone," they would say.

"But I think I remember part of its tag number. It was a New York plate, I think," I would say. Then I would give it to them piecemeal, hemming and hawing, blurting out a number here and a letter there, leaving out the last digit. I could put them onto Mr. Gordon, whoever he really was, without putting them onto Slava.

My eyes squeezed shut; that's what I was thinking about when my cell buzzed on the nightstand.

"Yeah, who is it?" I said, sounding groggier than I expected.

"Did you have a rough one last evening, boyo?" It was Bill.

"You could say that. What's up?"

"Brother Vassily."

"Who?"

"Brother Vassily, my friend from the Holy Cross Monastery in East Setauket. He's translated that newspaper article for you. He is very anxious to speak with you. He's willing to free up time for you today."

"Today won't work, Bill. Can't I just call him?"

"Face-to-face, Gus, is the only way he'll discuss it with you."

"Tomorrow, then, after one."

"I'll set it up and call you back. Does that suit you?"

"Sure, that would be great," I said with all the enthusiasm I could muster, which wasn't very much. "See you, Bill."

I spent a long time in the shower, rehearsing my lines for the detectives, but they didn't sound any less artificial than they did when I was horizontal.

28

They were waiting for me out in front of the building, and when I pulled up to the curb, Narvaez motioned for me to unlock the doors. When I did, he pushed the passenger bucket seat forward and climbed in the back. Dwyer waited until her partner settled in before pushing the bucket back and getting in next to me.

"Get a warrant or get the hell out."

"But it's such a nice car," Dwyer said, a surprising coo in her voice.

"You guys ever hear of this thing called the Fourth Amendment? You know, the one about illegal search and seizure?"

"Four? I can't count that high," Narvaez said.

"I didn't figure you could, but I had hopes for Dwyer."

"Me," she said, "I can count all the way up to a hundred on a good day."

"Is this a good day?"

"Depends, Murphy."

"On what?"

Narvaez wasn't in the mood for banter. "Shut your piehole and drive to West Twenty-first and park where you parked that night."

That made up my mind for me. Whether Narvaez was playing a part or whether he really was an asshole was beside the point. I hated bullies and I detested being bullied, especially after my talk with Mr. Gordon. I wasn't going to share a fucking thing with these detectives, not a description of the van, not a single digit of its tag number. But I did drive over to West Twenty-first and parked where I had the night Goran was murdered.

"Okay, here we are," I said.

They asked me the same questions they'd asked me at the Paragon coffee shop and got about the same answers. They were just trying to soften me up in order to start in on my relationship with Slava. They decided the interior of my Mustang wasn't the proper venue for that.

"Getting stuffy in here," said Dwyer. "Don't you think, Richie?"

Her partner seconded that. "Yeah, c'mon, let's go for a little walk."

I didn't protest. I could be cooperative and uncooperative all at once. They walked me over to where Goran Ivanovich had been shot.

"Recognize this stoop?" Dwyer asked.

"Maybe."

"Christ, he's back to 'maybe,'" Narvaez said. "You know what's funny, Murphy?"

"No, but I get the sense you're going to tell me."

"What's funny is that just before the vic got plugged, he was having a conversation up there with two other men." Narvaez pointed at the landing at the top of the short stairs.

"So?"

"So why didn't you mention that when we came out to that shithole you work at?" Narvaez wanted to know. "You think maybe that might've been a helpful detail, a description of those men, maybe. What do you think, huh, Murphy?"

"If I had seen them, yeah, maybe," I agreed. "Or if you had mentioned them when we first spoke, my memory might've been jarred."

"Will you listen to this guy, Dwyer? He's chock-full of ifs, might-haves, and maybes. He's also chock-full of shit."

I didn't react.

Dwyer, who had been eyeballing me, picked up the conversation. "And it was pretty convenient for you not to mention that one of those men on the stoop having a conversation with Ivanovich was a coworker of yours, Slava Podalak."

"And you know this how?"

"Listen, asshole, we ask the questions," Narvaez said, bumping me with his chest, trying to get me to take a swing at him.

"Stop with the bullshit, Narvaez." I decided to beat him at his own game. "Real brave with that shield in your pocket, huh? If I ever hit you, you wouldn't get up. Try me sometime when you can't use that shield and your female partner to protect you."

That did it.

"Any time, motherfucka," he screamed, ripping his jacket off and tossing his shield case onto the ground.

Dwyer rolled her eyes and stepped between us, her back to me. She put her hands on Narvaez's shoulders and pushed him back.

"Calm the fuck down, Richie. You're embarrassing yourself and it's not helping anything."

"Don't do that, Dwyer," I prodded. "The neighbors want a good show. I wonder how many of them would be willing to report your partner for taking a swing at me. Come on, let him. It's what he wants, and then I can kick the shit out of him."

She turned her head and said, "You, shut the fuck up and get back by your car. Now!"

I complied happily, having changed the subject.

Dwyer didn't look half as pleased as she approached. Apparently, she'd convinced Narvaez to stay where he was and to leave the rest to her.

"You're not gonna do that to me, Murphy. I'm not a hothead and I don't get distracted. So I'm going to ask you again, why didn't you tell us that there was a conversation going on on the stoop prior to the homicide?"

"You're a detective, Dwyer. You know how it works. Were you taught to volunteer answers to questions that aren't asked? Were you taught to expand on your answers or were you taught to answer specifically only what you were asked? But look, forget that. Let me save us both and your asshole partner some trouble. I'm going to tell you a few things, but once I do I'm not going to answer any more questions without a lawyer present. I will tell you that I do know Slava Podalak. We do work together on the night shift at the Paragon Hotel. We even have a meal together every now and then. He told me he was going to Poland to attend a relative's funeral. Is that last part true? I don't know. Maybe not. But I can tell you I have no idea where he is if he's not in Warsaw. Now, I don't suppose you're gonna tell me how you got Slava's name in the first place?"

She made a face and shook her head. "Afraid not. And just to let you know, Murphy, this is getting more serious by the minute for you and your pal Mr. Podalak."

"How so?"

"Because the list of victims is growing. Last night we fished a floater out of Sheepshead Bay. His balls and cock were cut off and shoved down his throat. They taped his mouth shut with an entire roll of duct tape. ME says it was done while he was still alive. ME also says that probably wasn't the worst of what was done to him. Apparently the guy had more broken bones than unbroken ones, and I won't even describe how his skin was flayed off parts of him."

"Who was the vic?"

"According to the papers we found on him, Mikel Borovski. Here," she said. "He don't look so good, but at least he wasn't in the water very long. A day, maybe. They wanted us to find him. Didn't cut his lungs or stomach. Didn't weight him down."

"How do you know he's connected to the first vic, Ivanovich?"

She didn't answer, just smiled at me.

"Oh, I get it," I said, answering my own question, "the same way you got Slava's name. Someone's feeding you guys information."

She reached into her jacket pocket and came out holding a photograph. "It's Borovski. Do you recognize him?"

I did, even after the way he'd been abused. It was Slava's friend Michael Smith, Mikel, the man I'd picked up from MacArthur.

"Sorry." I handed the photo back. "Never saw him before."

"Funny thing is we found a credit card receipt in his wallet from the Paragon Hotel, that dump you work at. Receipt was for a Michael Smith. That jog your memory any?"

I shook my head. "If he was in the water, how'd you find all this stuff intact?"

"Because the fuckers who killed him wanted us to find this stuff the same way they wanted us to find him. They wrapped his wallet and papers in a plastic bag. They're sending somebody a message. Want to hear something weird?"

"Sure, since you're going to tell me anyway."

"He was a cop in Russia, or at least he used to be. Along with his fake credit card and papers we found his badge and ID. These Russians are sick bastards. They aren't fucking around here, Murphy. Give us Podalak and we can protect him. And if I was you, I'd think about getting some protection for myself. The only rulebook these guys play by is that there are no rules."

I was churning inside, but I made sure not to react. All I said was, "Can I give you and Narvaez a lift back?"

"How sweet of you to ask, but we'll manage," she said, and gave me the finger. "Go find that lawyer you keep talking about. You'll need him. We'll be in touch."

Dwyer turned and walked back toward her partner. I got in my car and split before Dwyer had second thoughts about letting me leave.

On the ride home to the island, I put in a call to Alvaro Peña, gave him the tag number from the white Dodge van, and asked him to run the plate for me. He was quiet for a few seconds, his gears turning, deciding if he wanted to ask me what it was about. He decided not to ask. Smart man.

29

I had time to think as I drove east along the Belt Parkway, the sun behind me and big jet after big jet paralleling my course along Jamaica Bay as they headed to the runways at JFK. We didn't get big jets at MacArthur, 737s mostly, some commuter turboprops, and weekenders in their single-engine Cessnas. I guess when they built MacArthur they thought it would be a natural to take the spillover from Kennedy and LaGuardia. We were still waiting at MacArthur for the crumbs. That's why the Bonackers had bought the Paragon in the first place. They heard that Southwest was going to go big-time at MacArthur and that JetBlue was this close to moving some of their flights over from JFK. But all that promise turned out to be what much of life is made of, false hopes and fever dreams. It was kind of like how people think of Long Island. They dream of the Hamptons and the Gold Coast, Fire Island and wine country, but what they get is Ronkonkoma, Middle Island, and Mastic Beach. Not awful places, just not anybody's dream.

I considered trying to have Bill rearrange things so I could meet with Brother Vassily before my shift, but when I noticed Maggie's condo complex looming ahead of me as I turned off the Cross Island onto the Northern State, I changed my mind. I had to clear the air with her and I wanted to make sure she was okay. I didn't like that we hadn't spoken since the other night, which was as much my doing as hers. It was just really hard for me, harder than I ever would have believed, to think of my life without her in it even if it was for only a few months. Four months ago, we were still just feeling our way around each other, trying each other on for size. I don't think either one of us saw love coming. Does anyone ever?

There was an African-American woman at the security gate, a square badge I'd never seen at the complex before. That was good and bad. It meant I wouldn't have to deal with the snarky asshole who was always at the gate, but at least he recognized me and didn't make me go through the whole song and dance to get in. I gave the woman my name and told her who I was there to see, her building and apartment number. She told me to hold on, that she'd have to call up to get clearance. I'd wanted to surprise Maggie, but maybe it was better this way.

"Okay, mister, go on ahead. Do you know where to park?" she asked, the gate raising up in front of me.

"I do, thanks."

Maggie was waiting by the door, a wary look on her face. She looked tired, her hair was a mess, and her face was free of any makeup. The call from security must've woken her up. Pulling the door back to let me in, she said, "I don't want to fight."

"That's not why I'm here."

"Then why?"

"Because I love you. Because I don't like that we haven't spoken. Because I don't like how we left things."

"You were the one who walked out of here, Gus, when I asked you to stay." Maggie headed for the kitchen. I followed. "You want something to drink?"

"Glass of red wine?"

She poured the last few ounces of cabernet in the bottle into a stemless glass, handed it to me, and poured herself a few fingers of scotch. We raised our glasses to each other and drank with no joy. I put my empty glass in the sink and rinsed it. She lit a cigarette, arched her neck up, and blew the smoke toward the ceiling. I loved when she turned her head up that way.

"I know I was the one who left, but what's the expression they use now, I needed time to process it?"

"Have you . . . processed it?" she asked, more than a little sarcasm in her voice, and then gunned down her scotch. She took a long drag on her cigarette and tossed it into the sink. It hissed when it hit a few stray drops of water.

"I think so. I was happy—*am* happy—you got the part. Nobody's prouder of you than me. I just wasn't prepared for you to go and to be gone for so long. I made assumptions I shouldn't have made based on things I really hadn't thought through. You can understand that, right?"

"I've been burned a lot in my life, Gus." Maggie poured herself another. "I've let myself be used by men too many times. My ex used up everything I had in the tank so that I was running on fumes by the time we were through. I need someone who is on my side."

I knew that when she brought up her ex, it was serious. She never brought him up. I used to think that was because we had a rule about harping on our exes. Nothing is less attractive than bitterness. Then I thought it was for my benefit, but really it was for hers. Whenever he came up, she relived the pain more than a little bit.

"No one has ever been more on your side than me, Magdalena. No one. Ever. I fucked up the other night. I'm sorry. I know I was being selfish. I guess I came here to say that. I don't want to lose you and your going . . . when you told me . . . it felt like I was losing you."

She came to stand by me, put her glass down on the counter, and laid her head on my shoulder. I wrapped my arms around her and we melted into each other. I raised my hand up and stroked her hair. We stood there like that, with no need to speak, for a good five minutes.

"Can we go lay down?" she said. "I worked last night and didn't get home until ten this morning."

"Sure."

We walked into the bedroom and arranged ourselves in bed much as we had while upright in the kitchen. There were times when long, silent embraces were more powerful than any spoken declarations of love. She fell asleep in my arms and I guess I nodded off for a little while there myself. When I opened my eyes I checked my watch. Time to go. I gently rolled her onto her side, sliding my arm out from beneath her.

She was awake when I came out of the bathroom. I told her I had to get to work.

"I know, Gus," she said, lingering sleepiness slurring her words.

I leaned over and kissed her forehead. "I love you."

"I love you, too."

Then it occurred to me that I'd been rude and hadn't asked her about last night's job. We always talked about her jobs. "Where'd you work last night?"

"A private party on . . ." She yawned and stretched. "A private party on a huge yacht in the Hudson. Paid great, amazing tips. Gave me a cushion for when I'm on the road. I'm sorry. I shouldn't have brought that up."

"Don't be silly, Maggie." I sat down on the bed beside her. "We can't pretend about that. Let's enjoy the time before you go, okay? So whose big yacht was this?"

She shrugged. "Some super-rich Russian guy."

I went cold and rigid. Maggie noticed.

"What is it, Gus?"

I lied and changed the subject, sort of. "Nothing. Listen, I'm thinking of taking some time off before you go. How about we spend our nights together. You can come stay with me at the hotel or I can come stay here. We'll go to the movies. I'll even go to the theater with you."

She laughed at me and pressed her hand to my forehead. "You have a fever or something? You hate the theater."

I ignored the question but faked a smile. "What do you say? We can make a week of it and you can come work a case with me." I explained

WHAT YOU BREAK / 149

about Linh Trang and Micah Spears. I didn't mention a word about Slava or the very dead Goran Ivanovich.

"Let me think about it. I have a lot to get ready before I go."

"Sure."

I kissed her hard on the mouth. "I love you, Magdalena."

As I drove out of the complex, the square badge smiled at me, winked, and waved me past, but I stopped.

"What is it"—she looked down at her sign-in sheet—"Mr. Murphy?"

"The guy who's always here, the guy you replaced, what happened to him?"

"I hear he's in the hospital over at Long Island Jewish."

LIJ was just down the road from Maggie's condo.

"He have a heart attack or something?"

"Nah, it wasn't like that," she said. "Some big Russian guy beat the piss outta him when he refused to let him through. That ain't gonna happen to me." She lifted up the right side of her tunic and showed me a nine holstered on her hip. "I worked Rikers for twenty years. That's why they put me on the gate."

I was only half conscious of the words she was saying to me. Between the Russian's yacht and the beating at the gate, there was just too much coincidence going around to suit me. I tried Slava's phone again.

30

'm not sure there's such a thing as inheriting friendship, but I had. Smudge was a spidery little man, an ex-con with every reason in his heart to despise the universe or God or happenstance, to hate whatever conspiracy of circumstance had led to his fate. He'd had botched surgery to his pronounced harelip, which, in a perverse way, served to draw attention away from the muddy, silver dollar–sized birthmark nestled between his right ear and cheek. The muddy birthmark was where the name Smudge had come from. But the cruelest thing of all about him was his born ugliness. The harelip and birthmark were like bad icing and a rotted cherry atop an already ruined cake. And if all that wasn't quite harsh enough, he spoke in a nasal voice with a lisp so that when he said his name it came out as Thmudge. Yet in spite of the avalanche of karmic shit that had buried him beneath it, Smudge had faith. The kind of faith that was even the envy of Bill Kilkenny.

"Christ in heaven, if there was ever a man to turn his back on God, it would be that poor ugly little fella," Bill had once said to me. "If I'd half his faith, I think I could have changed the world."

Although Bill had left the church behind him after the rediscovery of his own faith, he had taken to attending Mass with Smudge about once a week. For his part, Smudge went to morning Mass every day. With Bill's help, Smudge had landed a part-time job with a Catholic charity, delivering meals to elderly shut-ins. With the public assistance and food stamps he received, it was enough to keep his head about water, barely. And when I could, I got him odd jobs. He was a pretty resourceful guy.

"Hey, Guth," Smudge said, opening the door to his Copiague apartment. He gave me what passed for a smile. "Come on in."

Copiague was a bit of a dodgy town next door to Amityville—yes, that Amityville—not too far east of Massapequa. But Smudge could deal with dodgy and dangerous. He had a lifetime of dealing with it. Maybe that's why he was such a resourceful SOB. He was used to dingy, too, always living quietly at the fringes. That kind of explained the affinity he and Bill had for each other. Both were used to having very little and living at the edges of where most of the rest of us lived.

"Hey, yourself," I said, patting him on the shoulder, stepping into the little studio apartment above somebody's garage.

"Can I get you a can of soda or water?"

"No, I'm good."

"Sit down."

There wasn't much to choose from in terms of seating. Just a Salvation Army couch and a wobbly office chair that was now more duct tape than Naugahyde. I went for the couch. I looked around the place. There were piles of used paperbacks all over the place. The paneling was warped and bulged on either side of the crucifix hanging precariously in the center of the longest wall. The linoleum floor was shiny from wear, not from wax, and the place smelled of mold and neglect. Like I said, Smudge was used to dingy. Compared to prison, this was the good life.

He'd done a bid. That was where he'd met Tommy Delcamino, the man from whom I had inherited Smudge's friendship. In fact, the only photograph in the place was a framed shot of Smudge and Tommy D, Tommy hugging his little friend, both of them smiling. So self-conscious of his mouth, Smudge didn't smile a lot. When he did, it meant something, and by that smile on his face in the photo you could feel the love he had for Tommy.

I nodded at the photo next to the TV. "You miss him?"

"Tommy D? Every day. I pray for him and TJ at Mass. Like I told you once, without Tommy I never woulda made it through my time inside. He risked a lot for me to survive in that place. He was the only real friend I ever had . . . I mean, before you and Father Bill."

I didn't correct his hanging the collar back around Bill's throat. I still thought of him that way, too, a lot of the time. It was like when an old teacher of yours asks you to call her by her first name. You do it, but it takes some getting used to.

"So, what's goin' on, Guth?"

"What's your work schedule like over the next few days?"

Smudge's eyes got big. "Whatever you need it to be. The sisters are pretty flexible with me. They know they don't pay me enough to bust my chops. What do you need?"

"I need you to keep an eye on someone for me."

"Who?"

"Maggie."

He tilted his head, confused. "Your Maggie?"

"My Maggie."

"Did somebody hurt her?" Smudge's voice got squeaky with anger and fear.

"Threatened, not hurt."

I explained about Mr. Gordon, but didn't go into details about the whys and wherefores. Besides, Smudge didn't need to know that stuff. He would only want to know, need to know anything that would help him do his job.

"That shitbox of yours still drivable, Smudge?"

"Yeah, sure. The sisters paid to have it fixed up so I could do my deliveries. Runs good these days."

"I'll take your word for it."

I shouldn't have. The reason Smudge had gone to prison was because he was part of a scheme to con people out of charitable contributions. Pretty ironic, given his current job. As he once told me, it was easy for people to feel sorry for him. "One look at me and they reached into their pockets."

"If you hang back," I said, "I think you'll be fine. All I want you to do is scream fire if there's any sign of trouble."

"You know what's funny, Guth? When you look like me, people notice you and then they don't. They wanna forget you and they make you disappear. No one will see me watching Maggie. I promise."

One thing I admired in Smudge more than anything was his brutal honesty. He didn't want you to lie to him to try and soothe his hurt. His hurt was too deep and his truths too evident.

"What's your rent here?"

"Six."

"Six bucks? Sounds about right."

He laughed. It was kind of a snort and a honk, but it made me laugh, too.

"Six hundred," he said between honks.

"A hundred a day plus gas and meals. And don't insult me by giving me fucking receipts or trying to turn the money down."

"Okay, Guth."

We shook on it. I took three twenties out of my wallet and told him that was just for some gas and a meal, that there'd be a hundred on top of it when we settled up.

I looked at my watch. "She's home now, but leaving for a bartending gig in Chelsea in about an hour."

"I'll have her back. Don't worry about it."

Of course I was worried. Yet in spite of Mr. Gordon's threats and his obvious skills at violence, my ugly little friend's assurances eased my mind.

31

S mudge woke me up to give me good news. Maggie had worked a party at a Chelsea art gallery from eight last night until midnight. Afterward she'd gone into Hell's Kitchen with two women who met her at the gallery. They ate dinner, had drinks. Maggie drove one of them home to Astoria and got back to her place around two.

"You want the details, Guth, I can give 'em to you."

"No, that's okay, Smudge. All I want to know is if something doesn't smell right or if you see somebody who doesn't belong. Go get some rest so you can pick her movements up later. I'll call her in a little while to see if I can't get you a heads-up about if she's working tonight and where. Even if she's in for the night, I want you to sit on her place, okay?"

I'd just about hung up and shut my eyes when my phone buzzed again. It was Alvaro Peña.

"You got something to write on?" he said.

"Wait a second."

I rolled out of bed and found a piece of Paragon stationery and a pencil. The stationery was a leftover from the people who'd bought the hotel two sales ago. They thought they were going to turn the place into the Waldorf. Instead the hotel turned them into paupers. The Paragon pencils were a recent addition, because the pens those Waldorf dreamers had purchased ran out a few months back.

"Yeah, Alvaro, go ahead."

"That tag you gave me is registered to a Kimberly Mark, Thirty-four Ocean Court, Brooklyn, New York one-one-two-two-nine. Any help?"

"Maybe. Thanks."

"Any progress on the Salazar thing?"

"Nothing yet."

He was off the phone. This time when I closed my eyes, they stayed shut for a while. When I opened them again, there was someone knocking at my door and screaming at me.

"For fuck's sake, Gus Murphy, open up."

When I pulled back the door Bill Kilkenny was standing there, looking as badly dressed as ever. Sometimes I could swear a blind man picked out his clothes, but I guess that's what you get from a man who wore black with a dash of white for most of his adult life.

"Good morning, Bill."

"Morning! If it was morning I wouldn't be here dislodging your arse from bed. It's near one in the afternoon and I've called you twice, to no avail."

"Sorry," I said, trying to shake the sleep out of my head. "It's been a long week, Bill, and I work the club this weekend. What's up?"

"You, just barely. But I've Brother Vassily downstairs in the lobby and the both of us are famished. Ten minutes, lad," he said, tapping his watch crystal. "Ten minutes. And remember, lunch is on you."

I don't know that I had formed an image of Brother Vassily in my head, but if I had, it wouldn't have done justice to the hulking giant of a man who stood up from the lobby couch as I approached. He was wearing lay clothing—a plaid flannel shirt, ill-fitting jeans, and work boots. Brother Vassily must have been six-six and thick as an oak tree, though it wasn't his size that made the most impact on me. Twenty years Bill's junior, he had long, unruly black hair, a matching mountain-man beard threaded with silver-gray, and possibly the most intense dark brown eyes I had ever seen. They truly seemed as if they might cut right through me. There was a broad smile on his face as I approached. I held my right hand out to him, but instead he embraced me and kissed my cheeks several times.

"Forgive me, Brother, I am sorry for being late."

"Not to worry, Mr. Gus. Let us eat and discuss. There is much curiosity about this thing I am translating for you," he said, his voice deep. His English was much better than Slava's, if just as heavily accented.

"Come on, my car's in the lot."

There weren't many decent sit-down restaurants in the area around the Paragon, so we ended up at the new coal-fired pizza place across from the airport. We had just missed the lunch rush and were basically alone in the place but for the help. We made a little small talk—I mentioned to Bill that I had some questions for him about Micah Spears—but it was evident that Brother Vassily was very anxious to discuss the newspaper article Bill had given him on my behalf. When Brother Vassily asked me where I'd gotten the article, Bill put his hand on Vassily's forearm.

"That's between Gus and me," he said to the Russian.

Brother Vassily nodded that he understood.

"So," I said after we'd ordered, "what's it about—the article, I mean, Brother Vassily?"

"Please to call me Vassily."

"Okay, Vassily, what's the article about?"

"It is from April eighteenth, 2003, an obituary for a man named Sergei Yushenkov."

"Sorry, Vassily, but the name means nothing to me."

"I had already left home by then to come here. But according to story, Yushenkov was a man who was part of a commission looking into the Chechen apartment building bombings."

When he said "Chechen," I froze up. I wanted to say something but couldn't. Bill asked what I would have asked, had my head not been going in several directions at once.

"The what?"

"In three cities in Russia in September 1999 bombs exploded in apartment buildings killing many, many people. Three hundred I am thinking is the number, or something close to this. The Chechens, those crazy Muslim bastards, they did it, killed men, women, and children as they slept. They are animals, the separatists like those Muslim brothers who make the Boston bombing. They were from Dagestan, but is the same. Murderers! Murderers!"

Brother Vassily was red-faced and agitated. He leaned forward and was pointing his finger at Bill. Then, noticing that he was almost out of his seat and losing it, the Russian sat down and took a second to gather himself.

"The next day, Prime Minister Putin is bombing Grozny and making war on—"

I cut him off. "Excuse me, Vassily. Did you say Putin?"

"Yes, Putin. He was not yet president then. Yeltsin was president. But many people are saying it is not the Chechens making these bombings of the apartment houses, but the FSB . . . state security like American FBI. They are saying that the FSB are killing our own people so Yeltsin and Putin can make war on Chechnya. It is madness to say this. Look what the Muslims have done in the theater and at children's school. But still to make happy those foolish people who believe lies, a commission was convened. This man Yushenkov was on commission. He was shot in his apartment by robbers. This is what newspaper is saying."

Before Bill or I could ask any more questions, the pizzas arrived. It was just as well. The rest would be details about the situation given to us by a man who had very strong opinions on the matter. It hadn't escaped my notice nor Bill's, from the looks on his face, that Brother Vassily had emphasized religion in his description of these events. I wasn't judging him. Who was I to judge? Fourteen years later, 9/11 still resonated with me. I couldn't drive into Manhattan and not look for the Twin Towers. Even now with the Freedom Tower built, I looked. Everybody on Long Island knew somebody who'd been killed that day. Me, I knew two firemen and a Port Authority cop who'd died at Ground Zero. Annie had worked at the Trade Center for a year before she got pregnant with John. And I knew, like any cop knew, how easy it was to stop seeing people as individuals. There's a kind of perverse comfort in group blame. That's the soil hate grows in best.

Afterward, I drove them back to the Paragon and the car Brother Vassily had borrowed for the day. I thanked him for his help and told him that I'd drive Bill back to his apartment. There was another round of hugs and cheek kissing. It was almost comical to see the blade-thin Bill in Vassily's grasp. It was good to smile after what I'd heard from Vassily.

"Nice car," Bill said, as I headed down Locust to Sunrise Highway. "I bet Maggie thinks it's a wee bit of a step up from the van."

"She hasn't seen it."

"What? Don't tell me you and Maggie—"

"No, Bill, it's not like that. She got a big part in a show that opens out of town. She's leaving in about a week from today."

"Look out, world. You're apt to be a miserable bastard for a while."

"That about sums it up, yeah. So, I've spoken to Linh Trang's boyfriend, her college roommate, and her sister. I've found out some hard stuff about the girl herself and maybe something that might help explain her murder. Might not."

"Will you tell Micah?"

"Not until I get more. Right now it's only an idea in my head. I need to do more checking around before it even becomes a real scenario."

"I trust you'll do as you see fit and do the right thing."

"Why did Linh Trang think her grandfather was a monster?"

Bill blanched. He was pale to begin with, but he truly went white.

"I can't discuss it with you, Gus. I truly can't."

"Sanctity of confession?"

"Something like that, yes."

"But he is a monster, isn't he, Bill? Or at least he used to be."

Bill's continuing silence for the remainder of the ride to North Massapequa was answer enough for me. The answer was yes.

32

Gyron Machinery Inc. was located in a stucco-coated factory building just a mile or two north of the Paragon. Their bland building looked about the same as the others clustered together in the industrial park south of the LIRR tracks in Ronkonkoma. Several industrial and office parks dotted Suffolk County, many of them flanking either side of Vets Highway. In only a little while, many of the workers from these places would be cramming themselves into the bar at the Paragon for Friday happy hour. Some would be back again later to prowl the dance floor when the bar was transformed into the Full Flaps Lounge.

Though I probably should have gone back to the hotel and rested for a while—shifts at the Full Flaps could be long, loud, and rough—I decided to have a talk with the people Linh Trang Spears had worked for from the time she graduated college until the day she was murdered. Most of her grumpiest Facebook posts were about working in the accounting department at Gyron. There weren't any red flags in those posts. Nothing that indicated she was being stalked or sexually harassed by other employees or her bosses. Nothing that hinted at anything inappropriate in their business practices. Her posts were what I imagined

Krissy's posts might be like when she discovered that working for a living was tougher and more boring than she might have imagined. Krissy had a year or two more before she would discover the reality of the working life.

Gyron's logo was featured on the lighted orange, blue, and black sign that ran across the front of the building and on the like-colored freestanding sign at the entrance of their parking lot. It wasn't a terribly original logo—a large black G superimposed over a smaller black M in the midst of a series of interconnected cogs and sprockets. It looked like something that might have been picked out of an online logo catalog. The lot was half empty, but I parked in a visitor's spot just the same and followed the signs to the office entrance.

The reception area was actually more sumptuous than I would have thought for a light industrial factory in Ronkonkoma. The carpeting was custom-made—dyed orange, blue, and black to mimic the signs outside—and the logo, woven into the carpeting, greeted visitors as they entered. The walls were covered in polished mahogany. The photos on those mahogany walls were signed and numbered, artfully shot black-and-white prints of industrial machinery. The seats were steel and black leather, still new enough to give off that strong leather scent akin to new-car smell. I liked it but could understand how it might turn some people off.

Unlike the decor, the fiftyish woman at the reception desk gave off the vibe that she had been there a long time, long enough to have been rooted to the chair she sat in. She was attractive but wore too much makeup, and her hair was too brown. She was half paying attention to her cell phone, half paying attention to the *People* magazine on the desk in front of her. With her attention so divided, there was no room for me. I cleared my throat, loudly, and she deigned to look up. She didn't exactly snap to or apologize, but she did acknowledge me.

"Yeah."

"Can I speak with the owner, please?"

She laughed. It wasn't a pleasant laugh. More sneering, like the look on her face.

"Good luck with that. He's fishing in the Keys," she said.

"The plant manager, then."

"Why, you selling something?" She turned and looked at the clock behind her and turned back to me. "'Cause you're so cute, let me give you a piece of advice. Friday afternoon at almost four ain't exactly the best time to be peddling your goods."

"Thanks for the compliment and the advice," I said, "but I'm not peddling anything. I'm here to talk about the homicide of Linh Trang Spears."

The receptionist shook her head and seemed genuinely shaken. "Nice girl. Beautiful soul," she said. "Hang on. I'll get Carl for you."

She tapped the keyboard and spoke into the small mic on her headset, "Carl, there's a cop here to talk to you about LT's . . . about LT."

I didn't correct her mistake. I would save that for when I spoke to Carl.

"What's your name?" I asked the receptionist.

"Lara."

"Nice to meet you, Lara. I'm Murphy. Gus Murphy. What can you tell me about LT?"

Lara had a lot to say, but it was mostly commentary on LT's looks, her polite manner, and the horror surrounding her murder.

The man I assumed to be Carl came through a door behind Lara. He was about my age, a few inches shorter, tanned in April, and had a mouth full of the whitest, straightest teeth this side of Hollywood. He had a shaven head and a salt-and-pepper goatee, was good-looking in a tough-guy kind of way, and was built like he spent time in the gym. He was dressed in khaki slacks and a black golf shirt featuring the company logo.

He offered me his hand. "I'm Carl Ryan, factory manager. And you're Detective . . ."

I shook his hand but didn't answer his question. "Can we speak some-place privately?"

"Sure, this way." He headed back toward the door through which he'd come.

I thanked Lara and followed.

Carl had a slight hitch in his walk. Not a limp exactly, but his strides were uneven. He took me down a corridor that was much more of what I expected to find in a machine factory. The green walls were grease-stained; blue vinyl flooring was grungy and worn-out in spots. None of the framed prints on the wall were signed or numbered, and they were also about as current as my aunt's harvest-gold refrigerator. And you could smell the factory odors in here—the petroleum tang of industrial lubri-cants, the odd odor of hot metal and plastic, and overcooked egg vapors of some sulfuric chemical. At the end of that corridor, we turned left. From here you could look out onto the factory floor through a Plexi-glas wall. Although the place smelled of activity, there was frankly very little going on. Mostly a few guys in dirty coveralls, cleaning. Like Lara said, it was four on a Friday afternoon. What else could I have ex-pected?

Eventually we came to a row of offices, mostly vacant, some fan-cier than others. Carl Ryan's was handsomely appointed with the same mahogany-veneered walls and leather furniture as the reception area. Same carpeting as well. Ryan's desk was a sleek Scandinavian thing that looked like it was moving even as it stood still. His desk chair was one of those expensive ergonomic things that was as easy on your back as it was ugly. As he sat down, he gestured for me to sit across from him in a leather chair.

"Mr. Ryan—"

"Carl, please, Detective."

"That's the thing, Carl. I'm not a detective, though I am SCPD, re-tired. Name is Gus Murphy."

He didn't seem fazed or get indignant. "Private, huh?"

I nodded. I suppose that still counted as a lie, but it seemed less of one. And it beat saying I was the courtesy van driver at the Paragon by the airport doing a favor for my ex-priest friend.

"I was wondering when the family would hire one of you guys."

That made me curious. "Why would you say that? The cops have the killer."

"But they don't know why he killed her," Ryan said. "If it was my kid, I'd wanna know why."

"Exactly."

"I wish I could help you there. I really do. All I can tell you is that we loved her as an employee. We knew we would lose her eventually when she got certified. Besides, she was bored to death here. Sorry, that was a stupid thing to say."

"Forget it."

"She was sharp, had a curious mind. This wasn't the kind of place for her, but her granddad sells us our electricity and gas, and the owner, Steve Randazzo, and him are kinda friendly. So when she graduated Hofstra, we hired her."

I went through a series of questions with Ryan but got nowhere. I didn't think there was anywhere to get with him, really. Finally, I asked him if it would be all right if I came back at a later date to talk to some of her coworkers.

"Sure. I don't think it'll help, but . . ." He shrugged and turned his palms to the ceiling. "C'mon, let me walk you out. I'm heading home, anyway."

Instead of retracing our steps, he walked me through the factory.

Walking into the machine shop, he said, "Normally, I'd have you put on a hat and safety glasses, but we're done for the day."

As we strolled through the place, Ryan would stop occasionally and say a word or two, mostly in Long Island–accented Spanish, to one of his employees. Then he'd finish in English.

"Luis, you in tomorrow," or "Diego, don't let me catch you taking an extra ten at lunch."

The workers eyed me with suspicion. I didn't blame them. A lot of the people who worked the dirty, dangerous jobs on the island were illegals. If you deported all the illegals off Long Island, there'd be no open restaurants, our lawns would overwhelm us, and no one would be available to repave driveways or lay tiles. About three-quarters of the way through the building, I spotted a worker coming out of a huge room, closing a humongous steel door behind him. The door had all sorts of warning signs in English and Spanish on it about hazardous chemicals and protective clothing.

The guy coming through the door didn't seem to have paid any attention to the signs, and Ryan chewed him a new one. I knew some Spanish, half of it simple stuff like "Please," "Thank you," and "What's your name?" The other half was curses. Most of what Ryan was screaming at the guy was in Spanish, and he wasn't saying "Please," "Thank you," or asking for the guy's name. When he was done screaming, the guy basically shrugged and walked past us.

"Fucking idiot," Ryan whispered, as much to himself as to me. Then, in full voice, he said, "No matter what you tell these *cholo* motherfuckers, they don't listen. There's all sorts of dangerous fumes and shit in there. You think they care? You think they give a shit if one of them gets hurt and OSHA shows up at my door?"

He didn't want an answer, so I didn't give him one. We walked through a door, past the loading bays, and into the lot. When we got outside, he walked over to a sleek, aggressive-looking, smoke-gray Maserati GranTurismo coupe. A car that, like his desk, looked as if it was moving, although it was as stationary as the building we'd just exited.

"Business must be good," I said. "She's a beauty."

"What the hell good is life if you don't enjoy it? Where are you parked?"

I pointed to the visitor parking spots.

"Nice car. I've got a weak spot for muscle cars myself, but . . ." He stroked the roof of the Maserati. He opened its door. "Listen, Murphy, sorry I couldn't have been more helpful. Have a good weekend."

And with that, he slammed his door shut and the Maserati's low, throaty rumble filled up the air. As I turned to walk back to the Mustang he tore past me, waving as he went.

33

The Full Flaps Lounge was hopping. I wasn't sure why. Well, maybe it was that it finally felt like spring. It hadn't rained for a couple days and the sun felt a bit warmer on your face with each rotation of the planet. I was never much for spring fever. Still, I had to confess, I enjoyed the prospect of shedding my Costco leather coat, which, by this time of year, always begins to feel like a leaden straitjacket. A cop had to be part shrink, part sociologist, and part social worker, but who knew why one Friday night at the club had more energy than the one before it? The DJ played the same music, often in the same mix, and the crowd was saturated with regulars. Like I said, who knows?

It was hopping, but things had gone smoothly. Sometimes more energy meant more drinking, which led to beer-muscle flexing, which meant more trouble. It was a simple equation. Our usual crowd contained a lot of divorced men and women, many of them so bitter you could feel it coming off them in waves. I'd overheard some conversations at the bar that boggled the mind, men and women comparing their settlements, their lawyer fees, and the relative satisfaction in their vengeance sex. *I could never stand his brother Joey. What a loser. But I don't think I ever enjoyed fucking a man more in my life. I think the only thing I enjoyed more was telling my ex about it.*

Annie and I had escaped most of the bitterness because what blew us apart had nothing to do with the usual reasons couples split up. What blew us apart was loss and fury, and if we hadn't exactly come to be at peace with it, we had, at least, come to understand it. That wasn't the case for many of the people in the club. Tonight just happened to be about more dancing, not more drinking or bitterness. I knew better than to assume it would be the same tomorrow night or that it would even last until closing.

I was working the door when she walked in. It was near eleven, ten-fifty-seven, to be exact. I knew because I'd just looked at my watch to figure out when I should start giving the guys their breaks. Her face didn't register at first, and then it did: Lara, the receptionist from Gyron Machinery. She cleaned up very nicely for a woman in her early fifties. She kept her body in shape, something I couldn't see while she was behind the reception counter at Gyron. But before I could say anything, she beat me to it.

"Moonlighting, Detective?"

"Something like that."

She turned to the woman at her shoulder. Her friend, like Lara, was in her early fifties. "See, I told you I recognized him."

Lara turned back to me, cash in hand.

"Not necessary, ladies," I said, stamping their hands for reentry. "If you go over by the bar, I'll buy you both a drink. Give me a minute."

Lara eyed me with suspicion. Lara's pal eyed me, too, but suspicion had nothing to do with it. I signaled one of the guys to take my place at the door and ambled over to the bar. Lara and her pal were loaded for bear, both wearing spangly black tops light on fabric, heavy on cleavage. Lara had on a short silvery skirt and high heels that showed off her legs and other physical assets. Her pal went for the painted-on-black-slacks look with even higher heels. Wisely, Lara had less makeup on than she wore at work so as not to draw too much attention to her age. Her pal took the opposite approach and laid it on thick. At least they were smiling. Sometimes smiles were in short supply on Fridays at the Full Flaps. Men and women who came to drink and dance and have a good time usually did. Coming in on the prowl was always an iffy proposition.

"Barry," I shouted to the barman, wiggling my finger above the heads of Lara and her pal, "these ladies' first two rounds are on the house."

He nodded and came right over. "Ladies, what'll it be?"

Lara spoke up first. "A mojito, please."

Her pal was less decisive, or maybe she was the type of person who when she knew something was free went for top-shelf. She proved to be the latter.

"Rémy Martin, if that's the best cognac you have," she said, without the least bit of embarrassment.

"Anything for you, Gus?" Barry wanted to know.

"Coke."

Lara introduced me to her pal as we waited for the drinks.

"This is Kim."

"Gus Murphy." I shook her hand. She held on to it an uncomfortable beat too long, and not for the same reason Micah Spears had.

"You're a detective?" Kim said.

"Suffolk PD, retired. I'm private now." It still sounded odd to say.

That got Lara's attention, but the drinks came before she could say anything. I put a five on the bar for Barry. We toasted and drank.

"Lara," I said, after she had made a dent in her mojito, "I was wondering if we could chat . . . privately for a few minutes after you finish your drink."

Kim gave Lara a nasty look when she turned her head. I noticed. Kim noticed me notice and didn't much care. It didn't take long for either Lara or Kim to finish. I nodded at Barry and he put up another round. I put up another five.

"Listen, Barry, introduce Kim to some of the guys," I said. "This is her first time here."

I didn't know if that was true or not, but Kim liked the sound of that and managed not to give Lara the death stare when I walked her and her second mojito outside.

"I'm sorry I didn't recognize you earlier," I said, as we leaned on a car fender, staring into the night sky. "I mostly focus on people's IDs, their cash, and their hands when they come in."

It was a lie, but one that would make her feel better. Where was the harm in that?

"That's okay, Gus."

"Also sorry about the lie of omission earlier at your work. It's just easier to get to speak to people when they think you're a cop. The fact is that I was hired by a member of LT's family to look into why she was murdered."

Lara bowed her head, but when she summoned up the strength to speak again she repeated much of what she had told me earlier. That LT was good at her job, if a bit of a stickler. *But all kids are like that. They get outta college and they think they know everything.* That LT was well liked by everyone at Gyron. That she felt a kind of motherly protectiveness about LT. *Factory full of men and just LT and me.*

"But she was never harassed or bothered by any of the workers?" I asked.

"No, never. Carl would never have put up with that, especially because LT's grandpa did business with us. Hell, he doesn't even like it if the guys flirt with me."

"But I bet you like it."

She laughed, and this time it lacked the sneer and snarkiness I'd heard in it this afternoon.

"Maybe a little."

"Did she ever talk to you about trouble at home or boy trouble, anything that you could connect to her murder? Anything, even if it seems like a stretch?"

She shook her head. "Sorry."

"C'mon," I said, "let's get you back inside, get you another drink, and have Barry introduce you around."

She liked that idea.

"Of course, there's be no need to introduce me around if . . ."

"Sorry, Lara, I'm taken and I'm damaged goods."

"We're none of us undamaged. We're all dented cans, Gus."

"But some more dented than others. Still, don't think I wouldn't be tempted."

She liked that, too.

As we walked back toward the entrance, I just happened to say that business at Gyron must be good. I mentioned Carl's car and the fact that the boss was busy fishing in the Keys.

"Yeah, in the last year things have been booming. Before that we were pretty close to shutting the doors. Then Carl landed this big Internet account and it's been great."

The small talk was at an end when we worked our way back to the bar and I gave Barry the heads-up to introduce Lara around and to give her another round on the house.

"Thanks, Gus," she said. "You're sweet. If there's anything you ever need to know about LT or if you become untaken, let me know."

I winked at her and went back to my spot at the door.

34

went through different phases with the music at the club. The first few months, I guess I kind of liked it, even found myself bopping around to it occasionally when no one was looking. Helped remind me there were some things other than grief and pain to life. Then it became just so much background noise. That didn't last. A man can only hear "My Sharona," "Disco Inferno," and "Paradise by the Dashboard Light" so many times before losing his mind. And when I heard the twangy guitar intro to "Rock Lobster" . . . well, that was my cue to take a break. It became an inside joke between the DJ and me, so that he knew to play the song around midnight, when I liked to get out and stretch my legs.

My getting out served a dual purpose. It helped me regain whatever little sanity was left to me and I got to walk the hotel perimeter to make sure things were as under control outside the club as in. Our crowd was usually well behaved, but there was the occasional spillage of hard feelings out of the club and into the parking lot. A few months ago, word got back to us that there was a guy selling weed and Molly outside the club. I'm not sure where he relocated after getting out of the hospital. The last thing the Paragon needed was a bad rep with the SCPD. The precinct commander gets pissed at you and the next thing you know there's a cruiser sitting just on the other side of your parking-lot exit. Takes only one or two DWI arrests for word to get around and to kill your business. I knew how it worked. I had once been that uniform in the car, sitting, waiting.

When I stepped outside I found the usual group of smokers huddled together, whining about their rejections, comparing notes on prospects, laughing, too. Word was more hookups happened out there than inside the club. You could still hear the music, dance if you wanted to, but you could also have a conversation without having to shout above the din. The regulars, as always, greeted me as I walked past, offering me smokes or to buy me a drink when I got back. I never took them up on their offers. I was never tempted to.

At the corner of the building, turning from the side of the Paragon where the club was located to the front of the hotel, I knelt down to take my gun out of its ankle holster. Since last December, when I came this close to getting my skull kicked in by three guys with coal in the cavities where their hearts should have been, I'd gotten a little more cautious when strolling the perimeter. I always waited until this point in the walk to grab my gun because I didn't want any of the clubgoers to know I carried or where I carried. All I wanted them to focus on was dancing, drinking, and having a good time.

As I was reaching for my little Glock, I sensed him coming at me from over my left shoulder. Maybe it was the sound of rushing footsteps or his breathing. Whatever it was that caused me to react, I was better for it. I ducked, tucking my chin to my chest, and felt the downdraft from his swinging fist. He was an amateur, had to be, him putting everything into a haymaker like that. But even amateurs and fools sometimes came armed with more than their stupidity and inexperience. So when the punch flew over my head, I rolled backward on the sidewalk and came up with my Glock in my hand, its muzzle aimed at the center of my would-be attacker's back.

"Hands against that wall, motherfucker, feet spread. Do it right now! There's a nine-millimeter pointed at you and I *will* use it."

Before I could finish the sentence, he was raising his hands up, placing his palms against the wall, and spreading his legs. I watched him very carefully as he did so, looking for any sign that he might try something even more stupid than rushing at me the way he had. As I watched, I tried to see if there was anything about him that seemed familiar to me. Nothing. I patted him down, pulled a cell phone out of his jacket, keys, and a leather wallet out of his pants pockets. When I stepped back he made to face me.

"Stop! You almost just got yourself shot. Now stay that way. Don't move. Don't speak until I tell you to. Understand?"

"I understand."

I didn't recognize his voice, but when I flipped open the wallet and saw the name and the face on the driver's license, I don't suppose I was shocked.

"Kevin Spears," I said. "LT's father and—"

"Linh Trang! Linh Trang!" He was back to shouting. "Her name was Linh Trang."

"You're in no position to be correcting me, Mr. Spears, or to be shouting at me."

He started once again to turn around.

"Don't fucking move until I tell you to. You look like your dad and you act like him. The rules just don't apply to you guys, huh?"

"Don't say that!" he screamed at the wall, fighting the urge to turn and scream it at me. "I'm nothing like my father."

"Suit yourself. Now, what was this bullshit about, you coming at me like that?"

"My family's been through enough. Leave it alone, please. Linh Trang is dead and nothing is going to bring her back. Nothing. Leave it alone. Leave us alone."

At least he wasn't shouting any longer. I probably understood his frustration better than he could have imagined. I tossed his wallet down between his spread feet.

"Pick it up and turn around."

He did so. He looked even more like his father in person than he did in his license photo. Same eyes, same cut of the jaw. I handed him his cell phone and keys.

"Jesus, you really were pointing a gun at me."

"I still am. It makes me angry when people act the way you just did. Makes me think if you had a gun you would have used it. Upsets me to think that."

"I'm not my father. I would never own a gun, but I will protect my family."

"You keep saying that, Mr. Spears. Protecting them from what?"

"From you, from my father."

"Look, I mean you no harm, and so far I haven't approached you or your wife. Abby seemed okay with me talking to her, relieved almost. You Google me and you'll see that I understand a little about what you're going through. All I'm doing is trying to find out why your daughter was killed. Your father wants to know and, frankly, I'm surprised you don't want to know."

He did a very odd thing. He laughed. It was a laugh not unlike Mr. Gordon's, icy and cruel.

"Listen to me, Mr. Murphy, my father is interested in Linh Trang's death for one reason and one reason only: his own skin. It's the only thing he's ever cared about or ever will."

"How does that work?"

He laughed that laugh again.

"You're an investigator of some sort and a cop. That's what you're telling people, anyway. Figure it out for yourself. In the meantime, stay away from my family and my friends."

I had to get back to the club and I wasn't in the mood for empty threats or warnings.

"I'm sorry about your daughter. From what everyone's told me, she was a great person. That she was happy and had it all together. I get that you must still not have your feet back under you. Took me a long time. But to be clear, I've been hired to do a job and I'm gonna do it. Now get outta here."

As I watched Kevin Spears walk to his car, I realized that I had lied to him about his girl. From what everyone but Lara had told me, LT had issues. John Jr. had issues, too. He didn't know what he wanted to do with his life. He worried about it a lot—too much. But the young can't hear that. They lack perspective. What did any of that matter now? What does anything matter after you're in a box in the ground, when who you are is only who you were and where you're going is where you are. Forever.

35

For the second time in the last few hours I got that funky feeling that something wasn't right, but this go-round there were no rushing footsteps or nervous breaths. Nothing obvious I could point to as I ambled down the hallway toward my room. I felt nearly spent, as if I'd run a marathon or if I'd been swimming for an hour against the tide. There wasn't anything particularly unusual in that, nor did I dislike the way I felt. It was a kind of satisfied exhaustion. Shifts at the Full Flaps did that to me, wore me out even on nights when no one tried to coldcock me or kick my head in between cars in the parking lot. The crush of people, the volume of the music, the heightened vigilance all took a toll on me, and then we usually finished the night with me and the guys having a drink or two. I always slept well, and then I'd go have a late breakfast with Slava.

I tried talking myself out of feeling apprehensive, telling myself that it was just my exhaustion playing tricks on me. Or maybe it was a sign that I was off my game and that I was already missing Maggie. Oddly, as much as I hadn't wanted her to go, I now wanted her to leave early for her own safety and my peace of mind. I thought that maybe I was thrown off by fear for Slava, that not only weren't we going to have breakfast later that morning, but that we might never have breakfast together again.

After getting back to the hotel from Gyron, I'd done some Internet research on the incidents Brother Vassily had talked about at lunch. I wasn't a hundred percent sure of who Mr. Gordon was or why he was trying to kill Slava, but I now had a pretty good idea of just how high the stakes were. I also understood the depth of Slava's shame. That's what I was thinking about, Slava's shame, as I came up to my door and nestled my gun in the crook of my hand.

I stood to the side of the door, flat against the wall, and very carefully slid my keycard into the lock with my left hand. The lock made its familiar mechanical click and sang its muted electronic song. I turned the handle, shoved the door open as best I could, pressed against the wall as I was, and waited. There was nothing: no gunfire, nobody rushing at me, nothing. The door swung slowly shut, the lock engaging with its double click. I repeated the routine once more. Again, nothing. *Click. Click.* Still, I could not shake that strange feeling that something wasn't right. On the other hand, I couldn't stand out in the hallway until sunrise and I was getting pretty desperate for sleep. I did the lock thing one more time, only on this occasion I didn't let the lock engage. Instead I kicked the door open just before it closed and kept my gun at the ready. Inside, I flicked on the lights and saw that I'd been right to feel something was off. There was a man sitting on the edge of my bed—Slava.

"Is good morning, Gus? How was club going tonight?"

"Small talk, Slava? C'mon. How did you get in here, anyway?"

He answered with that big, ugly grin of his. I wiped it right off his face.

"I know, Slava. I know."

I don't know what made me say it. It wasn't generally in my nature to blurt things out that way or to expose people, certainly not a friend. It wasn't my nature to say "Gotcha!" or to hurt someone. But of course that was ridiculous. I wasn't at all sure what my nature was anymore. I could've made excuses for myself, told myself that it was anger over Maggie being threatened or of my being caught up in a mess that wasn't my mess to begin with. But last year Slava had saved me from more than one mess that had nothing at all to do with him.

"You know. What are you knowing?" he asked, his voice full of anger and defeat. But he knew the answer. Slava was nothing if not intuitive. He was good at reading people. Even better at reading me.

"C'mon on, Slava, you and me . . . we can't start making believe with each other."

"No, Gus, there is no making believe between us. You are understanding my shame now. I see this in your eyes. I am killing men and women and children who are doing nothing to me. I have made killing because a man says this is what I must do like making order for me to sweep floor or taking out garbage."

"You don't have to explain yourself to me."

"That is why I am wishing to tell the only friend I have had for many, many years. Please, for our friendship, you are letting Slava explain."

And then he did something I never thought I would see him do—he cried. And when he cried, the bed shook. I swore I could feel the intensity of it through the floor and the soles of my running shoes. I think he must have been saving up those tears for sixteen years. Then the tears stopped as suddenly as they had begun. He turned to me, eyes red, wet, wiping his nose on his sleeve.

"How you are knowing?"

"In Mikel's room, after I was attacked, I found an old newspaper article about the murder of a man on the commission investigating the apartment building bombings. One of Bill's friends translated it for me. It wasn't hard to figure out from there."

"My father was an electrical engineer, a Pole and a communist. What you are calling a true believer. After the Great Patriotic War—"

"Huh?"

"In Russia is what we are saying is World War Two."

"Okay."

"So he was true believer and, with help from Soviets, resettled our family in Grozny, Chechnya. Stalin is doing this, putting Slavs in places that are ethnically different. I become a policeman there when I get out from school. The Chechens, they are hating us because they are Muslims and Soviet Union has no place for religion. For Muslims especially there is very little liking. For many years there are small terrorisms, but then, after Soviet Union is collapsing, there is madness. The Muslims are wanting us out and to be their own country. Many police are being killed. My best friend on police, I am loving like brother, he is being tortured to death and his body is left burning in middle of street in Grozny."

"So," I said, "when they came to you, you volunteered to do whatever had to be done."

"Like a stupid child, yes. I was full of hating for them. Such hate . . . but what am I knowing? I am a dumb policeman who doesn't see the bigger things in the world. What am I knowing about Yeltsin and Putin and their plans to making war on Chechens because they are not being popular with the people? With blood in my eyes all I am seeing is revenge for my friend. When FSB man is coming to me to be part of death squad and says they have tracked Chechen rebels to buildings here and here and here, I am blind to truth."

I told him about Mr. Gordon's ride in my van and his threats. That shook him up. He began pounding his huge right fist into the palm of his left hand. His eyes got a very faraway look in them.

"He is wanting me, not Maggie."

"I know. I have Smudge keeping an eye on her. He'll let me know if something's up."

Slava grinned his ugly grin again. "Smudge. Ha! Strange little man."

"But I trust him and he's had to watch his own back for so long. He'll be good at watching Maggie's." Then I returned to what we had been discussing. "So Mikel, Goran, you, and this Mr. Gordon who threatened Maggie, you were all part of these death squads?"

"This Mr. Gordon's real name is Bogdan Lagunov," Slava said, finally standing and walking over by the drawn window shade. "He is not from the squads. He is ex-Spetsnaz, Russian special forces, working for rich oligarch who is acting on behalf of Russian politicians that were involved in helping make bombings possible. It is how it is working in Russia. Corruption there is like cancer in a body spreading so there is being more cancer than body. The rich and the politicians, they are being in bed so close that they have the same face. Do you understand what Slava is meaning by this?"

I nodded that I did.

Slava still had his back to me, ashamed to face me when he spoke about this. "You know what is amazing, Gus?" He snorted and gasped. That's how Slava laughed, a series of snorts and gasps. "I am telling you. One of bombing squads was caught, how Americans say . . . red-handed, yes?"

"Yes."

"One of the bombing squads is caught red-handed before bombs can explode and they are all Russians, not Chechens, but still we let politicians blame the Chechens and make war on them. This is when I knew I must run or be dead myself. I got to family still in Poland and then people there are helping me come to America. In Brighton Beach there are people who are making a new person of me. Many of us ran. Many others who are not running are dead."

"But why come after you now after so long?"

"Because of how Putin is taking back Ukraine. It is making people remember how he makes manipulations with Chechnya. He wants to shut the door on this, I think. It would be bad for him to having one of us show up at UN or on television. Slava is an untied end."

"A loose end."

He snorted and gasped and slipped into Russian. "*Da*, *da*, a loose end, that is Slava. A very loose end. I want you to know this, Gus, I am having no love for the Chechens. They have done many terrible things."

"I know about the murders at the school and what they did in the theater."

"But I am no better than them. Worse. I make terrorisms on my own people. Even with the hate I am having I know most Chechens, like Russians, are wanting to just live lives with no bother to families. I have much blood on my hands and must live with this shame. I must live with it as long as I can. Dying is too easy for Slava."

"What are you going to do now?"

He handed me a slip of paper with another phone number on it.

"If Bogdan Lagunov is approaching you again or he is making threats on Maggie, give to him this paper or number is on it."

"But—"

"No, Gus." He shook his massive head. "You give paper and is not your problem no more. I have read once in a store a sign in the mall that is saying 'What you break, you own,' or something like that. What has happened back in Russia, all those people I killed . . . I am breaking. I cannot fix, but I must own it, not you."

"I heard about Mikel."

"His pain is no more."

"Where are you going after this?"

"It is better for you to not knowing."

I didn't argue the point.

"I'll go take a walk, so you can go as you came," I said.

"Good."

"Breakfast next Saturday?"

"Yes, Gus," he said, his big, beefy hand covering and shaking mine, "breakfast next Saturday."

He wasn't smiling as he said it. I don't know that I had ever seen a man look any sadder, not even in the mirror after John's death. In a strange way, Slava's sad face made me wonder not about his shame or about the long-ago bombings in Russia, but about Micah Spears. I now knew of Slava's shame, why he considered himself a kind of monster. I left the room and walked back to the lobby. As I did, I wondered some more about monsters and men and what turned one into the other.

36

(SATURDAY, AFTER SUNRISE)

When I got to the lobby after my talk with Slava, tired as I was, I didn't head back to my room. Instead I sat down in what passed for our business center and began hunting monsters. I knew it didn't make any sense to worry about Micah Spears's past. Monster or not, he'd clearly had nothing to do with Linh Trang's murder. That was the odd thing about this case, the needle on the compass kept pointing away from the murder itself and to Micah Spears. But why? What was his pull on the needle? It was like I felt I couldn't get anywhere with LT's murder unless I found out about the old man. And I couldn't get Kevin Spears's words out of my head. *Listen, Mr. Murphy, my father is interested in Linh Trang's death for one reason and one reason only: his own skin. It's the only thing he's ever cared about or ever will.*

I didn't waste a lot of time concerning myself with the reasons Kevin Spears seemed to hate his father so. I'd been a cop too long for that, seen too much to be surprised. I'd seen husbands murder their brides on their wedding nights and wives murder their husbands after forty years to-gether. I'd seen just about every combination of relative killing relative as you could imagine. Wherever there's potential for intense love there's also potential for intense hate. But I didn't have to plumb the depths as far as murder to understand that sometimes relatives just didn't get along. I didn't need to look any further than to my own drunk of a father and my poor reticent mother. One was never going to take a baseball bat to the other. No, they seemed too content to grind each other down with the drip, drip, drip of insults and the vacuum of passive-aggressiveness.

There was plenty of stuff about Micah Spears's businesses and how he had smoothly parlayed a profitable COD home heating oil business into two ESCOs—energy service companies—selling natural gas and electricity to commercial and residential accounts. Apparently, he was quite the entrepreneurial superstar and was much admired for his business acumen. There were several glowing pieces written on him that had appeared in the business section of *Newsday*, Long Island's lone newspaper, in *Long Island Magazine*, and several business-oriented publications. A lot of it was the usual up-by-the-bootstraps bullshit. *I started out with one used truck, a thousand bucks in cash, and a determination to succeed in the oil business.* Like that. You know, the kind of stuff us Americans have had drilled into our heads since we could crawl. He might just as well have said he began with one mule, a ten-dollar stake, and a fierce desire to prospect for gold. Or the updated version about the guy in the garage and his idea for a personal computer.

At least one thing did show through in the stuff online as in real life. Micah Spears did not come across as a happy-go-lucky family man. Not that most of the pieces or interviews with him gave him much room for talk about his family or his personal life, but still there was an iciness, a sort of refusal on his part to ever take the conversation in that direction. Even when asked the rare direct question about his family, Spears would shut the interviewer right down. He was a classic compartmentalizer. It was a skill I was familiar with. Cops have to develop the ability to compartmentalize or they don't last on the job. You open up the gates between the separate parts of your life and it's trouble. Yet in spite of Micah Spears's chilliness and hard-nosed business practices, there was nothing evidently more monstrous about him than the head of any privately held corporation, large or small.

There were two things I came across that got my attention, though. One was a black-and-white photo of Micah Spears from the early '90s at a chamber of commerce event, but it wasn't him I was so much interested in as the woman standing to his left, her arm looped through his. The caption identified her as Roberta Spears. From what I could glean, Roberta Spears was quite an attractive woman and probably ten years younger than her husband. What I found fascinating was the look on her face. Her expression, as far as I could tell, was one full of love and admiration. For his part, Micah Spears had the same expression he wore the first time we met: distant, superior, knowing, with hints of blackened soul. I didn't bother trying to reconcile their expressions. Nor did I try and reconcile the fact that two years after the photo at the chamber of commerce function was taken, Roberta Spears and Micah were divorced.

Although she now used her maiden name—Malone—Roberta Spears had been easy enough to research. She was fifty-nine, currently living on Shelter Island. She was, even now, quite a beautiful woman. She had let her long, straight hair go silver-gray, and in many of the photos on her Facebook page, it fell carelessly over her shoulders. Her eyes were on the brown side of hazel. What was gone from those eyes and from the curve of her lips was that look of love and admiration. There was a sadness there in their place, a look of bewildered disappointment. I don't know. I was so overtired that I might well have been reading things into her face and eyes that weren't there. It didn't take too much more research to get her house number and phone numbers. Like I said, privacy was dead.

The other thing that caught my attention was the fact that Micah Spears's history seemed to go back only as far as 1973. And unlike with his ex-wife, no matter how much key tapping I did, I could not penetrate the wall of years preceding '73. I knew he'd been in the military during the Vietnam War. At least that's what I understood by Bill's comments about his association with Spears. I tried a few sites that had histories of

Army and Marine units that had served in 'Nam, but that was more a stab in the dark than anything else. Frankly, I would have been shocked had I stumbled upon a mention of Spears on those sites. Having grown up after the war, I never realized the depth of our involvement there. I knew more about World War II or, as Slava had called it, the Great Patriotic War, than I knew about Vietnam. I guess you hear more about the wars you win than the ones you lose.

I scribbled down some notes for myself with one of those Paragon Hotel pencils, clicked off the computer, and headed, finally, back to my room. This time there were no funky feelings as I approached my room. Even if there had been, I was so tired, it wouldn't have mattered. I was ready for sleep. I don't think I'd ever been more ready for it in my life.

37

It was a conspiracy against sleep. My sleep, particularly, because not only was there someone knocking at my room door, but my cell was buzzing, dancing happily along the top of the nightstand. And it had been such a sweet, deep sleep, a drool-on-the-pillow sleep with pleasant dreams now unremembered. Dreams gone to where dreams go. I sat there for a moment, ignoring the phone and the door, thinking about that, about forgotten dreams. I wondered if we could be hypnotized into remembering them the way witnesses could be manipulated into recalling apparently forgotten details. And if we could, would we want to? I didn't used to concern myself with questions like this. Seemed I thought about them a lot these days. More and more. I stopped wondering and answered the phone.

"Yeah."

"Guth, are you okay?" It was Smudge.

"Just sleeping. Why? Is anything wrong?"

"No. Just wanted to let you know Maggie's at the Paragon. She came straight from her job in the city. You want the details?"

"Anything suspicious?"

"Nothing that I could see."

WHAT YOU BREAK / 189

"We'll talk later. Thanks for the heads-up, Smudge."

Armed with that knowledge that it was Maggie knocking, I got out of bed, stripped down to full nakedness, and flung my door open. Only it wasn't Maggie. It was Laticia, a new housekeeper, who took one look at me in my birthday suit and ran screaming down the hall past Maggie. It was almost worth it just to see the look on Maggie's face.

When the shock wore off, she said, "Should I even ask?"

"You know me, Magdalena, I have a thing for husky Mexican women in brown polyester housekeeper's uniforms."

She smiled at that, but when she thought about it, the smile disappeared.

"You knew I was coming. How did you know I was here?"

I deflected, grabbing her wrist. "Get in here."

She looked spent. Her eyes were bloodshot and her hair was all over the place. Her mascara had run a bit and her eye shadow was smeared. She smelled of ambient cigarette smoke, sweat, and musky perfume. The tails of her satiny black blouse hung over the waist of her short black skirt. But there was something about her like this that I found incredibly sexy. I can't explain it, but I found her as appealing this way as when she was fresh and perfectly made up. I kissed her hard on the mouth.

But she wasn't having it. She closed the door behind her and pushed away from me.

"Go brush your teeth and then you can explain why you thought that was me at your door."

I brushed my teeth and as I did I thought about how I should answer her. One thing that had helped cement our relationship was the truth. I'd already chipped away at that by omitting to tell her about Lagunov's ride in my van and his implied threats. Omission was one kind of sin. Straight-up lying was something else. There'd be no rationalizing that away, no pretending. The thing I had to balance out was risk. If she found out I was lying to her, I'd risk losing her. If I told her the truth and she acted in a way to set off Lagunov, I was risking her life. I was using my time in the bathroom to stall. Maggie caught on.

"If you brush those white teeth of yours much longer, Gus, you'll be down to the roots."

I put my toothbrush down, rinsed, and shut the water off. I walked back into the room, so preoccupied that I forgot I was still naked. I remembered when I noticed that Maggie noticed, too. I went to grab my shorts.

"I didn't say I wanted you to get dressed. I wanted an answer."

"I'll answer you. First you have to answer a question of mine."

She didn't like that and opened her mouth to protest, but she could see by the look on my face it wasn't open for debate.

"What?"

"During your last few gigs, has anyone hit on you in a way—"

She didn't let me finish. "Guys always hit on me. You know that. Are you getting jealous now? Now, after all—" She stopped herself, her beautifully tired face turning angry and red. "Are you having me followed?"

"I know guys hit on you, and no, I'm not getting jealous. Let me finish. Has anyone hit on you in the last few nights in a way that got your attention? You know, in a way that made you feel especially uneasy?"

"Why are you asking me—"

"Maggie!"

"Well, one guy, yeah."

"At the Russian's party on the yacht?"

She nodded, looking pissed off and frightened all at once.

"Russian guy with cold eyes," I said, "thick accent, but spoke almost perfect English?"

The anger and fear in her face doubled. "How could you know that? You *are* having me followed."

"No . . . well, yes. Now, not then. How could I have you followed on that yacht?"

"Back up, mister. What do you mean, not then but now?"

"Smudge."

"Smudge what, Gus?"

"Smudge has been following you, but only after you did the gig on the yacht."

"You better start explaining yourself or you better dance pretty quickly."

"The man who creeped you out on the yacht, his name is Bogdan Lagunov. He works for the man who threw the party on the boat. He's an assassin and his next target is Slava."

"Slava? Why would anyone want to kill the doorman at a third-rate hotel in Suffolk County?"

"Second-rate."

"Gus!"

"Sorry. The answer is I can't tell you. Even if you threaten to walk out that door right now and never come back, I can't tell you. Please just take my word for it. Slava is in serious trouble."

"Why doesn't Slava go to the police?"

I laughed in spite of myself. "He can't. Sometimes there are things we—the cops—can't solve or even know about."

"But what's any of it got to do with me?"

"Lagunov thinks I know where Slava is, and by proving to me he can get close to you, he's trying to motivate me to give Slava up."

"Do you know where he is?"

"No, not really, but that won't matter to this guy." I walked up to her and clamped my hands around her biceps. "Maggie, will you do something for me?"

"Depends. What is it?"

"Will you go to Detroit now? I'll drive you back to your place and pack with you. I'll pay your airfare and hotel until the rest of the cast shows up. Just please do this for us."

"First you don't want me to go, then you can't get rid of me fast enough." The worried expression on her face gave the lie to her words.

"C'mon, Maggie."

"I can't . . . not today, at least."

"Then you're thinking about it?"

She rested her head on my shoulder, pressing her face against my chest. "Of course I am. I'm no hero."

"Tomorrow?"

"Okay, Gus, tomorrow or as soon as I can. I have some stuff to cancel and to get coverage for, but that should work."

I just stood there holding her for a minute, my guts all torn up inside. After John's death I had vowed that I would never let anyone get close enough to me to hurt me the way he had, that I couldn't risk suffering like that again. But here I was and it was already too late for me to do anything about it.

"What are you doing here, anyway?" I asked finally, trying to avoid the knot in my belly.

She pushed her head back and stared up at me.

"You're not the only person in this who's going to miss someone. I needed to be with you. Thinking about not being around you for months . . . it's getting to me, Gus. Last night I could barely get through the gig. I was aching for you."

I cupped her chin in my hand and kissed her softly on the lips. "Let me make the ache go away . . . at least for a little while."

She didn't argue or say another word.

38

The ferry ride across to Shelter Island from Sag Harbor was a short one. The ride from Bohemia had taken considerably longer, though not nearly as long as it might have taken after Memorial Day. Any trip out to the Hamptons after that becomes a test of a person's road-rage threshold. Most people don't realize just how far it is from the middle of Suffolk County to "out east." Even in the unlikely event you have smooth sailing on the LIE, it comes to an abrupt end once you hit Montauk Highway. Then you crawl, and that's on a good day.

There was a time when I was a kid that there had been a plan to widen the roads out east along the route of the high-tension lines, but it never happened and now it never would. The people who lived out here wouldn't put up with it. They had too much money and too much influence to be ignored. It was to laugh, I thought, as the little flatbed ferry pulled away from the dock, Shelter Island looking close enough to swim to. The poor people in Wyandanch or North Bay Shore didn't have enough clout to get their streets plowed in winter or their potholes fixed in spring, let alone dictate to the politicians how wide to make their streets or where to put them. Most people can't understand desperation as a by-product of powerlessness. Cops see its effects every day.

I tried forgetting about how the poor got the shit end of the stick, at least for the moment, focusing instead on the approaching shoreline. I'd lived my entire life on Long Island, but I'd never been to Shelter Island. I'd been close, been to Sag Harbor a few times with Annie for fancy seafood dinners on our anniversary and on my thirtieth birthday. I'd been out here once with Maggie to see a friend of hers do a dramatic reading. On a map, Shelter Island looked like a forgotten piece of food stuck between the jaws of a prehistoric crocodile. What it was, in fact, was an irregularly shaped wedge of land in the waters between the North and South Forks of eastern Long Island. Like the rest of Long Island, it had once been home to an Algonquin Indian tribe. These days it was home to twenty-three hundred mostly white people who liked and could afford privacy. I was interested in only one of them—Roberta Malone, the ex-wife of Micah Spears.

When I got off the ferry, I took a ride around the island. It was a sleepy place in April. Maybe it was always so. I had no way of knowing. Although some huge, inappropriate houses dotted the landscape, most of the houses had an old Long Island feel that harkened back to the East End's fishing past. Many of the homes, even the newer, larger ones, were done up in wooden shingles and I liked that there weren't stockade fences everywhere. Once I'd satisfied my curiosity, I wound my way around to the southeast corner of the island to a street called Bootleggers Alley. If my information was correct, Roberta Malone lived off Bootleggers in a house overlooking Crab Creek.

I was glad to see that the house matching the address was a lovely but simple little saltbox with a gravel driveway. There was a weathered gray Range Rover parked on the gravel. No wax had touched the four-by-four's body in years. I parked at the edge of the driveway, walked straight up to the door, and rang the bell. As I waited, I noticed the air smelled different here. Unlike much of the rest of Long Island, which smelled of car fumes and wet grass in April, this piece of Shelter Island was relatively free of exhaust. Instead, the air had the slightly sour tang of marsh-land and salty grace notes of brackish water.

"Back here!" a woman's voice called out. "Come on around."

And there I found Roberta Malone, dressed in a ragged, paint-dappled sweater. She was seated on a stool, her back to me, an easel and canvas in front of her. To her right was a snack table on which were an assortment of silvery tubes and brushes. She used about a third of the tabletop as her palette. She was swiping at the canvas with a wide brush, broad swaths of azure appearing on the off-white material where I assumed the sky would be. Then she dabbed the brush in a glob of white and swirled it. I liked watching the way she moved the brush. There was an air of confidence and skill, of grace about her.

"How can I help you?" she asked, only half turning to look at me, continuing to paint as she did so.

"Micah Spears."

Her bearing changed. Her square shoulders rounding, her yardstick-straight posture slumping. She put the brush down on the snack table. Whatever inspiration she'd been feeling before I came around back seemed to have disappeared with the mention of her ex's name. She spun on her stool to face me, but her lovely face was distorted by pain. I recognized that sort of expression. I knew what it meant. She was trying to smile at me, but her lips just wouldn't cooperate and the corners of mouth turned down more and more with each quivering attempt at good humor.

"Who are you?" she asked.

"My name is Gus Murphy."

"Is that supposed to mean something to me?"

"I'd be shocked if it did."

She took the blue-and-yellow scarf off her head and shook out her hair. "Then why are you here?"

"Like I said, I'm here about your ex-husband."

"But what about him, and what makes you think I'd talk about him to a stranger?"

"Because I'm working for him."

Her pained expression shifted to a sort of bemused confusion.

"You have my sympathy, Gus Murphy, and you've also got my attention. The question is, what are you going to do with it?"

"How about I explain myself?"

"That would be a good place to start."

"I'm a retired Suffolk County cop," I said. "Mr. Spears hired me to look into his granddaughter's homicide."

That bemused expression of hers vanished, replaced by something else. It wasn't grief. I knew grief. This was something else. More like sadness than grief.

"She wasn't your granddaughter?"

Roberta Malone shook her head. "No. I was Micah's second wife." She cleared her throat and said, "I'm confused. I thought the police had the man that murdered Linh Trang. Some sort of gang thug."

"They do, but they don't know why he killed her. That's the reason I'm working for your ex. He wants to know why."

Then she did the same odd thing her stepson Kevin had done. She laughed. It was a knowing laugh, with a sneer and resignation in it.

"Micah would want to know, wouldn't he, especially because it was Linh Trang?"

Now I was confused. "Why would you say that? Why especially because it was Linh Trang?"

Seeming not to have heard the question, she stood and moved past me toward the back door of the saltbox. Her strides were as long and graceful as her brushstrokes.

"Would you like something to drink, Mr. Murphy?"

"Gus."

"Would you, Gus? I would."

She disappeared into the house and I disappeared after her. I found her in the tiny kitchen, mixing herself a vodka and lime juice.

"A gimlet," she said. "Very old-fashioned stuff, but I've got a real taste for them. Please, have one. I would say I don't like to drink alone, but that would be a lie. I don't like lying, Gus. Do you?"

"Lying? I didn't used to. I'm not so sure anymore."

"What changed?" she asked, mixing me a drink. "I mean, for you not to be sure."

"My son died a few years ago. Just like that." I snapped my fingers. "He was playing basketball and then he was dead."

"I'm sorry."

"You're sorry. I'm sorry. Everybody I know is sorry and he's still dead. That's why I'm not sure anymore."

She nodded, said nothing. I was thankful for that. Her silence and nod were more eloquent than the thousands of heartfelt words spoken to me on the subject of John's death. All those words . . . I came to resent them. She handed me the short glass with the greenish drink in it and raised her glass. "To your boy."

I raised my glass and we both drank. The drink was tart and a little bit sweet. My taste ran to bourbon, but I liked the gimlet just the same.

"It's my turn to be confused again, Gus. If you're working for Micah and it's about why Linh Trang was murdered, what are you doing here? You don't think I had anything to do with it. I know it got ugly there at the end between Micah and me, but—"

I laughed. "No, it's nothing like that. It's just that I can't get anywhere, not really. But I got this crazy idea in my head that I won't get anywhere about Linh Trang until I know more about your ex."

"Micah was right to hire you, Gus," she said, mixing herself a second. "You're a perceptive man."

"Then you'll help me out?"

She laughed again. "Shall we go outside?"

It wasn't a question. Roberta Malone took her fresh drink and headed out the way she had come. Outside, she plopped herself down in a lounge chair, its back raised. Even that she did with an almost balletic flair. She patted the arm of the Adirondack chair next to her.

"Sit, Gus. Sit."

I did.

"So," I said, "can you help me out about your ex?"

"I can't."

"You can't or you won't?"

She rubbed her chin and cheeks with her right hand, a smear of blue paint spreading across the line of her jaw. I didn't point it out. I wanted to hear what she had to say.

"Technically, I suppose, I won't help you, but for all practical purposes, it's that I can't. You see this house, this property, that car in the driveway, and the vodka you're sipping? Most of it's paid for by your employer, my ex-husband. It's all part of the settlement. Micah was very generous with me. I won't want for much for the rest of my life, but the terms of the settlement are quite clear and specific. If I discuss my past relationship with Micah or divulge any information about him, any at all, I risk all of this. Now, you seem like a really nice man, and if I was about twenty years younger, there's no way you'd be leaving here without bedding me, but nobody's that nice or sexy enough for me to jeopardize my future security. No one."

"I'm wounded," I said, putting my hand on my heart. It was easy to see she was girding herself for pushback and that if I went at her straight on, she'd slam the door shut on me. "But I understand. I mostly depend on my pension now and I wouldn't do much to jeopardize that, either, not even for you."

She smiled at me and there was no mistaking the glint of mischief in her eyes.

"Did you love him? Are you allowed to tell me that?"

She hesitated, sipping her drink, thinking.

"I loved him something fierce, Gus. Never loved a man more in my life. I'll never know that kind of love again. It had a kind of life of its own."

"But then something changed that. What?" I said. "Did you know Linh Trang had been forming a kind of secret relationship with him and then something happened? Blew it all apart."

She took the remainder of her drink in one swallow and her jaw clenched tight. She said nothing.

"Look, your ex isn't the nicest guy I ever met, but I've gotten the sense that people think he's some kind of monster. I was a cop for twenty years and I met some monsters, but—"

Roberta Malone stood up. "I think it's time you leave, Gus. I've enjoyed meeting you. I really have, and if I'd had another drink, those twenty years in age would have stopped mattering to me. But you're straying into territory I can't go to. I won't go."

"Okay. I get the sense you want to talk to me. I'm pretty good at reading people. If you decide to point me in the right direction, I'm at the Paragon Hotel in Bohemia. Just ask for me and they'll put you through."

She shook her head. "That won't happen."

"Okay. Thank you, anyway." I offered her my right hand. "I enjoyed meeting you."

She pushed my hand away, clamped her palms on my cheeks, and kissed me square on the mouth. Nothing silly. She didn't part her lips or thrust out her tongue. There was an oddness to it. Though her lips were soft and warm, there was a grayness and chill in the kiss. It was a kiss born of alcohol and some desperation, I think. I didn't encourage it and I didn't fight it. I let her play it out. She needed to, and sometimes you just have to let people do what they need to do. There are all sorts of kindnesses in the world. When she was done, she moved her cheek along mine until her lips were touching my ear.

"Micah Spears wasn't always Micah Spears."

That was that. She let go of me and retreated into the house without looking back. I took a last look at Crab Creek and another at her unfinished canvas. The canvas was mostly empty but for those broad blue strokes I'd witnessed her apply when I first got there. I spent a few seconds thinking about how the painting might come out in the end. Mostly I wondered about what she had whispered to me after the kiss. When I looked in my mirror to back out of the end of her driveway, I noticed some blue had rubbed off on my cheek. I took a napkin out of my glove compartment and wiped it away. The paint was gone, but the chill of her lips on mine lingered.

39

got the call on the way back to the Paragon. In the jumble of the last few days I either forgot or hoped the call wouldn't come. You'd think I would have learned my lesson about hoping by now. Where had hoping ever gotten me? Where had it ever gotten anyone? It was Detective Dwyer on the other end of the line, and all the hoping in the world wasn't going to stop her from saying what she'd called to say.

"Monday noon, at the Sixtieth Precinct. The ADA will be there, so you might want to bring that lawyer you like threatening us with."

"Tuesday."

"Monday."

"Dwyer, I'm working late tonight. I'm taking Sunday off. Besides, my memory is especially bad on Sundays. So it's Tuesday, and then only if my lawyer is available."

"Tuesday, noon."

She hung up without a goodbye or telling me to have a good day.

I put in a call to Asher Wilkes, expecting to leave a message, but he picked up.

"Gus Murphy, is that really you?" he asked, his resonant voice clear as ever despite the road noise. "Hell, I haven't heard from you since—"

He stopped himself abruptly, remembering that the last time we'd dealt with each other was after John's death. Parents spend a lot of time, once they reach a certain age, preparing for their own deaths, planning how to divide their estates among their children. For all the right reasons they spend very little time preparing for their children's deaths or planning the division of their assets. Nonetheless, John's savings and his few possessions had to be dealt with, and Asher had helped us through the surreality of it. He didn't do divorce work and wouldn't have gotten between Annie and me even if he had, so the dissolution of our marriage was handled by strangers.

"How are you doing, Gus? I read about you in the papers last year. Fucking Jimmy Regan," he said. I imagined him shaking his head. "I knew he was no saint, but I never would've figured him for that."

Of course he knew Jimmy Regan. He knew a lot of Suffolk cops because Asher had been an assistant district attorney in Suffolk, and not just any ADA. He was a high flyer, a superstar. Word was that he was being groomed for the top spot after the old man retired. He would have been the first African-American elected DA in Suffolk's history. The Department of Justice got to him first and made him a prosecutor for the Southern District of New York. Once again, Asher rose quickly through the ranks and was being talked about as a future attorney general, but one day he threw his big future away, trading it all in for a job as a public defender back in Suffolk County. He'd given that up a few years ago to start a small private practice.

"And how many people would've figured you to throw away a shot at being AG?"

"You know why I did it," he said, his tone suddenly somber. "You were one of the good guys, Gus. You saw how the system chews kids up."

"I know, Ash. I saw. I was just saying. From the outside, you never really know someone. Shit, sometimes we barely know ourselves."

"Amen to that. So, to what do I owe the pleasure?"

"What are you doing in the office on a Saturday at this hour?"

"I got some tough cases coming up, but never mind that," he said. "Why are you calling?"

"I need help."

"People who call lawyers usually do."

"Good point. Tuesday, I need you to come with me to Brooklyn."

"Why, you turning hipster on me, Gus? We going to Greenpoint or Williamsburg?"

"Funny man. No, the NYPD thinks I'm a material witness and believes I'm holding out on them."

"I suppose I shouldn't inquire as to the validity of their beliefs."

"Not unless you're in the mood to get lied to."

He laughed at that. "A client lying to his lawyer, how novel. So, what time?"

"I need to be in Coney Island at noon."

"Hold on . . . hold on, let me . . . Pick me up at my office at ten. You can explain the situation on the way in. Afterward, you can treat me to some hot dogs and Nathan's fries or some other Brooklyn delicacy. Though I do love me some of them Nathan's fries. Best on the planet."

"Ten it is."

Asher was a good man, maybe the most honest human being I'd ever known. He'd thrown his big career away because of a kid named DeShawn Pickette. Asher was connected to Pickette because he'd prosecuted him. I was connected to Pickette because I'd arrested him. DeShawn was a sixteen-year-old black kid from Wyandanch—the same town Asher had come from—who'd been in the system since he was eleven, so that when he and two fifteen-year-old friends used a toy gun to rob a 7-Eleven on Jericho Turnpike in Commack, nobody was looking to give him the benefit of the doubt. Especially not Asher Wilkes, who, with the blessing of the then DA, charged DeShawn as an adult and steamrolled his inexperienced and overwhelmed public defender. Not unexpectedly, DeShawn got the max.

Asher admitted to me once that he'd pretty much forgotten DeShawn Pickette fifteen minutes after he was sentenced.

"I was too busy steering my own ocean liner to give a shit about some asshole fuckup kid who came up out of the same streets I did. You don't lose sleep over a swatted fly and I didn't lose any over that kid."

Asher's attitude changed in February 2009 when he read in the paper that Pickette, after four years in Dannemora, had hung himself in his cell.

"The name sounded familiar," Asher said. "So I went back and reviewed the case. And when I saw that he was sixteen when I prosecuted him, that he'd been kicked around from one foster home to another and that his lawyer wilted when I blasted him for even suggesting a plea bargain, I took a hard look in the mirror and a harder look at the system. I didn't like what I saw wherever I looked. Suddenly, Gus, I wasn't so interested in power and a title, my record or my pride. I realized there could be no broader justice without individual justice. DeShawn Pickette deserved punishment for what he did, but he deserved justice, too, and maybe a little bit of compassion. He got way too much of one, some of another, and none of the last."

I didn't suffer from the same guilt as Asher. All I did was arrest the kid and his pals, but Asher and I would always be connected through DeShawn.

When I pulled into the lot at the Paragon, I made another call. This time I got what I expected—Charlie Prince's voice mail. I told him that I was curious about Linh Trang Spears's movements on the day of her murder and asked him to call me back. I sat there for a few minutes, thinking about John Jr., about TJ Delcamino, Linh Trang, and DeShawn Pickette. I didn't reach any grand conclusions beyond the fact that there was a lot of pain in the world and that it wasn't likely to end anytime soon.

40

I was distracted that night, so distracted that I had one of the other guys work the door, something I almost never did. It wasn't like I was confused about the cause of my preoccupation. I had a grocery list of reasons to preoccupy me, not the least of which was getting Maggie the hell out of New York. How many people, I wondered, go to Detroit to be safer? Since my initial shock at hearing the news about Maggie getting the part, it hadn't really struck me again that I wasn't going to see her for months at a time. Well, about an hour into my shift, it hit me like a sledgehammer. Sure, I had time and money enough to go see her wherever the play went, but that would be a day or two here and there on either side of that night's performance. At least she was coming to spend the early morning with me before I took her to the airport and put her on the plane. I took some small comfort in that.

The waves of heartsickness over Magdalena's leaving were kind of the baseline distraction. There were also the worries I had about Tuesday's meeting with the detectives and the Brooklyn ADA. Slava had given me the number to give to Lagunov if I had no other choice, though with Maggie out of town, that wasn't going to happen. I wouldn't turn it over to the cops. I owed Slava that much.

Although my confidence was bolstered by knowing Asher Wilkes would have my back, my fucking with the cops didn't sit well with me. Narvaez and Dwyer may have made it easy for me to see the situation as me against them, but it wasn't. Not too long ago, *I* was one of them. Nor had it escaped my notice that Micah Spears had hired me because Rondo Salazar wouldn't talk to the cops. Hypocrisy isn't relative or situational, and mine was starting to give me a bellyache. There were parts of the new me I guess I didn't love too well.

But the thing I couldn't get off my mind was the weird scene that had played out between Micah Spears's ex and me. Through the course of the night I found myself touching my lips, remembering her kiss, the smell of lime and vodka on her breath, and replaying the words she'd whispered in my ear. Though it had been a fine first and final kiss, it wasn't that I was recalling it as the beginning of a fantasy or because I'd been aroused by it. As handsome a woman as she was, what I recalled most was the desperation and the chill in Roberta's kiss. I couldn't shake the feeling of darkness about it and about what she had said about Micah Spears not having always been Micah Spears. Was she playing games with me, being cryptic? Was Spears not Spears in the way I was no longer who I used to be, or was she telling me something so obvious I was blind to it? That's what I was thinking about when Mike Parson came over to me.

Mike was a retired city cop I went to high school with and who did some Saturday nights with me at the Full Flaps.

"You okay, Gus?" he asked, concern on his face.

"Yeah," I lied. "Why you asking?"

"'Cause the DJ's playing 'Rock Lobster' and you haven't moved."

When I laughed, he laughed. It never occurred to me before that everyone who worked the club noticed my habits. But of course they did. They were all cops like me.

"I missed my cue," I said, standing up from the barstool I'd been keeping warm. "I'll be back in a few."

Outside, the air was pretty raw for April and you could smell the coming rain, sense it looking for any excuse to start. The cigarette smokers were huddled even closer together than usual, the men's collars turned up against the chill, the women furiously rubbing their bare arms, still pale from winter. Tonight they mostly nodded their greetings to me as I passed, many of them shuffling from foot to foot. I looked at my watch. It was just past midnight and the sound of the B-52s seemed to carry better in the thick air. There was just no escaping them.

As I approached the corner of the hotel, somebody threw a heavy fist into my gut that felt like it tore through my skin. It knocked the wind right out of me and sent me to my knees. Even as I scrambled to get up, I thought that this was getting ridiculous. This time I hadn't heard or seen him coming, nor had I sensed his presence. Well, I sure as hell knew he was here now. My attempt to get up was futile. My body was preoccupied with trying to get some oxygen back into my system. Though even if I had managed to make some progress toward the vertical, my friend with the heavy fist seemed more interested in keeping me right where I was. He drove his foot into my ribs, twice, making sure I felt it good. I felt it, all right, but nothing about it was good, and those kicks didn't exactly help me catch my breath. I rolled over on my right side and reached for my ankle holster.

"That was for Jimmy Regan, you piece a shit," he screamed at me after delivering that second kick.

I didn't recognize his voice.

"And this," he said, busting me in the gut again, "is for sticking your nose into my case, asshole."

Now I knew who it was: Tony Palumbo, Charlie Prince's partner.

"Yeah, you cocksucka, I heard your message. Who the fuck do you think you are, messin' around in my business?"

He was screaming, his face a twisted, angry mess, and I saw him swing his right leg back to kick me again. I tensed, but the kick never came. Tires screeched and I saw Palumbo jump out of the way. I recognized the car. Maggie's.

A door slammed and Maggie was screaming, "Leave him alone. Leave him alone."

Palumbo froze for a second, not sure what to do.

"Get back in your car!" Palumbo said, pulling his shield out of his pocket. "Suffolk County Police. This is a police matter."

Maggie wasn't having it. "Oh, yeah, good. Do you usually beat suspects like that? I think I'll call nine-one-one and see what they have to say."

The car blocked my sightline, but I got the sense that Maggie had her phone in her hand.

"There's no need for that, ma'am." Palumbo's voice was suddenly brittle.

"I disagree, Detective. You are a detective?" she asked, knowing the answer. "That's a detective shield, right? What's your name, Detective?"

He didn't answer, but Maggie had given me time to catch my breath, grab my gun, and get to my feet.

"Thank you, ma'am," I said, racking the slide to get Palumbo's attention. I figured with all those improv classes, Maggie would catch on. "I'm okay now. Please, go ahead and call nine-one-one."

"Yes, sir. I will definitely be a witness to what this detective was doing to you."

Palumbo raised his arms, facing his palms out, alternating his gaze between Maggie and me. "Whoa! Whoa! Wait a second! Wait a second! Ma'am, give me a minute to talk to this guy before you call." He turned to me. "Whaddya say, Murphy?"

I waited a few seconds to make Palumbo sweat. "Miss, could you give us a minute? Please wait in your car. If you see this man make any sudden movements, please call nine-one-one immediately."

She didn't answer, but sat back in her car and slammed the door shut. I heard the locks click.

Tony Palumbo was smaller than me, but that didn't make him a small man. He was a solid six feet of muscle and orneriness. He'd made detective and moved into Homicide because he'd been one of Jimmy Regan's chosen boys, not because he necessarily had any skill at the job. Now that Regan was dead, guys like Palumbo were on the fraying high wire without someone to catch them. They knew that the brass was looking for any excuse to cut ties with them and put as much distance between the department and Jimmy Regan's legacy as possible.

"Start talking, Palumbo."

"Fuck you!"

"Wrong answer, asshole," I said. "You hear that?"

"What? I don't hear nothing except that shitty music."

"You don't, huh? I hear it. It's the sound of your pension going up in smoke and of that cell door slamming behind you in Riverhead. You think anyone in the department is gonna run to defend you? One wave to the woman in the car and you're fucked."

Of course, he had no way of knowing that Maggie and I were connected or that she'd be in Detroit by Monday afternoon. All he knew was that she was a citizen who'd caught him in the act. He looked worried in spite of his bravado.

"What do you want?"

"Your complete files on the Spears homicide."

"No fucking—"

"You really are deaf, aren't you, Palumbo? I'm not fucking around with you here."

"You're bluffing."

I raised my left hand up to my ear to pantomime making a phone call and Maggie got the message. She held her phone up, the lighted keypad visible to Palumbo and me. She tapped nine, then one, then . . .

"Okay, okay, all right, for fuck's sake," he said. "The file's yours."

I banged on the roof of Maggie's car for her to stop. Then I looked inside. She'd gotten the message.

"I want something else. And when I tell you what it is, just say yes, because I won't stop her from dialing next time."

"And what do I get out of it?" he asked.

"You get to keep your pension and your shield and pretending you're any good at your job."

"What is it? What do you want?"

"If I need to speak with Salazar, you arrange it for me."

He laughed at me. People were doing that a lot lately and I wasn't so sure I liked it.

"What are you laughing at, asshole?"

"You. You wanna talk to him, fine, for all the good it'll do ya. I'll drive you there myself."

"No, thanks."

"How do I know you won't fuck me and have her call—"

"Because you don't know, Palumbo. Because I keep my word and because I like your partner." I gave him the hotel card. "Fax the file, the whole file, to the number on the card. And if I need to see Salazar, I'll call Charlie. That happens, this is all forgotten. Now get the fuck outta here."

I watched Palumbo leave and then got into the car with Maggie.

"Are you okay?" she asked. "What was that all about?"

"My sore ribs are sore again, but other than that I'm good. What was that about? It was about misguided loyalty and stupidity. You packed?"

"Bags are in the trunk. I'm gonna miss you, Gus Murphy."

"Not tonight you're not. Not tonight."

I grabbed her and kissed her and told her I loved her. She told me to shut up and to just kiss her again.

41

Airport goodbyes in the age of terrorism are empty, tearless affairs, usually marked by quick curbside kisses and rushed hugs in the face of honking horns and cops yelling at you to move on. Goodbyes were a bit more leisurely at MacArthur. Since Southwest had moved many of its flights to LaGuardia and all but one other airline had abandoned it, MacArthur was almost as popular as a pork store in the heart of Jerusalem. There were seldom tears shed by the people I dropped off at the airport. No one was going to mourn leaving the Paragon or scenic Bohemia, New York. I didn't drop off any parting couples or parents sending kids off to college or to the military. My usual drop-offs were bleary-eyed salesmen or tech guys impatient to get to their next stop. But Maggie was anything but my usual drop-off.

We'd spent all day Sunday alternating our activities between icing down my re-injured ribs and making love. There were tears, lots of tears. None of them tears of joy. We were both kind of heartsick at the prospect of being apart and of being forced apart sooner than we had to be. One day she would be there and we would have each other and then she would be gone. I don't think Maggie realized how it had felt to me the night she told me about getting the part, about leaving. It didn't have to make sense. It didn't have to be fair. I had long given up beating myself up over those constraints.

Maggie was also torn. She had to leave me behind to pursue her long-dormant career. I had helped push her into it. She was thankful for that, too, for my pushing her to get back to what she missed, but hurt by it, too. Life didn't have to make sense, and when it came to emotions, it seldom did. She was upset at me for making her leave earlier than she would have had to, mad at herself for loving me, for letting herself.

It had been my experience that there was never a shortage of hurt or anger anywhere in the world, that we were an angry species by nature and that we could more easily summon up anger than any other emotion. Certainly with more ease than love or fear or hate. It seemed that anger was always there, lurking just below the skin, a breath away, or around the next corner. Cops work in a world of it, were surrounded by it. I had fooled myself for most of my waking life that it wasn't so with me, that I had been spared the gnawing hurt and anger that seemed to come to everyone else so readily, eagerly. I had been spared from nothing. John's death had supplied me with all the hurt and anger a man could ever need.

As I drove the few blocks to the airport, I kept checking my rearview mirror. I was making sure that Smudge's shitbox was there behind me in the distance. This was a trick Slava had taught me. If you want to make sure you weren't being followed, have someone follow you. It was probably a waste of time, but if a man like Slava was afraid of Lagunov, I was going to be cautious. I guess I relaxed a little when I saw that the only thing between the ass end of my Mustang and the front end of Smudge's car was empty space.

I pulled up to the curbside check-in by Southwest and made to get out of the car. Maggie, who had been silent since we left the Paragon, grabbed my forearm.

"Don't," she said. "Please."

I opened my mouth to say something, but nothing came out. We had already set up plans for her to call or text at each stage of the trip. We'd set up an emergency word, an innocuous word that nobody else would recognize as a warning, in case she spotted trouble.

"Even if you think it or something seems wrong, you let me know," I'd told her.

She was angry at me for that, too. For letting her suffer the rebound from violence that happened sixteen years ago in Russia. Something that she couldn't have had less to do with even if she tried. I was angry at me for that, too.

Maggie slung her bag over her shoulder, walked around to the trunk, yanked out her suitcase, slammed the trunk lid shut, and rolled her suitcase to the outdoor check-in counter. I watched every movement she made, soaking in the little things she did, took deep breaths of the perfume she had left in her wake. She never once looked back, eventually vanishing from my view behind the walls and clouded glass of the terminal. She told me that this was only temporary, that even if the play was a big success, nothing ran forever, that casts changed. But nothing about this felt temporary. It felt very much like a last goodbye.

42

Felix called to me as Smudge and I headed to the coffee shop. I told Smudge to go ahead to get us a table.

"Gus, please come over here when you have a moment." His voice was high and he sounded agitated. The rich, dark skin of his Filipino face was paler than I'd ever seen it and he looked like he was fighting back a bad bout of nausea.

"You okay, Felix?"

"This came in the fax tray for you while you were gone."

He placed a thick pile of paper on the desk counter.

"Thanks."

"It is very disturbing, Gus. Please do not have other police files sent here if they are like that."

Felix's paleness made sense after I looked at the top several pages and saw arrays of Linh Trang Spears's crime scene and autopsy photos. They were rough to look at, even for me. One set of photos was worse than the other, but in different ways. The crime scene photos of her body, clothing soaked and crusted with blood, dumped into a pile of leaves and garbage, her milky, opaque eyes left open, were hard to take. Her lifeless body had been tossed away like a ball of dirty tissues thrown out a car window.

And an animal, maybe a fox, had gotten to her. So much blood had drained out of her that her skin was a ghostly bluish white.

But in their way, the autopsy photos were even more difficult to take in. The knife attack on her had been vicious, more brutal than I had pictured it in my head. Some of the wounds were more like gashes than punctures, as if Salazar had pushed the knife into her then yanked the knife across her body until he hit bone or something else that prevented him from going any farther. There were two of those wounds. Most of the other wounds were less horrific, but probably no less painful. Puncture wounds can be terribly painful, and depending on where the wounds were, it could take a long time to die. Given the nature of Linh Trang's wounds, I didn't imagine death had taken a long time in coming, and I'm sure shock set in pretty quickly. Every time I was on duty at a violent homicide scene or saw photos like these, I was glad families were spared the added burden of having these images haunting them. I could only imagine how hard they'd hit a gentle soul like Felix, given what they were doing to me.

"Sorry, Felix. It won't happen again."

He nodded, regaining a little color and turning to answer the phone.

Well, I thought as I walked toward the coffee shop, at least Palumbo had kept his word. I wondered if I would have to call in the marker on Rondo Salazar. After seeing what he'd done to Linh Trang, I was pretty sure I never wanted to be in the same room as that piece of shit. It was hard enough sharing the same island. I never had any moral objection to the death penalty, and after twenty years on the job . . . Let's just say that I wouldn't have lost a second of sleep if Rondo Salazar got put through an industrial meat grinder one limb at a time.

My objections to capital punishment were practical ones. I knew too much about the system to think it was close to mistake free. Juries were kind of like computers: the verdicts they churned out were only as good as the information they were fed and, even then, not always. Cops, prosecutors, judges, lawyers, juries—they mostly tried to do their jobs as best they could, but they all had different agendas and there was too much room for errors, lies, and loss of perspective. Executing the wrong person was worse than murder because it made everyone complicit. Besides, in New York State, it was practically academic. Rondo Salazar would be spared his life and spend the rest of it inside a cell somewhere upstate, preying on the weaker inmates.

It was no accident that I was having that thought as I sat down at the booth across from Smudge. Smudge had once been one of those weaker inmates. Everything about him screamed "prey animal," but with Tommy Delcamino's help, he'd managed to survive.

"How was it for you inside?" I asked, pouring the half-and-half and two Sweet'N Lows into my coffee.

"You know . . . it was rough. There's a lot of bad feelings inside. Everybody is pissed off all the time for like everything and for nothing. And they all need bitches and punching bags, and sometimes they're the same person. Look at me, Guth. I wasn't going to be anybody's bitch."

"You got smacked around a lot."

"Not too bad. Not as bad as some other guys. I was almost too easy to pick on. Then Tommy put the word out to leave me alone, and mostly they did. Tommy was a gentle guy in his heart, but when he got into a fight he always won."

I was going to drop it, but Smudge had something else to say.

"I don't know who thought of prisons, but they're fucked-up places. I mean, I know there are some people who belong in them and deserve them, but they're not good places for people. I don't know many people who come out better for being inside."

I didn't say anything to that and waited a beat or two to make sure he was finished. When I was sure he was done, I took out an envelope with cash in it and slid it across the table to him. He just folded the envelope in half and put it in his back pocket.

"There's a little something extra in there for you."

"But—"

"Forget it, Smudge. It's not a grand, so don't argue. You helped me out and it was Maggie you were watching for me, not some mutt."

He nodded and looked down at his coffee. "What's going on with you and Maggie?"

Before I could answer, my cell vibrated twice in my pocket. I looked at the text. It was Maggie. She was on the plane to Baltimore. That was all it said. Although the plane hadn't taken off and less than three miles separated the gate at MacArthur where it sat and the booth at the coffee shop, Maggie felt a million miles away.

"I don't know, Smudge. I don't know."

43

got four more texts. Landed in Baltimore. On the plane to Detroit. Landed in Detroit. Checked into hotel. There was no phone call. I wondered if there would be another phone call, ever. Last night had been so full of anger, hurt, and longing, and this morning's goodbye had been so strained that I didn't know what to think. Does everyone learn the hard lessons in middle age or was it just me? If I hadn't been so heartsick, I might have laughed at myself. When Maggie and I first met, when she was still Magdalena to me and the plan was that we were going to be just friends, I couldn't have imagined being this deeply involved. Could I have envisioned sleeping with her? Fuck, yeah. I was a straight man with a pulse, for chrissakes. But I didn't think I'd fall in love with her or think I'd be saying goodbye, not this soon. Shows you what I know.

After the last text, I shut off the Yankees game and looked through the murder file Tony Palumbo had sent me. I skipped the photo sheets, figuring I could go back to them if I had to, if I found some inconsistencies between Prince and Palumbo's notes and what I'd seen earlier in the photographs. Otherwise there was no point. That was what was so weird about my task. I knew who did it and I knew how he did it. There was little in the photos to suggest where he did it or why. Well, no, that was wrong. There was a lot of evidence in the photographs to suggest why.

An attack that vicious usually indicates rage on the killer's part. But where had the rage come from? Had I been wrong to dismiss the newspapers' convenient narrative about a childhood connection between victim and killer? Or maybe my scenario about LT going to a bar and coming across the wrong man at the wrong time had more to it than I had been willing to believe. Once I had a sense of her movements that day, I'd be better able to judge.

There wasn't much that I could find in the file about LT's movements on the day of her death. She'd left the house early to walk down by the water and to get a bagel and coffee. Abby said LT came back in at about nine with half a dozen bagels. There was a notation in what I assumed was Palumbo's handwriting—*Vic had everything bagel with cream cheese.* I understood the note. You never knew what would be important, and sometimes stomach contents could help establish time of death. Still, the note saddened me because it again made LT something more than just a perforated corpse. She was a complicated woman who struggled with her identity and who liked everything bagels with cream cheese.

As I read on I could feel sleep imposing itself on me and I'd had to snap my eyes open a few times. I found myself shaking my head to wake myself up. As if that ever really worked. I kept reading as best I could. After the bagel, Linh Trang had showered, then told her mom she had to go into work for a few hours. That got my attention. I wondered why LT had to go into work on a Saturday. It was mostly curiosity. Her movements after leaving work were of more interest to me than anything else, but I didn't get that far or, if I did, sleep blotted out whatever else I'd read.

I woke up to the sound of the hotel phone, loose pages scattered across the bed. My heart raced at the thought of Maggie at the other end of the line. All I could think about was how badly I had handled the situation, from the moment she told me about getting the part to making her leave town early. But it wasn't Maggie at all.

"Have you forsaken me, ya bastard?"

It was Bill, and though the sound of his phony lilt was a distant second to Maggie's voice, I couldn't recall being happier to hear it.

"Never. I'm glad you called."

"How's that?"

"I'm low, Bill. Feeling very low."

"We can't have that, now, can we? Come my way. Pick us up some chow and I'll supply the wine. What do ya say, boyo?"

"I say that I'll see ya in an hour."

"Whatever food you choose is fine with me. You can only imagine some of the food I've been forced to suffer through over the years. Christ in heaven, if I see another green-bean casserole, I'll be unable to turn the other cheek."

"No green-bean casseroles, Bill. I promise."

44

Asher Wilkes looked the part, which was another reason why he was always the guy singled out for the bright future and the brass ring. At six-three, two hundred ten pounds, he had a commanding presence and an athletic physique. If that wasn't enough, he was a handsome son of a bitch, with flawless dark mocha skin, a shaved scalp, and perfectly groomed facial stubble. Asher could have been Kobe Bryant's older, better-looking brother. And anyone who tells you good looks aren't a huge advantage in life is either willfully stupid or blind. The only crack in his armor was that he could no longer afford to dress as he once had. When your practice is grounded in lost causes, custom-tailored suits aren't part of the scene. I didn't mind that his blue suit didn't hang on him just so or that the collar of his white shirt was pilling. I'm sure none of his other clients much cared or even noticed. With Asher Wilkes at your side, no matter how bleak the outlook, you always felt like you had a puncher's chance.

"Nice ride," he said, folding himself into the front seat of the Mustang.

Asher turned to me and shook my hand. That was where the small talk and pleasantries ended. From that point on, he was all about business. He had me explain to him everything I could about the night in

Coney Island when Goran Ivanovich was executed. I was careful to do it in such a way as not to cause Asher any ethical dilemmas. People forget that lawyers are officers of the court and that there are certain things they cannot know and do not want to know. Cops never forget that. You learn early on how to skirt up right to the edge of things with the ADA and defense lawyers. Funny, everybody makes a big thing about cops lying in court—testilying, they call it. Maybe they should make a big deal about it, but you know what? Everybody lies and the biggest lies I ever heard in court didn't come out of a cop's mouth. It doesn't make it right. I know that. I haven't changed that much. I just wish the truth wasn't always in such short supply.

I told him about my previous encounters with the detectives and gave him my assessment of the partners handling the case.

"Narvaez is a prick and as subtle as a howitzer. He assumes everybody's lying and he goes from there. Dwyer is sharp and plays it close to the vest. She doesn't give much away. I don't think there's a lot of love between them beyond partner loyalty. Maybe you can use that."

Then I gave him some deeper background about Slava, Mikel, and Goran Ivanovich, but I neglected to mention the bombings and the three hundred murders they had been duped into committing. Were they duped? I only had Slava's word for it. It was odd that I trusted Slava without question. I hadn't asked myself whether I would have accepted the same story from another human being. From Spears? Maybe I hadn't asked myself because I knew the answer.

"Okay, Gus. Do you know where Slava is?"

"No."

"That the truth or something approximating it?"

"In between," I said. "I have an emergency number for him, but it's not for the cops."

"Who, then?"

"You don't want to know that and you don't want to know why."

"So we have no real bargaining chip if they decide to squeeze you?"

I knew what he was asking without asking directly. He wanted to know, if push actually came to shove, whether or not I'd be willing to give Slava up.

"If I was willing to give him up, Asher, I wouldn't have bothered you. I could have gotten any half-assed schmo to bargain me out of this. I could have done that myself."

"Fair enough. You let me do all the talking. All of it. You just sit there and look pretty."

"I can sit there. The other part . . ."

We didn't talk for the rest of the ride.

Inevitably my mind drifted back to my dinner with Bill the night before. He did have the gift of making me feel better about things even if there was no logic to it. Bleak didn't seem to be part of his vocabulary. I had to give him that. I'm pretty sure the two bottles of Sangiovese we drank with the fried chicken and biscuits didn't hurt. But now, out of Bill's orbit, the wine having long worn off, bleak was exactly how things looked.

Maggie still hadn't called. I was no closer to finding the reason why Rondo Salazar had killed Linh Trang Spears, nor did I have any idea if Bogdan Lagunov had gotten to Slava. I didn't know if I would ever have that answer. It was hard enough imagining my life without Maggie in it. I didn't want to think about my shifts at the Paragon without Slava there to pass the time. I hated the way people could become important to me without asking my permission.

THE SIXTIETH PRECINCT wasn't exactly a garden spot. A '70s concrete-and-light-brick shitbox, it lacked the character of the classic New York City cop houses and it was just old enough to be falling apart. A bored-looking uniform led us to the squad room, and when Asher and I walked in, Narvaez checked his watch to make sure we were on time.

"You're three minutes late," he said, that familiar nasty tone in his voice.

"Parking. We were actually ten minutes early."

Dwyer sat at her desk, facing her partner. She looked on impassively: always watching, always listening, always waiting for her opening. Behind Dwyer was a rumpled suit of a man. A rumpled, fifty-five-year-old brown suit, to be exact. He had unkempt gray hair and dandruff-speckled glasses and lapels. He looked like a lifer. The type who'd gone to New York Law at night, finished in the middle of his class, barely passed the bar, and who was thrilled to get a civil service job. It didn't make him incompetent, but he wasn't making me shake in my shoes, either. Asher's face didn't give anything away. I didn't introduce Asher. I wasn't going to talk. I knew he had meant what he said. Once we got up to the squad room, my mouth was only there for breathing and drinking water.

Asher stuck out his right arm to the rumpled suit. "Asher Wilkes," he said.

Rumpled Suit's eyes got big behind his glasses, real big. "Asher Wilkes," he repeated in a half-whisper. "*The* Asher Wilkes?"

Asher nodded.

"I'm Assistant District Attorney Michael Cohen. It's a pleasure to meet you."

They shook hands, Asher resisting any impulse he might have to ask Rumpled Suit if he was *the* Michael Cohen.

Asher nodded. "Pleasure's mine, Michael."

And then, as if on cue, Narvaez said, laughing, "Asher Wilkes, like in *Gone With the Wind*. Miss Scarlett, Miss Scarlett, I don't know nothing 'bout birthin' no babies. That Asher Wilkes? Like that?"

The only one laughing was Narvaez. Asher remained cool, his face impassive, but on the inside I knew he was clapping his hands together. Cohen looked like a pigeon had flown into his mouth and lodged in his throat. I stared down at the floor. Dwyer rolled her eyes, shook her head, and said, "You asshole!"

"What?" Narvaez asked. "What? I was only busting the counselor's balls a little. He's a big boy. He can take it."

Cohen moved his lips, but nothing came out.

"Excuse me, Detective Narvaez, but, for the record, that was Ashley Wilkes. And, just out of curiosity, did you just call me a boy? Do you have any notion of how racist and offensive your behavior is?"

"What? You're kidding me, right, Counselor? You telling me nobody ever—"

"Shut up, Detective Narvaez. Now!" Cohen found his voice, not as much of a rumpled suit as he appeared. He turned to Asher. "I'm sorry about that, Mr. Wilkes. Detective Narvaez is a little overzealous at times and—"

Narvaez shot out of his chair. "Who the fuck do you think you are to tell me to shut up, you little weasel?"

"Shut up, Richie!" Dwyer screamed, coming around her desk. "Just shut the fuck up."

She grabbed him by the sleeve and marched him out of the squad room. Listening to her alternate between screaming at her partner and trying to calm him down was sweet music to Asher's ears. I didn't mind it too much, either. Asher kept his expression fairly unreadable. Me, not so much.

After a minute of listening to the two partners going at it, Cohen said to Asher, "Do you think the two of us could have a quick chat?" He pointed at the interrogation rooms. "We could probably arrange to get your client out of here without much more bother."

"Let me consult with my client."

"Absolutely, Counselor. I think I need a drink of water. Take your time."

When Cohen walked away, Asher smiled at me and said, "Your take on Narvaez was dead-on. What a putz. I think I can make sure these two don't bother you again, or at least not until there's more violence connected to your friend Slava. There is going to be more violence connected to him, isn't there?"

I said, "You told me to keep my mouth shut."

He shook his head and made a face. "I'll take that as a yes. But let me see what I can do."

When Cohen came back in, Asher headed straight toward the interrogation rooms. Cohen followed. Dwyer came back into the squad room without Narvaez in tow.

"Where's your partner?" I asked, no gloat in my voice.

"Taking a walk to cool off."

"Where's he walking to, China? He was pretty hot."

She ignored that, pointing at the ADA and Wilkes, who were visible through the interview room's glass. "Cohen busy bargaining away our leverage with you?"

"No comment."

She twisted her mouth into what passed for a smile. Cohen stuck his head out of the room and asked Detective Dwyer to step inside.

"Here's where he tells me to leave you alone. But remember, Murphy, anyone innocent gets hurt, it's on your fucking head. Remember that, because I will." She put her face very close to mine, her breath smelling of stale coffee and failed peppermint. "Blood gets spilled and I don't care what the suits or the brass say. I'm coming straight for you. My partner will be the least of your worries."

She about-faced and marched into the interrogation room. I took her words to heart. As I'd suspected from the first time I met the partners, Dwyer was the dangerous one.

45

Lunch was part of my deal with Asher and he chose pizza instead of Nathan's, so we went to Tony O.'s. I may not have known much about this part of Brooklyn, but I knew about Tony O.'s. It was one of those pizza places, like Di Fara and Spumoni Gardens, that everyone knew about. Tony O.'s was all about the super-thin crust. We ordered two pies and waited.

"The execution of that guy Ivanovich," I said.

"What about it?"

"Happened only a few blocks from here. I didn't realize it until we parked. I drove right past this place when I was heading back to the island."

He didn't say anything to that.

"So, Gus, to be clear, you are probably not going to have to do this song and dance with the detectives again. They should stop harassing you now, but as I said at the precinct house, if there's more violence—"

"I understand. I get it. Dwyer made it pretty evident to me that she would eat my lunch if anybody else is killed. If I was in her shoes, I'd feel the same way."

"I hope this Slava guy is worth it."

"He saved my life, and I'm not being dramatic with you, Asher. If it wasn't for him, you would have either been at my funeral or defending me at trial."

"Do I want to know any of this?"

I shrugged. "It was all connected with what went down with Jimmy Regan and Pete McCann."

"Any fallout from that?" he wanted to know.

"Some," I said, rubbing my abdomen where Tony Palumbo had tried punching through me. "And some of it more subtle than others. People love their heroes and they don't like it when you expose clay feet, even when those clay feet are covered in other people's blood."

"I had a professor at Stanford who was fond of saying that when presented with a preponderance of hard evidence that refuted a popular myth, people will almost always choose to continue believing the myth. It's an important lesson for a trial lawyer to understand."

I didn't bother arguing with him. His professor was right and I sensed that I would be dealing with my destruction of Jimmy Regan's popular myth for years to come. Maybe for the rest of my life. The pizza came first. We did more chewing than talking, Asher and me.

My mind drifted back once again to my meal with Bill Kilkenny the night before and how I tried to pry more details out of my favorite ex-priest about Micah Spears. I'd detailed for him the strange encounter I'd had with Roberta Malone.

"She kissed you, did she? You do have a way with ladies, Gus Murphy. You surely do."

But I wouldn't let Bill slither out of it that easily.

"There was only the slightest hint of sexuality in the kiss, Bill. It was more a way of her to open up to me as much as she could. Apparently, she traded in part of her soul for her divorce settlement."

"And she said what to you, boyo?"

"Something about Micah Spears not being what he seemed. It wasn't so much what she said as the kiss and how she said it. It felt like I was cursed with knowledge."

Bill was a bit unnerved by that. Not much unnerved Bill Kilkenny. In the midst of my family's implosion following John's death, Bill was a rock—caring and sympathetic, available and loving, but never shaken by our fury and grief, not even when it was misdirected at him. He had served in Vietnam. He had been forced to kill, yet those few words I'd just said seemed to shake him.

"What is it, Bill? What's the deal with Spears?"

He tried deflection. "Cursed with knowledge, you say. A positively biblical phrase from a nonbeliever. There may be hope for you yet."

"Nice try, Bill. What is it with Spears?"

He shook his head at me. "I can't, Gus. I can't. I won't."

I didn't press. I owed him too much to push him, and it would have done me no good in the end.

I looked up from my pizza to see Asher taking a rest between slices. There was a distance in his eyes. It seemed I wasn't the only one whose mind had drifted.

"Where are you, Asher?"

"Just thinking."

"About what?"

"Not what. Whom."

I knew the answer. "DeShawn Pickette."

He smiled knowingly, sadly. "It happens when I'm around you, Gus. Hard not to think of him. Worst part is, there is a pile of files on my desk with the next DeShawn in it. Legal Aid lawyers in Suffolk got bigger piles on their desks and the ones in the city have even bigger ones on theirs. Sometimes I just want to throw my hands up and walk away."

"But you won't."

He laughed. "No, I guess I won't."

I changed subjects.

"Listen, Asher, if you were Googling someone and his history seemed only to go back to 1973, what would you think about that?"

"You mean if I was certain he was born before 1973?"

"Exactly."

"This a hypothetical?"

"I wish. No. I've gotten myself involved in something."

I told him the sad tale of Linh Trang Spears, her grandfather's desire to know the motives for her murder, and his offer of a foundation in John's name and a research donation.

"And this has nothing to do with your friend Slava and the reason we're here today eating this incredible pizza?

"Nothing at all," I said, raising my right hand. "Scout's honor."

"Sounds like somebody changed his or her name in 1972 or 1973. Easy enough to do. You petition the court for a court order. Name changes are public record, at least in New York State they are, and they have to be accompanied by a public notice in a newspaper. Wonder how that's going to work after there aren't any newspapers anymore." He shrugged, picked up a piece of crust, and said, "Give me the particulars. I'll have one of my paralegals or another lawyer look into it for you."

"Thanks, but I'm sure they have better things to do. Remember what you just said about the next DeShawn."

"I've got more volunteers than I know what to do with. They're young and they don't know any better. They have yet to develop that flat spot on their foreheads from banging it against the wall." He reached his arm across the table and put his hand on my shoulder. "Let me do this for you, Gus."

"Okay."

"Good, because the bill I'm going to send you for today isn't going to be a small one."

I made a stunned face. "What? I figured lunch would cover it."

"Figure again."

We both laughed at that, him harder than me.

The ride back to his office was a quiet one. Mostly I was thinking about Maggie and how I might make things right with her. I wondered if I would get the chance. I wasn't sure what Asher was thinking about, but I knew that at least part of the time he was wondering about how to make things right.

46

Traffic wasn't too bad, and we made it back to Asher's office relatively quickly, which, by Long Island standards, meant in less than two hours. With a bellyful of pizza, I was feeling pretty good about how things had gone in Brooklyn with Narvaez, Dwyer, and Rumpled Suit. When you have a lot of balls in the air at the same time, even one less to worry about is a big deal. Yeah, I was feeling all right until I noticed Building 40 of the Creedmoor Psychiatric Center looming before us. Building 40, with its mass and beige brick, looking like a perverse cross between a high school, a prison, and an Egyptian tomb, was one of only a few tall structures in the borderland area between Queens and Nassau County, the others being the three buildings in Maggie's complex.

I tried to squeeze thoughts of Maggie out of my head by filling it full of facts, half-truths, and stories I'd heard about Creedmoor. Like how Woody Guthrie had died there and how Lou Reed had been electroshocked into deeper madness in the place in 1959. It gave a whole new meaning to "Walk on the Wild Side." Before I got totally serious with Annie, I'd dated a woman who worked there. She told me how the full moon really did make the patients harder to manage and that by Friday the only difference between her and the patients was that she had the keys. I'd considered sharing those stories with Asher, considered making small talk to keep thoughts of Maggie at bay. In the end, I kept my mouth shut, because by trying to stop myself from thinking of Maggie, all I could think about was her. I swore I could smell her, her perfume, how it mixed with the rawness of her natural scent and how it filled the air after we fucked. It made me a little dizzy, gave me a knot in my belly, thinking that I might never experience Maggie again. I don't think I'd ever hurt that much before just from staring at a building as I passed.

After dropping Asher off, I thought about heading back to Bill's to hang out and kill time before my shift. I started his way and then decided that I had real work to do and that I'd only get frustrated with Bill's un-willingness to enlighten me about Micah Spears. It was still early enough to head back to Gyron, to talk to Carl Ryan about why Linh Trang had been called into work on a Saturday in late November. I knew from Jim Bogart that LT never made it home that night. So if I could find out when LT left work, I could narrow the time frame I had to investigate. The narrower the window between the time she left work and the time she was murdered, the easier my task would be. Maybe she had said something to one of her coworkers about where she was going after she was done. If she'd left around noon or one, she might have gone to get something to eat and I could check out the restaurants and delis in the area. If it was much later, I would check the local bars. I felt sure that if I knew where she went from work, I would have a good idea about how she had come to cross a fatal path with Rondo Salazar. If I knew where and when they crossed paths, I would almost have the why I was search-ing for.

Pulling into the Gyron parking lot, I didn't see Carl Ryan's Maserati anywhere. That was okay. The place was still open, but it was late enough in the afternoon that management types might head home. And I had learned over the course of my time on the job that you learn more from receptionists, secretaries, and clerks than you learn from management. Management types always felt like they had something to protect.

Whether it was their jobs, an image, a piece of the company, or stock options was beside the point. People with less to protect didn't choose their words as carefully. They didn't worry as much about saying the wrong thing or keeping things politically correct. I didn't have a problem with Carl Ryan. He had been friendly enough and seemed fairly straightforward when I'd spoken with him, but he said what I would have expected him to say about both the company and Linh Trang.

Lara was at reception, flipping through a different gossipy magazine than she had been the first time I'd come calling. And this time when she saw me, she smiled. It was mostly a warm, friendly smile, but there was still a hint of the lean and hungry in it. It wasn't predatory or anything. I'd seen a lot of such smiles at the Full Flaps Lounge, and not all of them directed at me. There was a lot of loneliness in the world and a lot of lonely people sharing it. Appeared to me the cure for loneliness was so simple and so available, but very few people seemed to be able to overcome the low hurdle of jumping it. I projected myself ten years forward and wondered if I would someday be smiling at someone like Lara was smiling at me.

"Hey, Lara."

"Gus. How are you? Still taken?"

"Afraid so," I said, though I wasn't so sure anymore. "And still dented."

"You look pretty fine to me."

"Thanks. You're not looking too shabby yourself, you know. You coming to the club this weekend? I'll make sure your cover and first round's taken care of."

She lit up. "I just might come. Your bartender introduced me to a few guys. I just might have to date one of them."

I winked at her. "You wouldn't be trying to make me jealous, would you?"

"A little, maybe." She winked back.

"Is Carl here?" I asked, playing dumb. "He said I could come back and ask around if I had any questions."

"Sorry. He split about an hour ago. Can I help you with anything?" She wriggled her eyebrows and smiled that come-and-get-it smile.

"You are persistent, Lara. I'll give you that."

"Girl's gotta do what she's gotta do. How else do you think I rose to this high office?"

"Pretty and funny. As a matter of fact, I think there might be something you can do for me."

She tilted her head and smiled. "Like?"

"Linh Trang was here the day she was killed. It was a Saturday, the Saturday before Thanksgiving. Were you here that day?"

Lara made a face. It was part confusion, part disappointment, and part . . . I wasn't sure what that third component was.

"When I make a face like that," I said, pointing at her, "my therapist always says to put it into words."

"Therapist? What does a man like you need a therapist for?"

"My son died suddenly a few years ago and I've been struggling with things ever since."

I couldn't quite believe I heard those words coming out of my mouth so easily. For a year, two years after John died, I couldn't bear talking about it. Hell, I could barely put one foot before the other. I hated when people brought his death up or expressed any kind of sympathy or sorrow. Now, here I was, telling a woman who was pretty much a stranger about my therapy and about John. Then I felt a little sick at the thought that I had said those things not because my therapy was working or that I was finally accepting the reality of the world without my son in it, but because I was trying to manipulate Lara. *Christ*, I thought, *I hope that isn't it.* Then I laughed at myself inside for that, for thinking of Christ and hope.

Lara looked as if I'd kicked her in the belly.

"Oh, God, how terrible. I'm so sorry."

"It's okay, Lara. I promise. I am better now. So what was that face you made just before about?"

She exhaled, making a kind of resigned sigh. "Linh Trang was killed on a Saturday, Gus, right? So, no, I wouldn't have been here. There's no need for a receptionist on Saturdays. To tell you the truth, Gus," she said, putting aside her magazine and leaning forward as if she was going to tell me a secret, "I don't even know why they need a receptionist at all. We get maybe five calls a day and half of those are solicitations."

"But you told me about that big account you guys landed last year. Carl says the business is doing good and he's driving around in a Maserati."

She made another face. "Yeah, I guess, but it ain't like it used to be when I first started here. Back then the phones were always ringing and the floor . . . the floor was busy. Now"—she shrugged—"not so much."

"Well, a lot of the business must be done over the Internet these days, so the phones wouldn't be as busy."

"I guess." She was unconvinced. "I don't know. I guess it's because so many of the old-timers here, the guys who were around even before I started, are gone. Like I said, this place used to be humming. Now I don't know most of the guys, especially the ones who work in the box. They—"

I cut her off. "The box?"

"That's the area on the factory floor with all the warning signs and stuff."

"Yeah, I noticed that the last time I was here. What's all that about?"

"Oh, I don't know. It's some special manufacturing process using plasma cutters and lasers and stuff. The things in there use all these exotic gases and there's all special shielding. But it's whatever we do in there that pays my rent and helps pay for my daughter's treatment." Seeing the confused look on my face, Lara said, "Bella's autistic. She's why my asshole husband left me. It's why they all leave in the end. I used to be afraid to tell the men I dated. I would always go to their houses or to motels at the end of the night, but they would always find out about Bella. No one wanted that responsibility. I can't blame them. I don't want it sometimes. It's hard. It's really hard." Then she caught herself. "I'm sorry, Gus. I didn't mean to go there."

"That's okay."

"See, my can's pretty dented, too."

I moved the conversation back to where it had been earlier. "So you've never been inside the box?"

She shook her head. "No. Too dangerous. I got curious once, a few months ago, and Carl nearly bit my head off. He was screaming at me about insurance rates and what would happen if there was an accident. I guess I couldn't blame him. I don't even go on the floor anymore. Not worth getting yelled at."

My curiosity about the box was over.

"So you don't know why Linh Trang would have been here on a Saturday?"

"I guess because she had a lot of work, but I don't see how, really. She was so bored all the time, claiming there was never enough for her to do. Who knows? Maybe she was getting some end-of-year stuff ready. Usually only Carl and a few guys come in on Saturdays to get the shipping pallets prepped for the week, so you'd have to ask him."

"Maybe you're right about the end-of-year stuff. I'll ask Carl when I come back."

I looked at my watch.

She said, "You have to go?"

"I do. I've got to get back to the hotel. Remember, if you can think of anything that can help me or if someone here says something that might point me in the right direction, call me at the Paragon. They'll connect you to me or take a message."

"Got it."

"So I'll see you Friday night?"

"Count on it."

"If I'm not working the door, tell the guy that Gus says you're a special friend and he'll understand."

"Am I?"

I was confused. "Are you what, Lara?"

"A special friend."

"I think so, Lara. I think so. Would it be all right if I left the way I did last time, walking through the shop? I'd like to talk to some of the guys."

Lara's demeanor changed again. I could see she didn't want the responsibility, but I didn't come to her rescue.

"I don't think so, Gus. I'm sorry. Carl's the only one who can let you do that. Like I said, I have to protect my job and—"

"Forget it. I'll come back soon. Tell Carl I was here. Okay?"

"I will."

I waved bye and told her I'd see her at Full Flaps on Friday night.

Walking to my car, I took a mental snapshot of Gyron's building and wondered if there was something I was missing. Was I looking in the wrong place for the first falling domino that led to LT's murder? If I was, I was fucked because I had no idea where else to look.

47

My shift on the van had been like many in my time at the Paragon, like many of my shifts on the job: filled largely with downtime, empty minutes, and coffee. I had spent a lot of my adult life in between, waiting. I'd had to learn to wait without the stress of anticipation, without wondering what was coming next. To survive twenty years on patrol you have to teach yourself to take what comes when the dispatcher's voice calls your number. I thought I had mastered the skill, that it would serve me well in my retirement. I would just relax, free of expectation, free of anticipation. And it worked for about a year. Then one day the hospital called and I was reminded that there was no such thing as that kind of freedom. There is always something lurking around the corner. Always.

At the Paragon, my potential stress was limited. My stresses were like those of an old elevator operator. The route was easy to learn and my duties confined to pickups or drop-offs at the airport and the Ronkonkoma station. It was comforting to know that the next call wouldn't entail approaching a car with tinted windows on a dark street in the rain or walking into a living room where a woman with a black eye and bloody broken nose was still holding the kitchen knife with which she had resectioned her husband's intestines. I suppose it was why I had taken the job at the hotel in the first place. That and the free room. But there is no such thing as insulating yourself from the world. Annie used to just show up at the hotel at odd hours of the morning, unannounced. She would come to fight, to fuck, or both. She came to do something, anything, with the pain and grief. Then months would go by without her visits. I didn't miss those post-midnight visits, not for a second. Still, even without them, there was no escaping intrusion, because I never knew when darkness would hitch a ride from the airport the way it had when I picked Mikel up from MacArthur.

I woke up thinking of two women, missing them. Maggie, of course, for a thousand reasons, but I was also thinking of Aziza. Aziza was a Pakistani girl who had worked at the Dunkin' Donuts shop at the railroad station. I had seen Aziza almost every van shift I'd worked at the Paragon and we'd developed an odd kind of bond, a silent understanding between near strangers. We knew nothing about each other outside of the donut shop, but what we knew of each other, we knew perfectly. I knew that she was young and painfully shy. Still, she would nod, smile a gap-toothed smile at me whenever I'd walk through the door. She didn't nod at everyone or smile for anyone else, not while I was around. I know. I watched. What did she know of me? My coffee order, she knew that. She knew she didn't need to ask it. She knew to put the change directly in her tip cup. It was a ritual, a brief dance of the shy and the lost, something for two humans to hang on to when at least one of them desperately needed even a small reason to hold on.

One day last month I walked into Dunkin' Donuts and Aziza was gone. Gone with her was her shy nod and smile. Gone was our dance, forever. Khalid, the night manager, a fleshy, brooding man who had always eyed me with deep suspicion, told me that Aziza had gone back to Karachi to be married. He smiled as he said it. It was the only time he had ever smiled at me. He hasn't smiled at me since. Was I thinking about Aziza because I'd stopped in for coffee last night, waiting for a guest to get off the train at Ronkonkoma? Yeah, maybe. But I didn't think it was that simple, especially since I was thinking of Maggie, too. I guess what I was really thinking about was loss. I thought a lot about it.

When my cell buzzed, I didn't jump to grab it. I considered not bothering with it at all, but scooped it up on the way to the bathroom.

"Yeah."

"You're an enthusiastic bastard. Don't make me sorry I called."

I stopped talking.

"Maggie? Magdalena!"

"Well, you haven't forgotten my voice in two days. I guess that's something."

"I was just thinking about you," I said, my voice cracking. "You're all I've been thinking about, really. I'm a jerk."

"You expecting an argument from me?"

"I'll take anything you've got to give to me. I miss you. I really miss you."

"Then you should've married me when I offered."

"But you'd still be gone." *And you'd still be in danger.* I kept that last part to myself.

"I know," she said, this time with some ache in her voice. "I miss you, too, a lot. I don't know if I can do this. I don't want to be away from you for so long. You're the first good thing—shit, the only good thing—that's happened to me since my marriage broke apart. I wasn't really alive again until I met you at the club that night."

"I know all about that, Maggie. *All* about it. But don't come home. You need to do this for yourself and for us." I heard the words come out of my mouth, though I couldn't believe I was saying them. "Look, I'll be here when you get back, whenever that is. I don't want you to resent me for making you lose the one thing you've always wanted. Bitterness ruins everything, and I don't want that again."

"But it's lonely here, Gus."

"The rest of the cast and crew will be there in two days. And I may not know anything about acting, but I'm guessing you're having a bad case of nerves."

"Since when are you an expert on me?"

"Since the minute we met."

She laughed. I don't think I'd been that happy over a sound since I heard both of my kids cry at birth.

"I love you, Maggie. Make me proud of you."

"I will." She cleared her throat, hesitated, then said, "Any progress with . . . things?"

"No lying between us, right?"

"No lying."

"No, in some ways I feel like things are getting farther away from me. I haven't heard from Slava in days, but I haven't had any threats, either. And my other thing . . . I really don't know what's going on there."

"I love you, Gus Murphy."

"I love you, Magdalena. Go practice your lines. I'll call you tomorrow to check on you."

"Only if I don't call you first."

And that was the end of our conversation, my bladder reminding me that happiness can delay things for only so long.

After I was done showering, shaving, and getting dressed, I picked my phone back up. During the long periods of last night's downtime, I'd spent hours on the Internet, searching for absolutely everything I could find about Micah Spears. I mean everything, and not one thing I could find predated 1973, so he had to have changed his name. That said, I couldn't find any official record of the name change. But I wasn't calling Asher, not yet. He said he'd check into it and I trusted he would. I had no choice, anyway. Short of dropping in on every local county clerk and digging through their records, Asher was my only option.

No, I was calling Charlie Prince. The time had come, I decided, to pay a visit to Rondo Salazar. To see for myself if his silence was unshakable and absolute. Nothing else I was doing seemed to be getting me anywhere with the murder of Linh Trang. I don't know what seeing the murdering piece of shit was going to do to help, but it was worth a shot. It wasn't that I wanted to stare into the killer's eyes, to see into his soul. Not at all. That was bullshit for books and movies. I wasn't interested in his soul, if he even had one. I had stared into killers' eyes before and seen nothing, learned nothing. I figured it was either going to see Salazar or going back to the Spears family—who were unlikely to receive a visit from me with open arms—and trying to piece together whatever fragments of what LT's movements had been on the day of her death or starting from the absolute beginning. The thing was, piecing her movements together without knowing exactly where she had been killed felt like it would be impossible. Finding out where she had been killed was key, but there was nothing, not a single word or indication in the murder book that even hinted at where Salazar killed her.

"Prince," he said, picking up on the third ring.

"Gus Murphy. I'm calling in a favor your partner owes me."

"Yeah, I heard about that. How you feeling?"

"My ribs have felt better and I got a fist-size bruise on my belly, but I'll live."

"You sure you wanna go to Riverhead? I mean, this Salazar is a real motherfucker and he won't talk to you."

"Probably not, but go ahead and set it up anyway. Sometimes you gotta see for yourself. You know what I mean."

"I do. Give me a little while and I'll get back to you."

I clicked off and spent the time reading through the file again, this time making sure to look at the crime scene and autopsy photos.

48

had been to the jail in Riverhead before, but not as often as you'd think. Unless you're on a special detail or squad, uniformed cops spend most of the time with prisoners at their precincts or at the courts. Transporting prisoners after their arraignments or to and from Riverhead or Yaphank once they were in the system was the job of the Suffolk County Sheriff's Office. The same office that was in charge of the jails. I was glad not to be so familiar with the place. It was a max-security facility and about as welcoming as a third-degree burn.

Charlie Prince had made it all happen quickly and got back to me within fifteen minutes. There were four times during the day when you could visit prisoners: 2:30, 4:00, 6:45, and 8:15. Charlie had given me the choice. Although I knew I'd be cutting it pretty close, I'd picked 2:30. I wanted to get it over with and to give myself some time to do a little digging before my shift on the van if Rondo Salazar gave me anything to work with. I wasn't optimistic that he would. I mean, there wasn't a single indication that he would speak to anyone about the case and there was nothing magical about me. I had no secret words to say, no presto change-o, no abracadabra, to loosen his tongue. He didn't know me. I'd be just another Anglo fucking cop to him. I don't know what I was thinking, but by the time I pulled up to the booth at the entrance to the jail compound, it was already too late for thinking.

I gave my name to the sheriff's deputy in the booth, told him why I was there, and who I was going to visit. He didn't react, just told me where to park and waved me on. That said a lot about a place like River-head. Not even the mention of a killer like Rondo Salazar raised an eyebrow. There were several Rondo Salazars inside. Some worse than others. Some men who had beaten crying babies to death. Men who had raped, tortured, and strangled women. Rondo Salazar was special, but only to me. And then only because of who his victim had been. That said a lot about me and about the rest of us, too. We had grown so used to violence that as long as it didn't touch us, we weren't horrified by it. Or if we were, not for very long. The sad thing is, as any cop with a brain in his head and a heart beating in his chest can tell you, it does affect us, me and you, every one of us, even if we pretend otherwise.

I parked the Mustang in the lot to the left of the building under an array of solar panels. These things were turning up in parking lots all over the island, like at the Deer Park LIRR station and the state office building complex in Hauppauge. I'm sure they seemed like a good idea. Many things did on paper or in planning. These solar arrays were won-derful until a foot of snow slid off a panel onto your head or sheets of rain soaked you if you stepped out the wrong side of one. Luckily for me it wasn't raining, nor had it snowed in two months.

As I walked to the building entrance under a bright sun it was hard not to notice how the areas bordering the paths had been beautifully landscaped. Maybe the landscaping had been done in the hope it would draw your eye away from the endless coils of razor wire at the tops of all the fencing. Or maybe it was to remind visitors just how close they were to the Hamptons. Somehow I doubted that was it. I didn't imagine the people inside—prisoners or corrections officers—spent much time con-templating the polo matches or regattas that took place just a few miles east of where their days ticked by, slowly. Sure, the COs went home to their families after their shifts, but I couldn't help but think it had to rub off on them a little. Inside is still inside. My grandma on my mother's side, a rigid woman in a black dress, full of disdain and superstition, was fond of saying that if you danced with the devil long enough, it was the devil who changed you, not the other way around.

"You'll see, John Augustus Murphy, you will see," she would say, wagging her finger, with unmistakable glee in her voice.

It was never surprising to me that my poor mother was so reticent and shy.

At the end of the path, just before you got to the main entrance, there was a drop box for contraband. If people used their senses to begin with, we could build smaller prisons. But they don't. Basically the contraband drop box was a reminder to visitors that once you walked into the jail, you could end up in a cell yourself if you were carrying drugs or a weapon. You could toss whatever it was that you shouldn't have been carrying in there without penalty. It was sort of like that warning sign on the road about the last exit before the toll, only the toll here was much more costly.

Inside the door was a visitors' waiting area, with benches lined up like church pews and a TV up in one corner. There were rows of gray lockers in which visitors would place all belongings not allowed within the visiting area. Most prominent was a raised counter, behind which three COs sat, checking IDs and surveying the waiting area. The counter was raised up for a reason, the same reason a judge's bench was raised. Height equals authority. But I wondered if the people in authority ever considered how it made the people on the other side of the bench or counter feel. No one likes being looked down upon. No one. And the people here visiting loved ones probably didn't need any extra motivation to resent or hate authority or "the man." The place had a purgatory feel.

The purgatory pews were crowded with black and brown faces, with a few white ones sprinkled in here and there. Most of them were women, many with kids. Many of the kids crying or crawling along the benches,

WHAT YOU BREAK / 247

some running around the room. The expressions on the women's faces were frighteningly blank. *Been here. Done this. Let me see my man and get the fuck gone.* There were some tears, too. Tears in the eyes of mothers or wives or girlfriends who hadn't been here before, who didn't know the drill, who hadn't practiced the look. It was the kind of place for tears. I'm not saying that the guys inside didn't deserve to be there, most of them did. They knew the price to be paid for doing what they had allegedly done or if they didn't, they should have. It's the price everyone else paid that was hard to take, the price paid by the people in the visitors' waiting room with me. What had they done?

It didn't really matter. The citizens of Suffolk County had a low tolerance for crime and an even lower one for criminals. Maybe because their taxes were astronomical and they paid their uniformed services so well, they wanted to get the full bang for their bucks. Whatever the reason, the DA's Office got the message loud and clear. Their conviction rate was something like ninety-five percent. If you were poor, black, or Hispanic, their conviction rate was even higher. Once they charged you, you were pretty much fucked. It's why Suffolk County was known as Suffering County and why Asher Wilkes had switched teams.

One of the corrections officers at the desk recognized me. "You're Gus Murphy, aren't ya?"

I nodded, trying to figure out where I knew him from or if I knew him at all. He could tell I didn't have a clue by the look on my face. I wasn't the only one who could read faces. It was important for COs to nurture that skill. They spent their entire working lives in a hostile environment where one careless moment could end your life.

"I'm Joey Pezzullo, Ralph's little brother. We played a season of softball together back in the day."

Ralph Pezzullo and I had been on the job together. He had already been ten years on when I was assigned to the Second Precinct. He'd long since retired. I reached up and over the counter and shook Joey's hand.

"How is that hard-on brother of yours? Still a prick?"

Joey laughed. "Down in some buttfucksville town in South Carolina, playing golf and getting fat."

"You give him my regards, okay?"

"I'll do that." Then his expression changed. I knew the look and knew what was coming, but I had to let him say it. "Oh, shit, sorry, Gus. I heard about your boy. My condolences. How you holding up?"

"I'm surviving. It's better now than it was." I changed the subject. "Listen, Joey, I'm carrying and I didn't want to leave it in the car."

He smiled. "No problem." He reached out his hand. "Give it here. I'll locker it for you. Just come collect it on your way out."

I bent down, removed the baby Glock from my ankle holster, and handed it to him.

Joey took it. "Who you here to see?"

"Rondo Salazar."

"That piece of shit?" He made a face. "Why?" he asked, his voice low enough so that only I heard him.

"Doing somebody a favor, a relative of the vic's."

Joey shook his head. "He won't talk to you, you know."

"So I've been told, but I gotta see for myself. Charlie Prince, one of the detectives on the case, he set it up for me."

"No problem, Gus." He looked at his watch. "Go over there by the scanner now. We're gonna get started here any second."

"Thanks."

Basically, Joey Pezzullo had put me to the head of the line. I didn't mind. I would get through fast enough. I emptied my pockets into a tray and went through a body scanner like the ones at the airport. The CO on the other side of the scanner was about to wand me, but Joey Pezzullo called to him and shook his head to let me go on. The next piece of security I had to pass through was something called a sally port. I have no idea why it's called that, but it was kind of like an airlock, only with bars instead of doors. There's two sets of bars facing each other with a space in between them. One set of bars slide open, you step inside, and those same bars slide shut, locking behind you. When those bars show they are secured and locked, the bars in front of you open to let you into the visiting area. It's a way to guarantee no one on the prisoner side of the visiting area can get into the waiting area and then out through the doors.

On the other side of the sally port, we were met by a CO with a clip-board who matched our names to the prisoners we were scheduled to meet. The prisoners, mostly young men in yellow jumpsuits with the word VISITING printed on the back, were already behind low Plexiglas barriers. Holes had been drilled into the Plexiglas to make it easier for the prisoners and their visitors to communicate. The visiting area was arranged in a squared-off reverse S-shape that allowed for the maximum amount of visitors. The S-shape also gave the COs on either side of the glass a good view of what was going on between the prisoners and their visitors.

The CO with the clipboard held me back as he matched names to seat numbers to the prisoner on the other side of the glass. When he was done with everyone else, he said, "You're Murphy, right?"

"Yeah."

"Joey P. called ahead. Says you're meeting with Salazar. He's not here yet. But even if he shows up, he won't talk to you."

"That's what everybody says."

"Anyways, I'm assigning you a place that gives you a little privacy," he said, pointing toward the ass end of the room. "If he shows, maybe if nobody's in earshot, he'll do more than fart or tell you to go fuck yourself. He don't talk much, but he likes that phrase."

"I've heard it once or twice before."

"If he's not down here soon, I'll call over to Four West and see what's up."

He didn't seem hopeful. He gave me the number and I went over to the seat farthest away from the sally port, but one which afforded me the best view of the entire room. For a brief moment, when the visitors got a look at their loved ones behind the glass, the room went eerily silent. Even the crying, fussing kids seemed to sense that this was a big moment. Then the silence vanished as they made their way over to the seats on the visitors' side of the Plexiglas barriers. Some reached over the Plexiglas barriers to hold hands or kiss. The CO kept a careful eye on the activity but didn't bust balls about it, at least not at first. After a minute he told everyone to sit down. Everyone sat.

I waited, not overreacting to the fact that Salazar was MIA. I knew he probably didn't want to meet with me and that he was the type to resist until they forced him through the door. He had an image to uphold with his gang brothers. After all, they were the ones who protected him in here, and inside you needed protection from rival gangs. Even in a max-security facility like Riverhead, prisoners would risk longer sentences and additional charges by trying to get at rival gang members. It was part of their code, part of what kept them protected by their own gangs. The first person who observed that violence begets violence was a shrewd SOB, or maybe he'd spent time inside.

After a minute or two without Salazar showing, I got an uneasy feeling. I walked back over to where the CO was stationed to ask about Salazar.

"I'll check," he said and picked up the wall phone.

Somebody on the other end was talking to him. I could even hear some of the conversation, but I could only make out part of what was being said.

"Figures," the CO said to me after hanging up the phone. "The motherfucker chose yard even though he knew he had someone waiting for him down here. Most of the time we can't force these assholes to come see somebody if they don't want to, but for you, Murphy, we'll ask real nice. Go back over to your seat. He should be down in a few minutes."

I turned, but before I'd taken five strides, an announcement came over the loudspeakers.

"Cease all inmate movement. Cease all inmate movement."

And all of a sudden that uneasy feeling became a basketball-sized knot. Behind the Plexiglas, all the prisoners gave one another knowing looks. Some nodded in agreement. Others smiled.

One young black guy with a shaved head, his arms and neck covered in tattoos, shouted out what all the other prisoners were thinking. What I was thinking, too.

"Somebody be gettin' his ass kicked."

A few of the prisoners laughed. All nodded again. Some of the visitors looked horrified, but most of them kept that practiced blank stare. Maybe this time with a dash of impatience. *Yeah, uh huh, ain't none of it my worry. Jus' let me get on with my own business now.* I could see the CO was back on the phone, having a lively conversation.

"Murphy," the CO called me over, the knot in my belly getting bigger and tighter.

He whispered very quietly, "Somebody just stuck your boy in the throat in the yard."

"Dead?"

"Not yet, but he's making a red mess of his pretty green jumpsuit. If you're interested, they'll take him over to Peconic Bay hospital. From what my guy says, he doubts the piece of shit will make it there alive. There's a shiv sticking out of his neck."

"You know what happened?"

The CO shrugged. "Who the fuck knows with these clowns? Maybe he looked the wrong guy in the eye or he told somebody to go fuck themselves and that somebody was in a bad mood."

I left it there.

"Thanks."

I went back to my seat and waited until they determined it was all right for us to leave. As I waited I watched as the rest of the people in the room went back to their visits. It was as if nothing had happened, as if things were back to normal. But there wasn't anything normal about this place, about what had happened to Salazar, or about me being there.

49

'd gotten word to Charlie Prince about what had happened to Rondo Salazar. He thanked me for the heads-up and told me he'd get back to me. I had no idea that when he said it that he would do it in person, but when I returned from my first run to the airport that night, Prince was waiting for me on one of the threadbare couches in the lobby. The lobby was pretty dead, but Charlie wondered if we couldn't go someplace where we couldn't be overheard.

"Sure."

I walked him past the aviation mural and into the coffee shop. Although the coffee shop was closed by seven, management kept some lights on in case the guests wanted to get out of their rooms and find a quiet spot to work. We were alone and sat at the same booth I always sat at, the one with the wingtip for a table.

"Is he dead?" I asked, as we were sitting down.

"Nope, but the prick might as well be."

"How's that?"

"Salazar lost a lot of blood, a lot of blood. Fucked up his brain. He's in a coma and the doctor says he's gonna stay that way until he craps out down the road. You think people in comas can have nightmares, Gus?"

He wasn't really asking. He was hoping. "I'd like to think so. I'd like to think that motherfucker's gonna have one long, long nightmare."

"I don't know, Charlie. So what happened?"

"The sheriff's investigators are doing their thing as we speak, but it looks like it was planned out to get your boy. Had a bull's-eye on his back. Seems there was a kinda bullshit fight between a few guys on the yard. One Crip and, get this, a *cholo* from the Asesinos. Real loud, a bunch of screaming, pushing, and shoving. Lotta sound, but not much fury. Salazar was off to the side in a big crowd, whole bunch of guys around him, so it was hard to see what happened. At one point Salazar ducked down and disappeared from view. When the fight broke up and the crowd went back to doing whatever they were all doing, Salazar was already down and leaking all kinds of oil. Somebody tried to give old Rondo a lesson in dental hygiene by trying to brush his pearly whites through the side of his neck. Whoever it was giving the lesson used the sharpened end of a toothbrush on him. Stuck it in good and deep. It wasn't a warning, no sir. They meant to kill his murdering ass. Even better this way."

"No trial."

"Maybe in fifty years from now, when doctors figure out how to wake up the comatose asshole. By then I'll be retired or dead and beyond giving a shit."

But Prince's being here belied his words. He gave a shit, all right, or he would have just given me a call. No, he was here for a reason and I wanted to know it.

"Charlie," I said, "I'm glad you came by to tell me all this in person, but what are you really doing here?"

His expression changed reflexively, almost as if he was wounded by what I'd said. He even started to raise his palms in protest. It was no good and we both knew it. He put his hands back down before they got to his chest.

"Okay, all right, Gus. It's a feeling I got."

"Which feeling is that?"

"The feeling that tells me your poking around the way you been got somebody nervous, real nervous, and they were anxious to make sure Rondo Salazar wasn't ever gonna talk to nobody about nothing ever again, not in this lifetime."

"But he wasn't talking to anybody anyway."

"C'mon. You know how it is. He wasn't talking yesterday. He wasn't talking now. Maybe he wouldn't talk tomorrow, but there's no statute of limitation on homicide. He spends five, ten years in Attica and he don't like it so much. Too cold, so cold it makes his little nipples hard and he decides to talk up, to trade his story for time in a downstate facility. This way, hey, that's never gonna happen."

"Good point, but I gotta tell you, Charlie, I'm getting nowhere." I shrugged. "Until we know what happened to Rondo Salazar for real, it's all guesswork. Like the CO at Riverhead told me, maybe Rondo gave the wrong guy the wrong look or told somebody to fuck off and that was that. We've got no way of knowing whether his ending up on the wrong end of a sharpened toothbrush handle had anything to do with Linh Tang Spears's murder or my poking around."

Prince tapped his nose. "I trust my feelings and I trust this."

"Charlie, if every cop was right about their feelings . . ."

"I know. I know. Everybody from green rookies to Chief thinks he's fucking Sherlock Holmes and can look into a perp's eyes and tell he's lying or smell when this one's guilty and that one ain't. I know. So let's assume I'm wrong. Tell me what you been up to anyhow and I'll be on my way."

I told him about my conversation with Abby Spears, my meeting with Jim Bogart, and my little run-in with Kevin Spears. I told that I'd talked to LT's old roommate, Kaitlin Fine. I explained to him about LT's issues with her identity and her acting out. That's when Prince's eyes lit up. I knew exactly what he was thinking.

"Yeah," I said, "I was thinking the same thing after I met with the Fine woman and the boyfriend."

He gave me a look and made a skeptical face. "How you know what I'm thinking?"

"I wasn't a detective, but I was on the job for twenty years, Charlie. Give me a little credit. You're thinking that LT had a fight or something or saw something on TV or the net that made her feel insecure and she acted out. That she went to a bar and got completely shitfaced. That she ran into Salazar somewhere when she was drunk off her ass and things got out of control. Maybe she was gonna fuck Salazar and then changed her mind and Rondo wasn't in the mood for a woman to change her mind."

"So, okay, you do know what I'm thinking. Remind me to give you a medal." He reached over and clapped me on the shoulder. "You read the report, right? She had alcohol in her system when we found her. She would have had to have a lot of it in her for us to find some still in her."

"Maybe. Like I said, I had the same thought."

"But not anymore, huh?"

"I like it less than I used to. Even with her acting out, I guess I don't see her and Rondo ending up in the same bar. And say they did, say the scenario is just like you painted it, why didn't he rape her first if it was about that? And don't tell me because he was too polite or it went against his upbringing. It was okay for him to cut her up like that and murder her, but not rape her when she changed her mind? See, I think that's where it falls apart."

Prince stood up. "Well, I'm gonna check it out anyways. There's bars all along the South Shore where the Asesinos boys hang out."

"I thought you were done with the case, Charlie, now that Rondo is in a long-term coma."

He shook his head at me. "Still bugs me that he never spoke to us about it. I want it to make some kinda sense to me, even if it's fucked-up gang-thinking sense."

"I've also been to her old job twice," I said.

"Anything?"

"Not really."

"Okay, then, I'm outta here," he said, turning to go. "You think of anything else, you let me know."

"I'll do that. Same for you."

"Will do, Gus."

And he was gone. After he left, I had trouble not going over our conversation in my head. There was just something about it that bugged me. I couldn't figure out what it was, though. Maybe it was Charlie's delighting in Salazar getting stabbed in the neck. I wasn't exactly crying about it, nor was I clicking up my heels, either. Whatever was bugging me, I'd have a long shift to think about it.

50

was caught in between, and in between is never a good place to be.

It had been a pretty normal shift for a Wednesday night, which is to say, a quiet shift. Most of the activity at the Paragon is on either side of the weekend. My few runs were themselves quiet ones. No chatty guests wanting to be my best pal. No moaning guests bitching about the overwhelming floral odor of the soap or the poor quality of the towels in the hotel. It was my experience that people could find almost anything to complain about. When I first took the courtesy van job, it was all I could do not to pull over and scream at them about perspective. *My son just died, you fucking moron, and you're gonna sit there and cry to me about the goddamned fucking soap?*

On the job, I had always been able to control myself that way. When the gawkers would come over to me near a murder scene or fatal accident and whine to me about their neighbor's dog pissing on their lawn, I had all the patience in the world. Now, not so much, not on the inside. Inside me these days there was rage. A little less lately, but it was in me deep, right where the universe had planted it, and I didn't think it would ever go away. I used to fantasize about being who I once was, about having my old life back. Not anymore. The world was stuck with me. I was stuck with me, stuck in between who I once was and who I would become. But my current issue was less global. I still couldn't forget my talk with Charlie Prince. It was like that catchy but annoying song you can't get out of your head no matter what you do. I was also thinking of Maggie and how badly I wanted to hear her voice.

The plan was to sleep for a few hours and then call Maggie's hotel at a reasonable hour, but after fifteen minutes of squeezing my eyes shut and hearing Charlie Prince's voice describing what had happened to Rondo Salazar, I decided the sleep part wasn't going to happen, not yet, anyway. It was still too early to call Maggie, so I showered, shaved, and took myself to breakfast. Breakfast by myself kind of depressed me. It made me think about Slava, about how we hadn't had breakfast last Saturday and how we might never have breakfast together again. For all I knew, he was dead. I didn't like to think that. Sure, I was close to Bill, but that was different. Slava and I understood each other in a way only one cop can understand another. And we shared an unspoken bond, too, one that didn't have anything to do with wearing a badge or carrying a gun. I couldn't explain it even if I tried, but it was powerful.

After breakfast, I decided to go back over to Gyron and have that talk with Carl Ryan. I don't know why I was bothering except that I had become more stubborn as I aged. Maybe because Gyron was only a few blocks from the airport diner or maybe it was that I just didn't buy the scenario that Prince had latched onto, the one I had thought of myself when I met with LT's friends. I figured I'd talk to Ryan and move on. Move on to where? That was the question. I wasn't sure I had any answers. With Salazar in a coma and with no idea of where LT had gone after leaving work that Saturday, I had no real hope of ever finding the why behind her murder. This whole thing was like swimming in wet concrete. I had worked hard to get exactly nowhere, and if I didn't make progress soon, I'd sink.

I pulled into the lot just as Carl Ryan was getting out of his Maserati.

I didn't know if the car was any good, but it was beautiful to look at. I came up on him before he was aware of me and startled him.

"Sorry, Carl."

He didn't seem pleased at my being there, but I put that down to the startle. Men don't like looking scared in front of other men, most especially in front of athletes, guys in the military, or cops. It's the uniform thing. No matter the lip service we pay about equality and sameness, men feel a little less than what they are in front of other men who take real physical risks. Men spend their whole lives measuring themselves against one another, and anyone who tells you otherwise is full of shit. Everything from the size of our penises to our bank accounts is fair play. In some ways, that's what Ryan's Maserati and my Mustang were about. Some men accept it and make it a small part of their lives. Some men, men like Pete McCann, made it what their lives were about.

"That's okay. You are a persistent bastard," he said with a laugh, patting me on the shoulder. "Lara told me you were back."

"Yeah."

"Not getting anywhere, huh?"

"Worse. I feel like I'm getting farther away than closer. Did you hear about what happened to the guy who killed Linh Trang?"

He hesitated, went a little pale. "Hear what?

"Someone stabbed him in the throat with the sharpened end of a toothbrush. He's in a coma and it doesn't look like he's coming out of it anytime soon."

Ryan's color returned. He turned, spit on the ground, and said, "Good. Fuck him. Come on, walk with me."

We headed toward the offices. He held the door open for me so that I entered first. Lara's face lit up and she leaned forward, opening her mouth to say something, but when Ryan walked in behind me, her whole body language changed. Her face went cold. She looked nervous.

Ryan seemed not to notice. "Any calls, Lara?"

"Nothing yet, Carl."

"Okay, Mr. Murphy and I are going back to my office. No calls for, say . . . how long do you think this will take, Gus?"

"Ten, fifteen minutes, tops."

"No calls for fifteen minutes. C'mon, Gus," he said, holding the door for me once again.

I waved bye to Lara and headed into the back.

We settled into our seats—Ryan behind his desk, me in front. He offered me coffee. I turned it down. He made himself a cup. I let him take a few sips before I asked my questions.

"Why was Linh Trang here that Saturday?"

"She had some financials to see to that probably could've waited until Monday, but she was really diligent about her work. Now I wish . . ." His voice drifted off.

"What do you wish?"

He looked genuinely ill there for a moment. "I wish she hadn't come in. I can't help but think if she had stayed home that day . . . you know. Maybe she wouldn't have done X or Y and she would never have run into that scumbag."

I considered saying something about the futility of wishes, but just moved on.

"You told the detectives that she got in around ten, went to her office, but that no one saw her leave. Is that right?"

He looked impressed. "How do you know all that?"

"Just because I'm retired doesn't mean I don't have sources."

"Yeah," he said, winking, "don't we all? But yes, that's about right. I stopped in to say hi to her when I saw she was in. She said she'd be done in a few hours and I left it at that. I was out on the floor with the guys most of the day, getting shipments packed up for pickup on Monday morning. We were very busy because of the short week ahead."

"But nobody saw her leave?"

"No, but she did punch in and out. Well, not really, not like in the old days. We have a digital time clock that works on the employee's finger-print. No buddy clocking in or out for you." He reached into the top drawer of his desk and came out with a folder. He handed it to me. "When Lara told me you'd come back and said you would probably come again, I got that out. It's Linh Trang's daily time record reports from the month she was killed."

"Yeah, I've seen a copy of it." I handed it back to him. "So there's no way to fake this?"

"Why would anyone want to fake it? And, no, otherwise what would be the point of having a fingerprint reader?"

"I guess."

"So you would have no idea of where she was going once she left here?"

He shrugged. "None. Like I said, I just popped my head into her office to see why she was here. We couldn't have spoken for more than twenty seconds."

I kept at it because I didn't want to have to come back if I forgot to ask even a stupid question. Ryan had been pretty patient with me, but I could tell he was tired of answering these questions again and I had no official standing.

"Just one or two more questions. Anyone else here that day that might have an idea?"

"I doubt it," he said, his annoyance getting a little closer to the surface. "The guys in the shop and on the floor have very limited contact with the office staff."

"But they might have some contact? I mean, no one keeps tabs on all their employees' movements. We had cops who were dating each other, but no one knew about it."

"Off the record?" he said, leaning forward.

"Sure."

"Listen, Gus, most of the guys in the shop, they're . . ." He waved his hand. "They're illegals. Oh, they come in here with Social Security numbers and driver's licenses and stuff, but we don't ask too many questions. It's how we survive against foreign competition and how we keep our employees happy. Most of them don't speak a lot of English. When they're here, they keep their heads down and their mouths shut. They don't want to notice anyone or get noticed by anyone."

"How did Linh Trang feel about your arrangements?"

"She didn't love it, but she was a realist and none of us was doing anything strictly illegal. Besides, she was going to leave soon anyway."

"Look, I know I'm being a pain in the balls, but I'd still like to talk to the guys who were here with you that day?"

His patience was nearly at an end. "I don't even remember who was here that Saturday."

"But you would have their time sheets, no?"

That did it. Patience over. He stood up, face red, "Okay, Gus—"

But I didn't let him finish. My cell buzzed, and when I saw that it was Maggie calling, I raised my palm to Ryan to stop him and answered the phone.

"Just give me a second, okay?" I whispered to her. "I'm working the Spears thing. Or let me call you back."

"No, Gus, please. Don't hang up." She was breathless and sounded frightened. "Joe DiMaggio. Joe DiMaggio," she repeated, using the code word we worked out if she felt she was in danger.

"Okay. Give me a second."

I held the phone away from my ear and looked up to Ryan.

"Is there a place I can take this call, an empty office or something?"

"An emergency?"

"Yeah."

"Out the door, turn right. Two doors down is a break room. No one is in there at this hour."

"Thanks."

As I walked quickly out of Ryan's office toward the break room I put the phone back up to my ear.

"What's the matter, Maggie? What's going on?"

"I'm not imagining things, Gus."

"What aren't you imagining?"

"Someone is following me, a man. I've seen him a few times like lurking around when I've gotten off the elevators or coming out of the hotel restaurant. He keeps his distance, pretends like he's not watching me, but he's watching me. I know. Men have been watching me my whole life. He's almost always at the edge of my sightline, but he's there."

"Describe him to me."

"Big man in his thirties, muscularly built, bad mustache. Shaggy brown hair. He wears sunglasses and a leather jacket. You don't think I'm crazy, do you?"

"Of course not. You were right to call me. Where are you right now?"

"In the hotel," she said, voice trembling slightly.

"Where in the hotel?"

"In my room."

"You have the privacy latch and the security lock closed?"

"Uh-huh."

"Good. Stay there. I'm gonna get back to the Paragon. It'll take me about five minutes from where I am now. Then I'm going to make some calls. Don't open that door up for anyone until you hear back from me. Understand?"

"I understand."

"When someone comes to the door, they will use the words "Father Bill" to you. If they don't use those two words in that order, don't open up and call nine-one-one immediately. Don't yell, don't fight, call. You got it."

"You're scaring me, Gus."

"Okay, call, then scream and fight. Is that better?"

We both laughed at that, too loudly and for too long.

"Listen, Maggie, you'll be okay. I'm gonna take care of this and you'll be fine. Remember, Father—"

"—Bill," she finished the sentence. "I remember."

"I'm going now. I'll call you back in a little while and explain how it's being handled. I love you, Magdalena."

"And I would have to love you to put up with this shit."

Good, I thought, she had some anger in her voice. It would help her focus. I hung up.

I ran back into Carl Ryan's office, thanked him, and apologized for being such a pain in the ass. He assured me that it was okay and, seeing the panicked look on my face, asked if there was anything he could do.

"One thing," I said. "Can I get out through the shop floor? I'm in a hurry."

"Come with me."

As the Gyron building disappeared from my rearview mirror, I realized that when it came down to it, I didn't really care about Micah Spears's past or his money and promises. It was hard not to care about what had happened to Linh Trang, but the sad truth was that nothing I could find out about her murder would change her fate. It was a lesson I would keep relearning: Knowledge of the dead changes nothing. What mattered was keeping Maggie safe.

51

Maggie was as safe as I could make her from seven hundred miles away. I'd had Kurt Bonacker get in touch with the hotel manager where Maggie was staying and the manager let me speak to his head of security. I probably could've gotten in touch with security by myself, but I knew the way the world worked. If word came down from management to help the guy on the phone, it carried a lot more weight than if I was asking a favor.

It turned out that the head of security at the hotel was a retired Detroit PD sergeant named Vernon Boston. Vernon and I got on just fine and I made the threat to Maggie as clear as I could without going into too much detail. I left Slava out of it, telling Vernon that I had some old enemies from my time on the job.

"Don't we all?" he said. "Don't we all? Shit, I'd need more fingers and toes to count up mine."

Hotels, especially big ones like the hotel I'd booked Maggie into, have all sorts of passageways that guests never see or even know exist. He took Maggie down to the loading dock in a service elevator and had her driven in a cargo van to another hotel.

"Do you have a reliable personal protection firm out there?" I'd asked before he moved her.

"It'll cost you, but sure we do. Ex-Blackwater types, you know what I mean?"

"Perfect. Twenty-four hours a day until I say otherwise."

"I'll set it up."

That was the easy part. The hard part was calling the emergency number Slava had given me. I wasn't going to hand him over to the Russians without first discussing it with him. In any case, I had bought us both a little bit of time now that Maggie was safe. He didn't pick up. I didn't figure he would. Sometime during the day, when it suited him, he would call me back. The voice mail box wasn't set up, so there was no chance of leaving a message. I wouldn't have had to, anyway. Slava would know why I was calling. Now all there was to do was wait, but the universe doesn't operate as neatly as that. So even before I put my phone back in my pocket, it buzzed in my hand.

"Gus." It was Charlie Prince.

"Yeah, Charlie, what's up? Making any headway with the case?"

"That's where I am at right now. I'm in a bar in Bay Shore known to be a Asesinos hangout. Third place I've been in the Brentwood/Bay Shore area. So far, no luck. But that's not why I called."

"I didn't figure it was. So what's the reason?"

"I heard from the Sheriff's Office investigator this morning."

I asked, "What, Rondo's dead?"

"Nah, looks pretty good he's gonna spend the rest of his short, miserable life in zucchini land. He had a stroke last night and they helicoptered him over to Stony Brook University Hospital. Brain function is gone. Hey, Gus, you think if I volunteer, they'll let me pull the plug on the motherfucka?"

"You'd have to take a number like at the Stop and Shop deli counter. Thanks for calling to let me know, but—"

"That's not why I called you, either. Well, yeah, it's part of the reason, but there's something else."

"Something else like what?"

"Looks like the guy who stuck his toothbrush into Salazar's neck was one of his own."

"One of his own?" I asked, not knowing exactly what Prince meant.

"One of his own, another Asesinos *cholo*, Martín Gutiérrez, a real badass. Gutiérrez makes Salazar seem like a fucking choirboy, if you can believe that. Remember the drug deal that went bad a few years ago in Freeport?"

"Sorry, Charlie, I haven't been much for the news for the last few years."

"Five dead, three men, two women. Throats slashed. Then the bodies were mutilated postmortem. You don't want me to draw you a picture, do you? It wasn't pretty. A CI for the Nassau County detective who caught the case pointed to Gutiérrez and two other Asesinos members, but they didn't have any physical evidence to make it stick."

"So what's he doing in Riverhead?"

"Awaiting trial for homicide. A bouncer at a bar in Huntington Station threw Gutiérrez out when he was harassing a woman who wanted no part of him. Early the next morning, Gutiérrez, full of enough meth to keep all of Suffolk County lit, came back and waited for the bouncer to leave work. When he did, Gutiérrez beat him to death, slowly, with his fists. It's on video, there were witnesses and tons of physical evidence. He's going away for the rest of his life anyway. I guess Rondo must've said or done something to his gang brother to really piss him off."

"Come on, Charlie, let's be honest with each other here," I said. "You don't like it and you don't think for a second Gutiérrez tried to kill Rondo because of some breach in gang etiquette. A guy who beats another man to death on video and in front of witnesses isn't going to plan a fake fight in the yard as a distraction. If it was some gang etiquette thing, Gutiérrez would've walked right up to Salazar and stabbed him on the block."

"It was a hit," he said. "It had to be, but why?"

"The answer's pretty obvious, isn't it? The gang wanted Salazar dead to protect themselves. Gutiérrez was already fucked, so they had him do it. My guess is Gutiérrez doesn't even know why he was ordered to kill Salazar or they gave him some bullshit story. He'll be a dead end, not that he would talk in any case. There's no incentive you could offer him to talk."

"But I'm gonna go speak with him later anyway, after they arrest him. You want in?"

I thought about it. "Thanks, but no, I don't think so. I'll just be in the way, and I've got other shit I'm dealing with right now. You find anything out, I'd appreciate hearing about it."

"You got it, Gus." But he wasn't done. Although he stopped speaking, I could almost hear him formulating his next sentence. I waited. "You know, I can't help but think we don't have any idea of why Linh Trang Spears was really murdered. I sure am curious now, though."

"Me, too, Charlie. Me, too."

"I'm gonna keep checking the bars for now. I'll let you know if I find anything."

That was it. I got the sense he knew he could check every one of those bars and clubs and he would get nowhere. If Charlie Prince was right, if I was right, that Gutiérrez had been ordered to kill his gang brother, it was progress of a sort. It might mean someone was nervous, that my poking around had, in fact, started a chain reaction . . . or not. In spite of what I'd said to Charlie, there might be a hundred reasons for Gutiérrez to make an attempt on Salazar's life that those of us on the outside of the gang could never know about or even understand. For the moment, I had plenty of other things to worry about, but very little I could do about them except wait.

52

Bill Kilkenny was confused but happy when I showed up at his door with a cold antipasto plate and eggplant-parm heroes.

"Smells grand, but to what do I owe the pleasure?"

"I'm not sure you'll like the answer."

He laughed. "Experience has taught me that the Lord cares little for my preferences. My likes or dislikes tend not to change the facts."

"Nothing changes the facts, does it, Bill? There are plenty of facts I'd like to change."

"No less true for me or any of us, I think. You're thinking of your lad, then?"

I shook my head. "No, actually, I'm not."

He patted my cheek. "Then you've come far, Gus Murphy. You've come very far. Now, will you stop tempting me with those aromas—Italian, if my Arthur Avenue–trained nose isn't lying to me—and get in here. I've the perfect red to go with it."

We didn't talk much as we sipped our Chianti and shoved hunks of provolone, Genoa salami, soppressata, roasted peppers, and olives into our mouths. But whenever I looked up, I could see Bill studying me for cracks and fissures.

"What is it, Bill?"

"You show up here unannounced with lunch, but you haven't much to say. You tell me, boyo. If your mood's not about John Junior, then what, or is it who?"

I explained to him about the man who was following Maggie and about the choice I had to make about Slava.

"I don't envy you, but is it really a choice between Slava and Maggie? Is it one life for another?"

"I didn't ask for any of this."

"Who among us asks for what we really get, Gus? It is our fate. Some of it is of our own making, but most of it is out of our purview."

"Don't go all God squad on me, not now. Next thing I know, you'll be shoving a rosary in my hand and asking me to kneel beside you for a little praying."

"If I thought you would mean a word of it, I wouldn't hesitate to do just that."

I laughed. "Well, if you're in a praying mood, Bill, you might ask the Holy Trinity why one of his own gang brothers tried to kill Rondo Salazar yesterday."

He was stunned. "The man who killed Micah's granddaughter was himself killed?"

"Sort of. He's in a coma for which there are no return breadcrumbs."

"That's artfully put for the likes of you."

"I'm thinking about the breading on the eggplant heroes."

"They'll keep," he said, in about as stern a voice as he could manage. "Have you made any progress there with what Micah asked of you?"

"In terms of concrete progress, no, but one of the detectives on the case thinks that my nosing around about Linh Trang's murder might be stirring the pot. I don't know what to believe. Now can we eat?"

Bill nodded. And as he set out plates for the heroes, I was tempted to ask him yet again about Micah Spears's dark past. I didn't bother. It wouldn't've worked any better now than it had the last two times I asked.

Besides, I couldn't praise the man for keeping my confidences and things I'd revealed at the lowest points in my life and at the same time fault him for keeping the same covenant with others. Oddly, it was Bill who broached the subject of Micah Spears, if in an offhanded manner.

"So then, if there's all this gang shite involved, the poor girl's murder might have no connection at all to Micah?"

"Why would Linh Trang's murder have anything at all to do with her grandfather?" Because Bill had brought up the subject, I figured I might finally be able to get some information out of him. "Maybe if you'd tell me why Spears changed his name, I could give you an honest answer."

Bill looked like he was considering the proposition when my cell vibrated. Before he answered, I reached into my pocket.

"Sorry, Bill, I've gotta get this," I said, and walked outside.

I picked up, simultaneously hoping and dreading that it was Slava. It wasn't Slava, and I sighed in disappointment and relief.

"Hey, Asher."

"Christ, Gus, I know nobody wants to hear from his lawyer, but could you fake a little enthusiasm? It makes up for the lack of pay."

"Sorry, Ash. My bad. What's up? The NYPD back at it again?"

"Nothing like that," he said, almost in a whisper. "Are you working tonight?"

"Yeah, but tell me what's going on and let me worry about work."

"There's someone I think you should talk to." His voice was now a whisper. Although there was a lot of background noise, he clearly didn't want anyone to overhear what he was saying.

"Where are you?"

"At the courthouse in CI."

"How is Central Islip these days?"

"Same as it ever was, only more depressing. Listen, can you get out of work tonight?"

"If I have to."

"You have to."

"Okay."

"Do you have a piece of paper and a pen?"

"No. Text me the info, Ash."

"I can do that."

"What's this about, anyway?"

"Just show up tonight."

"Should I thank you?"

"Maybe not," he said, his full voice back. "Depends. I've got to go."

He was good to his word and was gone. Before I went back inside, I called Fredo, the other van driver who was always looking for extra shifts. He never turned them down.

"Is everything okay, Gus?" Bill asked when I stepped back inside.

I shrugged. "Is everything ever okay? At least it wasn't about Maggie and it wasn't Slava."

"That's something. It's good, I think, to remember to be thankful for the small graces."

"Like what?"

"Like eggplant-parm heroes, for fuck's sake. Now can we please eat?"

I had nothing to say to that.

53

Y ou didn't have to live on Long Island for more than a few months to discover the North/South divide, the LIE acting as our own version of the Mason-Dixon Line. The general theme being that, with the exception of the Hamptons and a few scattered towns along the Atlantic, the North Shore had better schools, was wealthier, cleaner, safer, whiter . . . I mean, Gatsby didn't live in Merrick, for chrissakes, nor did the Astors, Roosevelts, and Vanderbilts build their mansions in Mastic Beach.

But the North Shore was no less free of the bullshit dividing lines that existed in places like Bellport. Only on the North Shore we liked to pretend that there was no such thing as the wrong side of the tracks, only the best side and the gradually, marginally, slightly less good sides. It's sad how easily we let ourselves fall into that tribal nonsense, the who-is-better-than-whom crap. Even in Commack, the place where Annie and I had raised the kids, our neighbors got haughty about North Commack having it all over South Commack. As if it mattered in the scheme of things. Ask any real estate broker on the island and they'd tell you I was certifiable, that of course it mattered, that nothing mattered more. That on the North Shore, the descriptor "North" could mean several hundred thousand dollars in asking price, that on the South Shore the descriptor "South" could mean the same. *Right, what could possibly matter more than fucking real estate values?*

I guess I had real estate on my mind as I drove north up Nissequogue River Road, the silent river below to my left, Smithtown Landing Golf Course along the opposite bank. Not that I could see the golf course in the dark or make out the phase of the moon through the mournful blanket of clouds that had descended upon Suffolk in the last several hours. I had grown up in Smithtown, on Blydenburgh Avenue, squeezed between Main Street and the Long Island Rail Road, the tracks not seventy-five feet away from our back door. I'd driven past the old house on my way to the address Asher Wilkes had texted me. I used to like to take the short drive from our house in Commack with the kids to show them where their dad had grown up. I guess I liked reminding them that I was a kid once, too. I used to feel like a kid a lot of the time, not even the job could beat it out of me. I didn't feel much like a kid anymore, nor did I go by the old house. It just didn't have any meaning for me the way it used to.

Nissequogue was part of Smithtown, the rich part. It was located on a scenic, steer's head–shaped piece of land between the river on the west, Stony Brook Harbor on the east, and Long Island Sound on the north. There were municipal beaches at the tips of the steer's horns: Short Beach on the river side, Long Beach on the harbor side. As a teenager I'd spent a lot of time at both beaches, but I hadn't spent a whole lot of time in Nissequogue itself. Nissequogue didn't really have a lot of there there, except for the country club and beach club, and the Murphys were never going to be members of either one of those. There weren't even a lot of streets in Nissequogue. When you have huge houses on giant lots, who needs streets? I had never been in any of the houses up there, never even been close to one except for the time I had taken a wrong turn and ended up halfway down some rich asshole's driveway. The fucker actually came out of his house toting a shotgun.

I turned left off Nissequogue River Road onto Horse Race Lane, then left again onto Boney Lane. I stayed on Boney just past Pheasant Run and came to the private road Asher had alerted me to. It was down this private road, so I was told, that my streak of never entering a house in Nissequogue would end. I parked my Mustang in front of the four-car garage that had either once been an actual carriage house or been built to resemble one. I walked back to the front entrance of the house along a crushed stone driveway, the stones making crunching sounds beneath my feet. It was so quiet up here that my footfalls seemed to fill up the night. I was very close to the Sound and to the wetlands along the river. The air didn't smell so much of salt water as it did of rotting vegetation, like at Roberta Malone's house on Shelter Island. Wetlands, marshes, and swamps have a very distinct odor of decay, and that odor was heavy in the air.

The house itself was tastefully huge in that it didn't overwhelm the big old-growth oaks and maples around it, nor did it push at the borders of the lot, which were far enough away that they were impossible to make out in the dark. My guess was that the lot was a good three acres, give or take. It also helped that the next closest house that I could see at all was at least a third of a mile away across Boney Lane on Pheasant Run. The house before me was a three-storied, two-gabled affair. The section of the house that featured the main doors showed an old brick façade to me, the bricks rising up from the ground to the tip of the gable. The rest of the house was English Tudor style, with gray slate roofing. The place was all very tasteful: no poodle-shaped topiaries or bizarre sculptures, no elaborate fountains, giant prayer wheels, or wind chimes.

The odd thing was that I was told I would be expected, but I had no idea by whom. What did I know about the person or persons on the other side of the big black doors? I knew he or she had lots of money. Just how much, how they'd gotten it, or if they still had it was in question. I also wasn't quite sure exactly why I was asked to be there in the first place, though I figured it must've had something to do with Micah Spears. Why else would Asher have sent me here? Still, I would be sure only after I rang the bell. I did that.

The right side door pulled back and an older man, a few years the senior of either Bill or Spears, stood in the vestibule. He was bald-headed and age-spotted. His blue eyes were faded and his shoulders stooped slightly. Still, he was a pretty imposing figure, one I thought I had seen somewhere before but couldn't quite place. He wore a heavy blue wool sweater, frayed at the sleeves and around the collar. Beneath the sweater he wore a crisply collared white shirt. His pants were fine gray wool, the cuffs of which fell over beat-up brown slippers. He held a cut crystal glass of scotch—expensive single-malt, from the campfire smell of it—in his left hand.

"You'd be Gus Murphy," he said, his voice steady and rich with easy authority. "Come in. Come in. I'm in the study." He didn't bother introducing himself.

The old man had a lumbering gait with a slight limp. As I followed him along the parquet flooring, under the pendulum hall fixture, past the sweeping staircase, I struggled to place him. And, after hearing his voice, it was even more frustrating. I knew this man, but from where? He turned left down a hallway and opened a door onto his study. I laughed to myself because studies weren't standard issue in most of the houses I'd ever been in. They were the stuff of movies and the books I read to kill time during my shifts. But this was a study, all right.

The walls were lined with carpet-to-ceiling bookcases, with a fancy wheeled ladder on a rail off in one corner. There was a fancily embroidered daybed by the fireplace and a massive desk near the huge picture window. The room smelled distinctly of old rum and fruit-scented pipe smoke. The neat display of pipes on the big desk confirmed what my nose told me. Rows of framed photos, black-and-white and color, sat atop a black baby grand piano. The piano partially obscured a cabinet and dry bar featuring an impressive display of bottles of single-malt scotches.

The one wall free of bookcases was lined with artfully framed certificates and degrees and photos of my host with the rich and powerful, but I didn't need to read the degrees or certificates to spark my recall.

"Judge Kaufman," I heard myself mutter.

He smiled a yellowy-toothed smile in spite of himself. "Indeed, Gus. You've testified twice in my courtroom. I have a good memory for those things."

"Yes, Your Honor."

Judge Julius Kaufman was a Suffolk County legend. He was a legend because he was that rare judge all sides hated, but everyone respected. He was neither a hanging judge nor a soft touch. He wasn't the type to issue a warrant on the whims of a prosecutor, nor was he the type to demand unreasonable proof before issuing one. He was a fair man. Fairness may be something people outside the legal system may think is the ultimate goal of the system. The truth is anything but that. It was adversarial, a competition, and when humans compete for anything they look for an edge. And when you're looking for an edge, fairness is often the first casualty.

"I see you admiring my pipes. I'm afraid they're for display purposes only these days, vestiges of things past," he said, his eyes looking far away to a place I could not see. "My late wife wanted to rip up the carpeting in here when I was forced to give up smoking. She thought the smell would make quitting more difficult, but I enjoy the memories too much. I find a comfort in it. Excuse me, Gus. Old men get foolish and wistful at inappropriate times."

"'Foolish' isn't a word I ever heard anyone use to describe you, Your Honor."

He laughed a deep, hearty laugh, one that made me smile just hearing it.

"No? I can only imagine the words your fellow officers and the prosecutors used to describe me."

"Well, they were certainly colorful."

"Excuse my rudeness, Gus. Please sit," he said, gesturing toward a green leather wing chair across from his desk. "Would you like a glass of scotch? I have many to choose from. If you name one, I probably have it."

"I'm not much of a scotch drinker."

"Bourbon?"

"Sure." I didn't want to be a pain and I did eventually want to get to the point of my being summoned. "You pick."

A minute later, he handed me a cut crystal glass like his own, and sat behind his desk.

"Cheers. *L'chaim*," he said, lifting his glass to me, and sipped.

I sipped mine. It was pretty heady stuff for bourbon.

"Gus, I have held the oaths I have taken over the years very dear, and considered the words in them seriously. I have tried always, with a good rate of success, to keep the promises I have made, both personally and professionally."

"I sense there's a 'but' in here somewhere."

He laughed again, only this time there was a sadness to it and no humor.

"Yes, let me cut if not directly to the chase then closer to it. In 1967, fresh out of University of Michigan Law and passing the New York Bar, I did a foolish thing. To the horror of my parents, I enlisted in the Marines. I looked around me and saw black kids and Puerto Rican kids being drafted left and right, being made fodder for the war machine, and I saw also that upper-class and middle-class kids had options. They could become cops or doctors or go to college and get deferments. Remember, this was before Nixon came in and put an end to that." He laughed a real laugh. "Of course, you don't remember that at all. How could you? Thank God for that. It was a terrible time. Anyone with fond memories of the sixties is being willfully stupid.

"Excuse me, I digress. But truthfully, my parents needn't have worried. Once I got through officers' training school, there was very little chance I was going to see combat. I was assigned to the Judge Advocate

General's Corps. Believe me when I tell you, we didn't lack for cases during Vietnam. It was also during this period that I discovered I was a good lawyer, but that I was a particularly gifted prosecutor. Not only was I good at it, Gus, I had a taste for it. You didn't want any blood in the water around me. No, sir."

I must've reacted, because he stopped and smiled at me.

"You seem surprised," he said. "I know my reputation. I'm aware that I was known as a fair judge, but fairness is learned behavior, Gus. And it was as a prosecutor in the military and then as a civilian that I learned it."

"Judge Kaufman, no offense, but is there a point to all this? I mean, your life sounds pretty fascinating, though I can't see that you'd be interested in telling it to the likes of me. The reason I'm here must have something to do with Micah Spears. I know that a friend of mine met Spears in 'Nam and won't talk to me about—"

"Yes, that's why you're here, but I'm afraid you're going to have to suffer through a little bit more of my background before we get there." He scowled at me. "You haven't touched your drink. I'm getting myself a little more. Do you mind?"

I shook my head and I sipped some more of the bourbon as he refilled his glass.

He returned but didn't sit behind the desk. Instead he sat on one corner of it, close to me.

"So let me skip forward to 1971 and my final case in the JAG Corps. It was a very ugly case, a very ugly case indeed. It involved three soldiers whose unit had been involved in a firefight in Kon Tum Province near the confluence of the borderlands of Laos, Cambodia, and South Vietnam. The three soldiers in question claimed they got separated from their unit during the fight and resurfaced eight days later at a fire base about twenty klicks northeast of where the original skirmish had taken place. The three of them held to the narrative that they had lived off what they scrounged and foraged and that they had spent much of the time hiding from enemy patrols. When they were sent back to their unit, their CO would have none of it and had them charged with desertion under fire, a crime punishable by death. They were escorted back to Saigon to await court-martial.

"About a week after that, intel reports surfaced—I had a lot of pals on the intel side of things—about a massacre at a small village just on the Cambodian side of the border. The reports were horrific. Whole families murdered in the most gruesome ways imaginable. The ones shot to death were the lucky ones. There were drowned babies, but according to the reports, the young women of the village got it worst of all. They had all been raped, beaten, tortured, and stabbed like pincushions. Naturally, our first inclination was to blame it on Charlie—sorry, the Vietcong. That it was retaliation for the villagers collaborating with us or the South Vietnamese. It wouldn't have been the first time during the war that it had happened, but we were keen to make PR hay with it after years of getting killed in the press, most especially after the My Lai Massacre trials the previous year. Do you know about My Lai, Gus?"

"Unfortunately, I do."

"So you can understand why many people in the armed forces were anxious to get play out of an even more brutal, if smaller-scale, incident by the enemy. We sent in our best forensics people, documented everything. Photographed, filmed, made site maps, sketched it all. We autopsied each victim. There was just one problem, but it was a big problem."

"The Vietcong didn't do it."

"No, they did not. The bullets and shells recovered at the scene were from standard-issue U.S. Army M16s and Colt 1911 .45s. The stab wounds were from M7 bayonets, our bayonets."

"Could have been the enemy making it look like us," I said, not believing for a second the words coming out of my mouth.

"I suppose, if not for personal items belonging to the careless soldiers actually responsible for the slaughter."

"The three soldiers you already had in custody in Saigon."

The old judge smiled as sad a smile at me as I had ever seen.

"But, Your Honor, that begs the question, how did he ever get back here. I mean, never mind the massacre, those guys were already charged with desertion under fire."

"As I said before, Gus, thank God you weren't around in those days. It would be hard to explain to anyone who hadn't lived through those times the incredible levels of insanity, dissention, and chaos. This was post–My Lai, and the year after we invaded Cambodia, essentially expanding the full-blown war into a neighboring country. We were negotiating peace with the north while the country was being torn apart at home."

"So what does any of that have to do with—"

"Come, come, Murphy." He stood up, his tone of voice becoming authorial, even impatient. "You're a grown-up and an intelligent man. What do you think happened?"

I asked, "Was it a weak case?"

"To use the vernacular, it was a slam dunk. I had enough evidence to get those men executed enough times to vanquish all nine lives of the three most curious cats to have ever lived. No, I was told to make it go away. Ordered to drop it. To forget it. That the last thing the armed forces needed, that our negotiators needed, or the country needed was another public airing of our dirtiest laundry." He walked around behind his desk by the window and stared out into the darkness. "You know the most galling aspect of it all, Gus?" He wasn't really asking. "The most galling part of the whole disgusting charade was that I was ordered to help facilitate their name changes and to ensure the records were sealed.

"I would like to tell you that I had done as I was told, that I had forgotten it and left the whole sordid horror story in my past until Asher Wilkes called me last evening. But I can't tell you that. I have thought of it every single day of my life since and have suffered the most appalling guilt over having played along. I have thought of it every time I've sat in judgment on the bench, every time I have instructed a jury, every time I sentenced a man or woman to prison.

"I'm a sorry old man and I've got a weak, tired, and sick heart. I haven't done you any favors, Gus, by sharing this with you. Believe me, I haven't, not in the long run. At least you didn't have to look at the photos of those poor mutilated girls or drowned babies or the old men and grandmothers hanging from the trees. I've spared you that much." He turned to face me. "I hope it's worth the burden to you."

"So do I. What are you going to do now, Judge? Will you finally go public with it?"

He laughed that sad laugh. "To what end? I'll be the one to suffer the shame of not having come forward sooner. And the innocents will suffer, too. Spears's family, the other men's families . . . why should they suffer? Their families are no guiltier of the crimes than Hitler's dog was guilty of her master's. I won't do that to them, and I hope you have the good sense not to."

"No, Your Honor. I won't. I promise."

I stood and placed my nearly full glass of bourbon on the glass-topped desk where the judge had sat looking down at me a few minutes earlier.

"Good. You know what I think I'll do now, Gus?"

"What's that, Your Honor?"

"I think I'll smoke a pipe and finish my scotch. That's just exactly what I think I'll do. Good night, Murphy."

"Good night, Your Honor."

I let myself out. The sky had opened up, but not so much that I got soaked walking back to my car. As I turned right off the private road, I realized that I was, as had been suggested to me, in the employ of a monster. That I now understood Kevin Spears's words and why Linh Trang had cut off her burgeoning relationship with her grandfather. Judge Kaufman's words had the strongest grip on my attention. *Why should the innocents suffer?* I thought of the bodies of the mutilated girls of that Cambodian village and the photos I'd seen of Linh Trang Spears. Maybe, I thought, it was too late. The innocents had already suffered.

54

Nissequogue River Road was fairly straight, but narrow—one lane in each direction—and dark, even though the leaves hadn't yet bloomed on most of the trees. The clouds and the rain weren't exactly helpful, either. Still, I had the road to myself and my thoughts. I couldn't help but wonder how Kevin Spears and his daughter had found out about what and who Micah Spears really was beneath the fancy clothing and frosty exterior. I couldn't bring myself to believe he had, in a weak moment, confessed his boxcar load of hell-worthy sins to either his son or granddaughter. No way. Men like Spears don't have weak moments and they don't confess. They compartmentalize and move on. They rationalize their actions, then bury their transgressions deep, pouring time and layers of concrete over the graves. But what did I really know about monsters? I'd crossed paths with murderers, rapists, and baby killers before, though never in a single package.

When I passed Parson's Lane, a pair of headlights appeared in my rearview mirror. So ended my temporary ownership of River Road. I was happy for more company than the silent river afforded me. There are occasions in life when alone time with your thoughts is as destructive as an all-night drunk or picking a fight with the wrong guy at the bar. I actually smiled at the mirror in relief. The relief was short-lived, because before the smile had left my lips, the headlights rushed up close to my bumper. The rain and the glare of the headlights made it impossible for me to make out anything about the car or its driver. I checked my gauges. I was already driving ten miles an hour over the speed limit, so I didn't think my slow driving was the issue. And if that wasn't the issue, trouble was.

I was all too familiar with this particular brand of trouble. Last Christmas morning, three bikers from the Maniacs motorcycle gang tried to shotgun me and run me off the road. Although two of them were killed trying and one wound up with a life sentence, they'd come a little too close to accomplishing their goal for my comfort. I didn't know if that was what was happening here, but if it was, I wasn't going to fuck around. I grabbed the Glock out of my ankle holster, holding it in my right hand across my left thigh. If the guy behind me meant to do me harm, he had no choice but to come along the driver's side of my Mustang. The river to my right and the houses that dotted the riverbank limited his options.

I wasn't in the mood for cat and mouse, especially when I was cast as the rodent. Nor was I up for a game of chicken, so I decided to force the action. I eased my foot off the gas, gently slowing down. The car behind me almost hit my rear bumper, but then slowed in kind. My guess was I'd confused him some and he was now aware that I was fully aware of him. Then I sped up at a sharp bend in the road where it veered away from the river. I figured I knew this area of Smithtown better than almost anyone who might be following me. I'd hoped to put enough distance between us for me to duck my car into a driveway and let him scoot past. But before I could even think about it, there he was again, his rear end fishtailing a little on the wet pavement as he gave his car more gas to catch up.

The angle and distance between us did cut down on the glare in my mirrors enough to allow me a better look at the car behind me. It was a two-door orange Honda Civic that had been transformed from a used econo-box import into a street racer. When I was on the job, I hated chasing these things down in my Crown Vic. They were nimble and the fastest ones had nitrous oxide injection systems. Yeah, laughing gas, but there was nothing funny in it for me. So I knew that as much straight-line speed as my Mustang could deliver, it might not be enough to let me shake this guy if I found a stretch where I could floor it. The lack of glare also revealed that there were two men in the chase car, a driver and some-one riding shotgun. My sense was that in this instance "shotgun" wasn't just a figure of speech.

As I approached Edgewood, I slowed just enough to turn left without rolling over. I didn't figure that I would lose him simply because I ne-glected to use my turn signal. Edgewood was fairly straight and narrow, with traffic in both directions, and might allow me to test how much speed his car could deliver. The rear end of the Mustang got a little loose in the turn and my right rear tire kissed the curb pretty hard, but not enough to throw me into a spin. As I fought to get the car straight, I re-alized for the first time how dry my mouth was and how hard my heart was hammering. My shirt was sticking to my back and I thought I could smell my own sweat. My leg muscles ached and twitched, and I made sure to keep my right index finger away from the Glock's trigger. I didn't want to shoot through my door—not yet, anyway—or, worse, through my own leg. When I got the Mustang back under control, I put my foot all the way down on the gas and not gently. The tires spun a little on the rain-slicked blacktop, then gripped. And when they did, I was thrown back in my seat. I didn't bother looking at my speedometer, because I knew there was only one traffic light between me and 25A.

I did, however, check my rearview. It had nothing positive to show me. The Civic handled the turn onto Edgewood with less difficulty and was gaining ground, and as it came closer to me, it began to veer slowly into the oncoming lane in order to get beside me. I was too far away from 25A to outrun him. The roads just ahead of me that I might turn onto led into twisty streets and dead ends that would put me at an even greater disadvantage. Besides, if I tried a turn at this point on wet pavement at this speed, I had zero chance of keeping my car from going airborne. No, my only chance was to get as far as Fifty Acre Road and try a left turn there. Fifty Acre was also straight and narrow.

When I checked my mirrors again, his front right fender was next to my rear driver's side wheel well. I couldn't risk any more speed, so I put my gun hand on the steering wheel just long enough to hit the window switch. As the window lowered I changed hands again, put my right arm across my chest, and rested the barrel of the Glock on the windowsill. Then I caught a break. Horns blared and headlights appeared in the opposite direction, forcing the Civic to fall back behind me. The light ahead of me turned red and I slowed enough to make the guy behind me believe I might actually stop. I didn't, zipping right through it. He hesitated, but not long enough for me to gain much advantage.

Almost immediately, he veered over to get next to me. I slowed some to prepare to turn and as I did I saw another pair of headlights appear behind the Civic. Something flashed, flashed again, again. *Gunfire?* I didn't stop to check. As I swung hard left onto Fifty Acre, his front end nearly sideswiped my rear quarter panel. There were more flashes and the Civic slowed, then spun out of control. I made it onto Fifty Acre Road, my rear end fishtailing like mad. It probably took me fifteen hundred feet to get the car steady again, but there were no headlights in my mirrors. He hadn't made it. I raced straight up Fifty Acre, slowed to subsonic speed, turned left onto Branglebrink, left onto Old Mill, and finally back onto Nissequogue River Road. The only things I saw in my mirrors were darkness and beaded rainwater on my rear window.

Once again approaching the intersection of Nissequogue and Edgewood, I hit the window switch and put the gun back on my thigh, the muscles in my right arm aching, the ones in my hand cramping. I shook my arm and flexed my hand. I was spent, but not beyond curiosity. I went over it all in my head: the Civic, the chase, those other headlights, the flashes. It didn't make any sense. None of it. I shook my head, as if that ever did any good except in cartoons. When I got to the intersection, I actually stopped at the light and noticed the sky to the left was brighter than it should have been.

This time I stopped at the light and when it turned green, I crossed slowly onto Edgewood. As I did I noticed the fire and heard the sirens. I was pretty far away, but guessed the fire was coming from close to where Fifty Acre met Edgewood. I thought about not turning, about just getting back to the Paragon and collapsing. I mean, I already had all I could handle with what Judge Kaufman had revealed to me about Micah Spears. I didn't think about it for very long and, like a summer moth, turned left and headed directly for the flames.

55

Two Fourth Precinct white-and-blues in full throat, light bars flashing, screamed by me as I rolled toward the fire. When I got there, the two SCPD cars were parked at angles across Edgewood, blocking any traffic coming from my direction. I pulled over to the curb, holstered my weapon, got out of the Mustang, and walked past the patrol cars.

The Civic that had chased me was now orange with flames, its paint blackening, charred, and peeling. The smell of a car fire is all about the acrid stink of melting plastics and synthetic rubber. You could taste the hot metal on your tongue, feel it at the back of your throat. And just beneath all the chemical stench and taste of smoking-hot metal were two other odors familiar to a retired cop who'd been at lots of car fires: burning flesh and burnt human hair. Those things have distinctive odors all their own. And when I saw the one body stretched out on the pavement, I knew the other guy hadn't made it out. Besides the smells, the heat was intense, the flames snapping at the night.

"Yo, yo, buddy," a uniform yelled at me, his hand raised. "Where the fuck you think you're going?"

As I began to answer, the sirens and blaring horns of two St. James Fire Department trucks, coming up the other side of Edgewood, blotted out my words. The cop shook his head and rolled his eyes at the noise. The cop was young. I didn't recognize him and he didn't recognize me. No shock there. Once you retire, you might as well go live in a museum with all the other fossils and dinosaurs, for all the new guys care.

When the trucks came to a stop and they cut their sirens, the cop waved at me impatiently to come on and finish.

"My name's Murphy," I said. "I used to be in the Second Precinct. I was coming back from visiting a friend up in Nissequogue when I saw the flames. I wanted to see if anyone needed help. What's up?"

He thought about busting my balls or simply shooing me away like a good old man, but he decided I was all right.

"What's up? Nothing good. Car blew up. One of the occupants is toast." He laughed at his own joke. "The other's dead on the pavement over there."

"An accident?"

He shook his head and shrugged at the same time. "Yes and no."

"Huh?"

He threw a thumb over his shoulder at the body. "That guy there has two entrance wounds and an exit wound that I can see. Looks like he had enough life in him to crawl out and die."

"Yeah, fire can be a great motivator."

He laughed at that. "Can I steal that line?"

"Sure. It's a big hit at parties."

That confused him a little bit. Like I said, he was young.

"I wouldn't feel too sorry for them, Murphy. Looks like they got it before they were gonna give it to somebody else. The vic over there with the gunshot trauma, he has a Glock .40 in his waistband and we recovered an AR15 over on the other side of the vehicle. These two weren't going wild turkey or deer hunting."

"Any ID?"

"Nothing on the two vics, but the car's registered to some guy in CI."

"Central Islip," I mumbled to myself aloud.

"I gotta go," the cop said. "And do me a solid, get back over by your car. The civilians are starting to come out to have a look."

"No problem. Thanks."

I did as he asked and walked back toward my car, head down. I had been in his shoes plenty of times and I didn't want to make the kid's job any harder than it would already be. Given that this was now a crime scene with bodies and weapons, it was going to be a long night for a lot of people with badges and shields. When I looked up, I froze. There was another car—a black Cadillac CTS coupe—parked directly behind my Mustang. A tall man, a man I recognized, was leaning against the front fender of the Caddy.

"Good evening, Gus Murphy," he said, with a smile in his voice. The smile didn't reach all the way to his gray eyes. He managed not to have his mouth look particularly feral as it did when he was in my van.

"Mr. Lagunov."

"Please, please, I prefer Mr. Gordon. When in Rome . . . You know this saying?"

"I know the saying, but we're a long way from Rome."

He laughed a chilly laugh. "But not so far as Grozny."

"No, not that far. Are you here to threaten me again?"

"On the contrary, I am here to save your life, Gus. Or, to be more correct, I did just save your life. You don't suppose those two men were making an attempt to drag race with you, do you?" There was that laugh again. "I think not. You are good, though, resourceful. I am willing to wager that you had your sidearm on your thigh as you tried to evade the other car. You might even have killed one of them. Yes, I am confident you would have gotten at least one. And if you were lucky . . . who knows what the outcome might have been. Most men, even most policemen, would have panicked. You did not, did you?"

"Panic? No. Believe it or not, I have some experience with this stuff."

"Yes," he said, "the motorcycle gang. You did quite well there. Three of them. Two dead. One in prison and you are still standing."

"You seem to know an awful lot about me."

"I am prepared. It is part of my job. Still, Gus Murphy, I do not think your lack of panic comes from experience."

"I guess I have a different way of looking at life now than when I was on the job."

His expression changed to one that looked almost human.

"The death of a loved one changes you, yes? No man should bury his son. In Russia, our history is too full of fathers burying sons."

"How many fathers have grieved because of you?"

There it was, that feral smile. It was a hunter's smile, but one tinged with pride and vanity.

"Many, I suppose. Very many. Some in warfare, but some not. Two more tonight. Would you have rather me let them murder you?"

I ignored the question. "Who were they?"

"I am not certain." He gave a careless shrug. "Is it of consequence? Their intent was very clear to me."

"You were following me?"

"Obviously."

"Even if I knew where Slava was, I would never have risked leading you or one of your men to him."

"But you have spoken to him. Otherwise you would not know my name."

"That was careless of me."

"This man you know as Slava is proving to be more resourceful than I would have believed for a police thug. And before you start defending him, Gus Murphy, let me inform you of his sins. He, too, has made many fathers and mothers bury their young."

"I know what he did," I said, maybe a bit too loudly. "But he was lied to and tricked into it."

Lagunov laughed at me. "So if he had blown up Chechen women and children and their terrorist husbands and fathers, this would have been good, then?" He shook his head at me. "No, Gus, this is what you

Americans call splitting hairs. He might have been tricked into blow-ing up those buildings and maybe he did kill many innocent people without wanting to, but he was still willing to kill with bombs. Bombs are stupid things, blind things. They do not see a difference between Mus-lims and Christians or women and men, old or young. Why do you pro-tect this man?"

"That's my business."

"I like you, Gus Murphy. More, I respect you. But your business now is my business and I will do my job no matter what is required. For in-stance, killing those men to protect you."

"Why do that? Why kill those men? Why protect me at all?"

"Because you are my last best link to Slava." He spit on the ground in front of him. "My idiot subordinate, he used very poor judgment in his handling of Mikel. As you might say, he got carried away and Mikel expired before he could reveal what he knew. For now, that leaves me with you and you with me."

"You forgot to mention Magdalena."

"Ah, yes, the beautiful Magdalena." He smiled that smile again. "How is she enjoying her new accommodations in the Royal Dearborn Hotel? My compliments to you and your security people. See, you are a re-sourceful man. You did that on the fly, did you not? No one instructed you how to go about protecting her. That was good and the people you have hired to guard her, they are excellent. I have even done business with some of them, but I do not have this job because I am a fool. You cannot afford to have her guarded twenty-four hours a day for very long. And why risk her for such a man as Slava? Give him to me and I will end his suffering and guilt quickly, painlessly. You have my word. I have too much respect for you to offer you financial incentive and I have no enjoy-ment from threatening a woman. But, as I said, I will do—"

"Your job no matter what." I thought for a moment and suddenly all the noise from the fire, the snapping flames, the fire chief screaming instructions, the swooshing of the fire hoses all came rushing in to fill the vacuum I had been in since I'd spotted Lagunov leaning on his Caddy. "I am waiting for a call from Slava," I heard myself say. "I will tell him what you are offering. That's the best I can do. Give me a number I can reach you at."

He made a puzzled face as he reached into his wallet. He handed me a card. It was heavy stock and embossed, though the only thing on it was a telephone number. No name. No address. Only a number with an area code I did not recognize.

"Day or night," he said.

"You know you are awfully calm for a man who just killed two people."

"Would you have me shed tears for the men who were going to kill you?"

"Do you shed tears at all?"

"I am Russian," he said, as if that explained everything. If it did, I was too thick to understand.

He saw the confusion on my face.

"Russians cry easily. But we do not cry like the people here or in Europe because things are hard or sad. Life is hard. Life is sad. No, Gus, we cry for sentimental things. The sight of an old woman's face or of a baby. We cry at the sight of an old friend we have not seen for years or at the sound of an old folk song. We cry for sentimental things, things of the soul."

I was tempted to ask if he believed he had a soul, but who was I to ask? He stared at me for a moment, nodded, and said good night. I waited until I couldn't see his taillights before getting into my car and leaving. I was pretty numb during the ride back to the Paragon. I kept checking my mirrors to see if I could spot Lagunov behind me. I could not, though somehow I knew he was there. The craziest part was that I found some measure of comfort in that.

56

By the time I'd gotten back to the hotel, I was dead tired. Adrenaline rushes are great until the rush is gone and the exhaustion takes over. I had called Maggie from the parking lot. Told her I loved her and assured her everything would be all right. I knew one part of it was true, the part about loving her. I didn't have any idea if everything would be all right. That all depended on people and things out of my control. *Control!* I used to think I had control of my life. Then again, I used to believe in Santa Claus and the Tooth Fairy. I guess I got past those myths by the time I was six. The myth of control persisted into my forties. I kept checking my cell phone for a call back from Slava. I might just as well have expected Santa and the Tooth Fairy to be waiting in the lobby for me with a sack of toys and a shiny silver dollar.

I neglected to tell Maggie about my evening. I didn't want to go through the whole bloody saga of Micah Spears. I still couldn't quite believe it myself. And as I listened to Maggie tell me how much she was looking forward to the start of rehearsals in the morning, I realized I hadn't even bothered asking Judge Kaufman for Spears's real name. I'm not sure it would have mattered. Whatever name you knew him by, whatever shape he took, the devil was still the devil. *The devil.* It was almost funny. Somehow it was a lot easier for me to conceive of the devil than to conceive of God. All I had to do was live in the world to find proof of the devil. I'd just had an evening full of proof.

"Gus, are you okay?"

"I'm tired, but why are you asking?"

"You were laughing, kinda."

"Sorry, I wasn't laughing at you at all."

I'd gotten off the phone quickly after that because I could feel myself shutting down.

I zombie-walked through the empty lobby and was glad to see no one was at the front desk. I wasn't in the mood for more conversation. When I got upstairs, I took off my jacket, unstrapped my holster, and literally fell into bed. I must've turned the TV on, too, since it was on when I opened my eyes. I was disoriented, thinking I was late for something—I didn't know what—and jumped up onto the floor. I remembered that feeling from when I was a kid and would wake up on a Sunday morning thinking it was Monday and that I'd missed the school bus.

Then I remembered where I was and who I was and ached like I'd been shot as the last few years flooded over me all at once. The call. The hospital. The wake. The burial. The raging and the pain. The blame and the mourning. The grief and guilt. Annie's affair. The divorce. Krissy's self-destruction. Tommy and TJ Delcamino. Kareem Shivers. Pete Mc-Cann. Jimmy Regan. Richie Zito. And now there were more bodies on the pyre. Some fresh. Some old and nearly forgotten. Some paid for. Some not. I had suffered through a few of these everything-all-at-once moments since John Jr.'s death. I wondered how Lagunov would have assessed my calm and resourcefulness if he had been there to witness my moment on the cross of recent history.

When I caught my breath, I checked the time. Five thirty-seven. I felt much better than I had when I'd fallen into bed, but the panic had taken a bite out of me again. I shut the TV off, got fully undressed, went to the bathroom, and came back ready to sleep. But I noticed the message button on the hotel phone flashing red. Had I slept through the call or had I been so spent when I fell into bed that I'd just missed it? It was beside the point now. I listened to the message.

Gus, it's Lara. You know, Lara from Gyron. Please call me when you get this. Please, it's really important. Something's not right. Call me on my cell when you get this. Whenever you get this. On my cell.

She ended the call by giving me her cell phone number, but she needn't have bothered telling me something wasn't right. I could hear it in her excited, breathless whisper. The problem was that she didn't give me a clue as to what wasn't right and where it wasn't right. I was guessing it was at work, but that's all it was, a guess. I listened to the message again, this time taking note of when she left it. She'd called only about ten minutes after I'd left for my mystery date with Judge Kaufman. It had been my experience that when people tell you to call them whenever you get a message, that they mean it. So that's what I did. After five rings, the call went straight to voice mail. I hung up and dialed it again to try and wake her up. Same result. It was my turn to leave a message. I didn't want to make her anxiety any worse by leaving a worried message or to make too much of her message.

"Hey, Lara, it's Gus Murphy returning your call. It's early and I'm going to get some more sleep, but call me whenever." I clicked off and put the phone on the nightstand.

The next time I opened my eyes, I knew where I was and who I was and there was only that little sting I always felt in my chest where my whole heart used to be. The sun was peeking through the curtains and the clock told me it was nearly eleven. The sun was a nice change of pace from last night's misting rain. It would have been grand if my cell wasn't buzzing. I didn't figure it was Maggie. She'd be in rehearsals by now or meeting up with her castmates. That left Slava or Lara. It was Lara's number, but the person at the other end of the line wasn't her.

"Gus?"

"Al Roussis? What the fuck are you—"

I didn't finish the sentence because there would only ever be one reason for Al Roussis to be calling me on Lara's phone. He knew by my sudden silence that I had my answer and let me absorb the reality of it.

"How?" I asked.

"Looks like a home invasion. She was raped, beaten to death, and robbed. The place is a mess. She's a mess."

"Oh, fuck! Her daughter! She has an autistic daughter. Is she—"

"She wasn't here, Gus. A neighbor says the kid started living in a group home in January."

This is where most people would have said "Thank God." I passed on the opportunity. Tough to thank a God who is okay with what had been done to Lara, but had, in a moment of divine largesse, kindly spared her daughter.

"Gus, I need to talk to you . . . officially."

"Can we do it off-premises?"

"Sure."

"Why don't I come over there? Where is there?"

He asked, "You don't know where she lived?"

"Is that the first official question, Al?"

"If you'd like it to be, yes."

"I knew where she worked, but not where she lived. She also used to come into the club."

"No, Gus, I don't think here is a good idea. They've taken her away, but . . . don't come here."

"What's the time frame?"

"ME says between nine and eleven last night. Why?"

"You know why. Because you'll want to know if I have an alibi. And yes, I have about the best alibi you've ever heard."

"I'm listening."

"Give Judge Kaufman a call."

"Julius Kaufman? What were you two doing?"

"Discussing jurisprudence. What else?"

"This isn't funny, Gus."

"I'm not trying to be. Let's just say the judge and I had a private matter to discuss that doesn't concern you. He'll tell you the same."

"Okay, but I caught the case and there's still stuff I need to know. Meet me at Antics Pub on Hawkins Avenue in Ronkonkoma in an hour. It's close to you."

"I'll be there."

I knew a lawyer who liked to say to juries that he was dumb but not stupid, and that the ADA was treating them as if they were both. I felt that way at the moment. Suffolk County may not be the Garden of Eden, in spite of what local real estate brokers might tell you. We had our share of violent murders, but I thought it was a little bit too much of a coincidence that two women who worked at the same company should be brutally murdered within months of each other. And since Rondo Salazar couldn't have done it, I knew it had to be somehow connected to Gyron. But how? Why? There was that question again.

57

(FRIDAY NOON)

ntics Pub was on Hawkins Avenue just north of Exit 60 on the
LIE, next door to a PSE&G substation, and across the street from
a funeral home. Cozy. Antics was somewhere between a low-rent
shithole and a passable dive. It had come into the world as a single-family
house that, with middling success, had been turned into a bar-restaurant.
The only decent meal I ever had there was on St. Paddy's Day. Then
again, it was tough to fuck up corned beef and cabbage. But it was a local
mecca for the cheap-beer-and-cigarette crowd.

I got there a few minutes before Al and found a booth for us by the
front window. A waitress came over the minute I sat down. She wore
black slacks that fit her five years and ten pounds ago and a top that
showed too much sagging, tanning-salon cleavage. Yet none of that is
what caught my eye. She had the look of surrender about her, a look I had
seen in Lara's face, a look I had seen on many women's faces at the club.
The expression that said she had gotten as far as she was ever going to
get and if this was as good as it was going to get, well, then do as you
will. It wasn't resignation, exactly. No, it was surrender. She had been
pretty once, my waitress, maybe beautiful, but too much sun, too many

Marlboros, too many late-night threesomes with Jack Daniel's and last-call Romeos had taken their toll.

"What'll ya have to drink?" Her mouth made the proper friendly shapes, her hazel eyes as disinterested as could be.

"Corona, no lime. I'm waiting for someone."

"Aren't we all?"

"Any specials?" I asked just to ask.

"Menu's on the placemat." She made a nasty face, pointing to her left. "Specials are on the board."

Al gave me a quick wave from the parking lot, then came in. As he was sitting down, the waitress delivered my Corona, a lime sticking out of the top of the bottle. I didn't bother complaining about it. Al said he'd take a Corona, too. The waitress seemed pleased not to have to talk to him.

"Are we going to eat?" he wanted to know.

"Not me."

"You mind if I do?"

"Menu's on the placemat. The specials are on the board."

Al was one of those people who, in spite of an unimposing stature, could eat like a moose. On any other day I might have taken a delight in listening to what he might order. But when the waitress delivered his beer and took his order, I paid their conversation little mind.

"Okay, Al, ask your questions."

He took out a pad and put a voice recorder on the table. He made some official-sounding statement that I barely paid attention to and asked me if I was aware I was being recorded and if I consented. When I nodded, he gave me a look.

"Yes, I am aware, and yes, I consent."

I gave completely honest answers to his questions, describing how I'd met Lara, how many times I'd met her, the nature of our interactions, why I had her phone number, why I had called and left a message on her cell, etc. All this while he was eating his soup, Buffalo wings, salad, cheeseburger, and fries. He told me he was shutting off the recorder.

"I called Judge Kaufman," he said, wiping ketchup off his fingers. "He wasn't pleased, but he alibied you a hundred percent. You wanna share with me what you were doing up there in with Julius Caesar?"

"No."

"You wanna share what you think about Lara's homicide?"

"Truth?"

"Truth."

"I'm not buying the home-invasion scenario."

"You would if you had seen the door busted in, the blood everywhere, and the condition of her body. She was bleeding all over the place, if you catch my meaning, Gus. It was at least two, three guys, and they didn't treat her with much respect. Then when they were done with her, they broke her up with baseball bats. They left the fucking bats behind."

"I think it was meant to look like a home invasion gone out of control just like Linh Trang Spears's murder was meant to look like some random encounter gone wrong. This is about something going on at Gyron, where they both worked. I'm sure of it, Al. That's what Lara's call to me was about. She must've found something out. Maybe she stayed late at work and didn't want to say anything for fear of being caught . . . I don't know."

"Any proof?"

I shook my head.

"I didn't think so. That doesn't mean I won't check it out. You know I will. But frankly, I have to check out the guys she dated, her ex, the men she met at your club. You know how it works, Gus."

"But when you get around to Gyron, they'll know you're coming."

"They always know I'm coming."

"Can you get search warrants? There's an area of the factory they call the box, that—"

"Search warrants! Based on what? You're getting way ahead of yourself here. C'mon, Gus. We're talking two separate homicides of different natures, committed by different assailants with different MOs in different locations months apart."

"I think it might have something to do with their finances. Lara said they weren't really busy anymore, but the factory manager is driving around in a hundred-grand Maserati."

"Saying they weren't as busy as they used to be isn't exactly an accusation of wrongdoing. And no offense to the lady, but she was a receptionist."

"But Linh Trang wasn't. She worked in accounting."

"Gus, like I said, I'll do my job. I'll check it all out, but it's not going to happen overnight. I have to work the case the way it presents itself to me, and how it presents itself to me right now is as a home invasion, rape, robbery, and murder. You get something concrete, something I can use, and I will make the quickest fucking U-turn you've ever seen. But until then . . ."

I wanted to argue with him, but it would have been a waste of time. He was right and he *was* the Homicide detective. I was a courtesy van driver who had worked patrol with the occasional plainclothes assignment. Last year, that thing with Tommy Delcamino and his kid, I kind of stumbled into that and found my own way. I'd made headway mostly out of luck and stubbornness. I supposed if I wanted the evidence Al was talking about, I would have to do it again. The difference between Al and me . . . I didn't have to play by the rules.

"Okay, Al, you've gotta follow where the evidence leads you. I get it. Then let me let you get back to it."

"I'm glad you're off the suspect list. You know there are plenty of guys on the job who want to hurt you because of Pete and Jimmy Regan."

"Believe me, I know," I said, rubbing my belly where Tony Palumbo had tried to put his fist and foot through me. "Now get outta here and do your job. I got this."

"You sure?" he asked, already slipping his jacket back on.

"As long as you keep me updated on the case."

"Fair enough, Gus. Take care. I'll get these guys."

He had a great clearance rate, but still I couldn't help but wonder how many times those words had been uttered and how many times the implied promise in them had gone unfulfilled. I watched Al walk past me and get into his car, my mind churning the whole time.

"I'll take this when you're ready," the waitress said, dropping the check.

"Wait."

I gave her the cash and told her to keep the rest. It was a nice tip, but not even twenty-five percent got a rise out of her. At this stage, I wondered what would.

As I was leaving Antics, I saw a *Newsday* on the table next to me, the front page facing up. There were booking photos of young, hard-looking men with facial tattoos staring blankly into oblivion. But more than their photos, the headline caught my attention:

ASESINOS ASSASSINATED
GANG VIOLENCE IN SMITHTOWN

58

That did it.

I had all the ingredients called for in the recipe, but not the recipe itself. There had to be a connection between Gyron Machinery, the Asesinos, and the murders of Linh Trang and Lara. There had to be. I couldn't see what the connection was, not yet. I was close, though, otherwise why come after me, why murder Lara? Charlie Prince had been right, after all. It was definitely my poking around that had started the chain reaction, but what I couldn't see before was that my turning up at Gyron had been the catalyst.

As I drove, guilt whispered Lara's name in my ear, each whisper louder than the one before it until the crescendo of her name was deafening. Even the jet engines overhead as I pulled into the Paragon lot seemed to me to be screaming Lara's name. Although as a cop and a basically rational human being I understood that the only persons responsible for Lara's murder were the men who killed her, it was going to be hard, if not impossible, for me to absolve myself. A chorus of discordant what-ifs joined the din of guilty accusation. *What if I hadn't gone to Gyron? What if I hadn't been a wee bit flirtatious with Lara? What if I hadn't bought her drinks at the club? What if . . . What if . . . What if.* If I thought it would have helped, I would have clapped my hands over my ears. I knew better. Eventually the chorus would die down, but the whispers would never leave.

"Gus!" Felix shouted to get my attention as a hurried through the lobby. "Gus."

His voice broke the spell, at least temporarily. I was glad of it. I retraced my steps back to the front desk.

"What's up?"

"A man called for you after you left this morning. I asked him if he wanted to leave a voice mail message on your room phone, but he refused."

"What did he sound like?"

Felix screwed up his face as if he'd bitten into a rancid piece of meat. "It was an odd voice, like in the movies, like when they use a distortion machine."

"Did he say anything else, this man?"

Felix slid a piece of paper across the black granite countertop. "He gave me this number and then he hung up."

Slava.

I thanked Felix and then went straight up to my room. I wasn't sure who to call or what to do first, because as much as I wanted to save Slava's life, as much as I owed it to him, I had now incurred another debt, a bigger debt, so said the renewed screaming in my ears. Besides, I knew if I called the number Slava had left for me, he wouldn't pick up and it would be impossible for me to leave a voice mail. He would call me again when he was sure he was safe and beyond detection.

I wondered why he just hadn't run. He had no more connection to the USA than he had to East Timor, for chrissakes. He was an adaptable bastard, with a survival instinct like none I'd ever seen. I don't know. Maybe he figured that with the oligarch's money, running was a waste of time and that if he was going to make a stand, it might as well be here. Whatever his reasoning, I hoped he lived long enough to explain it to me. Lagunov was right, I couldn't very well keep Maggie protected round the clock, but I could afford another few days without seriously depleting my savings. So for now, I decided my new debt came first.

I called Bill and asked him to invite Micah Spears over to his apartment. I was prepared to be insistent about it. There was no need. Bill was perceptive. I'm not sure how he knew, whether it was the tone of my voice, the cadence, or the phrasing. What mattered was that he understood. I suppose good priests, like good cops, have to be able to sense trouble coming around blind corners. And before leaving the church, Bill had been a good priest. I didn't know another man who could have sustained people the way he had in spite of having lost his own faith for forty-plus years.

Spears was already there, sharing a glass of wine with Bill. They weren't exactly all smiles and good cheer, nor were they at each other's throats. It must be tough for priests, doctors, and lawyers to keep in confidence some of what they know. Hardest for priests, I thought. Sin and forgiveness was their business, but they were humans, too. At least some of them were. The ones who preyed on children belonged in a zoo. Not on display, but as meals for the big cats and hyenas. And when all was said and done, I'm not sure I would cry if Micah Spears, Rondo Salazar, and the men who killed Lara wound up in the lion enclosure with a brief head start. My bloodlust was tempered by Lagunov's words about what Slava had done in Russia. Many people would want to add him to the lions' diet. A few would happily add me.

The minute Spears and Bill saw my expression, they knew something was up with me but were unsure what. I didn't leave them guessing for very long.

"Been to Cambodia lately, Mr. Spears, or whatever the fuck your real name is?"

Bill looked sick, but Spears reacted exactly as I knew he would. He smiled at me, what passed for a smile, anyway. Then he turned to Bill.

"You were right about him, Bill. He is good at this." He turned back to me. "I've guarded that secret for quite a long time with very few cracks in the walls, and in less than two weeks you found out the whole story, didn't you?"

"I did."

"Care to tell me how?"

"Fuck you."

Now he was laughing. I thought he and Lagunov would have been a fine pair. Maybe not. Possibly because Lagunov had saved my life, I thought better of him than Spears. I couldn't picture Lagunov doing to women and children what Spears had done and I was again thankful not to have seen photographs of the Cambodian village.

He stopped laughing. "But somehow I don't think you called me here just to tell me what a horrible monster I am. You've made progress about Linh Trang."

I ignored him. "You're very wealthy, aren't you?"

"I am wealthier than most, but I don't have really big money. What has that to do—"

"Three things," I said, "and then we'll discuss your granddaughter."

He was all business now. "They are?"

"A woman was murdered helping me find out about Linh Trang. You'll hear about it on the news and read about her in the papers tomorrow. She was a single mother with an autistic daughter. I want you to take complete financial responsibility for the daughter for the rest of her life."

"If what you say is true, and—"

"You didn't hear me too well, I guess. This isn't a negotiation. The answers I need are yes, yes, and yes or I walk away and I make public the fact that a prominent Long Island businessman drowned babies, hung old people from trees like Christmas ornaments, and raped and butchered women. And I have the file to back it up," I lied.

Spears actually looked shaken by that.

"Yes, I'll take financial responsibility for the girl."

"Swear to it in front of Bill."

"I swear it, Bill, as I have never lied to you about what I did or what I was. What else?"

"I'm having someone kept under twenty-four-hour protection and the bill could run as high as twenty grand. Will you cover it?"

"Yes. Done." He snapped his fingers at me. "Move on."

"Tell Bill the real reason you were interested in me finding out why Linh Trang was killed. You lie and I'm walking out the door."

Spears hesitated, finally opening his mouth to answer after collecting himself. But it was Bill who spoke.

"Gus, for fuck's sake, don't be daft. Arnold over here—Yes, that's his name. Arnold Mason. Not the name you would figure for a monster, is it?—was in fear that after all these years his bill was coming due. The way poor Linh Trang was killed, mirroring so closely the way he and his squad mates had killed those women in the village, shook him to his core. There's no surprise in that for me, but if you think for one moment that this man didn't love his granddaughter and that his only reason he was curious as to motive was a selfish one, you are wrong."

"We can have that debate some other time," I said.

"It's a fair debate who knows more of monsters, cops or priests, but this one I'm well acquainted with. Indeed, we'll talk of this at a later date."

"So," Spears said.

"I'm not there yet, but I'm close."

"What is that supposed to mean. Is this all going to be about oaths and riddles?"

"Linh Trang and Lara, the woman I was telling you about before, were killed because they found out something about the things going on at Gyron Machinery. That's right, Spears, the place where you got her the job."

Whatever perverse pleasure I might've taken in the irony of it was extremely short-lived because for the first time since I'd met him, maybe for the first time in his whole miserable fucking life, Micah Spears looked broken. The frosty exterior cracked into a million pieces, a billion, not all with sharp edges. I gave him a moment to make some sense of it before I said any more. And that moment helped me recover from the pang of shame I felt. It was a comfort to see that part of who I once was still remained.

"Whatever the reason Linh Trang and Lara were killed is in that building, and I think I know where."

That seemed to get his attention and his icy demeanor returned, this time, though, with eyes on fire. Humpty Dumpty back together again, but red in tooth and claw. I read that phrase once—red in tooth and claw—in a poem in high school, I think. It never made sense to me before.

He said, "What are we going to do about it?"

"We?"

"That's right. We."

"Well," I said, "I'm probably not going to be able to get in there alone."

"I'm coming."

I thought about arguing with him, but I didn't see that I had many options. Slava, my first choice, was unavailable. Smudge was great in a fix, but not this kind of fix. Bill . . . I couldn't do that to him again. He had already had to bloody his hands on my account. The guys who worked the club with me were either still on the job or recently retired. And while they might've been willing to stretch the law a little, they wouldn't be willing to go as far I would be. And they would be right, because at the moment, I was prepared to go pretty fucking far. I had put Lara in danger, as Spears had put Linh Trang in danger. Neither one of us meant to, but what did that matter now?

"Okay. You wanna come, you're in. You're probably gonna have to get your hands dirty and you might not come out the other end of it."

"Do you really think that bothers me?"

I didn't answer directly. "I'm not sure how we're gonna do this yet, but we'll have to move fast. Once the Gyron people see the cops are sniffing around, they'll stop doing whatever it is that got Linh Trang and Lara killed. At least for a little while. From what I know of how they operate, Saturday is our best bet. The factory floor is pretty much shut down, but they have a few guys in to crate orders and prep shipments."

"Shipments of what, I wonder?" Bill said.

"Exactly, Bill. Exactly."

Spears's jaw clenched. I looked him in the eye.

"Do you have a gun or a rifle?"

Before I could finish the question, he peeled back his tweed jacket and showed me a Smith & Wesson 9 mm clipped to his belt. "I have a carry permit and I have some more questionable weapons at my disposal."

I nodded.

"When I come up with a plan, I'll call you. Whatever we do, it'll be tomorrow."

There wasn't anything left to say. I could see worry in Bill's eyes, but he kept his concerns to himself. Bill wasn't a gassy sort. He never spoke just to hear the sound of his own voice. And in this case he knew there would be nothing to stop what others had already set in motion. The issue for me now was coming up with a plan that wouldn't get us killed or arrested.

59

I was about to head downstairs for my usual Friday shift working the door at the Full Flaps when my room phone rang, its red light flickering, its ring an annoying electronic chitter. Since getting back from Bill's apartment, I'd accomplished exactly zero—sitting up in bed, mindlessly, blindly, flipping from channel to channel. No matter how hard I thought about it, I couldn't come up with a plan for Spears and me that made a lick of sense or wouldn't get us both shot or arrested. I liked to think I was a pretty smart person, fairly well read, too, for a cop, but sometimes that stuff didn't count for shit. And my twenty years on the job wasn't helping me much, either. Being around mutts and skells doesn't transform you into a criminal mastermind. Osmosis doesn't work that way. Besides, the thieves, arsonists, and killers I'd been around were the ones who got caught.

I'm not sure what it was, the chirping, the flickering light, or knowing that it was probably Slava on the line that flipped the switch. Whatever it was, it kicked me in the ass and sparked an idea of how it might be possible for Spears or me to get a peek at what was inside the Box at Gyron Machinery without signing our own death certificates. And in that same moment, I realized there might also be a way to get Slava out of his mess alive. Odds were against it. A lot of stuff had to go just right for it to work, but any chance at all was more than he had now.

If I didn't need Spears alive to take care of Lara's daughter, I wouldn't have spent a second worrying about keeping him safe. Spears, unlike Slava, seemed incapable of real guilt. Slava needed to live in order to suffer. He explained to me that his shame was something he needed to live with as long as he could breathe. Death, he once confided in me before I knew the details of his old life, would be too easy and would only add to the insult of what was in his past. I knew Slava to be capable of aching regret, shame, guilt. Did Micah Spears regret his part in his granddaughter's murder? Yeah, he did. I saw that for myself, but I think that was about the extent of his humanity. Did I think he spent more than fifteen seconds over the last forty years regretting what he and his friends had done in Cambodia? Probably not. The only thing he'd spent the last forty-plus years worrying about was the blowback, waiting for what he'd done to catch up to him. Hoping like mad it never would.

It was an odd equation to ponder. I don't think that's the kind of balance the universe seeks. And even if it did or even if there was a God, would the brutal murder of an innocent young woman somehow pay down the debt on the slaughter of an entire village? How could it? The dead in that village were gone, incapable of asking for restitution, incapable of receiving it, incapable of anything. And would the tortured dead take a second's pleasure in more innocent brutality? Those were the kinds of equations for God's defenders, philosophers, and physicists to ponder. I left all questions of balance behind once I picked up the phone.

"Gus Murphy," I said, trying unsuccessfully not to sound happy.

"Is Slava, Gus."

"I hoped it was you."

"You are calling Slava, yes?"

"Is it a secure line to talk on?" I whispered, as if whispering mattered.

"Is safe."

I explained to him about Maggie, about the twenty-four-hour protection she was under and why. I explained to him about how Lagunov had saved my life by killing the Asesinos. I waited to tell him my idea about Gyron because I wanted to give him a moment to take in what I had just told him. I also knew his first instinct once he did absorb it would be to sacrifice himself in order to protect Maggie. The thought of any innocent blood being spilled on his behalf was worse than the shame and guilt he was already dealing with.

"Slava is stopping this, Gus. I am giving myself to Lagunov and this is all being over with," he said, as I suspected he would. "I cannot having your beautiful Maggie hurt for my sins and stupidness."

"I have an idea, Slava. It's not much of one, but if it works, I think you have a chance and we will all come out of it okay."

From his end, there was silence. Then finally, "What are you having in mind?" he asked, some hesitation in his voice.

I was glad he asked. He was a man who would see the holes in my plan. He listened very patiently. When I was done, there was more silence.

"Much can be going wrong with this. Is very risky for you, Gus, and for this other man. For Slava, not so much."

"In the end, Slava, if it works and we get that far, the risk will all be yours. Your life will be in my hands."

"You should be forgetting this other man, let Slava go in with you. My life is worth very little and I have no worries of dying."

"No," I said, "it won't work if you expose yourself like that. This only works if you hang back. You can't be out front with me."

"This other man, you are trusting him?"

"In this? Yes."

"He is not hesitating to use weapons?"

"He has killed."

"Is not what I am asking."

"He won't hesitate," I said, though I had no way of knowing.

Spears or Mason or whoever he was under his skin might have happily killed dozens of people, but that was a long time ago. I didn't think he had necessarily changed. People don't change unless they want to or unless events change them. I had all the proof of that I needed. But Spears was an older man now, and old men, even old monsters, might hesitate. They have more to protect. I'd find out soon enough.

"Why not go to police?"

"I already have, Slava, but I have no real proof of anything. They have to work their cases the way they work them. You know that. And once the police start sniffing around—"

"The Gyron people will be disappearing all evidence," he said, finishing my thought.

"Are we set?"

"I am not liking this, Gus. What if you are wrong? You could be going to prison."

"I'm not wrong. Are we set?" I repeated.

"Tomorrow, Slava will be there as you are saying."

There was little joy in his voice about the prospect of getting out from under the hangman's rope. Neither of us had any illusions about our odds for success. He realized that part of his chance of escaping a death sentence depended on me putting my neck in the noose. I realized it, too. That's why my next call would be to Maggie. I wanted to tell her that the end to the worries about her safety was at hand. I wanted to hear about how the first day of rehearsals had gone. But mostly, I wanted to hear her voice and thank her for loving me. Before I called, I gathered myself. It wasn't going to be easy to not give myself away.

60

The monster and I sat in his black Mercedes SL550 convertible, the roof down in spite of the late-afternoon chill. Having the roof down allowed us to stand on the seats and use binoculars to keep tabs on the comings and goings at Gyron. We were in the parking lot of a "To Let" factory building across the way and slightly down the road from Gyron, a convenient row of overgrown hedges affording us some cover. And we needed as much cover as we could get. Although we were at an oblique angle and the street separating us from the Gyron building was a wide one, Saturday in this industrial park was almost free of activity. A few FedEx trucks had passed by, an eighteen-wheeler or two, and a useless security cruiser had made a few cursory laps.

In opposition to the rest of the park, there had been a flurry of activity across the way. We'd been there for two hours, and in that time the loading dock's bay doors had rolled up seven times. The strange thing was that the vehicles backing in and out of the bays weren't what I would've expected. Not a single semi or box truck had backed in. The largest vehicle had been a brown step van that kind of looked like a UPS truck but wasn't. The other six times the bay doors had gone up, they'd been raised for smaller vans and even a few cars. I'd taken down all their tag numbers. Five of seven were out-of-state plates. The corrugated steel doors rolled down each time a vehicle backed into the dock, so we couldn't get peek at what was going on or what was being loaded.

"Whatever it is they're loading, it can't be that heavy," I said. "They come out of there not riding much lower than when they back in. Only the brown step van rode noticeably lower on its suspension."

He grunted back at me. We hadn't talked much for most of the time we waited. He kept track of the vehicles in the parking lot, trying to figure how many men were inside. And like I said, I was keeping tabs on the vehicles pulling in and out of the loading bays. We figured our best chance to strike would come when they began closing up shop and the workers started to leave. It was simple math. The fewer of them on the premises, the better it was for us. But it was a tricky calculation because we couldn't wait too long. We needed Carl Ryan to be there when we moved in. The whole first part of the damn plan was a tricky calculation based mostly on guesses and very little solid information. The second part was even shakier, based solely on wishful thinking and my less-than-encyclopedic knowledge of human behavior.

"Is the gray Maserati still in its spot?" I asked, though I knew that it was. The wait was getting to me. "We can't let him leave."

Spears ignored the question about the Maserati. "You're a queer duck, Murphy, you know that?"

"How so?"

"We've sat here for two hours and you haven't asked me."

"Asked you what?"

"Don't go thick on me now, Gus. You haven't asked about what happened *over there*."

"I haven't asked because I'm not in the mood for lies and revisionist history. And even if you told me the truth, what would it matter? And what would you have me ask, anyway? Should I ask about how you went about it? Whether you systematically killed the older villagers first, drowned the infants, and then raped the women? Should I ask if the old people were dead before you hung them from the trees? Should I ask if the women and girls were still alive when you butchered them? What? Do you think I'd be curious about that? Should I ask why? No. I already know why. You're a fucking monster."

He didn't shrink from my assessment, nor did his expression change. He wasn't going to try to persuade me otherwise. I'm not sure he much cared about my opinion of him. For all I knew about what went on inside him, he may have brought the subject up simply to pass the time because he wanted an excuse to relive the incident. Killers do that sometimes. They agree to interviews with the press and with shrinks so they can relive the excitement of what they had done. I wasn't curious about the details of his inhumanity. That was true, but there were some things I *was* curious about.

"How did they find out?"

Spears was confused. "How did who find out what?"

"Your son, to start. How did he find out about what you had done? I can't believe it's a coincidence that he adopted a Vietnamese orphan."

Spears laughed a nasty laugh.

"A coincidence? No, not a coincidence."

"You sure didn't tell him."

"My first wife," he said. "Kevin's mother told him. Let me save you the trouble of asking how she found out: a letter. I came home late from work one night and I found her beside herself in the kitchen. There was a half-empty bottle of vodka on the table. It was clear she'd been crying and she was bleeding from her forehead as if she'd smacked it into the corner of an open cabinet door or something. Her face was covered in bloody tears, but when she saw me, she charged at me like she was shot out of a cannon. She came clawing at my face, kicking, screaming like a banshee. She was calling me your favorite word: monster. She also used some rather colorful descriptors along with it."

I guess I shouldn't have been shocked at his continued calm demeanor and cool voice as he described what I could have only imagined was a horrible scene. I was, nonetheless. That's the thing about real monsters, I think. The rest of us can never quite believe the depth of their depravity. We want to think they're guilty but with an explanation, that they aren't as evil as we think. That was why they could sneak up on us. We let them.

"When I got her slightly calmed down," he continued, "she walked back to the table, bent over, and picked up two sheets of paper that were on the tile floor. She shoved them into my hands. 'How could I not see you for what you are?' she said. 'How could I have fallen in love with you? How could I have been so blind and stupid?' Then she started raging again, but this time at herself, tearing at her own clothes, scratching her face. I slapped her. I had to. And you know what she did? She started laughing at me."

"She wasn't laughing at you," I said. "She was laughing at herself, at how ridiculous and absurd the world was. That letter was like an earthquake, tornado, avalanche, and forest fire all at once. One second she was happily married and had a family and the next it was gone. Believe me, Spears, I know. I know how that is."

He looked at me as if he had never before considered the possibility. But if I expected this small revelation to magically transform him from Mr. Hyde back into a human being, I would be disappointed. He shrugged. *So what? Next.*

"I moved into a hotel that night. Kevin was away at college then. I knew she'd call him as soon as she could. They were always thick as thieves, those two." Spears shook his head and smirked. "It was years before the kid would even speak to me again or acknowledge me, and then only because his ship was sinking and he was desperate for money when his first business was going under. He always was a fuckup like his mother. He couldn't even get it right about where to adopt from. I wanted to take the stupid idiot and show him a map." Spears jabbed at his left palm with his right index finger. *"This is Vietnam. This is Cambodia.*

After what Pol Pot did, there were plenty of Cambodian orphans to go around. What a silly, guilty fool, my son. What did he have to feel guilty about?"

I didn't want to go there, and asked, "Who sent the letter?"

"It was typewritten, unsigned, and the envelope had no return address. But whoever sent it got all the details right. I was sure it was Chris Farmer, one of the Lost Patrol." He smiled as he said it. "That's what we called ourselves, the Lost Patrol."

It was all I could do not to punch the smug asshole in the face, but before I could, he went on.

"Chris hadn't done very well after coming back and relocating. He was a hick, a real redneck from Buttfucksville, Arkansas, somewhere and just couldn't cope out of his world. He was always after me to help him out. Before too long his requests became what they always really were in the first place: blackmail threats. So I thought he had just finally made good on the threats."

"And who told Linh Trang?"

He shrugged. "Doesn't really matter, does it?"

"Humor me."

"I suspect it was Roberta."

"The second Mrs. Spears?" I said. "Telling LT about you would have risked breaking your divorce settlement."

He made a face that was part fury and part admiration, but said, "I would never cut her off. Unlike my bitch of a first wife, I loved Roberta. Only person or thing I think I ever loved in my life. Only loss I ever regretted before my granddaughter was murdered."

"I don't think it was—"

Spears cut me off. "Wait! Shut up. The van's pulling out with three guys in it. That leaves only two cars in the lot plus Ryan's."

"Time to move."

But we didn't move, not immediately. There was always that moment for me, that moment before a drug raid, before responding to a shooting, before going through the front door at a bad domestic call, when it floods in: the fear, the risks, the knowledge that things never go as planned. Never! I didn't know what was going through Spears's head, whether he was afraid or worried. I didn't care, just as long as he did what he was supposed to do and came out the other side of it alive.

61

(SATURDAY, LATE AFTERNOON)

I hopped out of the car, reaching back in for Spears's Benelli semiautomatic shotgun. The damned thing was as sleek and black as the Mercedes. Spears had offered me a whole range of weapons, some of which weren't meant to kill waterfowl or elk. They were human-specific. Along with his array of hunting rifles, he had a Romanian-made AK47 and a fully operational MP5. These days I was less familiar with the gun laws than when I was on the job, but it was a pretty safe bet that neither of those two weapons was legal for a private citizen to possess in New York State, gun permit notwithstanding. I don't suppose he gave a fuck about legality.

I slung the shotgun over my shoulder. Those two assault rifles were killing machines, and I had no desire to empty a clip and pile up bodies. I'd already killed all the people I ever wanted to, justifiably or not. Cops are comfortable with shotguns because just the sight of them scares the shit out of people. They're loud and they're powerful and you don't have to be a very good shot if you're forced to use them. With a pump-action shotgun, just the *cha-ching* of chambering a round was usually enough to stop someone in his tracks. But a pump-action shotgun was about the only hole in Spears's private little armory.

"This is it," I said, yanking the rolled-up ski mask down over my face. "You know what to do."

Spears didn't answer, not with words. He hit the gas and pulled out of the lot. I climbed the parking lot fence, wiggled through the hedge, and made my way across the street to the parking lot of the building that abutted Gyron Machinery. A low concrete-and-stucco wall separated the properties. I crouched behind the wall and waited. And then . . . *Bang!* The waiting was over. I peeked over the ledge of the wall and saw that Spears had T-boned Carl Ryan's Maserati, crushing in the passenger-side door. Spears's airbag deployed, but he didn't look any the worse for wear. As soon as the airbag deflated, Spears took off his shoulder belt and laid his head down on the steering wheel.

It didn't take long for one of the loading bay doors to roll up and for two guys to come running out to see what had happened. They were shouting at each other in Spanish, one gesturing wildly with his arm to get back into the building. I didn't understand a lot of what they were saying, but I heard Ryan's name mentioned a few times. It wouldn't be long now. My heart was pounding so hard I swore I could hear it in the quiet of the failing daylight. My mouth was cotton, the sound of my pounding heart suddenly drowned out by a high-pitched ringing, the by-product of rushing blood full of adrenaline. And as if on cue, Carl Ryan came running out of the office door, the guy who'd gone to fetch him trailing behind.

"Motherfucka! Motherfucka!" he screamed as he ran. "Look what this motherfucka did to my car. I'm gonna kill you, you cocksuck—"

Ryan went silent when he got up close to Spears's Mercedes. He was facing away from me, so I couldn't tell anything about his expression, but his body language changed completely. He stiffened as he slowly swiveled his head from side to side. I couldn't be sure if he was looking for accomplices or to see if there were any passersby who might've witnessed the crash. My guess was he recognized Spears when he got up close to the cars and then Spears, as was the plan, made sure Ryan knew who he was.

"You fucking murderer. You killed my granddaughter." Spears slurred his words as if he was drunk or concussed or both.

Ryan didn't deny it. He didn't call Spears crazy. He didn't make a move to call an ambulance.

Spears reached down and picked up the .38 he had hidden beneath his seat. When his hand came up holding it, he said, "I'm gonna kill you, you fucker. I'm—"

Ryan smacked the pistol out of Spears's hand, balled his fist to punch Spears, but held back because Spears played possum. He plunked his head back on the steering wheel, looking for all the world as if he had fallen unconscious. Ryan was swiveling his head again, making doubly sure there were no witnesses. He waved the two men over to the car.

"Cuchillo, get this asshole inside."

"Where we did the girl?"

"Yeah."

"You want me to cut him?"

"Not yet," Ryan said.

Cuchillo, I knew what that meant: knife. Knife was about five-seven, with broad shoulders and a V-shaped torso. He moved like a cat—nimble and steady on his feet.

"Alejo," Ryan called to the bigger of the two men, the one who had gone back into the building to fetch him. "Help Cuch carry this prick inside and then come out to see if his car runs. If it does, pull it into one of the bays for now, then meet us in the utility room. We're gonna see just how much the old man really knows."

With that, Ryan picked up Spears's .38, turned, and walked back toward the offices.

A minute later, Cuchillo carried Spears's arms, Alejo his legs. They dragged him into the shop through the open bay door. Spears was good. He didn't put up any kind of fight. He just sort of went limply along.

Five minutes later, Alejo was back. The Mercedes turned over when Alejo punched the ignition button. *Good.* I needed Alejo to be preoccupied with the car. When he put it in reverse, the Mercedes kind of lurched backward about fifteen feet and stalled out. The front end was pretty well crushed and there was fluid leaking all over the parking lot blacktop.

I thought out my next move as Alejo tried to get the Mercedes to turn over again. To me, Ryan's actions were as much an admission of guilt as a signed confession, but my standards meant very little in the scheme of things. I needed proof. On the other hand, I was satisfied that neither Alejo nor Cuchillo were innocent bystanders. One of my worries going into this was that some innocent, eight-buck-an-hour schmuck would get caught up in the potential crossfire. I wasn't worried about that anymore. What I was worried about was the one guy who hadn't shown himself. By Spears's count there were four men in the building. Ryan, Cuchillo, and Alejo accounted for three of the four. I'd have to watch out for the other guy, but I couldn't wait around much longer for the fourth man to show himself. I had to move.

Alejo was cursing up a storm as he kept pushing the ignition button, the Mercedes stubbornly refusing to turn over. He stopped moving, stopped cursing when I shoved the tip of the Benelli's barrel into his neck. In my heightened state I became acutely aware of the smells around the wrecked cars. The stink of heated rubber and plastic. The petroleum and chemical tang of gasoline, antifreeze, and motor oil. The rank odor of sweat and fear coming off Alejo. Maybe a little bit of that was from me, too. Maybe a lot of it.

"Get the fuck outta the car. Now!" I whispered, backing up enough so that he couldn't take a swing at the barrel of the shotgun. "When you're out of the car, walk toward the open bay door. You open your mouth before you're told or run or call out and I will blow your fucking head off. And believe, Alejo, at this distance with this gun . . ."

But he didn't move.

"Fuck your mother."

I stepped back in close and smacked the side of the rifle stock hard against his ear. It was a cushioned synthetic stock, but it hurt plenty.

"That was your last warning. Now, get the fuck outta the car."

He did it this time, still rubbing the side of his head.

"Walk slow."

As we moved forward, I noticed that Alejo was pretty much covered in tats. Some of them were colorful—red, blue, green, even yellow—and skillfully done, but many were sloppy prison tats. And then I noticed one on the left side of his neck, a spread-winged vulture, a human skull in its beak.

"Asesino," I mumbled to myself.

Alejo must've heard it, because he laughed.

"You got some big *cojones* on you, but you gonna die ugly, *cabrón*. You gonna scream like that old *puta* did when that baseball bat hit her the first time."

I came very close to pulling the trigger when he said that, thoughts of what had been done to Lara and LT rushing into my head. Instead I stuck the point of the barrel into his back and shoved him so hard he toppled forward. "Get up, shut the fuck up, and keep walking. You don't do it, I'll kill you right here and I'll start by blowing your balls off."

He kept walking. Although I couldn't see his face, I knew he was smiling. I'd be lying if I said that didn't unnerve me some.

"Stop," I ordered when we got to the open bay door.

He stopped. I told him to turn around. He turned slowly, the smile I knew was there still on his face. I didn't ask why he was smiling. I knew why.

"Call the other guy to come to the dock to help you."

"Other guy?"

"Not Ryan and not Cuchillo," I said. "The other guy."

"No other guy. Just Carl, Cuch, and me."

"Bullshit. Call him out here."

I didn't have time to argue with him. I kicked him flush on his right kneecap, hard. Something snapped inside his leg with a sickening sound. Alejo gasped in pain, collapsing to the concrete truck bay. I didn't give

326 / **REED FARREL COLEMAN**

him a chance to scream, sticking the barrel of the Benelli into his crotch. He pissed himself, a dark stain covering the front of his jeans.

"Call him out here, now."

"Fuck you," he said through gritted teeth. "Fuck you!"

That was it. He wasn't going to do it, no matter what I did to him. I'd already done the worst I could, I'd embarrassed him. Once he pissed himself, he was lost to me. I relaxed my grip on the shotgun, reached into my back pocket, and got out the telescoping metal baton Lagunov had left behind in Mikel's room. I laid it across the back of Alejo's head. He went limp and quiet. He'd be out for a while, and even if he came to quickly, he wasn't going anywhere with that knee.

I slung the shotgun back over my shoulder and got my old service Glock out of my jacket pocket. I had to go through the steel door and onto the shop floor. The door, which I had been through once on a previous visit, was heavy and had only a slit of a window in it. That slit wouldn't give me much of a view of who or what might be waiting for me on the other side. As powerful and loud as the Benelli was, a long barreled weapon was unwieldy to use coming through a door.

I looked through the window slit, moving my head from side to side to see as much of the shop floor as I could. It was fairly dark, none of the higher-intensity factory lights were on, but it was far from pitch black inside. Skylights in the factory roof provided some ambient light. I saw nothing moving on the floor at all. I gripped the handle, turned it, gently pushed open the door, and stepped through.

62

After I eased the door shut behind me, I let myself calm down before moving again. Pressing my back to the closed door, I listened. For what? For anything. For everything. But there was nothing to hear. No screams. No shuffling of feet. Nothing at all except for the sounds of my slowing breaths. Through the windowed wall at the opposite end of the shop, I saw the overhead lights were on in the corridor that contained all the offices. There was no movement there, either. I tried to remember if I'd seen a door marked UTILITIES or UTILITY ROOM during my previous visits, but it was no good. I assumed, mostly out of wishful thinking, that it had to be where the offices were. It didn't really matter. I couldn't stay where I was much longer. I had no idea of how long Alejo would be out of it. I had to get a look inside the Box and I couldn't leave Spears alone for too much longer.

I checked my watch. Although it felt as if an hour had passed since Spears crashed his car into Ryan's, less than fifteen minutes had actually elapsed. I put my service weapon back in my pocket, took the shotgun in my hands, and moved as carefully and quietly as possible to the area on the shop floor where the Box was located. As I moved, I kept an eye on the corridor windows. I was almost there when Cuchillo's silhouette appeared in the corridor. I froze, feeling as naked and exposed as the day I was born. The only cover I had was a shadow thrown from the corner wall of the Box. Cuchillo took his face away from the glass, moved down the hall, and opened the door onto the shop floor.

"Alejo! Alejo!" he shouted, his voice bouncing off all the hard, flat surfaces.

When there was no reply, he shook his head, said something I couldn't hear, and began to close the door. But he stopped, opened it back up, and peered into the darkened factory. He looked right at me, right through me. He seemed to sniff the air. He hesitated, then finally closed the door. I waited until he disappeared from view before moving again. The clock was really ticking fast now. If they were already getting impatient for Alejo, they would find him soon enough.

I stepped around the corner as quickly as I dared and found the thick steel door to the Box, which was kind of a cross between a bank vault and a restaurant refrigerator door. Once again, I exchanged the shotgun for my old Glock. I knelt down and touched my ankle where I had the baby Glock holstered. If I walked into something unexpected, the ankle holster was a kind of insurance policy. If they took the Benelli and the big Glock away from me, they might not think to check me for another weapon. When I stood up I didn't waste any time. I yanked on the handle. The door must have been counterbalanced because, in spite of its girth, it opened as if it weighed only a few ounces. As the door pulled back, a light came on, and what I saw inside made me sick.

To my left, along the wall, neat row after neat row of assault-style rifles, AR-15s and M4s were lined up in racks, waiting to be packed. There were several large computer-controlled milling machines at the rear of the room, but most of the Box was dedicated to a weapons assembly line. There were several long, parallel benches with bins of various rifle parts next to each of the assembly stations. Some of the stations had bench vises, coil-corded power tools hung from outlets in the ceiling at other stations. There was no plasma cutter here, no tanks full of exotic or flammable gases. I pocketed my Glock, took out my cell, and thumbed to the camera icon. I started at the rear by the milling machines and worked my way forward, documenting every aspect of the manufacturing and assembly process.

There were partially assembled rifles all along my path, but what I'd found most interesting were the piles of rectangular aluminum slugs by the milling machines and what those machines turned them into: lower receivers for assault rifles. The receivers were the business components of the rifle. The place where the firing mechanism was housed. The place where you locked in the clip. There were no markings of any kind on the receivers: no numbers, no place of manufacture, no nothing. These rifles would be completely untraceable weapons—ghost guns. I'd heard about ghost guns for many years, produced only on a very small scale in the garages and basements of overzealous gun enthusiasts, Second Amendment advocates, and antigovernment hate groups, but this was doing it on a large scale.

Suddenly I understood the whys and hows of things. Linh Trang and Lara had either seen inside the Box or spotted something wrong in the paper trail. After all, the other rifle components had to come from somewhere. Maybe the invoices didn't match up with what the bosses said was being produced. Maybe too much money was coming in. A thousand things, large or small, might've caught Linh Trang or Lara's attention. Gyron made the weapons and the Asesinos sold and distributed them. I remembered what Alvaro Peña had said to me about how the Asesinos were recently flush with cash. No wonder. There were long lists of potential customers for ghost guns, and most of them scared the shit out of me. Drug cartels and white supremacists were the least of my worries. With these things available on the street, it was easy to imagine a scenario where terrorists got hold of them, walked down Sixth Avenue or into the Smith Haven Mall at Christmas, and sprayed innocent people with clip after clip until bodies were piled three deep. I was picturing that when I heard something at my back: someone racking a slide.

"Don't turn around, asshole. Put the shotgun on the floor," Carl Ryan ordered, his voice thick with menace. "When it's on the floor, kick it forward."

I didn't argue.

63

(SATURDAY EVENING)

placed the Benelli gently on the floor and kicked it less gently back toward the milling machines.

"I also have my old service piece in my pocket," I said.

"Same drill."

I did as I was told, but if I thought that would satisfy him, I was wrong.

"And the ankle holster, dickface," he said. "I'm not an amateur."

When I had unstrapped the holster and kicked it toward the back of the room, he told me to turn around.

Ryan, a SIG in his hand, was flanked on his right by Cuchillo, holding Spears's .38 on me, and on his left by a heavyset, older man with sleepy eyelids, holding a shiny automatic pistol aimed right at my chest. Now everyone was accounted for, but too late to do me any good. Both Cuchillo and the fat man had the vulture/skull tattoos on their necks. Ryan waved his index finger at me.

"Come on, Murphy, let's go. We're gonna have a nice painful little talk and then I'm gonna kill you and Spears."

At least Spears was still alive, but I wasn't exactly comforted. They backed out of the Box and waited for me. When I stepped through the door onto the shop floor, Ryan kicked me in the balls. I went down and puked up what was left of my lunch onto the floor. I struggled to get my breath back, to come back into my own head and body. Before I could, though, he was leaning over me, shouting at me.

"You nosy motherfucka. Lara worked here for almost twenty years and because she was hot for you, she had to stick her fucking nose into things. Now she's dead, asshole. That's on you. That's on *you!*"

He swung his foot at my chin, the edge of his boot tearing open the skin along my jaw. I was bleeding pretty badly, but he hadn't actually make very solid contact. I faked it, sprawling back onto the floor and closing my eyes. It was all I could do not to get sick again as I landed face first in my own vomit.

Ryan, leaning over me again, spit on me. He missed my face. "Fucking glass-jawed pussy! Cuch, get him into the utility room with his friend. Jorge, go find out where that moron Alejo is. I ask him to do one simple fucking thing and he can't even do that shit."

I heard what I assumed were Jorge's feet heading toward the loading bay door, metal filings scraping between the soles of his work boots and the cement floor. A steel hand clamped itself around the front collar of my jacket and began dragging me ahead. When I thought it was safe to peek, I opened my eyes just a slit. Ryan was walking ahead, fast. Cuchillo was a strong bastard. He was almost keeping pace in spite of pulling my weight. Just as Ryan was opening the door that led from the shop floor into the office corridor, someone, Jorge, called out.

"Cuchi, ven rápido. Hay un problema. Ven rápido!"

Cuchillo said to Ryan, "There's trouble."

"Go see what's up. I'll handle him."

Cuchillo let go of my jacket, the back of my head thumping to the floor. I was still woozy and nauseated from the kick in the groin. Ryan slapped me across the face.

"Get up, motherfucka. Get up or I'll kill you right here." Ryan pressed the SIG to the side of my face.

I tried, but couldn't manage it, not at first. Then, on the second try, using the wall, I propped myself almost upright. I wasn't sure how walking would go, but I was pretty motivated not to die. I opened the door and took a tentative step through into the hallway.

"Go right, asshole."

Using the corridor wall for support, I took slow, measured steps. At the bend in the corridor toward the offices, was an unmarked, black steel door I hadn't even noticed when I'd been there before. Light leaked out the bottom of the door into the hallway.

"In there."

Some of my strength back, the nausea almost gone, I turned the handle and pushed in with my shoulder. My eyes immediately focused on the body in the center of the room, Spears's body. He wasn't moving and I couldn't be sure he was breathing. What I could say was that his face was a pulpy, red mess and that his eyes were swollen shut. His lips were wrecked and pieces of his shattered front teeth were on the floor next to his head. There was a puddle of blood by his left hand and then I saw his left pinky and ring finger were missing.

"Tough motherfucka," Ryan said, admiration in his voice. "He didn't give you up until Cuch cut off his ring finger. Sit down on the floor." He pushed me in the back with the SIG.

I sat down close to Spears. He was unconscious, but still breathing.

"When Cuch gets here, it'll be your turn, Murphy, and he won't be cutting off your fingers. Or you can make it easy on yourself. You tell me who you've told about this, which one of your old cop buddies you've clued in, and I'll just shoot you and him. Don't tell me now and you'll look worse than him. Worse, because it will be Cuch to start with, then I'll be doing the hurting. It'll be me. We got machines in the shop that'll do some awful bad things to the human body. You ever see what people look like after shop accidents? Either way, you're gonna tell me."

"Let's trade," I said.

"You're in no position to trade."

"Okay, fuck you. You try your best to get those names outta me. Who knows, maybe the cops are on their way."

"What do you want?"

"I know why you killed the women. They must've caught on to what you were doing here. But where did you kill Linh—"

"Right here," he said, anticipating the question. "Rondo did her right where you're sitting, right after we had her punch out. She was happy to cooperate after we forced half a bottle of scotch down her throat and told her we'd cut her fucking finger off and do it for her, that fucking pain-in-the-ass gook cunt. She was a ball-breaker from the moment she got here. *What about this invoice? What about this check?* I shoulda fired her ass the first week. Then she came in that Saturday and came looking for me on the floor about petty-fucking-cash receipts. She was told a hundred times never to go on the shop floor or anywhere near the Box, but she just couldn't fucking behave."

"And how did you get Salazar to do it?"

Ryan laughed. "He volunteered, the crazy motherfucka. He said he was probably going to go away for killing a MS-Thirteen guy over a drug dispute. These guys are the craziest motherfuckas I ever met. When it comes to their gang shit, I stay out of it. Helps me keep breathing."

"But they had Salazar killed."

"Like I said, when it comes to their gang shit, I stay out of it."

"And Lara. Christ, Ryan, you knew about her kid and you still—"

"Shut up."

But I didn't shut up. "Do you know what they did to her? They gang-raped her—"

"I told you to shut the fuck up."

"After they were done raping her, they beat her to death with baseball bats. Nice partners you got."

He charged at me, screaming, "That's on you! That's on you."

Ryan smacked me across the left side of my face with the SIG. Unlike the glancing kick that had cut my skin, the gun made solid contact at the back of my jaw. It was like getting Tasered with a sledgehammer, pain shooting up into my head, my mouth, my neck and shoulder. I felt it in the fingers of my left hand. My face swelled up almost immediately.

"They did that to her to teach me a lesson," he said, distraught. "They thought I was getting sloppy, that I didn't deal with you the right way, and they weren't happy about having to kill one of their own. So they were gonna show me how to do it and what happened to partners that disappointed them. That's why they tried to have you killed that night, too. They warned me that next time it would be me. They said they could always find some greedy Anglo to do business with."

He went silent, looked at his watch, turned to the utility room door. I didn't move. Didn't say a word.

"Where are those morons?" Ryan mumbled loudly enough for me to hear.

He turned toward the door, took a step, and raised the SIG. But when there was a sharp rap at the door and the handle turned, Ryan lowered the gun. The door flew open and locked in place.

"Where the fuck have you guys—"

He never finished the sentence. He never took another breath. Instead there were two hushed metallic barks and the back of Ryan's skull exploded. Blood, bits of bone and brain sprayed Spears and me. Ryan's body plopped to the floor like a handless sock puppet.

Lagunov stood in the doorway, removing the sound suppressor from the barrel of his gun, his face as impassive as if he had dropped an envelope through a mail slot. Stepping into the room, he pocketed the suppressor, holstered the weapon, and shook his head at me. But it was me who spoke first.

"It took you long enough to get here. Another few minutes and he might've killed me."

The corners of his mouth lifted in spite of himself. "You are very brave, but foolish, foolish man."

"I do what I have to do," I said. "Where are the others?"

He nudged Ryan's body with the toe of his shoe. "This man has plenty of companions for his travels in the next life."

"All dead?"

"All."

"Thank you."

"I, too, do what I must, but you took a dangerous risk. What if I had already gotten to Slava and eliminated him while you and this man here were doing this operation? My employer's interests would have been seen to and the cavalry would not have come to save you."

I smiled at him, my jaw aching as I did. "It was a safer bet than you think."

That actually unnerved him. "Why do smile at me?"

"Turn around very slowly and look for yourself."

What he saw when he turned was Slava standing in the doorway, the Benelli raised in firing position.

"As I have said to you, Gus Murphy, you are a resourceful man."

64

Slava spoke in Russian to Lagunov. I didn't understand a word of it, but the tone was clear enough. When Slava was done talking, Lagunov placed his holstered pistol, another one holstered to his ankle, a nasty-looking combat knife, and an ASP on the ground at his feet. One by one he kicked them to Slava, who did not move an inch. Neither Slava nor I had to be reminded of how dangerous a man Lagunov was. He had left proof in blood all over the premises, some of it at my feet.

Lagunov turned to me. "You will kill me here or at a different location?"

"We're not going to kill you at all unless you force us to."

He looked relieved but confused. Neither expression fit his perpetually chilly, stoic face.

"If Slava killed you and ran," I said, "what would that accomplish? Your employer would just hire someone to take your place, and that man would eventually find Slava, wherever he was. That and your employer might take my part in this as an insult to him, putting not only myself but all my loved ones at risk. I get the sense your successor would not be as . . . polite as you have been with me."

"I am afraid my employer would demand my successor do whatever was necessary to not repeat my mistakes."

"And even if we could elude your successor and his successor, one of them would get either or both of us sooner or later. Sooner, more likely."

"Agreed."

"So, you see, Mr. Lagunov, all three of us have a problem."

"How would you suggest we resolve it?"

"Slava and I want a meeting with your boss."

Lagunov laughed and said, "You are joking, no?" He turned back to Slava and said something in Russian, probably repeating what he had said to me.

Slava, his ugly face as serious as I had ever seen it, shook his head at Lagunov.

Lagunov looked at me, eyebrows raised. "Only a fool sticks his head in a hungry lion's mouth."

"If it's the fool's only real option, he would be a fool not to do it."

"But, Gus Murphy, what can you possibly accomplish by this?"

"For one, it'll save your life. And I think it might save ours as well."

"I repeat to you, you are a very brave man, a loyal man. But why risk so much for a man like this one?" He pointed at Slava.

"That's my business, but if for nothing else, he saved my life. As you, too, have twice saved mine, though for very different reasons. Look, Lagunov, we don't have much time. This is the deal. Both Slava and I will meet with your employer wherever he wishes. We will both be unarmed and I give you my word there will be no tricks. The only precondition is that he promises to listen fully to what I have to say."

"But what if he listens and decides that it is still in his interests to have your friend over there eliminated?"

Slava answered. "Then I am saying goodbye to my friend Gus Murphy and watching him leave. I will stay to be staring in the face what is coming for all men."

I pushed. "Can you make it happen?"

"I will have to if I wish to walk out of this building," Lagunov said. "You are not the only resourceful man in this room."

"You will take your men off Maggie immediately?"

"As soon as I leave the building."

"And Slava can come back to work and live his life until the meeting?"

"Agreed."

"I have your word?"

"You have my word."

"Slava, let him go."

Slava hesitated for a second, then, backing up into the hallway, he let Lagunov pass, carrying our fates with him as he went.

65

We had returned to our post-shift Saturday breakfast ritual, but Slava was not attacking his breakfast with his usual vacuum-cleaner gusto. Never before had I seen him leave a single potato, sliver of egg, or crust of toast on his plate. Christ, he hadn't even touched his sausages. Slava was a big man with big appetites. Not today. I didn't blame him. I wasn't very hungry, either. Besides the stitches along my chin and bruised jaw, I had been living in a kind of purgatory since the events at Gyron had unfolded. Slava, too. We had things hanging over our heads that were so completely out of the realm of our control that we couldn't even pretend to influence the outcome. It was at times like these that I understood the function of prayer. I understood it, though I knew better than to try it. Fool me once . . .

The cops knew nothing about Slava's part in what had happened at Gyron, but there was a chance, a slim one, that the Suffolk County DA's Office might charge Spears and me or go to a grand jury to get indictments against the both of us for our shoot-'em-up cowboy antics. Although we had broken up a major criminal conspiracy in the process, what we had done wasn't strictly legal and we had left a lot of dead bodies to clean up in our wake. Though neither Micah Spears nor I were responsible for any of those bodies, sometimes politics and the public's mood have a lot more to do with what a DA does than the truth. Asher Wilkes told me to sit tight while the DA held his wet finger to the political winds. Asher said we'd know soon enough. Soon enough for whom, exactly?

Spears, because of the severity of his injuries and his concussion, had been worthless to the cops. That left me as the only credible witness to the Gyron bloodbath. What civilians didn't understand about police work was that it wasn't always a search for the truth. More often than not, it was a search for a narrative that fit the facts and evidence of the crime. And that's exactly what I'd given the SCPD detectives. I didn't stray far from the truth until it was necessary. Lies that were as close to the truth as possible, as I was discovering, were best. For most of my life I had been a bad liar because I hadn't had a whole lot of experience at it. The last several months had changed all that.

Anyway, I told the truth, such as it was, about why Spears and I had done what we did. I told them the truth about what we had planned to do, what we did, and what went impossibly sideways. I told them the truth right up until the part where Lagunov entered the utility room and blew the back off Carl Ryan's head all over us. That's the point at which the truth train went straight off the rails.

"Listen, Detective, I don't know who those guys were in the masks, but my guess is they were MS-Thirteen or the Latin Kings. For all I know, they might've been Bloods or Crips or some other fucking rival gang. All I know is I was happy to see them. They came busting through the utility room door and put a hole in Ryan's head. The shooter took one look at me and Spears, saw we were in bad shape, and split. I mean, look at me. Look at Spears. Ryan and his guys fucked us up pretty good. Spears is half dead and I think my jaw is broken. I can only tell you what I saw."

I wasn't sure they even half believed me, but the facts fit the narrative and the narrative fit the facts. Of course it helped that my chin was still bleeding pretty badly and that the left side of my face was swollen up like a beach ball. And it was a good thing Slava had thought to take Lagunov's weapons with him when he left. Those would have been difficult if not impossible for me to explain away. If I was charged, Asher said he could beat the charges with any jury the DA could put me up in front of. Slava's limbo was worse.

Lagunov had been good to his word, calling me later that Saturday evening to promise he had taken his men off Maggie and that she was in no danger from him. He actually offered an apology for threatening her at all. I let that pass. He also said that Slava could return to his old life, at least temporarily.

"The meeting?" I asked.

He laughed, then clicked off before answering.

So I understood Slava's lack of appetite. The longer a man spends in limbo, the more it feels like hell. Waiting, even for the most patient of men, breeds a kind of self-torment.

"Gus," Slava said, noticing me looking at his plate, "come, we are going now."

I paid the bill. He left the tip.

In the vestibule I asked, as I always did, "Do you want a ride?"

He answered as he always answered. "Slava is walking home. I needing air to think."

But when we stepped outside, the sun now risen up, the air smelling both of spring and jet fumes, it was clear to us that the waiting was at end.

"Please, gentlemen," Lagunov said, "get into the van."

66

We weren't alone with Lagunov. There were two bruisers in the van with us. They were both bigger than either Slava or me, and both were armed. We didn't get much of a look at them since the minute the doors closed, bags were placed over our heads.

"Relax, gentlemen. This is only a precaution for us all," Lagunov explained in his cool monotone. "We will be in the van for some time together. If you need water, please ask. Unfortunately, there will be no rest stops. So maybe it will be better to be thirsty."

Slava grunted. I didn't even do that much. I was too busy concentrating. Because I knew the roads in the area so well, I could figure out part of our route. A lot of it was along the LIE. No other road on the island was so long, flat, and straight. I could tell we were heading west toward the city. Even on a quiet Saturday morning there were certain exits—43 for Syosset, 37 for Roslyn, 31 for the Cross Island Parkway—where traffic always slowed. After that it became a guessing game. Were we going to the Bronx? Westchester? To Manhattan? Brooklyn? It didn't matter, anyway. After a while I stopped trying to figure out our route, focusing instead on what I might say to Lagunov's master in order to keep Slava alive.

About thirty minutes after where I figure we'd crossed into Queens, the van came to a stop. When the doors opened I was hit with the powerful salt scent of the sea. That really wasn't much of a clue, since New York City was pretty much surrounded by water, much of it the Atlantic Ocean. We were led out of the van, my running shoes crunching gravel beneath them and then slipping slightly as I was led onto the wet boards of a pier. We were lowered into a boat and not a very big one. It was rocking pretty good under my feet. Someone shoved me down onto an uncushioned plank.

"Now would not be the time for you to get seasick," Lagunov said. "The bags will stay on no matter. Do you understand?"

I answered yes. Again Slava grunted. I could only imagine what was going through his mind. For all he knew, he was only a few minutes away from his death. The only thing standing between him and his execution was me. It had seemed like a good idea at the start. We'd gotten pretty far, but it seemed less and less of a good idea as time passed. A motor started up and we were moving. I don't think we were moving very quickly, but, with my senses distorted by the bag and adrenaline, it felt like we were traveling at the speed of sound. Each of the bow's confrontations with the light chop was jarring. The smell of the sea mixed with the fumes from the engine. I could also smell that someone was smoking a cigarette. The motor cut back. We turned gently. Our little boat banged into something and we stopped. Our motor was silenced.

Lagunov said, "We are going to help you onto a ladder that you must climb yourselves. There will be someone behind each of you if you slip, but do not slip. Especially you, Slava. My motivation to save you is very limited."

There was no grunt from Slava this time. No one slipped.

Once on board, I was led down some steps, along a short hallway, and through a doorway. A door closed behind me and the bag was removed from my head. The cabin was well lit, but subtly so. I was sure we were on a yacht, a big one, maybe the one Maggie had worked on, maybe not.

Even so, the cabin might have been the boardroom of a Fortune 500 company. There were eight seats upholstered in camel-colored leather around a beautiful green glass table. A map of the world was etched into the center of the table, and vases of bright orange, red, and yellow flowers stood on either side of the etching. The floor was covered in thick beige carpeting and the walls were lined in a tight-grained exotic striped wood the likes of which I had never seen before. And on the walls were paintings, some that looked vaguely familiar. Work by famous artists, but not paintings that I knew. What I knew about art couldn't fill a paper cup.

"You have an eye for art, Mr. Murphy?" said a short, bald man with a glint in his doe-brown eyes and a smile on his face. He rose out of his chair and waddled over to me.

I was surprised to see I was alone in the room with the short man. No Slava, no Lagunov, no helper monkeys. The little man was dressed in a blue blazer, a powder-blue polo shirt, khaki slacks, and rope-colored deck shoes. It all looked like expensive stuff and the blazer was definitely tailored, but he had the type of bowling-pin body that no amount of tailoring or fancy clothing could make attractive. But men with money never have to worry about their looks, or so I've heard.

"That painting behind you there is a Vermeer. This one," he said, taking me by the elbow and walking me to my right, "is a Christina Rossetti. I adore the Pre-Raphaelites. Here is an early Pollock. I'm not a fan, but my guests are impressed by it. That is a Warhol. I despise Warhol. He was a phony. He took other people's labors, did a bit of slap and tickle, and called it his own. And this, this," he practically squealed, "is my favorite. A very late Basquiat. So sparse. So vivid."

To me it looked like a skull drawn by an angry second-grader who wanted to use all sixty-four crayons in his box. But like I said, I didn't know art. I didn't even know who Vermeer or Rossetti were. I knew Warhol because it was impossible not to. And the only reason I knew the others was because I had once helped Krissy study for an art history test. The little man spoke with a funky accent. His English was Russian accented, but it was a more cultured one than Slava's or Lagunov's. And it sounded as if he had learned his English in the UK or Australia.

"Excuse me, Mr. Murphy. I have been a rude host. Can I get you something to drink? Something to eat. Ask for anything and we'll more than likely have it."

"Just some water. Thank you, Mr. . . ."

"My name is unimportant, Mr. Murphy," he said, walking over to a wet bar and pulling out a bottle of Fuji water from a small refrigerator. He twisted open the cap and handed the rectangular bottle to me. "May I call you Gus?"

"Sure."

"Please, Gus, sit."

He gestured at a seat close to the head of the table. It sounded like a polite invitation, but I recognized an order when I heard one. After I sat, he sat at the head of the table where he had been seated when the bag was removed from my head.

The little man leaned toward me, "Listen carefully to me, Gus. I have given you the courtesy of this meeting because Lagunov tells me you are a resourceful man, a man deserving of respect. He does not say things of this nature about many people. That you are here at all and that you do this thing out of loyalty to a friend proves to me Lagunov's judgments of you are correct. I could use a man like you. I could trust a man like you not because I paid you, but because it is in your nature to be trustworthy. Yet I must warn you that your prospects of saving your friend's life are not very good."

"I figured as much."

"I am told you are fully aware of what the man you know as Slava has done in the past."

I nodded that I was.

"We will not debate the morality of his acts here. I am no one to judge him. But it surprises me that a man, even such a loyal man as yourself, should risk your life for a man who has murdered so many people." He dismissively waved his pudgy little hand at me. "Yes, yes, he saved your life. I am aware. Still, I wonder."

"Slava feels he has to live to atone and suffer."

"Very Russian of him. I commend him, but you must understand my position. He is a problem, an inconvenience to my friends and business associates. These friends and associates, they are powerful people who have asked me to remove this splinter before it festers. This Slava, he can be a very troubling embarrassment to my friends."

"Lagunov trusts me. You seem to trust me. I give you my word that Slava will never divulge any information about what happened in Russia all those years ago. He never told me, and I am the only friend he has in the world. I had to figure it out for myself."

He smiled sadly at me. "Gus, you have just made the argument against yourself. If you could figure it out, then so can others. And these others might find a certain advantage in using Slava's knowledge against my friends."

"But he can't prove any of it. He has no documents. No recordings. Nothing."

"In Russia, there are records of him, of what has happened. Please, understand these are very high stakes. I am afraid even if I were to trust you and trust him to never speak of his role in those unfortunate incidents, it is safer if he is gone. Men can be forced to break their promises. If Lagunov had put just a little more pressure on you with your lovely Magdalena, you would have given up Slava, no? What guarantees would I have that Slava would not do the same with his secrets if you or a loved one were threatened? No, Gus, you must see my position."

I was getting that sick feeling in my belly as I felt Slava's life slipping out of my fingers.

"You said you would like to have a man like me work for you," I said. "Okay, I'm yours. I'll work for you. All you need do is spare Slava's life. Ask Lagunov, he'll tell you, I am a resourceful person."

The little man rubbed his chin. "It is a tempting offer. Believe me, it is. Lagunov is loyal, but I pay for his loyalty. A man like me cannot trust many people on their face and I would trust you. I *do* trust you, but you would be too small a cog in the machinery. These friends and associates of mine, they are worth more money to me than you can possibly imagine. So, Gus Murphy, I am sorry. You have been valiant and shrewd, but not shrewd enough, I am afraid. I will call Lagunov to come fetch you. Would you like to say goodbye to your friend? Maybe this would be too hard for you."

My mind was racing so fast I was dizzy and the knot in my stomach was about ready to squeeze the desperation up into my throat so I could choke on it.

"My father was a nasty drunk," I heard myself say, my voice distant and muted. "And I don't think he said five wise things to me in his whole fucking lifetime. But he once said something I think you should listen to."

The little man's eyes got wide and he tilted his head in concentration. "And what words of advice from your drunk father should I heed?"

"Your friends now may not be your friends tomorrow." My voice was back and strong. "It was easy to understand how he had lost his friends. But you don't have to be a nasty prick to lose friends. I had a best friend, a fellow cop, a pallbearer at my son's funeral, who fucked my wife only a few months after my boy died. I have lost many friends. Some you shed as you age. Some fade away. Some you piss off. Some piss you off. Is it the same for you?"

He was rubbing his chin again. "Yes, it is the way of life. Continue, I am listening."

"These friends and business associates of yours, can you guarantee that they will always be there as friends?" I asked, the knot loosening its grip on my intestines. "Okay, so you kill Slava and remove the splinter for them. Tomorrow, when they no longer need you or they need someone else more or it is in their self-interest to call you a splinter, what leverage will you have? But if you keep Slava alive, his knowledge becomes your leverage. Keep Slava alive and the splinter becomes a club, one to keep in reserve as insurance against the day they would put your head on the plate."

I stopped, not wanting to overplay my hand. If this didn't convince him, nothing would.

"And you, Gus Murphy, would you still offer your services to me if I should need them?" he asked after a moment of quiet consideration. "I might ask for something that would displease you."

"I won't kill anyone for you, if that's what you're asking."

He snorted at that. "You would be surprised at what you would do. Still, I have others for that. There are distasteful things short of killing."

"I won't take back my offer now."

He smiled, stood, and offered me his hand. His shake was firm and he stared me in the eye much as Spears had done weeks ago. Only when this little man stared into my eyes it was as if a cold wind blew through the cabin.

"I will call on you one day, Gus. Of that you can be sure. And when I do, do not disappoint me. No one will be able to talk me out of sparing you and Slava if you disappoint me. But we will not talk of that today. Today you should celebrate with your friend whose life you have saved." The little man wagged his finger at me. "Keep an eye on the splinter for me. As you say, I may need him."

"How will you convince you friends that Slava has been—"

He laughed, that cold wind blowing through the cabin again. "Do not concern yourself with such things. That is what I have Lagunov for. Now, Gus, please have a safe ride back to the diner parking lot. I don't suspect there will be a need for you to be blindfolded, as we have made our pact."

I suppose I should have been thrilled. Relieved, at the very least. Instead I felt as if I had just signed a stranger's death warrant and made a deal I would someday fiercely regret.

EPILOGUE

(MID-MAY, WEDNESDAY MORNING)

Bill Kilkenny, Asher Wilkes, Lara's sister Niki, and I sat around the mirror-polished tiger-maple table in the conference room at Barson, Mckee, Grimm & Mitchell PC. We were there to watch Micah Spears sign the papers establishing the trust for Lara's daughter, Bella. Spears had been out of the hospital less than a week and still looked considerably worse for wear. He had lost more than two fingers and a few teeth that Saturday afternoon at Gyron. He had lost the myth of his own immortality.

We all do, somewhere along the line, lose our sense that we will somehow escape what is waiting for us at the other end of the tunnel. I lost mine long before John died. You can't be a street cop, not even one in a relatively quiet sector like mine had been, and escape the sound of the ticking clock. I had seen so much death in its varied forms, innocent and otherwise, from car accidents, heart attacks, drownings, train wrecks, and plane crashes, to stabbings, suicides, shootings, bombings . . . It was a long list. We all come into the world in pretty much the same way, yet there are many, many ways to leave it. And leave it we will, inevitably and alone. I guess that some people can keep the myth going no matter what. But all walls crumble, no matter how mighty or thick, even the ones monsters build around their bloody transgressions. I no longer believed in judgment day. I'm not sure I ever really did. The former Arnold Mason probably hadn't believed in it either. Yet from the look of him across the table, he did now.

After the papers were signed, Lara's sister left, gently kissing Spears on the cheek and hugging me. She didn't ask a lot of questions about who and why and how. Those questions aren't as important to some people as to others. All she knew was that Spears and I had helped find the men who had brutalized and murdered her big sister and left her the guardian of a twenty-one-year-old autistic niece. All she knew was that there was a man with money who was going to make her burden much easier and that she was thankful for it.

After she left the room, Asher asked Erin Mitchell, Spears's attorney, if she could give us a few moments alone together. She left without a word and when he was sure she was gone, Asher spoke.

"You are both in the clear," he said, staring directly at Spears and me. "The Suffolk DA assures me he has no intention of pressing charges of any kind against either one of you. But from where I stand I have to say that was an awfully stupid and risky thing you gentlemen did."

I smiled and muttered, "That seems to be the consensus."

"What?"

"Nothing, Asher. Sorry."

Of the assembled, only I knew the whole story. Spears's recollections of that day were lost to him in a swirling haze of pain, blood loss, and concussion.

"You do realize," Asher continued, "that you might have tainted important evidence or completely ruined a long-term investigation with your cockamamie stunt. If I was the DA, I'm not so sure I would be as forgiving."

I said, "Maybe it helps that there was no long-term investigation and two homicides were cleared up in the process. Not to mention that we shut down the biggest ghost-gun operation in the history of the country.

And I handed the ATF and FBI leads to the distribution of the guns by giving them all the tag numbers of the cars and vans that had been at Gyron that day."

Asher still didn't like it. He was a great defense lawyer, but he had played for the other team, too. That's what made him so good. He still thought like a prosecutor, still understood their sides of things. Why these particular half-truths seemed to bother him more than the ones I'd told Narvaez and Dwyer or the ones his other clients rattled off as easily as they breathed, I couldn't say.

"How about the part where you could have been killed? If that other gang hadn't so very conveniently showed up and taken out Ryan and the Asesinos, we wouldn't be sitting here today. And just for the record, I don't buy that other gang bullshit for a second."

After the lecture, Asher left. He had done me the service of making sure the trust was set up properly and funded fully. I didn't trust Spears as far as I could throw him and I needed Asher to ensure Spears and his lawyers hadn't tried to pull a fast one.

Al Roussis, Charlie Prince, and his asshole partner Palumbo were pleased. Closed cases make for very happy detectives. Once I tipped Al Roussis off that Alejo had been one of the men to murder Lara, he had no trouble finding the other two men who had been part of her execution. They had left a lot of damning evidence behind. And when I told Charlie that Salazar had been the right man all along and why he had done Linh Trang, he seemed pleased and sad all at once. Alvaro Peña, the SCPD's gang expert, was surprisingly less pleased than I thought he would have been.

"Yeah, Gus, it's great you stopped these guys, but they put a lot of weapons on the street already. And the thing is with gangs, whether it's drugs or guns, protection or putang, when they find a cash machine that works, they keep going back. These factories are going to start showing up all over the place. Something else, too. Gangs are copycats. What works for one, works for all."

I didn't want to think about that.

Bill had come to visit me in the hospital once he made sure Spears would live. And when he did, he said he felt obliged to explain some things to me. The look on his face hinted that it was best to simply sit back and listen.

"I did a stint as Padre in a military prison in Saigon before I rotated back to the States. It was there I met Arnold Mason. He was cold as ice even then, a man with his own windchill. During my first visits he told me to fuck off, but one night he sent word for me to come pay him a call. I did as he asked, Gus, and came to sit with him. He told me he wasn't of the Catholic faith but that he wished to confess his sins to me. What did it matter to me if he wasn't a Catholic? I had lost my own faith by then. He could have been a pagan for all I cared at that point. I would have heard his confession.

"When we had dispensed with the formalities, he proceeded to describe in the most horrid, lurid detail the acts for which he and his friends were to be tried. After a few months in country, it was hard to shock me. And after I had been forced to kill, I thought there wasn't a blessed thing in the universe which could have shaken me. That I was immune." Bill laughed at himself. "The lack of humility and stupidity of that thought, the hubris!

"The things he described to me that night in his cell . . . I have never been able to rid myself of them. It's as if they were tattooed into my brain. I think I'll sooner forget my name in my dotage than his words. I can see the images now as I saw them then. I was disgusted, nauseated, furious, especially when he seemed to grow excited in his retelling. Yet there I sat, listening, taking it in as I had been trained and taught to do, as I had done for many others who had come to seek me out. And inexplicably, what I felt for him was sorrow and forgiveness. There was rage, but mostly sorrow and forgiveness. That's how I knew that although I had lost my faith, it would not escape me forever. I knew that even if Jesus had seemed to abandon me, that He was there somewhere and I would find my way back to Him or He to me. So you see, Gus, it was this monster who kept me from walking away from the church all those years ago. If we had never crossed paths, Arnold Mason and myself, I don't know that I would have survived long enough to have my faith restored.

"When he had his twist of good fortune and relocated to the island, I was easy enough to find when he came looking. I believe in some way he takes a strange comfort in my knowing who he is under that well-scrubbed and nattily dressed façade of his. I don't pretend to understand it. I don't pretend to understand him, but I owe him a debt of faith. But what concerns me now is our friendship, Gus. Can you forgive me for getting you involved in this?" Bill asked, bowing his head.

"Forget it, Bill. There's nothing to forgive."

I left it at that. I didn't ask if Bill had given absolution to Arnold Mason that night in a dark cell in Saigon. I didn't want to know. There were many things I didn't want to know about or think about, but I knew how that sentiment went with the universe. But just as Spears found an odd comfort in Bill knowing the full extent of his depravity, I took a similar comfort in the indifference of the universe to my whims and wishes.

Before leaving the law offices and heading to the airport, I told Spears that the only money I wanted from him was a check to cover the bill for Maggie's security and a few thousand bucks for my time. I told him to donate all the money he had originally offered me to a medical research program of his choosing in Linh Trang's name. Spears didn't argue. He didn't thank me, either. It was as it should have been. When I left that room, I didn't look back. I never wanted to see the monster, now broken and frail, ever again.

Bill stopped me in the hallway. "What was that shite about in there, Gus? What about the foundation in your boy's name?"

"Doc Rosen is always after me about facing the reality of things and moving on. The reality is that John is dead, Bill. He's gone and I have to let go of all the ways I can make myself pretend that he's not. A foundation might keep his name alive, but that wouldn't bring him back to his mom and me. Let the money work to keep other kids alive."

Bill opened his mouth to say something, but about-faced and went back into the room with Spears.

I had a one o'clock flight to Chicago out of LaGuardia. Maggie's play had been running there for a week and had gotten pretty good reviews. Two of the reviews had mentioned her performance in particular. We had worked things out as well as two people could work things out over the phone, nine hundred miles apart. I wouldn't know if we had really healed the wounds until we saw each other, held each other, and kissed. When we kissed, I would know. She would know. We would move on from there. All I knew was that I was so excited I could barely sit still for imagining the feel and taste of her, imagining what it would feel like just to have her smile at me again.

I was in the airport men's room when it happened. I found myself staring into the mirror as if staring into the distance and losing myself in my own reflection. Things were almost back to normal. My friend Slava was back at work and safe. I was back at work, driving businessmen and women to and from the airport to the train station to the hotel. Some of them chatted with me or at me. Most were silent in their discontent. In the last few weeks, no one who had gotten on or off my van had piqued my interest or raised my suspicions. And now, if I could make amends with Magdalena, the world would be right again. The mirror called bullshit on that.

Nothing was the same or would it ever be right, not in the way it had been right or normal as before. I was a different man from who I had been only a month ago. I had always considered myself a good man. I think most other people thought that of me, too. It is easy, I realized, to be good when you go untested or, like when I was on the job, you take the same tests over and over again. Since the night Mikel had gotten on my van and the day I met Micah Spears in Bill's apartment, the tests were new ones. What the mirror showed me was a menu of my own hypocrisies and lies. Over the past two weeks I had compromised everything I thought I believed in.

I was in league with monsters—one because I needed his money to help mitigate my own guilt and another to save a man who had, by his own admission, deserved punishment beyond death. I could no longer hide behind Slava's warnings that his past shame was too great to share with me. I knew who he was, knew what he had done. He had a hand in more deaths than Spears. Yet I felt no less warmth for Slava when we laughed together, thought it no less funny when he mangled his sentences. It seemed my morality, like police work, was not so much a search for the truth as a set of rationalizations that let me sleep at night.

As I stared into the mirror, I tried to find who I once was. The man who had so strongly believed in capital punishment. The man who would have damned the torpedoes and the potential fallout. The man who would have shouted to the world about the cover up of Arnold Mason's atrocities. The man who would have, should have let Slava meet the fate he deserved. I couldn't find that man. Instead I saw my black-clad maternal grandmother looking back at me, smiling cruelly, and saying, "I told you so."

ACKNOWLEDGMENTS

I owe a great debt to Chris Pepe, David Hale Smith, and Ivan Held, and to Katie McKee.

I'd also like to thank Erin Mitchell, Peter Spiegelman, Ellen W. Schare, Ming Liu Parson, and Mike Cascione.

But none of this would be worth it or mean a thing without the love and support of Rosanne, Kaitlin, and Dylan.